Edith was wide-eyed. "How could we be married without a priest?"

"They have taught you much from books and little from life. How could they . . . in an abbey?"

"The Abbess told me what was expected of a wife. I . . . I hated it."

"I would tell you a different story. Would you be willing to learn?"

"With you I would be willing."

"My poor little captive Princess! You must refuse to take the veil." His hands caressed her body under the rough serge. "To think they could condemn you to such a life. You will be a ready pupil. Oh, I have such delights in store for you, my dearest love. . . ."

Fawcett Books
by Jean Plaidy:

BEYOND THE BLUE MOUNTAINS C2773 $1.95

THE CAPTIVE OF KENSINGTON PALACE 23413 $1.75

THE GOLDSMITH'S WIFE 22891 $1.75

LIGHT ON LUCREZIA 23108 $1.75

MADONNA OF THE SEVEN HILLS 23026 $1.75

THE QUEEN AND LORD M 23605 $1.75

THE QUEEN'S HUSBAND 23896 $1.95

THE WIDOW OF WINDSOR 24151 $1.95

THE LION
of
JUSTICE

Jean Plaidy

FAWCETT CREST • NEW YORK

THE LION OF JUSTICE

THIS BOOK CONTAINS THE COMPLETE TEXT OF THE
ORIGINAL HARDCOVER EDITION

Published by Fawcett Crest Books, a unit of CBS Publica-
tions, the Consumer Publishing Division of CBS Inc., by arrangement with G.P. Putnam's Sons

ISBN: 0-449-24318-4

Printed in the United States of America

First Fawcett Crest Printing: August 1980

10 9 8 7 6 5 4 3 2 1

BIBLIOGRAPHY

Arnold, Ralph	*A Social History of England*
Aubrey, William Hickham Smith	*The National and Domestic History of England*
Bagley, J. J.	*Life in Medieval England*
Baker, Timothy	*The Normans*
Brooke, Christopher	*From Alfred to Henry III*
Brown, R. Allen	*The Normans and the Norman Conquest*
Bryant, Arthur	*The Story of England: Makers of the Realm*
Davis, H. W. C.	*England under the Normans and the Angevins*
Green, J. R.	*A Short History of the English People*
Milne, Duncan Grinnell	*The Killing of William Rufus*
Page, R. I.	*Life in Anglo-Saxon England*
Pine, L. G.	*Heirs of the Conqueror*
Poole, Austin Lane	*From Doomsday Book to Magna Carta 1087–1216*
Round, J. H.	*Feudal England*
Stenton, F. M.	*Anglo-Saxon England*
Stephen, Sir Leslie and Lee, Sir Sydney (edited by)	*The Dictionary of National Biography*
Strickland, Agnes	*Lives of the Queens of England*
Tomkeieff, O. G.	*Life in Norman England*
White, R. T.	*A Short History of England*

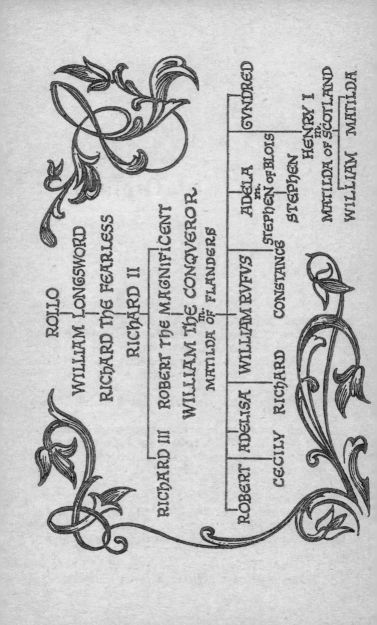

ROLLO
WILLIAM LONGSWORD
RICHARD THE FEARLESS
RICHARD II

RICHARD III   ROBERT THE MAGNIFICENT   WILLIAM THE CONQUEROR
m.
MATILDA OF FLANDERS

ROBERT   ADELISA   WILLIAM RUFUS   CONSTANCE   ADELA   GUNDRED
                                              m.
CECILY   RICHARD   STEPHEN OF BLOIS

                                         STEPHEN

                                         HENRY I
                                         m.
                                         MATILDA OF SCOTLAND

                                         WILLIAM   MATILDA

The Scottish Orphans

In her bedchamber the Queen of Scotland lay dying. At any moment she would send for her children to say her last farewell to them. The girls, Edith and Mary, sat gloomily in the schoolroom, their books before them; but they paid no attention to these as they thought of their mother who, from the time she had first come to Scotland, had been noted for her beauty and her piety.

Mary, the younger, was the first to speak. "Edith, do you think she will die before our father comes?"

Edith paused a moment before she turned mournful blue eyes on her sister and said slowly: "What if *he* should never come back?"

"Don't speak so, Edith." Mary shivered and glanced furtively over her shoulder. "It could bring ill luck."

"What I say will not bring us ill luck. It is the Normans who have brought that to our country and our family."

"But if our father defeats the King of England, our Uncle Edgar will be King. He *is* King in truth. If the

Godwin Harold had not usurped the throne and the Normans had not come..."

"If!" retorted Edith scornfully. "What is the use of saying If! And it all happened long ago. Twenty-seven years. And it is said that no one could have withstood William of Normandy. All his life he had conquered."

"It will be different with William Rufus. He is not like his father. And he is cruel. The people hate him. He cares for nothing but hunting and they say he has vices which are...unnatural."

"But what do you in truth know of him?"

"What I hear. And I believe that our father will defeat him and that very soon Uncle Edgar, the true King, will be on the throne. The English will welcome him. Of course they will welcome our dear Uncle Edgar. He's good, he's a Saxon and he is the true King."

"You talk like a child, Mary."

"And you of course are so wise. You have lived for sixteen years and because I haven't lived quite as long you think you are so much cleverer."

"Don't let us quarrel, Mary, while our mother is dying."

"She won't die. She'll get better and very soon we shall see a messenger riding to the castle with the news that our father has captured Alnwick Castle and is marching south."

Mary pushed her books aside and went to the long narrow window which was cut into the thick wall. Edith joined her, for what use was it to pretend to work at such a time? They should be praying—for the victory of their father and the soul of their mother. Yet how difficult it was to think of anything but: What will become of us?

*   *   *

Looking down to the moat and the drawbridge and beyond to the green hills, Edith was thinking how quickly everything could change. For sixteen years she had lived secure in her father's castle and it was only recently that she had been aware of a shifting pattern. Princesses became important when they grew up. Their

8

future could become a matter of state. They either married or went into a nunnery. Edith was not of a nature to wish for the latter. The brief glimpses she had had of her mother's sister, Aunt Christina, who was the Abbess of Rumsey, had decided her. How different were the two sisters! Her mother was gentle, beautiful and kind; she was good, too, for on every day in Lent she went to church bare-footed, dressed in a gown of hair cloth, where she selected the poorest people that she might wash and kiss their feet. She wanted her children to be good and happy—but most of all good, as she was herself. As for Aunt Christina she was far from beautiful and her black robes had frightened Edith when she was very young. Aunt Christina's sharp cold eyes saw every fault and no virtue; her knees were hard it was said because she had spent so many hours on them praying and this was considered saintliness of the highest order. Aunt Christina was so busy being good that she had no time to be kind. She thought all those who were not dedicated to the convent life were sinners. Even her sister Margaret, mother of Edith, had lived in what Christina called a worldly manner, bearing many children.

No, it would not be a nunnery for Edith if she could help it. She would beg her father to spare her that.

She hoped to marry as romantically as her mother had. She had heard the story many times. Edith's mother was Margaret Atheling, the daughter of Edward, who had been the son of Edmund Ironside; her grandmother had been the daughter of Emperor Henry II of Germany. When Edward the Confessor knew that his reign could not last much longer he had sent for Margaret's father Edward, as was presumed, with the object of making him his successor. Edward had died before the meeting could take place but he left a son, Edgar, as well as two daughters, Margaret and Christina.

Then William came and conquered England and because of Edgar's clear claim to the throne the Conqueror had kept him under surveillance. He treated him well but Edgar grew to suspect his motives and thought it an excellent idea to take his sisters to Hungary where his mother's relatives would welcome him.

He had set sail from England but ran into a storm and his ship had been thrown up on the Scottish coast. There was nothing to be done but to ask for asylum—which the royal Athelings did.

Malcolm Canmore, the King of Scotland, agreed to give them hospitality while they made their plans. Malcolm, young and comely, had recently come to the throne by driving out the usurper MacBeth, and was a romantic as well as a handsome figure. He entertained the fugitives in his castle and within a few days had fallen in love with Margaret and asked Edgar for his sister's hand in marriage.

What great good fortune! The dowerless young woman who had been on her way to Hungary to ask for asylum was being asked to share the crown of Scotland.

Her brother Edgar had expressed his pleasure; as for Margaret she was no less pleased, and very soon after her arrival in Scotland the marriage was solemnized and the spot where she had landed was for ever after known as Queen's Ferry.

It was a happy marriage and very fruitful. She soon presented her husband with a fine son who was named Edward after her father and this child was followed by another son who became Edgar after her brother—then Edith, Mary and the little ones followed. Her brother Edgar stayed at the Scottish court while her sister Christina entered a convent and became its Abbess.

So it had been a happy storm which had driven their ship in to the Firth of Forth.

Why could they not remain happy? wondered Edith. But how foolish to think that time could stand still. Uncle Edgar talked constantly of the Norman usurpation and dreamed of the day when he might regain the kingdom. It had been useless while William the great Conqueror lived but it was five years since he had died and during those five years Edgar had begun to hope again.

There was much talk about Rufus who was not the man his father had been. William I had been a harsh ruler but people had respected him. They realized that what he had done had been for the good of the country. His great selfishness had been his love of the hunt and people had been turned from their homes to make forests where wild beasts could roam. The penalties for killing wild animals had been very cruel; but because of the manner in which the country had prospered and law and order had been brought in, William was accepted.

Rufus would never be. He was different from his father by all accounts. William I had had great dignity; he was a tall man and although towards the end of his life he had grown so corpulent that only the strongest horse could carry his weight he had always had the appearance of the great ruler he was. Rufus was short of stature, broad and fat; there was a red tinge in his hair and his complexion was ruddy. When he was angry he would stammer and become almost unintelligible, but in the company of his friends he was said to be witty and able to laugh at himself. As his vices were many and his greatest friends were among members of his own sex, his joking references to them made those about him accept them with more leniency than they would otherwise have done. Like his father his greatest passion was the hunt. At this time Rufus had fallen ill and when the news had reached Scotland, Malcolm Canmore decided that the moment had come for him to take revenge on his old enemy for all the slights Scotland had received at his hands.

Malcolm's great ambition was to restore the Saxon line. If he could succeed, he would not only drive the Normans back to Normandy but set his own relations through marriage on the throne of England.

For this reason Malcolm had amassed an army and marched south; and it was while he was absent that his wife had become ill and that illness had so progressed that now she was on her deathbed.

*   *   *

Turgot came into the schoolroom his expression grave, his pallor accentuated by his black priestly robes. He was their tutor as well as their mother's confessor, but there would be no lessons today.

"How fares my mother?" asked Edith.

"I fear, my child," he answered, "that you must be prepared for the worst."

"If only our father would come!" cried Edith in despair.

Turgot nodded. "Soon she will wish to see you to say goodbye. I have come to warn you to be ready."

Mary began to cry.

"Do not let her see your tears," went on Turgot. "She will wish you to be brave. Kneel with me now and pray for strength to face this ordeal so that she will know that all my teaching has not been in vain."

There in the schoolroom they knelt.

Turgot wondered whether the girls realized the tragedy which was facing them. They lived in a violent age from which during their short lifetimes they had been miraculously sheltered. He had advised peace; he had been against Malcolm's marching across the Border. These Normans had come to stay. That seemed certain. And, although William Rufus might not be the man his father was, he was a wily general and the Normans were great fighters. Battle was in their blood. It had come from their marauding Norse ancestors who had roamed the seas in their long ships looking for lands to plunder.

Malcolm should have stayed at home. Turgot had not swerved from his conviction even though the news was good and Malcolm had laid siege to Alnwick castle and it seemed that the besieged could not hold out much longer. But if he took the castle that was but a beginning. Turgot hoped that Malcolm was not going to indulge in a long war which was most unlikely to bring any profit to either side as was the case with most wars.

Turgot was deeply involved with the family; he had been a part of it for so long. Of a noble Lincolnshire Saxon family he had become aware of the power of the Conqueror when, during one of the latter's punitive expeditions, he had been taken prisoner and held hostage. There had followed a time of privation in the dungeons of Lincoln castle, from which, with the help of sympathizers, he had escaped and, reaching the coast, taken ship to Norway. When the ship was driven back to the coast by the treacherous winds, he had landed in the north and because the north was then in revolt against the Conqueror and he was a man of some learning had found hospitality in Durham Abbey and there became a priest and eventually its prior. Having heard his story Queen Margaret had been interested and had sent for him. Their regard for each other had been instantaneous. She made him her confessor and the preceptor of her children and ever since the welfare of the royal family of Scotland had been his chief concern.

The death of the Queen would be as great a sorrow to him as to her family and he knew that before she died she would want him to swear on oath to continue to care for them after her death as he had during her lifetime.

As they now knelt in prayer there was a shout from below and the clatter of horses' hoofs could be heard.

Mary forgot she was supposed to be at prayer. "It is a messenger," she cried, and rushed to the window. The others were not long in following her.

"It is our brother Edgar," said Mary.

"He must have come from the battle," added Edith.

"How sad he looks!" went on Mary. "Oh I know something fearful has happened."

They followed him down the stone stairway to the hall and there was Edgar, weary, mud-stained, his eyes wild, and a look of such misery on his face as the girls had never seen before.

"My son," said Turgot, "you have ill news?"

Edgar answered: "The worst. I must see the Queen."

"The Queen is grievously sick."

"It cannot be . . ."

"'Tis so, alas. Tell me your news and I will impart it to her if she must know it."

Edgar shook his head and it seemed as though the words would not come.

Turgot prompted him gently. "Your father was besieging the castle of Alnwick and had reduced the inhabitants to starvation. They were on the point of surrender."

"Yes," replied Edgar slowly, "they did surrender. They surrendered on condition that they should deliver the keys of the city to none but my father."

"Yes, yes, my son."

"So...he went in person to receive them, and a knight brought them to him on the point of a lance. The knight knelt and as my father stooped to take them, this...this...treacherous dog forced the point of his lance through my father's vizor and pierced his eye."

"God in Heaven!" cried Turgot. "And the King?"

"He died mercifully soon. He was in great agony."

Turgot folded his hands and his lips moved in prayer.

The King dead, he was thinking, the Queen dying. What will become of these children?

*   *   *

They stood about her bed. How different she looked from the beautiful young girl who had come ashore at Queen's Ferry and captivated the King.

Her eyes, enormous in her pale wasted face, sought the children ranged about her bed—Edgar, the two girls and the little ones. She saw with relief that Turgot was there also.

"You would keep something from me," she said. "I know it. There is ill news. What of my husband and eldest son?"

Turgot nodded to Edgar.

"Mother, there is sad news."

"My husband...my son Edward...?"

"They are dead. Edward was killed in battle. Our father at the siege of Alnwick."

"Oh, God help you all."

She looked at Turgot. "Come close, my friend."

He approached the bed. "You will continue to care for these children."

"I will, with God's blessing."

"They are young yet, Turgot. Too young to lose both

14

father and mother. Swear to me, Turgot. Swear to me on the Black Cross."

The girls looked on in awe as the beautiful cross was taken from the black case which gave it its name. It was made of gold and enormous diamonds adorned it. On the gold the figure of Christ was engraved in ivory. It had been talked of often but always kept in a secure place and it was because the Queen was dying that it had been taken from that place that she might hold it in her hands during her last moments on earth. It was symbolic, that cross. It had belonged to the Saxon royal family for generations and must never pass into the hands of any other. While it was in the possession of the Athelings they believed themselves to be the true sovereigns of England no matter if William the Conqueror had snatched their lands from them.

Turgot took the cross reverently in his hands and swore that he would care for the Queen's children.

"My life is ebbing fast," she said. "Teach my children to love and fear God, and, if any of them should attain earthly grandeur, be a father to them and a guide. If the need should arise, reprove them if they should become proud; guard them that they may not offend God and forfeit their hopes of eternal life. Swear thus, Turgot, on the black cross in the presence of God."

Turgot knelt by her bedside and kissed the cross.

"So help me God," he said. "I shall serve you as faithfully in death as I did in life."

Her white fingers curled about the cross and she lay back and died.

*   *   *

The Queen was buried at Dunfermline and in trepidation the children waited for what would happen next. Turgot had told them that their brother Edgar was King of Scotland but this did not seem to be the case, for no one came to the castle to swear loyalty to him and there was no talk of a coronation. In fact, each day retainers disappeared from the castle and those who remained had changed subtly. They were furtive, expectant and they did not behave to the children as they had when their parents were alive. Only Turgot remained the same, stern and watchful.

Young Edgar did not know how to act. Was he the King or was he not? What could this strange attitude mean? Where were the lords who should come to swear fealty to him?

Turgot advised that they go on as though they were unaware of the changing situation, for soon there would be some indication of what was taking place.

He was right. Uncle Edgar Atheling came riding to the castle in great distress. He summoned Edith and Edgar and told them that he wished to talk to them very seriously.

They had heard of their father's half-brother, Donald Bane, had they not? Indeed they had. He had always been a troublemaker. He was illegitimate but that did not mean he had no hope of inheriting the crown. Turgot had said that he wished kings would be less prodigal of scattering their seed throughout the kingdom, for the results often ended in wars and disasters.

Donald Bane had declared that as Malcolm and his eldest son were dead, and young Edgar was not old enough to rule, he had stepped into the breach and had taken the crown. Scotland had a new King.

"But this is monstrous," declared young Edgar. "I will not endure it."

"You can do nothing," said his uncle shortly. "Donald Bane has the crown and there are those who will help him hold it. We have no means of wresting it from him. In time we will march against him, but first we must gather together a loyal army."

"Let us begin to do that at once," said his nephew.

But the older man shook his head wearily. "My dear nephew," he said, "we are in no position to do that. Moreover, King Donald has issued an edict. He orders all English exiles to leave his kingdom."

"Exiles!" cried young Edgar. "Is the King of Scotland then an exile in his own realm?"

"My dear nephew," replied his uncle, "against whom do you imagine this edict is issued? Am I not English? Am I not an exile? He wants me out of this country.

16

And why? Because then you, my boy, will be at his mercy. What hope do you think you have without me to protect you?"

Edgar stared at his uncle in dismay.

"It is true," said Edith. "I see it clearly. Oh, Uncle Edgar, what are we going to do?"

"We are going to escape Donald Bane, for you, Edgar, as the rightful King of this country, are in the utmost danger. Go at once to your nurseries and prepare your brothers and sisters. We are going on a journey. First send Turgot to me."

"Will he come with us, Uncle?" asked Edith.

"He will."

Turgot came with all speed. He had already heard the news.

"We are in acute danger," said Edgar Atheling to the priest. "In particular my nephew."

"We are leaving here?" replied Turgot. "And where shall we find refuge?"

There was a brief silence. Both men were remembering the occasion when they had been shipwrecked. They had escaped once. Could they hope to do so again?

Edgar replied. "In England."

"England! You think Rufus will allow us to stay there?"

"We have to risk that."

Turgot said: "I have recently taken a vow to protect these children."

"Think you not," replied Edgar, "that I will not protect them with everything in my power?"

"I know it well. But to take them into England where the King of Scotland has been fighting the English . . ."

"My good Turgot, I know Rufus. There was a time when we lived under the same roof. We were boys together. I became a friend to him and his brothers."

Turgot's brow furrowed. Edgar was of too gentle a nature to be a match for these treacherous Normans. He seemed to forget that he was the rightful King of England, that, had he been of an age to govern, King Edward the Confessor would never have named Harold, son of Godwin, as the future King; and it would have been Edgar whom William would have had to face

17

at Hastings. And if Edgar had been King how could William of Normandy have disputed the fact that he was in truth the King? Edgar had been too young at the time but he was no longer young; yet there was about him an air of gentleness which was in sharp contrast to what Turgot remembered of the mighty Conqueror, and admirable as it might be it was a characteristic which did not win battles and subdue rebellious subjects. Edgar might well have been a King such as Edward the Confessor but there was no doubt that he was the rightful King of England, yet he seemed to be of the opinion that the son of the usurper would happily receive him and shelter him when the Saxon community were constantly chafing against Norman rule. To whom would such people look but to the Royal Atheling to deliver them. And Edgar was suggesting placing himself into the none too scrupulous hands of William Rufus!

"How firm is such friendship when a crown is at stake?" asked Turgot now.

"Why, Turgot, Rufus knows I have no means of taking the crown from him."

"I hear there is dissatisfaction with his rule."

"There will always be dissatisfaction. His father instructed him for some years before his death. Rufus will never be the great leader the Conqueror was, but who could be that? Turgot, none knows more surely than I that the Norman rule has come to stay. I am concerned with restoring the Scottish crown to my nephew and I believe I can persuade Rufus to help me in this."

"You face a grave risk," Turgot warned him.

"Tell me, where else can we go? Or do you suggest that I leave my sister's children here to be murdered by Donald Bane?"

"Nay," retorted Turgot sorrowfully, "I see the situation is desperate."

"I prefer to trust Rufus rather than this uncouth Scot. I assure you I *know* Rufus. Once he is convinced that I shall make no attempts on his crown he will be my friend. We were boys together—he, and his brothers Robert and Henry. I was as another brother. They used to laugh at my Saxon ways, but all in good part. Well, Turgot, are you ready to set out for England?"

"I see that there is no other way open to us."

Rufus

When William Rufus heard what had happened to Malcolm of Scotland he lay back on his couch and laughed heartily.

"Our brother of Scotland was too clever," he commented. "He thought to harry me while I lay on my sick bed and look what it has brought him."

Those young men whom it pleased him to honour laughed dutifully. William Rufus was a man of violent temper. So had his father been but the anger of William the First was scarcely unpredictable. All men knew that if they gave him absolute obedience and never encroached on the strict forestry laws they were safe. Not so with William II; his red face could grow purple with rage and the unfortunate man or woman responsible would often have no knowledge of why this should be so. So, all must walk warily with the new King.

Like his father he loved possessions and looked in all directions in order to add to his wealth, but unlike his father he could be extravagant on occasions. That was in pursuit of his own pleasure. When he wanted something he wanted it fiercely and he was determined to get it.

Life had not been easy since his accession. There was certain to be trouble in the family. When he looked back over his childhood and remembered the stormy scenes in their various schoolrooms he laughed aloud. Robert would have run him through on one occasion but for the intervention of their father. Robert and he would always be enemies, because naturally Robert believed that he, as the eldest son, had more right to the crown of England than William Rufus had. It was true Robert was Duke of Normandy but it was a far better thing to be King of England than Duke of Normandy. And then there was Henry. Poor young Henry who was left without land—only five thousand pounds of silver and his father's prophecy that one day he would be richer than either of his brothers.

Following this train of thought Rufus sighed and said: "It was unfortunate that our father had too many sons. It is a common failing that kings either have too many or not enough. You see what a wise man I am, my friends, for I have no sons—not even a bastard or two. If all men were as I am how much more comfortable the world would be."

"It would not be over-populated, my lord," said his favourite friend.

"Oh, we'd keep a few studs for that purpose," laughed Rufus.

"My lord's young brother might be of use."

The young man laughed.

"What then?" asked Rufus. "Has he added another to his tally? I hear he was giving a good account of himself with the Lady Nesta of Wales."

"Exceeding good, my lord, and they say the lady grows larger each day."

"It keeps the young rake out of mischief," said Rufus. "But I have to keep my eyes on master Henry. It may surprise you, my friends, but he occasionally takes his

21

thoughts from the ladies' bedchambers and dreams of the battlefield."

"As my lord knows to his cost."

"We could have finished him at St. Michael's Mount but for my elder brother. Robert is a fool. There was not a drop of water in the castle; they were dying in the fortress for lack of it, and what did my chivalrous brother Robert do? He sends him water—and not only water, but wine for his board. I could have killed him when I heard. "This is our brother," he said, and he looked at me with those rather mournful eyes of his. He is very beautiful and he was my mother's favourite you know. He was always vain and hates the fact that his legs are too short. My father used to jeer at him. Curthose he called him. My father thought there was only one perfect man in the world—himself. And those of us who did not resemble him were poor things in his opinion. But when Robert rebelled against him and Richard died he turned to me. Richard was the first favourite. He looked like a Norman, you see. The rest of us had the Flanders touch...except Henry. He has a Norman look—tall and with that fine curly hair. I doubt not it is that which brings him so much favour in the ladies' bedchambers. But I was telling you that we could have been rid of Henry but for Robert. And what has he ever done but bring trouble and bastards into the realm?"

The young man laughed obediently.

"Come, my fine friend, what is there to laugh at? I am a man beset by brothers, and now Henry has squandered his patrimony and roams the countryside seeking consolation in robbing ladies of their virtue since he cannot rob me of my throne, and I doubt not his soul is stained purple with the sin of fornication. Listen."

There was a commotion below the window. Riders were approaching.

"Messengers mayhap. What now?" said Rufus. "No evil news I trust to spoil the pleasant evening I had planned for us."

The messenger was brought into his presence.

Rufus dismissed the man with the customary command: "Go and refresh yourself," and read the dispatch.

Then he said: "Edgar Atheling has arrived in England with his sister's brood."

"What will you do, my lord?" asked his favourite friend.

"That, my dear, remains to be seen," he answered. He narrowed his eyes. "Rest assured I shall have them under close surveillance."

* * *

William Rufus opened his eyes and sleepily surveyed his bedchamber. It had been a riotous night and as usual after such festivities morning came too soon. Sunlight filtering in through the narrow slit of a window shone onto the stone recess seat cut into the wall, but because this was a royal bedchamber it contained some modern luxuries such as the faldestol on which he sat when he entertained guests in his bedroom, letting them make do with the wall seats or the floor. A velvet drapery was thrown over it at this moment. His eyes went to the chest with its fine carving; in this were kept his clothes, and although he slept on a bag of straw this was placed on a bed the frame of which was elegantly carved.

In the early mornings he let his mind wander over state affairs. He was thinking at this time about the Atheling who had taken refuge in his country. Edgar had always amused him—pretty youth. He would never be a king though. He was not made of the right stuff. Still the people could rally to the Atheling if they hated the Norman enough, and he must face the truth: there had always been animosity towards the Normans.

Yet they could be persuaded, or could they? He had persuaded them once. That was when Robert had tried to take the crown from him. He had expected it. Naturally the eldest son wanted the greater prize.

But their father had nominated him, William Rufus, as his successor. What had he said to him on his deathbed, stern as ever? "What are you doing here? Why are you not claiming your kingdom?"

Rufus laughed. One had to admire the old man. He was the greatest they would ever know, and if he was without humour he was the finest soldier of his day and for most of that which was his and his family's today they had to thank William the Conqueror who had given it to them.

They could never be like him—any one of them. And did they want to? Not Rufus. He knew how to enjoy life—which he was sure his father had not—and he intended to go on doing it.

But now his mind was straying from Edgar Atheling because that fellow's being in the country reminded him of the early days of his reign when Robert had come against him. Robert was a fool; he could be relied upon to fail in any military exercise.

Rufus laughed to think of those days when the Norman barons who owned estates in England had declared that they would not accept Rufus as the King of England and prepared to set up Robert in his place.

Their uncle Odo had been Robert's general. Odo! That Bishop who had been in disgrace with the Conqueror because he had passed over much English treasure to Rome. The old fool had had a fancy to become Pope and believed that by bribing the Cardinals he could persuade them to elect him. Fortunately William had discovered this, and sent him back to Normandy where he had languished in a dungeon until his brother Robert of Mortain (like Odo, the son of their grandmother's marriage after their grandfather's death, to Herlwin de Conteville) misguidedly persuaded the Conqueror, on the latter's deathbed, to set him free.

Free to come against the King whom William himself had chosen!

Rufus had been in danger then and he prided himself that he had acted with extreme astuteness. He had asked the people of England whether they wished to put their necks in the Norman yoke. This amused Rufus for it struck him as highly amusing that he, the Norman son of a Norman father, should be pleading thus. But there was some truth in it for while Robert had remained entirely Norman, he, Rufus, had to some extent become Anglicized.

"My good people," he had declared, "rally to my banner, I swear to you that if you will stand beside me and thrust out the unwanted Norman, there shall be no more unjust taxation, every man shall enjoy his own hunts and chases in his own woods and wolds, and all abuses of the law shall be abolished."

How they had cheered him! How they had rallied to his banner. And when Odo arrived he was set upon and taken prisoner, and it was not until Rufus had won the day that Robert characteristically, put in an appearance. How typical of Robert! How had he ever thought he could outwit their father? That had been just another of his miscalculations, of course.

Rufus could not be hard on his captives. How could he be ... on Normans? Moreover many of them had been friends with whom he had played in his childhood. More important was the fact that he might need their support in the future for he knew that he would not be able to keep the promises he had made to the people; the taxation which the people called unjust, could certainly not be abolished; nor would he change the forestry laws for nothing was going to be allowed to interfere with his pleasure in the chase.

So he and Robert made a pact. If death should overtake either of them that one would pass over all his possessions to the other. Thus the survivor would have both England and Normandy.

It had been at this time that Henry had become so incensed against his brothers. He said they ignored his existence; they forgot that he also was their father's son, and he demanded to know what his inheritance would be.

"The ladies of England," retorted Rufus. "And I doubt Robert would debar you from enjoying the Norman ones when you visit his Duchy."

"And I'll leave the men to you," answered Henry, and for a while they hurled insults at each other. But Henry was indeed resentful. He had set himself up in the fortress of St. Michael's Mount with the intention of making himself a nuisance to both his brothers.

It was not possible to enjoy a peaceful reign. There would always be conflict. It was looming now in yet another spot. The Church! The Conqueror had been a deeply religious man and he had lived in harmony with his Archbishop of Canterbury, Lanfranc. Rufus lacked his father's devotion to the Church. Often he blasphemed against it and he did not suffer from those twinges of conscience which had beset the Conqueror when he considered his reception in heaven. Rufus had an inherent dislike of churchmen. Many of them were rapacious, a characteristic he understood perfectly being well endowed with it himself, but whereas he admitted this they hid their avaricious natures under a guise of hypocrisy. At least Rufus was not a hypocrite. In private Rufus could laugh at himself and did. Very few people of his time could do that; many of his intimates had whispered among themselves that it was only this characteristic which made him tolerable.

He could not accuse Lanfranc of hypocrisy. There was a man of great integrity and Rufus had never had any intention of removing him from his post. Death had done that. The See of Canterbury was very rich and Rufus had made a habit of keeping the abbeys and bishoprics under his own control whenever the occasion arose. He found this highly profitable; so when Lanfranc died he added Canterbury to those over which he held sway and was in no hurry to find a successor to the Archbishop.

Since he had been ill, however, even he had experienced a few qualms. His priests had shaken their heads over him as though they feared his future in Heaven if he did not repent and, although had he been in good health he would have laughed at them, it was not so easy with Death lurking not far distant.

It so happened that Anselm, the prior of Bec in Normandy, was visiting England and because of this man's qualities, Rufus decided that he should become Archbishop of Canterbury.

When the offer was made to Anselm, he thanked the King but shook his head. "My home is in Normandy," he told him. "I have lived so long at Bec that I could consider no other."

Rufus smiled grimly. We shall soon see about that, he told himself.

Craftily he ordered that Anselm should visit his sick room where he had ordered the leading churchmen to assemble. When the bewildered Anselm entered a crozier was thrust into his hands and a Te Deum was sung to celebrate his election.

The sick King lay back on his bag of straw smiling. He could never resist baiting the clergy.

Anselm looked sternly at him. "My lord," he had said, "you must understand that I am not one of your subjects. I am a Norman and owe obedience only to my Duke."

Rufus laughed at him. "So you would lay down the crozier we have bestowed on you, would you? Do so ... for a while. You will take it up again."

And he did, for Robert at the time was eager to come to terms with his brother after having been so disastrously defeated in his attempt to take the English crown that it was necessary for him to comply with the request of Rufus. So the reluctant Anselm had been obliged to take the post offered him and now presided over the See of Canterbury.

These fanatical men were a menace to peace. They had to question this and that. They could never let well alone; and now master Anselm was trying to prove that the Church was more important that the State, a belief which Rufus would never accept.

He had a power though, Rufus would admit that. These religious fanatics often had. He had preached to Rufus so eloquently of the dire punishment that befell sinners in hell that even he had become a little shaken and had released numerous prisoners, cut taxes and forgiven people their debts to the crown. But now he was well again and he had repudiated all that he had been persuaded into promising when the gates of Hell had appeared uncomfortably close and warm.

"Death has receded," Anselm had told him. "But do not imagine it will not return."

"Time enough to repent when I see it in the distance," Rufus had commented with a laugh.

"You are asking to be struck dead without warning."

"Must I give up all then for the sake of my future life?"

"That is the Christian way."

Rufus grimaced. "My good Anselm, my sins are so

many that I doubt they'd all be forgiven however many good works I performed. So I will do as I wish down here to make sure that I get what I want at least in one place."

Anselm was horrified. Let him be. Rufus was not sure that he believed all these pious men told him. He liked better the religion of his ancestors—feasting in Valhalla after death, a paradise to be reached through valour rather than pious deeds. He could have his place there with the utmost ease, for he had inherited his father's courage and was well skilled in the arts of war.

He might bait Anselm but all the same he knew that there would be trouble in that quarter.

The immediate anxiety though was the presence of Edgar Atheling in the country. Many of his advisers had said that the Atheling claim to the throne must never be forgotten.

It was true, but Edgar was no fighter. He did not believe Edgar would come against him. Such a pleasant boy, though more Robert's friend than his. He was too rough for the Atheling, but Robert with his charm and his extravagances and his love of poetry had been as a brother to Edgar.

One of his knights asked for audience and he received him in his bedroom. He must have important news to come to him thus in the morning when his temper might not be too good.

"What bad news bring you?" he growled. He like to see the alarm in faces. Why he could order the fellow to a dungeon and have his eyes put out if he offended him. Not that he would do this. That was a punishment he reserved for real offenders. But it gave a pleasant sense of power to set men trembling.

"One of your knights has been slain in combat, my lord."

"And what concern of mine should this be that I must be awakened at an early hour of the morning to learn of it?"

The hour was not early but the fellow dared not contradict.

"I believe you would wish to know, my lord, that he

was slain by a friend of Edgar Atheling because he said that he was raising up a family who would try to take the crown."

Rufus nodded slowly.

"So this man was slain by a friend of the Atheling. He has good friends, has he not? And indeed so have I for they bring me news when they think I should know it."

The man smiled slowly and Rufus broke into loud laughter.

"Brave man," he said.

"To take up the cause of the Atheling, my lord, 'tis so."

"Nay!" roared Rufus. "You are a brave man to disturb me from my rest. You know my temper. 'Tis not of its best at this hour, man."

But his humour was good. He was pleased with the fellow.

He wanted to think about this Atheling and his family. A young boy deprived of his crown by a usurping bastard; and the family taking refuge in England. Edgar was brave to come here where many would say he had more right to the throne than William Rufus.

Edgar was not a coward; he had always know that; but he was not a fighter either.

There was one thing that was certain. Edgar had not come to England to claim the crown. How could he? He had no army. All the same it would not be a bad idea to keep him occupied.

He decided he would send for Edgar Atheling.

*   *   *

Edgar came in answer to his summons.

They took stock of each other. He has grown coarser, thought Edgar. But he had always been coarse with his red face, thick form, his rather stuttering speech and his manner which could change from bantering friendship to haughtiness in the space of minutes. Edgar had always been more in tune with Robert.

Very handsome, these Saxons, thought Rufus. Some of them are good fighters though. I remember Harold's coming to my father's court when he was made to swear away his kingdom over the bones of dead saints. There was a handsome man, but a fighter too. Edgar was not that, but no coward. A dreamer more like. Another such as Robert.

"So Edgar you have brought your sister's brood here."

"And grateful we are for your hospitality."

"Well if I denied it where else would you have gone? To Normandy?"

"I had wondered whether I should throw myself on Robert's mercy."

"Robert is not my good friend at this time, Edgar. You know he fancied he would like my crown . . . or rather his barons did. Robert is too indolent to fancy much but extravagant living."

"You wrong him, William."

"You were always his special friend. But they were good times we had together, eh, Edgar? The trouble with my brothers and myself is that we're a fighting brood. Robert wants what I have. I confess I should not mind having what Robert has and Henry would like what we both have. What can you expect with a father such as ours?"

"He was one of the greatest men the world has known."

"Ay to that, but an uncomfortable one, Edgar. Though in the latter years he and I grew close. After Richard died he took me into his confidence. He was determined to make a king of me and I was determined to be one—and to remain one—that worked well. But, Edgar, I have not brought you here to talk of the past but of the future. What of these nephews and nieces of yours?"

"As you know, William, Donald Bane has snatched the crown of Scotland."

"And the poor little rightful king is too young to make an attempt to regain it."

"Too young and too poor."

"Well, he has an uncle who is not so young."

"But poor, William."

Rufus burst into loud laughter.

"Well, we shall see, we shall see. There are girls I believe of marriageable age?"

"They are over-young as yet. Edith, the eldest, is not yet sixteen."

"What do you propose to do with them?"

"I had hoped you would give your consent for them to be educated in an abbey with the nuns."

"You don't propose they should take the veil?"

Edgar shrugged his shoulders helplessly. "Who would wish to marry dowerless princesses?"

"Their coffers may be empty, Edgar, but their veins are furnished with good royal Saxon blood."

"'Tis true. Their parents dead though, their brother dispossessed, themselves penniless . . ."

"You tell a doleful tale. Is not their aunt the Abbess of Rumsey?"

"That is so."

"Well then, Edgar, that takes care of the girls. Let them go to their aunt and when the time comes we shall see whether it will be the marriage bed or the nun's veil for them."

"William, I was certain I could rely on your friendship."

"The younger ones may go to Rumsey too until plans are made for them. But it is your Edgar of whom we must think. There is a young King without a crown. This Donald Bane is a man who holds a high opinion of himself, I am told. He has displaced a young boy who had just become an orphan and who had no army behind him. He has installed himself in his castle and prates of marching below the border to harry my good subjects. You would have thought that which happened to his predecessor would have warned him, would you not, Edgar?"

"As I warned Malcolm."

"Ay, you were always a cautious man, Edgar. I have a proposal. What if I provided troops and placed you and young Edgar at the head of them and you marched into Scotland and displaced this traitor?"

"You would do that, William!"

"I would like to see this young Edgar. If I had as high an opinion of him as I have of his uncle, I might

well do that. I want this Donald Bane put down, Edgar.
And when I have set young Edgar on the throne I shall
expect him to be a good friend to me. He will swear
fealty to me. He will be a good vassal; then there will
be peace between me and the King of Scotland."

Edgar's eyes were gleaming. Rufus of course would
want repayment for his help. That was natural. But it
was far better for Edgar to be restored as King of Scotland, even though he was also vassal to the King of
England, than to wander about the world stateless as
Edgar Atheling had done for so many years.

The pact was concluded.

Edgar should have the chance to regain his kingdom
and when he did he would always be grateful to the
King of England.

*　　*　　*

The Abbess received the children in her sanctum.
The stone flags were cold to the feet and there was no
furniture, only a board on trestles and a rough stool on
which the abbess sat.

The children stood before her while her cold stern
gaze flickered over them.

The eldest, Edith, was the most handsome, she decided. Therefore she would need the most correction.
Her hair was in two thick plaits and as one of these
hung over her shoulder, the Abbess Christina assured
herself that her niece had placed it there for adornment
and must be cured of the cardinal sin of vanity.

"Pray remove that object. It disgusts me," said Christina, staring at her niece.

Edith had no idea to what she referred and stammered: "I do not understand . . ."

"That piece of hair which you have wantonly placed
where you think it will be admired. Hide it, I say."

Edith flushed and taking the plait threw it over her
shoulder where it could no longer offend the Abbess.

"You will learn how we deal with vanity here," she
said. "We pray that it shall be taken from us and if it
is not it is whipped out of us."

"I was not meaning to show my hair. I . . ."

"Silence," said Christina. "We do not excuse our follies. We admit them and pray for the power to cast them out. They are devils that possess us and need to be exorcised."

Edith silently prayed that Uncle Edgar would return and take them away from this cold unfriendly place and this hostile woman. But she knew that she prayed in vain. It had been her mother's wish that their Aunt Christina should care for them. Could their kind and gentle mother have known how harsh a life of religion had made her sister?

The little ones were cowering close to her. Mary was dismayed; but Edith knew that Aunt Christina had decided that she should be her main victim.

"You are here to learn to become worthy members of a great family," said the Abbess, "but first of all you must be children of God. Here we show no mercy to those who stray from virtue. Understand that, every one of you. You will now go to the apartments reserved for you and there you will find your garments ready. Those which you now wear will be taken from you. They are the vestments of the world."

A nun came into the chamber and the Abbess said to her: "Take them away, Sister. You know your duty."

Edith was about to protest and for a few moments she and her aunt looked into each other's eyes. When her parents were alive she had resisted Aunt Christina's efforts to put her into a nun's habit. Once Aunt Christina had brought the rough serge garment to her and forced her to put it on. It had scratched her skin and was uncomfortable and ever after Aunt Christina had always terrified her. There was something satanic about her for all her piety or perhaps because of it. She was so sure of her virtue that she did not care how much she hurt others in her efforts to make them as good as herself.

How angry her father had been when he had seen her in the nun's habit!

"Take that thing off," he had roared. And how happily she had done so. "My daughter is not destined for the cloistered life," he had shouted. "A match will be made for her. She is to be a wife and a mother."

33

Aunt Christina had been angry, but she could not stand out against the King of Scotland. Alas, her father's eye had been cruelly pierced by a traitor's lance and there was no one to protect her now and she was at the mercy of stern Aunt Christina.

The chamber to which she was taken was small and cold. There was a crucifix on the wall and a bag of straw on the floor. On the straw lay a black robe—of the same starchy material which she remembered. She shuddered with horror as the nun bade her remove her clothes. "Everything," said the nun, her eyes glinting. Off came the soft shift and it was replaced by the rough one and over that went the black robe.

Never in her life had Edith felt so desolate. Her parents dead, herself a prisoner in this gloomy place presided over by harsh jailors.

The nun left her and when she was alone she ran her hands over the hateful cloth; then in a sudden rage she took off the robe and throwing it to the floor, stamped on it.

"I will never, never take the veil," she cried. *"Never!"*

Then the realization of the futility of what she was doing swept over her.

What was the use of stamping on the cloth? What was the use of raging?

She knelt down by the straw and clasping her hands together prayed: "Oh God, help me. Save me from my aunt Christina."

She rose in despair, supposing God to be on the side of a pious abbess rather than on that of a young girl with thoughts of worldliness.

"What can I do?" she whispered in despair.

Then she heard footsteps, so hastily she picked up the robe and put it on.

For a while she must accept defeat.

* * *

A great enthusiasm had arisen throughout the Christian world to make what was called Holy War on the Infidel.

For many years pilgrims of all Christian nations had

taken the journey to Jerusalem believing that by doing so they would expiate their sins. Jerusalem was in the hands of the Infidel and this influx of visitors, often very wealthy, had become a profitable trade to them.

Robbery had flourished; worse than that, pilgrims had been seized and taken into captivity; many of them had been tortured and killed. For years men had been preaching against these practices; and one of these was Peter the Hermit, a man of great eloquence who had aroused indignation throughout Christendom.

Pope Urban II had called a council at Placentia and during this the suggestion had been put forward, and unanimously agreed upon, that there should be a crusade against the Infidel.

Those who craved for adventure seized on the idea. To make war, to fight and kill and earn a place in Heaven for so doing seemed an excellent plan; and very soon after the meeting at Placentia, the first Crusade was being made ready.

This was an idea which appealed whole-heartedly to Robert of Normandy. This adventurer, dreamer and idealist who had recently been defeated by his own brother, saw in the venture an escape from the tiresome business of making terms with Rufus, who was more wily than he was.

He had lived a life of great extravagance; he had squandered many fortunes; he had been guilty of self-indulgence. Now he would go and fight the Infidel for the glory of God and the Christian Faith and so earn a remission of his sins.

So must his grandfather—Robert's namesake—have felt. Robert the Magnificent, they had called him. He had been a second son and could not tolerate that his elder brother should inherit Normandy. So he had tried to wrest it from him and, legend had it, had poisoned him. After that his conscience had smote him so continuously that he finally decided to make a pilgrimage to the Holy Land in the hope of wiping out his sins. And he, the present Duke Robert? Well, he had chafed against his father's delay in granting him the Duchy and when they had met in combat had come near to killing him. So he had need of expiation too.

If he were to go to Jerusalem to join in this Holy War he would need more money, for he would have to equip an army which would be worthy of him. And how could he do this in his circumstances? He had never been able to keep money. Perhaps it was this failing which had incensed his father, for the Conqueror was avaricious in the extreme and never spent money unless it was going to bring him some good which would be more beneficial than the sum spent. But Robert could never resist giving money to his friends, to his mistresses, to any who asked for it. Money and possessions were to be enjoyed, not hoarded; and he found great pleasure in giving. Unhappily he often gave what was not his to give; consequent he was invariably in dire straits.

Now he was as penniless as usual and he desperately needed money to prepare himself to join the crusade.

What could he do?

He sent for Alan, Duke of Bretagne, his brother-in-law. Alan had married his sister Constance and was now a widower, for after a few years of marriage Constance had died. Alan was looking for a suitable wife and having been the husband of one of the Conqueror's daughters he was looking high.

An idea had come to Robert.

When Alan came to him, Robert told him that he had a mind to join the Crusade.

"I need money," said Robert, "more urgently than you need a wife."

"You would need a fortune, my lord, to equip yourself for this venture."

"And where should I find it? If my father had left me England..."

Alan was silent. Rufus was showing himself to be a more able ruler in England than Robert was in Normandy, and he doubted whether Robert would have been more able to equip a crusade if he had been King of England than he was as Duke of Normandy.

"I have been thinking of my brother Rufus for I believe I could get the money from him."

"Has he so much money?"

"He has means of raising it. He could tax the people of England."

"Would he do this for you?"

"If the bargain was attractive enough."

"How could that be so?"

"If I offered him something he would like to have ... in pawn say. For a sum of money to be repaid on my return from the Holy Land I would offer him ..." Robert paused and Alan looked at him in disbelief. Robert lowered his eyes and said: "Normandy."

Alan stared at the Duke.

Robert squirmed uneasily. "It would only be for a few years. He would be a kind of Regent. It would protect the Duchy against my enemies. I have decided that for a sum of 10,000 marks I will offer him Normandy. It is to be returned to me when I come back and repay the loan."

Alan was too dismayed to comment and Robert went on: "I want you to go to my brother and lay this suggestion before him. At the same time you might well find a wife. The royal Athelings are in an abbey at Rumsey of which one of them is the head. The eldest girl is Edith and marriageable. You might well find that she is a suitable bride for you; and in view of the project you will be laying before him, I think my brother will be in a temper to approve the suit."

So Alan set out for England.

*   *   *

When Rufus heard the proposition he was thrown into a great state of excitement.

Normandy for 10,000 marks. He would find that money no matter where he had to go for it.

Oh what a fool Robert was! What a mad dreamer! He did not deserve Normandy. That much was clear.

Yes, yes, he declared, Alan of Bretagne might go to the Abbey of Rumsey and see the girl. He waved his hand for him to be gone. He could not wait to call together a meeting of the men he would need to carry out his plans.

How were they going to raise 10,000 marks? There was one way of raising money known to him. Taxation. If his subjects had land and money and he needed it, they must provide it. And if they refused, there were dungeons waiting for them.

First he called in Ranulf Flambard, his greatest friend and favourite.

"Ha, Ranulf my boy, listen to this."

Ranulf sprawled familiarly on the faldestol. He roared with laughter when Rufus told him of Robert's proposition.

"We'll get the money," cried Ranulf. "We'll get the money and Normandy."

Rufus gazed affectionately at Ranulf—a man after his own heart. He had been attracted to him the first time he had seen him. His sexual tastes were similar to those of Rufus and they were immediately close companions. Ranulf was the son of a parish priest of Bayeux who had come to London soon after the Conquest. Hearing much of the King's manner of life he came to Court and his rude manners, his hearty laughter, his malicious tongue and a certain rough wit immediately appealed to Rufus.

Ranulf had quickly discovered that the best way to stay in the good graces of Rufus was to keep him well supplied with money and he had devised new methods of taxation. It was for this reason that he had been given the name of Flambard—the firebrand; for his methods of extortion were not over nice.

Ranulf now threw himself whole-heartedly into the matter of raising 10,000 marks. He instituted a new form of bribery. Men could pay their way out of trouble. Criminals were set free if they could raise enough money to buy their release.

"The church is rich," said Ranulf; and they laughed together. Ranulf knew how his sovereign enjoyed discomforting the clergy.

"Get to it, my good friend," cried Rufus. "And begin with our reluctant Archbishop of Canterbury."

*   *   *

Anselm was amazed to learn of the bargain into which Robert of Normandy had entered with his brother. He would have refused to help raise the money but he was warned by his friends that that would be unwise. He must remember that Rufus was a violent man and that Rome was too far off to offer him protection. He could be thrown into a dungeon and blinded—a revenge often taken by the King on his victims,—for the Conqueror himself had abolished the death penalty and decided that it was a more just punishment to rob rebels of their eyes than their lives.

Anselm therefore raised five hundred pounds of silver in answer to the King's command.

Rufus roared with anger when he received this offer.

"Of what use is that to me?" he demanded. "From the rich See of Canterbury I want more and shall have more."

Anselm replied that he could not give what he did not possess; and he sold the silver and distributed the proceeds among the poor.

Well, mused Rufus, five hundred pounds worth of silver was better than nothing. So he sent a messenger to Anselm to tell him that he would accept the silver after all.

Anselm was not displeased to reply that the silver had already been sold and the money it had raised given to the poor.

Rufus's face grew purple when he heard this.

He would have to show that insolent priest who was master in this land, he decided, and that soon. In the meantime his great concern was money ... money for Normandy.

"I want money," was the message sent to Anselm. "Have you not gold and silver boxes full of dead men's bones?"

That the King should suggest using the ornaments

on coffins was repugnant to the Archbishop and he ignored the King's request.

Rufus forgot Anselm temporarily. He had accumulated the 10,000 marks. The agreement was drawn up. Normandy was in pawn; and if Robert could not repay the loan and if he failed to return, then Rufus King of England would be also Duke of Normandy.

A Suitor at the Abbey

How dreary was life at Rumsey. There were lessons and prayers all through the day; and the girls were made to wear the black Benedictine robe of the order which had been founded by King Alfred.

They were rebellious as far as they could be. Edith had often taken off her robe when she was alone and stamped on it to relieve her feelings. One day when she was thus engaged she perceived a pair of eyes watching her through the aperture in the door of her cell and she was suddenly more frightened than she had ever been in her life. The eyes disappeared but shortly afterwards her aunt came into her cell, but by that time she had hastily put on the robe and was kneeling before the cross on the wall. The Abbess stood quietly behind her for some seconds; then a pair of hands was placed on her shoulders and she was forced down until her head was on the stone floor.

"Jezebel!" whispered Aunt Christina. Edith's head was pressed against the stones; she cried out in pain and Aunt Christina laughed derisively.

"Get up then, spawn of the devil," she said.

Edith stood before her.

The Abbess sat on the stone seat cut out of the wall.

"You like not the holy habit," she said.

"My father said I was not to be a nun."

"It may be that God has punished him for denying his daughter her vocation."

"I do not wish to take the veil."

"It may be that you will have no choice in the matter," said Christina. She narrowed her eyes. "Take off the robe you so despise."

"I do not despise it. It is only that I feel it is not for me."

"Take it off," said Christina.

Edith took off the robe and stood in the rough hairy shift.

"Take that off too," was the command.

"I have nothing beneath it," replied Edith.

"Well let us see this body of which you are so proud."

"Nay, you mistake me. It is not pride. It is . . ."

"Vanity!" The Abbess rose and taking the shift in her firm hands pulled it off. Edith stood naked before her.

She studied the girl. "Voluptuary!" she said. "So you wish to flaunt this do you?" She pinched the firm flesh and brought her face close to that of Edith. "Of what do you think when you lie in your cell? Of what are you thinking when you are on your knees? Pray tell me that. Nay, I will tell you. You are thinking sinful thoughts. You are thinking of men and this body in their hands."

"No, no, Aunt Christina, it is not so."

"Then you will take the veil."

"No, I will not."

"Why not, if your thoughts are as pure as you would have me believe?"

"I wish to marry, to have children."

"Did I not tell you what was in your mind? So you add lies to your many sins."

"My mother was a good woman—the best that ever lived," said Edith defiantly, "yet she married and had children."

The Abbess took Edith by the arm and pushed her down on her straw.

"So you long for men. You want this body you so much admire to be admired by others, to be caressed. I shall caress it in my way . . . in God's way." She called to one of the nuns who was waiting outside the cell. The woman came in carrying a long thin cane.

"There, my daughter. This is the child from whom evil must be purged. She dreams of the caresses of men; give her the caress of the cane."

"Mother," began the nun.

The Abbess turned her venomous gaze on the nun. "Do you disobey me, then?"

"Nay, Mother." The nun came to the prostrate figure of Edith and lifted the cane. It came down stinging her across the thighs. "Again," said the Abbess. "Are you so feeble that you can do no better than that? Again and again."

Edith turned her back on them and covered her face with her hands. "Oh, Uncle Edgar," she prayed, "why did you send us here?"

The Abbess had snatched the cane from the nun that she herself might use it. The strokes were more firm, more vicious.

"Aunt Christina, I beg of you . . ."

"Ah, the miscreant becomes a penitent. Yes, daughter, what have you to say?"

"Do not, I beg of you."

"Then you will wear the robe and love the robe, the outward sign of that which is holy?"

"Yes, I will wear the robe."

The Abbess laughed. "Your tender skin may rebel even more so than before. There are weals on your buttocks, girl. Do not strip naked and dream that they have been put there by a too eager lover. Come, get up. Put on your shift. Is it not shameful that you should stand thus naked. You will love the robe. You will remember that these are the robes of the Black Benedictines which our famous ancestor founded. You will pray that you may be purged of your worldliness. Come, I am impatient."

Painfully Edith rose to her feet. Over her head went

the hideous black hairy shift; she was enclosed once more in the black robes.

"On your knees," said the Abbess. "Ask for forgiveness, for you are in dire need of the intercession of the saints."

With lowered eyes Edith stood before her aunt. The Abbess was satisfied. She turned and with the attendant nun left the cell.

So she must wear the robes. But never never shall I take the veil, Edith promised herself. This could not go on. A time would come when Uncle Edgar came to visit them. Then she would remind him of her father's determination that she should marry. Her mother, it was true, had wished her to take the veil, but her mother had not known how vehemently she hated it.

She shuddered as the rough stuff touched her sore body.

She would never forget the sight of Aunt Christina, the cane raised in her hand, her eyes gleaming with a virtue so intense that it was like a fierce pleasure.

How she longed for the old days in the schoolroom under dear old Turgot.

But the beating had strengthened her determination to escape.

* * *

There were visitors to Rumsey Abbey. Alan, Duke of Bretagne, wished to pay his respects not only to the Abbess but to the Atheling ladies whom he understood were being educated there.

The Abbess was gracious yet haughty.

"It is not the custom of the Abbey to allow novitiates to receive visitors."

"Novitiates!" cried Alan. "I understood that the Princesses were merely here to receive an education, and were destined to play that part in the world so often reserved for ladies of their blood."

"They have a great desire for the convent life," said the Abbess and then to absolve her soul she thought: As yet they are not fully aware of this but it exists.

"I do not think it is the desire of their uncle and their eldest brother that they should take the veil."

"That is a matter for the future. For this time I must respect their youth. They cannot receive visitors."

"I understood differently from the King."

"You come from the King?"

"With his blessing."

The Abbess was taken aback. She dared not offend Rufus. She had to be grateful that he allowed her, a member of the Atheling family, to take up the post of Abbess in an English abbey. If Rufus had sent Alan of Bretagne here it could be with one purpose. He was a possible husband for one of the girls and as Edith was the elder her turn would probably come first.

This was disturbing, but the Abbess was not one to be disturbed for long. She could however not prevent Alan's seeing Edith and Mary.

She sent for the girls. A summons to the Abbess's apartment was a cause for apprehension, but Mary, who had not been selected as the butt for Christina's venom as Edith had, and for whom the Abbess had no special plans as yet, was less concerned than her sister.

When the girls stood before her in their black garments, their hair carefully hidden, the Abbess surveyed them critically.

Edith had a certain beauty but the habit was very effective in concealing it and if this man had thoughts of marrying her, it might be possible to hurry her into taking some sort of vow. The determination to thwart Edith's desire for a worldy life was growing in the Abbess. A strong woman, accustomed to having her own way, never forgetting her royal birth and that the crown of England should have belonged to her family, she was anxious to rule her own empire and that included her nieces who had become part of it.

She had considered Alan of Bretagne. A middle-aged widower, a man not without power and clearly a friend of Robert of Normandy and Rufus King of England since the former had sent him to England on some mission and the latter had given him permission to come and visit the Atheling girls at her Abbey.

Of course he was looking for a bride, although he was a little old for that, but if he were hoping for heirs he would select a young girl. Constance, his dead wife and daughter of the Conqueror, had been childless during their six years marriage. And his union with the royal family had perhaps given him a taste for Princesses.

Christina did not like it. Nevertheless she could not disobey the orders of Rufus. She shuddered to think of the man. He was crude and vicious. She was well aware of his perverted sexual tastes. She thought a good deal about such sinful practices, conjuring up pictures of the crude red-faced King and his favourites, the better she promised herself to implore the saints to put a stop to such evil.

She noticed with satisfaction that Edith was looking a little fearful.

She kept them standing in suitable humility.

"We have a visitor who has asked to see you. As you know it is against rules of the Abbey for our young novices to receive visitors. But this is an old nobleman who is visiting England on some mission from the Duke of Normandy and the King has asked if I would graciously receive him. I shall of course be present. Now, we will go."

Alan of Bretagne bowed low and said what a pleasure it was to meet the Princesses.

It was long since Edith had seen such a man. He was old it was true, but he was a warrior and he brought a new and alien atmosphere into the Abbey.

"I have recently come from Normandy on a mission from my Duke to the King. The King will I doubt not wish to have news of you." He had a commanding air, this man. He turned to the Abbess. "I would like a word in private with the Princess Edith."

The Abbess bristled. Her strength was as great as his and she was on her own ground.

"My lord Duke, I could not so far forget my duty."

"Then," said the Duke, "we will sit together in yon window seat while you remain here with us."

The Abbess looked thunderous but the Duke had bowed to Edith and she without looking at her aunt walked to the window seat with the Duke in her wake. Christina, reminding herself that he came with the blessing of the King, and being astute enough to ask herself what report he would take back, had no alternative but to sign to Mary that she be seated on the far side of the chamber with her while the visitor and Edith conversed—in sight of her alert eyes, yet out of earshot.

The Duke bent towards Edith; she noticed his big hands, his weather-beaten skin, his rather rough method of speech. He lacked the grace of her uncle Edgar. He repelled her slightly. Ever since that day when her aunt Christina had made her put on the nun's habit and her father had expressed his annoyance and said: "She is to be a wife and mother," she had dreamed of the man she would marry. Naturally he was young, handsome, courteous, learned, noble; this rough Norman soldier appeared to have few of these virtues.

He said: "I'll be blunt. I've the King's permission to woo you. I need a wife. I need heirs." His eyes swept over her body carefully concealed in the black robes. "My wife Constance was barren. It was a source of great concern to me. She died and now I look for another wife."

Was this courtship? It was not how she had imagined it would be. This man leaned heavily towards her. "You're young. You should bear me sons. I have large estates in Normandy. The Duke is a friend of mine and holds me in favour. I am, as you must know, his brother-in-law. You are a Princess but a dowerless one. Your father's kingdom has been snatched from him. I doubt not your brother would be pleased to give you to me."

Edith said hastily: "I am not sure, my lord, that I would make you a suitable wife."

"Why not?"

"I know little of the demands of married life."

He laughed and from across the chamber the Abbess watched uneasily.

He laid a hot and heavy hand on her thigh. "That is something I can teach you. I would not wish you

47

practised in such matters. The King would give his consent I know."

"There is my uncle to be consulted."

"Have no fear. If the King consents so will he."

"I should need time to consider."

"You know little of the ways of love you tell me, maiden. You know little of the ways of state. The King has decided that I shall have you if I like what I see. And I like it well enough." Leaning towards her suddenly he pushed back the coif which concealed her hair. The two thick fair braids were revealed.

"Why yes," he said. "I like it well."

The Abbess, her face pink with mortification, had come towards them.

"I gave you no permission, sir, to *undress* my charges."

"Why, Abbess, you put ideas into my head. You could not call removing the head-dress undressing."

"The interview must be at an end," she said.

"So be it. I have seen enough," replied the Duke.

He stood up; he bowed. Christina said to the girls: "Wait here." And she herself conducted Alan of Bretagne from the chamber.

Edith's face was scarlet; she was trembling. She could not forget the gleam in his eyes.

Mary was excited. "Edith, does it mean that you are going to be married?"

"He said he had come to look at me and I was well enough."

"Did you like him?"

"I hated him. I hated the way he looked at me. As though I were a horse. His hands were hot and strong. Oh, Mary, he frightened me."

"But he would be a husband. Oh, Edith, if you marry I shall be here alone."

"They will find a husband for you doubtless."

"I hope he will not be as old as yours."

"I am going to my cell."

"The Abbess said we were to wait."

"I cannot, Mary. I want to get away from this room . . . I can see him too clearly here."

"She will be angry."

"I don't care, Mary. I must go."

*　　*　　*

She lay on her straw. Anything, she thought was better than submitting to what he was going to teach her. He was not the lover whom she had imagined. He wanted to breed sons and he was going to enjoy the breeding in a manner which she did not think would be very enjoyable to her. In truth he repelled her so strongly that what she wanted more than anything was never to see him again. Anything . . . simply anything was better than marriage with him.

But the King had given his consent. She knew well enough that Princesses had no say in whom they should or should not marry. She remembered the story of her mother's being washed up at Queen's Ferry and being given the hospitality of the King of Scotland; and the King of Scotland had been handsome and young, a veritable fairy prince. He had said: "This Princess is without dowry. She has no great position, but I love her and she loves me." And so they were married. Her mother's attendants had often told the story. How beautiful she was and how the King had taken one look at her and had declared his intention of marrying her. That was love; that was romance; and if, as Aunt Christina had said, she had been guilty of dreams, they had certainly not been lascivious; they had concerned an idyllic romance such as that of her parents.

The door of her cell was opened; the Abbess came and sat down looking at her.

"What did he say to you?"

"He spoke of marriage."

"And you were all a-tremble to go to him! I could see you could scarcely wait. You should thank me for taking such good care of you. He would have had you with child by now had I left you together."

Edith rose from her straw. "It is not true. I hated him. He is coarse . . . and I would rather do anything than marry him."

49

The Abbess was silent for a few moments; her expression softened. Here was triumph.

Then her lips hardened. "You're lying. I have seen the wanton in you."

"Nay, 'tis not so."

"There was pleasure on your face when he removed your coif."

"I hated his hands on me."

"You hated that? Then what of the marriage bed? That will be more to your taste doubtless. Such a man would debase you. Your body would belong to him. You know little of such men. You know nothing of what marriage means. It is my duty to make that plain to you. You cannot fall into his probing lascivious hands without knowing what is in store for you."

"Pray do not tell me. I cannot bear to hear."

"But you shall hear." The Abbess bent over her. She forced her to turn so that she lay on her back and the Abbess stared down at her.

Edith wanted to stop up her ears. She could not bear to listen to what her aunt was saying. She could not believe it. Her saintly mother could never have done such things.

The Abbess was smiling to herself; she seemed to be looking into far-off pictures which she was conjuring up from her imagination.

She said several times: "This I tell you for your own good. That you may know the ways of men and what they expect from women."

"I want none of him," sobbed Edith.

"There is only one safe place and that is in the Abbey. And here the soldiers could come at any time. Wear the robe always; hide your hair; try to look cold and unsmiling. For if the soldiers should come to this Abbey—as they have done to others—then men would seize you and do to you unlawfully what Alan of Bretagne would with the blessing of the church. There is only one way to save yourself. I offer you that. You can tell the King that you have made your mind to become a nun. That you have already taken some of your vows."

"I have not."

"That can be remedied."

50

"But I will not. My father said . . ."

"You want to go to this man? You long for the touch of his probing hands; your body calls out to share in his filthy practices."

"No. No."

"Listen to me. It is custom in our royal family that a member of it shall always be an Abbess of Wilton Abbey. I am shortly to leave Rumsey for Wilton. I shall train you to take my place for you shall be the Abbess in due time. It is your duty to our ancestors and first of all to the greatest of them, King Alfred. Would you displease him? He would haunt you if you did. Alfred, the saints and God himself have decreed that you shall follow me. You will be in command of a great Abbey; you will be following our royal tradition. I have decided that I shall train you for this."

"My father said I was not to take the veil."

"And what happened to him? He was killed by a lance that pierced his eye. His was a painful death. A just punishment, some might say."

"He was good to us."

"Your mother wished it. She was an Atheling as we are. She understood the traditions of royalty."

"Mayhap Mary could be the next Abbess."

"Mary is not my choice. You are that. You can absorb learning. You do well at your lessons. You will be educated as few women are. And this choice has to be made. The noble life of the Abbey or the foul one with that rake who could not keep his hands from you even in my presence."

"Why must there be this choice?"

"Because you are an Atheling. The King may well offer you to the Duke of Bretagne. If he does the only thing that can save you is the veil. I will leave you to think of it. Do not forget what I have told you. Imagine yourself in that man's bed. Then think of the peaceful, dignified life you could have here."

"I have not been happy here."

"Nay, for it has been my painful duty to chastise you. If you took your vows, if you made the proper choice, you would find how kind I could be. Now I will leave you. You will have much to think of. I believe you now. You do not care for that man ... but all men are alike. You have learned much this day. Think on it."

She was alone. Images would not disappear although she longed for them to do so. She could not help thinking of that man's hands; the gleam in his eyes, the horrible words of the Abbess.

Then she touched the rough serge of her habit. Fiercely she hated it. But not more fiercely than she hated Alan of Bretagne.

*   *   *

What rejoicing filled Edith's heart when Uncle Edgar arrived at Rumsey. He had always been the kind and gentle mentor, more easy to talk to than her own father. She was greatly relieved, for since the visit of Alan of Bretagne she had been haunted by nightmares; she had dreamed that she was poised between two fearful alternatives. She was on a path which led to beautiful pasture lands, but to reach those pastures she must pass through two gates—one guarded by a black-robed figure waiting to incarcerate her for life and the other by a beast with slavering lips who would submit her to all manner of humiliation and pain.

She needed no soothsayer to interpret that dream.

What will become of me? she wondered. Oh, where was her good Turgot? Where was her dear kind uncle? How often had she prayed that they would come to her, and now her prayers had been answered. Uncle Edgar had arrived at Rumsey.

Aunt Christina was present at their first meeting so that it was impossible to throw herself into his arms and tell him how happy she was to see him.

He had changed a little. There was something remote, almost saintly, about him.

"Your uncle brings good news," said Aunt Christina, smiling and looking almost benevolent. She was always pleased to see members of her own family and of course Edgar was very important because he was the true King of England.

"Yes," answereed Edgar, smiling from Edith to

52

Mary. "We have had good fortune in Scotland. We have displaced the traitor Donald Bane and your brother is now King of Scotland."

"What excellent news," said Aunt Christina. "I hope the traitor has been made to answer for his sins."

"He stares blindly at his prison walls. His eyes were put out. He will never see the crown of Scotland again."

Edith shuddered. They had taken the kingdom from him, she thought, but they could have left him his eyes. Better to have killed him than to have blinded him. And yet an evil man had pierced her father's eye. It seemed a cruel world. But she must rejoice with the rest because her brother Edgar had regained the crown and they were no longer penniless fugitives living on the bounty of the King of England.

Edith wanted to talk to Edgar alone that she might discuss the dilemma which faced her. Her spirits were high. Now that Edgar had regained his crown there would surely be a place for her in Scotland.

She could not tell him of her anxieties with Christina looking on, but there would be an opportunity later.

She was dismayed to hear that her uncle intended to stay but a few days, but she did manage to convey to him her great need to see him alone.

They walked in the gardens together—he in his embroidered cloak, she in her black Benedictine robes.

"Oh Uncle," she said, "please help me."

"If God wills," he said.

"Alan of Bretagne has been to Rumsey."

"I know it well. He wishes to marry you."

"I cannot do it, Uncle."

"My dear child," said Edgar, "there comes a time in our lives when we have to do that which does not please us."

"This is no small matter. This is for the rest of my life."

"I have to tell you, Edith, that I am going away." A rapt expression crossed his face. "You have heard there is to be a Holy War. Jerusalem, the Holy City, is in the hands of the Infidel. Our pilgrims have been robbed and tortured. We have decided to take the city from the Saracens and put it where it belongs, in Christian hands. The Duke of Normandy will go into battle. He is amassing a great army. I shall go with him."

"You are going to leave us then?"

"I have in truth come to say farewell to you before I go to Normandy. I am joining the Duke's army and we shall 'ere long be leaving for the Holy Land."

"You must help me before you go, Uncle Edgar. What can I do? I cannot marry Alan of Bretagne."

"Why not, my child? He was good enough for the Conqueror's daughter. He was accepted as the great King's son through marriage. Why should you feel thus?"

"Because he is old, Uncle."

"He is not too old to beget children; and he is a man of power in Normandy."

"I cannot bear him near me. Please do not let them force me into marriage with him."

"The King of England approves the match."

"But my brother is now King of Scotland. You have won back his crown for him."

"The King of Scotland is the vassal of the King of England. If Rufus promises you to Alan of Bretagne there is no gainsaying his wish. Your brother owes his crown to the King of England, for it was his forces who won it back for him."

"It was you and my brother," cried Edith.

"We commanded the army, but the soldiers came from Rufus and the price he asked was that Scotland should be a vassal of England." Edgar smiled his gentle smile but she knew his thoughts were far away in the Holy Land. "If Rufus gives you to Alan of Bretagne there is no help for it. You will be his wife."

She covered her face with her hands.

"Little niece," said the gentle Edgar, "is marriage so distasteful to you?"

She lowered her hands. "Nay," she said. "I know there could be great good in it. My mother was the best woman in the world" ... she said that defiantly, thinking of Aunt Christina ... "and she bore many children. I wish to bear children. I wish to make a home. But I would rather anything than marriage with Alan of Bretagne."

"So it is his person that revolts you."

"He is old and he smells of horses and he is rough and he would not care for me only for the sons ... and the pleasure ... he could derive from me. Uncle Edgar, I want marriage but not with Alan of Bretagne."

"My dear niece, Princesses cannot choose these matters."

"I know it well, but not Alan of Bretagne."

"It will rest with the King."

"And you say he has given his consent."

"He will I believe. He is pleased with the man because he has satisfactorily given him Normandy in pawn. This marriage would be a kind of reward for the services he has rendered."

"And am I to have no choice then?"

"Oh come, Edith, you are young, and you have childish notions. Marriage to one or another ... what matters it?"

"It matters to me," said Edith.

"You will go to Normandy; you will be chatelaine of a great castle; you will have your children."

"No, Uncle Edgar."

But Uncle Edgar was smiling serenely. He was obsessed by his own future glory. He was seeing himself in the battle—not that he was a great soldier nor did he love the battlefield—but he loved a cause; and this was the holiest cause of all: the wresting of the Holy Land from the Infidel and placing it in Christian hands.

For his part in such an enterprise surely a man would win his place of honour in the life hereafter. And of what importance was an ignorant young girl's fear of marriage compared with such glory?

Edith looked at him sadly. He was very good, of course; he had always been that; and now he was even more good because he was going on this Holy enterprise; and when people were dedicated to the service of God they did not seem to care very much for the troubles of human beings.

"Uncle Edgar," she went on, "I *cannot* marry this man. Please, I beg of you, tell me what I can do."

With what seemed like a mighty effort he forced his

mind from the contemplation of Jerusalem. He took her chin in his hands and turned her face up to his.

"If the King of England consents to your marriage there is only one thing that could prevent it."

"What is that, Uncle?"

"You could take the veil."

She lowered her eyes; she wanted to give way to despair. There was no way out, wherever she looked those two unhappy alternatives confronted her.

Edgar left on his glorious adventure and Edith went back to her fears.

The Miraculous Escape

It was with reluctance that Rufus received his archbishop. As he had said to Ranulf, he had little love for
any churchman. It was his belief that a king had no
need of the fellows and it was a well known fact that
they fancied themselves as the rulers of the realm.
They liked to put their kings in leading strings.

"That's something I'll not endure," he told his favourite. "My father was a religious man—he had far
more respect for the church than I ever could have. He
gave Lanfranc much licence. We were all brought up
to reverence Lanfranc. But Lanfranc is dead and now
we have this man Anselm. I forced him to office but I
could take the crozier from him with as much vehe-
mence as I made him take it."

"They'd say you would have to have an archbishop,"
said Ranulf.

"Ay, that they would. Lanfranc fancied himself as
a statesman and he was. My father made good use of
him. He sent him to Rome when he was excommunicated for marrying my mother and Lanfranc served

him well. It would seem that this Anselm would wish me to serve him."

"He calls it serving God," said Ranulf.

They laughed together.

Rufus went on: "Why to expect us two to pull together is like putting an untamed bull and a feeble old sheep in the same plough."

"Well, what are we going to do with our feeble old sheep?"

"Let him know who's master. He'll be here soon."

"I'll enjoy the encounter between the bull and the sheep. Will the bull savage the creature?"

"Nay, my friend. But I'll have some sport with him."

They laughed together and in due course Anselm arrived to see the King.

He was brought into the chamber and was clearly not pleased to see the insolent Ranulf present.

"I would have speech with my lord alone," he said.

The arrogance of these priests, thought Rufus cocking an eye at Ranulf. They understood each other well and it was not always necessary to speak their thoughts. Ranulf raised his eyebrows in a manner which suggested he agreed.

"You need feel no shyness in the presence of my good friend here," said Rufus.

Ranulf smiled insolently at the Archbishop.

"What I have to say to you, my lord . . ."

"Can be said in the presence of Ranulf. Pray proceed."

"There is disquiet in the country because you, my lord, have not kept the promises you made to the people when the taxes were collected to pay the Duke of Normandy."

"Promises!" said Rufus. "What should they care for promises when their King now holds Normandy? My brother Robert is going to find it somewhat difficult to regain the Duchy."

"They only wish, my lord, that those promises which were made to them should be kept."

Dreary old Anselm! His place was in a monastery. They should never have brought him from Bec to try to play politics. Rufus for all his flippant manner was well aware of the conflicts which could arise between the Church and the State. It was like a measure they danced, each jostling for the better position. The Church of England would have to learn it could not usurp the power of the King. For all his religious feeling the Conqueror had never allowed that. He had respected Lanfranc; he had listened to Lanfranc and kept on good terms with him; all the same there had never been any doubt who was the ruler of England. Nor should there be now. William II's rules should be as absolute as that of William I.

"Tell me the true reason for your coming here," said Rufus.

"You know, my lord, the conditions of my accepting the See of Canterbury."

"Ha! Here we have a monk of a little Norman monastery making terms with a king."

"An Archbishop of Canterbury, my lord. And as such I ask that the lands of the See which were taken when Lanfranc died be restored."

"You would be a rich man, Anselm."

"I have no wish for riches. But there is much I would do for the poor—spiritually and temporally."

"Churchmen, I am of the opinion, enjoy rich living as much as do their kings and masters."

Anselm ignored the gibe which certainly could not apply to him.

"I asked that in all matters spiritual you should take my counsel."

"There is little in which I would seek your counsel then, for I am not a spiritual man. I like well the pleasures of the flesh and I need no man's counsel to tell me how to obtain them."

Ranulf ostentatiously suppressed his laughter.

"There is the matter of my pallium."

"Ah," said Rufus. "Did you know, Ranulf, that an archbishop cannot perform his duties without his vestments? Now a king is by no means so handicapped. I can go about my business garbed as I will and do it none the worse."

"Without my pallium I cannot consecrate a bishop nor yet hold a council."

59

"We have a surfeit of bishops," growled Rufus.

Anselm said: "It is necessary that I go to Rome to receive my pallium from the Pope."

"From the man who calls himself Pope," said Rufus narrowing his eyes.

"From Urban II."

"Ah, the man whom *you* call Pope."

"He is widely recognized as Pope."

"He is not so in England and you are in England now, my Archbishop."

Anselm was embarrassed. There were two popes at this time. One was Urban II who represented the reforming party and Clement III who was supported by the imperialists. As Abbot of Bec, Anselm had sworn allegiance to Urban, but the King of England had done no such thing.

"If I am to carry out my duties I must go to Rome and collect my pallium, and if I am to succeed in office the lands of my See must be returned to me."

"How can you go to Rome and take this pallium from a man who, in England, is not accepted as the true Pope?"

"My lord King, there are few countries who do not accept him."

"I have told you *I* do not accept him. Am I or am I not the King of this realm? My father swore that no Pope should be acknowledged in this country without the consent of the King. I agree with him and I have not acknowledged Urban." His temper was rising and as usual on such occasions his face had grown scarlet with fury. He pointed to Anselm: "If you do, you defy my authority. You serve the Pope not the King. You are a traitor to your King, Sir Anselm, and what you are trying to do is tear the crown from my head."

Anselm was pale and calm in contrast to the red fury of the King.

"If you will grant me permission to retire, my lord, I will do so. But I must tell you that it will be necessary for me to call together a council."

"Your departure will please me, but before you go let me tell you this, Sir Anselm. I begin to wish I had never set eyes on you. I hated you yesterday. I hate you today and I shall hate you more the longer I live."

"Then it was an ill moment when you thrust the crozier onto me."

"Ill indeed."

"For now," Anselm reminded him, "you cannot dismiss me without the permission of the Pope—and that will be the Pope accepted by the world if not by you, my lord."

"Get out," screamed Rufus.

"When he had gone he looked at Ranulf and his anger faded suddenly. They began to laugh.

"We must devise some plan," said Ranulf, "for teasing your naughty Archbishop for there is no doubt that good as he may be in the service of the mock Pope, he is bad for my lord's temper."

"He is an obstinate man," mused Rufus. "He will go on demanding the return of these lands and I shall continue to refrain from giving them to him. As for his pallium, he'll not go to Urban for it. And what care I if he has no pallium at all? He can dispense with all his churchman's robes for all I care. Although I fancy he would be far from handsome without them."

"Not of a kind to tempt my lord to the pleasure of the flesh."

"Be silent, fool. That man has plagued me too much. I have matters of moment to think of."

"And I see they do not include the naked Anselm. You should rid yourself of him. Send him back to Normandy and find an archbishop who knows that the King is King and will have no one gainsay it."

"These church men are too powerful. I see conflict ahead. Who is to rule—the King or the Pope?"

"For a man who fears hell's torments it is indeed a problem, but you, my lord, have few such fears."

"Nay. I was brought up to be a Christian but I never took to it. I like better the gods of my more distant ancestors. Odin the All father, Thor with his hammer, Valhalla, Ranulf, where men feasted and made love according to their inclination. That is a way more to my fancy. And in my heart, Ranulf, I doubt that their heaven awaits these Christians. And if it is peopled by such as Anselm who would want to go there?"

"Not you. Not I."

"So I'll make sure of my pleasure here and if they are right and hell fire awaits me, I must needs endure it. Now this Anselm would call together a council. If they decide he shall go to Rome to collect his pallium they defy me. I'll not have that, Ranulf. My father never would. And nor shall I. I will make known my anger to the men who form this council. I'll warrant you, Ranulf, they will not dare to go against me."

"Then," said Ranulf, "we must wait and see."

*　　*　　*

It was an uneasy council that met at Rockingham. Rufus had made it clear to all those concerned that his fury would be aroused if it supported Anselm. All knew that the outcome of Rufus's anger could be violent and it was greatly feared. On the other hand many of them felt that their souls could be imperilled if they supported the King against the Archbishop.

Anselm declared that he would obey the King and serve him well except where his actions would be in conflict with the Pope.

"Who governs this land?" roared Rufus. "Is it the King of England or the Pope of Rome?"

He ordered the council to rid him of Anselm.

This however could not be done without the consent of the Pope. Anselm had taken the crozier during a solemn ceremony. He was the Archbishop of Canterbury and only the Pope could depose him.

Anselm, calm in the face of the storm, and, as the King said, stubborn as a mule, declared that the only course open to him was to appeal to the Pope.

"Rid me of him," cried Rufus. "This man is a traitor."

But the barons and churchmen replied that they could not pass sentence of deposition on a man who was ecclesiastically their superior.

*　　*　　*

Alone with Ranulf the King gave vent to his rage.

"This land," he said, "is governed by the Pope, not by the King. I swear I will not countenance that. My father never did and nor shall I. Anselm! There will be trouble while he remains here. Would I had never kept him here. I would I had sent him back to Bec."

"Alas, my lord, but he is here and here he will stay until this Pope displaces him."

"In my own kingdom, Ranulf! My own kingdom!"

"There are herbs that are tasteless in wine."

"I know it well. But this is not the way with a man such as this. I want him removed in a manner which will arouse no suspicion. How Ranulf? How?"

They pondered it for long but could come to no satisfactory conclusion; and it was Urban himself who came to their aid.

Under the Conqueror, England had become a power of some importance and Urban chafed that he had not received recognition from that land. His spies kept him well informed of what was happening there and he sent a messenger to the King, implying that he might be willing to help him in return for recognition.

Rufus laughed when he received this letter. It appealed to his sense of humour that he should see a way out of his dilemma through the Pope himself.

As a gesture of his willingness to come to terms, Urban set the pallium to England with instructions that it should be placed on the high altar at Canterbury. Thus he had delivered it neither to the King nor to the Archbishop and the controversy had been solved in a most delicate manner.

It was true that Anselm, by the consent of all concerned, took the pallium and continued in office, but the Pope had intimated to the King that he would be willing to work in secret to bring about his desires providing of course he was satisfactorily rewarded.

*   *   *

One of the pages came to tell the King that Alan of Bretagne had come from Rumsey.

"Bring him to me," said Rufus, and in an aside to

Ranulf who was his constant companion at this time: "He has been inspecting the Atheling girl. What did he find, I wonder?"

Alan bowed and the King said: "Well, brother, so you are impatient for a wife and have found one to your liking."

"I have, my lord."

"So there is to be a wedding in the family?"

"If you give your consent, my lord."

"And why should I not? It was always my father's wish to pump good Norman blood into the Saxons."

"So I am to have the girl?"

"Have her. Take her back to Normandy and let me know when you get your first boy. Better luck than with my sister."

Alan hesitated. "There may be some barriers set up by the Abbess."

"That Abbess! She is Edgar's sister. She has too high an opinion of her royalty, I think."

"Indeed so," replied Alan. "She was anxious to show me that she was the ruler of her Abbey."

"Under the King, I hope."

"I doubt she recognizes that. She may try to stop the marriage."

"When *I* have consented."

"She may try but with your consent I'll marry the Princess in a week or so."

"May she give you all you want," said Rufus.

"Now I have my lord's consent that matter is settled," said Alan.

"You should ride back to Rumsey to tell the happy girl what is in store for her."

"When I have celebrated my victory, I shall do so."

Left alone with Ranulf, Rufus said: "If only it were possible to deal as easily with Anselm as with my brother Alan!"

"Alan is easily satisfied. A good bedfellow and a cask of wine will do for him. Anselm wants power and that is in truth another matter. You have no wish for the girl nor the wine—so he can have them. But the power is yours and not to be shared. Oh, never fear, my King, we'll settle Master Anselm—ay, and before the Princess begins to grow large with Alan's seed if need be."

* * *

Alan of Bretagne was very pleased with himself. He had the King's consent to his marriage. The girl was personable—young and royal. Her brother had now become King of Scotland. This marriage would be almost as advantageous as his first.

He sat drinking with the company he had brought with him from Normandy. It grew late as he enlivened the company with stories of his prowess both as a soldier and lover.

His little Scottish Princess had a treat in store.

The stories grew more wild and more ribald as the evening progressed and again and again Alan's goblet was filled.

"Well, my friends," he said, "it is time I left for Rumsey. The Princess will be anxious. She'll think I'm never coming to claim her."

He stood up. Hazily he saw the faces of those who had been drinking with him. He was vaguely aware of the smiles changing to expressions of concern as he fell to the floor.

* * *

The Abbess sent for Edith.

"I have a message here," she said grimly. "The King has given his consent to your marriage with Alan of Bretagne."

Then Edith knew that on no account would she take this man. Yes, even a life here in the Abbey was preferable to that. Moreover if she consented to take her vows her aunt would be less harsh to her. She had been so in these last weeks because she knew of the turmoil which was going on in Edith's mind.

"I will not marry him. I'll take the veil," cried Edith.

"You fool," retorted her aunt. "Don't you understand? It is too late. The King has given his consent. You have no choice."

Edith stared with horror at her aunt.

"Did I not warn you? Did I not tell you that God would avenge your renunciation of him? You have had opportunities given you and constantly you turned away. You could not decide. You were set against the holy life. You longed for a man and then when you saw one, some sense of decency prevailed. But it is too late. The King has decided."

"Perhaps I could go to the King."

"Go to the King? It is not possible."

"If I pleaded with him . . . If I could tell him . . ."

"You do not know the King. He would not be moved by the tears of women." The Abbess laughed as though momentarily enjoying the situation; but she was almost immediately grim again. "Nay, you have been chosen and you have rejected God's wishes. He has now decided to punish you."

"Oh, Holy Mother," whispered Edith.

"Yes, you may appeal now. It is too late I tell you. Had you taken your vows none could have touched you. They would not have dared. But no . . . you would not. You deserve everything that befalls you. You have chosen. You will be handed over to that vile man and he will make sport with you."

"Please . . ."

The Abbess laughed bitterly. "Your ancestors are mocking you. Go. I cannot bear the sight of you."

Edith went to her cell; she lay on the floor and trembled. Hideous images came in and out of her mind. "Oh God," she prayed, "save me."

*   *   *

It seemed that God answered her prayers in a most dramatic manner.

The Abbess sent for her. Rarely had Edith seen her aunt in such a pleasant mood.

"God has decided to be merciful," she said.

"How so?" asked Edith eagerly.

"Alan of Bretagne, celebrating his success in getting

the King's approval, drank himself to a stupor. When he stood up, God struck him down. That lustful body is now being consumed by the fires of hell."

A horrible image but how could she help but be grateful for her escape!

"Come," said the Abbess, "kneel with me now and give thanks to God."

*　　*　　*

But there was still the further problem. Aunt Christina was wrong if she thought the way was clear. Because one terror had been removed it did not mean that the other alternative did not remain.

I will not become a nun, vowed Edith.

It would begin again, the persecutions, the taunts, the persuasions. But she would be firm. She had never given her word.

Did God in truth mean that he had determined she should become the future Abbess? Had he removed Alan de Bretagne in such a dramatic way as a sign?

She did not know, but the fact that she was saved from Alan did not mean that she loved the black Benedictine robe any the more.

The Abbess declared she had had a further revelation of God's approval.

She was to be appointed to the Abbey of Wilton as its Abbess.

This delighted her. It was Wilton Abbey over which a member of the Atheling family had always presided.

She was to be its Abbess and she was determined to train Edith to follow in her footsteps.

The young Athelings could now return to their brother's court in Scotland. Only Edith and Mary, she insisted, must remain behind.

The Vices of the King's Court

The King was in his bedchamber with several of his friends. They were laughing together at Robert, a very special favourite of the King, who had come to show the new fashion he had created in shoes. Robert pranced round the room in his extraordinary footgear and coming to the King, bowed in an exaggerated fashion.

"Get up, you fool," cried the King.

"But like you not my feet now, sir King?"

"They become you well, Robert. You must see that I have the like."

Robert sat on the floor and drawing off his shoe presented it to the King.

"The long points are stuffed with tow, my lord, and corned up like a ram's horn."

"I never saw the like," laughed Rufus, giving Robert an affectionate push which sent him sprawling across the floor. "Get up, Horned One. Get up, Cornard."

"An' you wish it," answered Robert. "But I see my lord likes well my shoe."

"I like it well. What say you?" he demanded of the company.

"My lord, we like well Robert Cornard's horned shoes."

"Then Cornard he shall be named from henchforth. Come sit beside me, my Cornard, and tell me what adventures have been yours in the court today?"

"Such as would make a bishop blush, lord."

"He is a shameful one, this Robert Cornard," said the King. "But a pretty fellow albeit."

"And always thinking of new fashions to amuse my King. Look, like you well my curls, lord?"

Rufus pulled Robert's hair affectionately. It was long and had been curled with hot irons and parted in the centre, falling about his face.

He looked more like a woman than a man. He was scented and his robes swept the floor as he walked, or rather minced, about the chamber. He had a bad reputation, for it was said that he was an adept at many evil practices known to men of his kind. The King was amused by him and although he was not the friend Ranulf was, Rufus never seemed to tire of his company.

In the hall below a banquet was being prepared and shortly the King would descend to the hall surrounded by his friends. They were all rivals for his attention, these young men, and each tried to outshine the others. Scented, their hair long and curled, their robes like women's robes cut low at the neck, they crowded about him jostling for his attention.

Rufus could not help smiling as he watched them and wondered what his father would say if he could look into his successor's bedchamber..

Rufus had no illusions about himself. One of his great virtues was the rare ability to see himself clearly; and an added quality was that he never shied from the truth.

Well, Father, he mused, as he looked on that scene and listened to the high-pitched voices of his friends, we cannot all be alike. My court is a gayer place than yours ever was. You had no time for the pleasures of life. For you it was continual conquest. You were known through the latter years of your life and mayhap will be known for ever more as the Conquerer. What shall I be known as? Rufus! Shall I leave behind nothing to be remembered by except my red hair and ruddy complexion?

Yet I am a soldier—not as good as you, but who could be? I have followed the laws you laid down. I have kept the country intact. And I have now got my hands on Normandy. It may well be that I shall bring it under the English crown, for how is Robert ever going to pay me back? I have built even as you did. There is this noble hall of Westminster. I have added the White Tower to your Tower of London, and I have built a bridge across the Thames. Cathedrals, monasteries and churches have been built, although I confess I have had little hand in those. There is something about the Church I cannot stomach. Perhaps it is because churchmen seem to me such hypocrites and, sinner that I am, I am not that.

There'll be no son to follow me. I could not take to women, and marriage is too repulsive to me. I have brothers, Robert and Henry. Robert would be useless as King. I am not sure of Henry. He's ambitious and clever, they say. But he'll be an old man before I'm ready to go. There are the sons of my sisters. What a morbid subject! I'm not going yet. There is too much here to amuse me. I like life, Father. I enjoy it as you never could. These are my friends who amuse me— something you who were all man could never understand. The hunt... now there we are on common ground. It's something we could always share. The feel of a horse beneath one... the baying of the dogs... the chase!

Nay, Father, if you watch me from wherever you are, do not think too badly of me. I have followed in your steps as far as possible. I think of you and your wise laws. I follow them. But I am myself and must act accordingly.

Robert had brought his face to that of the King.

"My lord is thoughtful."

"Ay," said Rufus, "and it is time you dressed me for the banquet."

"My lord's hose," cried Robert, and a page came running with the garment. Robert's nose crinkled with disgust. He covered his face with his hands and pretended to weep.

"What foolery is this?" demanded Rufus laughing.

"It is more than I can endure," wept Robert. "My lord King to wear such hose!"

"What's wrong with them?" demanded Rufus.

"They are unworthy. I could bow to my lord but never to such a pair of hose."

"Have done with your jesting and dress me."

"'Tis no jest, lord; these hose are unfit for royal legs. Send for the varlet who brought them to you."

Rufus looked on with amusement as the man appeared trembling before Robert who had seated himself on the faldestol, cleverly imitating Rufus.

"Hose, man, hose!" he shouted.

"Yes, my lord," said the frightened man.

"You bring such hose to our lord the King!"

"They are the King's hose, sir."

"Tell me the price of these hose, man."

"I know not."

"Then find out."

The frightened man scurried away and Robert continued to amuse the company by murmuring: "Hose ... inferior hose ... an insult to my royal legs...." He even endeavoured to make his face grow red with feigned temper.

The page returned with another man and Robert signed for them to stand before him.

"These offending hose," said Robert. "Pray what did they cost?"

"Three shillings, my lord."

"Three shillings. You would encase the King's royal legs in three shillings' worth of hose? You should have your eyes put out for such treason."

The frightened chamberlain began to tremble.

"My lord," he began, "the King has never questioned ..."

"He is questioning now. A King should never wear hose that cost less than a mark. Bring me a worthy

71

pair of hose if you do not wish to see how fierce my displeasure can grow."

The chamberlain bowed and hurried off. In a few moments he returned with a pair of hose.

"How much did these cost?" asked Robert without looking at them.

"Two marks, my lord. They are very fine hose."

"They will serve. And, fellow, never on pain of death offer the King three shilling hose again."

The company was greatly amused and Robert minced over to the King holding the hose before him.

"They look no better than the others," said Rufus.

"Yet, they cost two marks and are therefore worthy of your royal legs."

Robert could always be relied on to enliven the company with amusing games and there was laughter while the King was dressed.

Then down to the hall they went to the banquet where three hundred ushers and doorkeepers had been placed at all entrances to keep out the hungry people, who attracted by the smell of roasting meat, and knowing the hour when the meal would be taken, had assembled outside and if not prevented would come rushing into the hall as the food was carried in and try to snatch it from the dishes.

Everything was in order. There stood the ushers, their rods in their hands, ready to keep out the rabble and make sure that the food and drink were carried to the table unmolested.

They feasted and in due course the King retired to his chamber accompanied by his chosen companions.

*   *   *

Anselm was preaching against the vices of the King's entourage. He declared that the King and his friends partook in the most abandoned sodomy. They were extravagant; the new fashions were disgusting to all normal men, for gentlemen wore long robes and mantles which swept the floor and their gloves were so long and wide, that a man could not use his hands when encased in these ridiculous objects. Their hair

72

was worn long and flowing; it was crimped and curled; their shoes with the ram's horn toes, their mincing manners—all these, declared Anselm, were an abomination.

It should be remembered what had happened to the Cities of the Plain. How soon before God raised his hand against the King of England and his minions?

"God curse Anselm," said Rufus, and he wished that he could rid himself of the man. When he thought of the rich lands of the See of Canterbury still remaining in the hands of Anselm he grew so angry that the veins knotted at his temples and his friends feared he would fall to the ground in a fit.

His hatred of the Pope had grown, for he had made a grave miscalculation concerning him. Urban had sent the pallium to Canterbury and saved a delicate situation, and Rufus had presumed, in view of the secret communications between them, that if he acknowledged him as the true Pope he would repay that recognition by relieving Anselm of his office.

Urban was wily. He was accepted in England. This was what he wanted, but since this had come about, why should he agree to the deposition of a man for whom he had the utmost respect in order to satisfy a king who lost no opportunity of stating his animosity towards the Church?

So Rufus having acknowledged Urban as Pope was still left with Anselm.

It was clever Ranulf who found a way. There had been a rising in Wales and all those in possession of goods and lands were by law forced to supply men and money to suppress the revolt.

The Welsh had been subdued but, pointed out Ranulf, Anselm had done little towards the victory.

"The forces he sent were ill equipped," declared the King's friend. "Why, with his resources he should have sent far more. This is an offence for which he can be summoned to your court and made to answer this charge."

"Let him be sent for," said Rufus, "and let him be accused. Let him be proved to be a traitor. Can I be

73

expected to allow a traitor to hold my See of Canterbury?"

Ranulf arranged that Anselm should be sent for, but Anselm did not answer the summons.

The King was furious. He wanted to have him brought by force, but he realized that this was not wise. Anselm was head of the Church and as Archbishop of Canterbury was not under the jurisdiction of the King. He answered to the Pope, and Rufus cursed himself for having acknowledged Anselm's friend and ally.

It was a false step, but Rufus was too honest to blame anyone but himself for that.

Anselm should be condemned and they would see what could happen then.

A messenger arrived from Anselm for the King. He would not come to the court and the King had no powers to force him. He in his turn must have the King's permission to leave the country and he asked for it now. He wished to go to Rome to discuss his affairs with the Pope.

Rufus's immediate reply was a refusal; but after some consideration it occurred to him that it would not be a bad step to get Anselm out of the country. Once he was out, what harm could he do? The Pope could rage all he liked, Rufus was King in his own country; and with Anselm no longer there why should not Rufus seize the rich lands of Canterbury? Archbishop! He could do without an Archbishop.

So he let it be known that he might possibly accede to Anselm's request and as a result the Archbishop prepared to leave for Rome.

He came to take his farewell from the King and give him his blessing.

"Spare yourself," shouted Rufus. "I've no need of your prayers."

"We all have need of prayers, my lord. A king more than his humblest subject."

"I'll do my own praying," shouted Rufus. "Go where you will but get out of my sight."

Anselm left and as soon as he had gone Rufus sent for several of his knights. "Go to Dover," he commanded, "and make sure you reach there before the

74

Archbishop. Search his baggage lest he be taking to Rome any of the treasures of the Church."

The knights left and Anselm was treated to the indignity of the search. Meanwhile the King lost no time in seizing the rich lands of Canterbury.

*　　*　　*

When he arrived in Rome the Pope received Anselm with all honours and even lodged him in his own palace.

News reached the Archbishop that the King had already taken the Canterbury lands which as Anselm was still Archbishop came under his jurisdiction.

"The King is a man without religious feelings," Anselm told the Pope. "He has no fear of God nor of hell."

"All men fear eternal damnation," replied the Pope. "If I threaten excommunication he may well restore your property."

The Pope sent a messenger to England with a letter to say that unless the King restored to the Archbishop that which was his due he should suffer excommunication.

When Rufus received this letter he roared out his fury.

His father was once excommunicated for marrying his mother without the consent of the Pope. The Conqueror had snapped his fingers at the Pope. Did they think that he, William II, would accept what William I had not?

He roared at the messenger: "Get out of my realm. If you are not gone from here by the end of this day I'll pull out both your eyes."

Back went the messenger to Rome, his eyes safe, and when his story was told the Pope called together a council to consider the King's way of life, his lack of religion and his quarrel with the saintly Anselm.

It was decided at the council that Rufus should be excommunicated and this threat would have been carried out but for Anselm who implored the Pope to wait awhile.

Rufus, he knew, would be quite unmoved by excommunication, a fact which the Pope, not knowing him, could not be expected to understand. No good would be served by the carrying out of the threat which Rufus would laugh to scorn.

Rufus was amused by the controversy. He declared that there was no question of returning the lands, for had not the Archbishop gone to Rome without his royal licence and having done so had he not forfeited the archbishopric?

Anselm realized that this in a way was a victory for the King. He was in England snapping his fingers at Rome; and there was nothing the Pope could do to frighten him.

Anselm settled down to the peaceful life. He was often in Rome with Urban and at times went into the monastery of San Salvatore where he worked on the treatise which was to become famous—the *Cur Deus Homo*.

He began to understand that Urban, after his first gesture, was not eager to pursue the threat of excommunication. England under the Norman kings had become too important a country for that. Rufus had acknowledged him and for this reason he did not wish to alienate him too far.

Anselm realized that he had made a mistake and that he could not expect more help from Urban, so he decided to leave Rome altogether. He had a great friend in Archbishop Hugh who resided in Lyons. He joined him and receiving a warm welcome decided to settle there until such a time as he could return to Canterbury. As it seemed that would never be while Rufus lived, it could be said that Rufus had won the battle.

Love Comes to Wilton Abbey

The thick stone walls of the Abbey of Wilton had become a formidable prison for Edith. On this spot had once stood a wooden building and Queen Editha (the wife in name only of Edward the Confessor who was, it was said, too saintly to have ever consummated his marriage) had rebuilt it in stone at the same time as the Confessor was building Westminster Abbey.

The order was, as at Rumsey, that of the Black Benedictines; and, now that they were at Wilton, Christina was more determined than ever that her niece should follow in her footsteps. She was delighted by the transfer. Wilton, she said, was the Royal Abbey. Atheling Princesses had received their education there ever since it had been founded in its present form by Queen Editha; and of course an Atheling had always been the Abbess.

The time would soon come for Edith to take her vows. It was a ceremony long overdue. This affair of Alan of Bretagne had postponed it, but now God had removed him there was no need to delay longer.

Edith was thankful for the company of her sister. Mary had never suffered as she had. Although she was forced to wear the robes of the order they did not irritate her skin as the did Edith's, and Mary was always sure that one day she would escape into the world.

But now even she was getting anxious.

Sometimes she would come into Edith's cell to talk to her. It would have been forbidden had they been discovered so they always had to talk in whispers and keep on the alert for prying nuns. Often Mary had hidden herself in the stone alcove while Edith stood before the cross as though in meditation until footsteps passed away.

"How I long to escape," said Mary. "And we are getting old, Edith. You are twenty-one years of age. Soon we shall be too old. Oh, if only our father had not died. I wish our uncle would come. I would ask if I could go back to Scotland. Perhaps then a husband would be found for me."

"Who can say what sort of husband?" replied Edith, remembering the leering eyes of Alan of Bretagne.

"Is not any husband better than living here for ever, wearing these fusty robes? I want to have jewels and an embroidered gown. Aunt Christina doesn't want us to marry . . . especially you. She feels that marriage is a sinful state and yet how would the world go on without it!"

Edith was silent, thinking of the conflict which had beset her when she could not make up her mind between the dreary existence under Aunt Christina and marriage with Alan of Bretagne. They were two extremes; there must be something in between. She did know now that if she could find a husband of her own age—or thereabouts—a gentle kindly man, she would be ready to go to him and rejoice that she had escaped Aunt Christina.

"We are tucked away here," said Mary, "and who is aware of us?"

"Alan of Bretagne was," Edith reminded her. And she added to comfort her sister: "It may well be that some others are."

She was right.

This time it was Mary's turn to be summoned to the Abbess's sanctum to be told that the King had given his consent to Eustace the Count of Boulogne to come to Wilton to see her.

Mary's expression betrayed her excitement.

The Abbess looked at her sternly. "I see that you, as your sister once was, are eager for the marriage bed."

Mary, emboldened by the possibilities of escape, replied: "It is the lot of most women, Aunt."

"I am filled with sorrow to think that after all my teaching, all the efforts I have made to instil some piety into you, you should harbour lustful thoughts."

Mary in her exulting mood could not help feeling sorry for poor Aunt Christina who would never have a husband and who hated the thought of anyone else's having one. So she did not reply but kept her eyes lowered that Aunt Christina might not see the pleasurable anticipation which she could not suppress.

"You must prepare yourself for this meeting. It disgusts me that he should come here to inspect you as though you were a dog or a horse. I would forbid it but he has the King's consent to come and none of us dare disobey that."

How wonderful, thought Mary, that Aunt Christina's sway was restricted.

"I will send for you when this man arrives. Be prepared."

Mary went to her cell in a state of great excitement. Edith came to hear what the Abbess had said.

"He is coming. Eustace of Boulogne. I shall be Countess of Boulogne! Oh, Edith, how I wish I had a rich embroidered gown in which to see him. What will he think of me in these hideous black robes?"

"He'll make allowances for them."

"With what joy shall I cast them off. I'll tear them off. I'll stamp on them."

"I did that but little good did I derive from it."

"Oh, poor poor Edith."

The sisters clung together and Edith said: "Have you forgotten, Mary, that when you go I shall be here alone?"

"Oh, Edith, I do remember it. That will spoil my joy."

"You must not allow it to be spoilt. It is better for one of us to be happy then neither of us."

She did not want her sister to know how desperate she felt. Mary's going away, herself alone and Aunt Christina increasing the pressure on her to take the veil!

It was a dismal prospect.

*   *   *

How like that other occasion when Alan of Bretagne had come to Rumsey.

They were both summoned to the great hall there to receive the suitor.

I pray that he is not old and lascivious and that Mary will be happy with him, thought Edith.

Aunt Christina brought the visitors into the hall. There were several of them and one was quite handsome.

The Abbess was looking angry, but of course she would, for although she did not wish Mary to succeed her as Abbess she would have preferred her to take the veil rather than emerge on what she could only think of as a lustful life.

The handsome young man smiled. He had a worldly look about him which was engaging. If Alan of Bretagne had looked like that she would not have hesitated to choose him.

The Abbess said: "Here are the Princesses."

They curtseyed; the men bowed. "The Princess Edith; the Princess Mary."

The handsome young man was looking at Edith and smiling. Fortunate Mary! He had a certain charm about him.

"The Count of Boulogne," said the Abbess presenting, not as Edith thought, the handsome young man, but another, much older man. Edith had scarcely noticed him. He took Mary's hand and said: "I would speak with you."

As before the Abbess insisted that this could only

be under her surveillance and as Edith had once sat in a window seat with Alan of Bretagne, so Mary would now sit with Eustace of Boulogne.

"And the Earl of Surrey," said the Abbess, indicating the man who had roused Edith's interest. He bowed and took Edith's hand and led her to another window seat.

What could this mean? Rarely had Edith seen her aunt so angry.

"I do not understand," she said.

"I have the King's consent to visit you," he replied.

"Why so?"

"If Eustace of Boulogne can visit the Princess Mary why should not William of Surrey visit the Princess Edith?"

"But . . ."

"Remember I come with the King's blessing. Let me tell you who I am. My mother was Gundred, the youngest daughter of William the Conquerer. She married William Warren, Earl of Surrey. My parents are both dead, and my uncle, the King, has always been kind to me."

"I see, and he has sent you here to see me."

"You know for what purpose."

"The Abbess . . ."

"Is a dragon. I see it. She was angry when she knew that I was here. She had been expecting only Eustace. My uncle had told me that she would not welcome me. The situation amused him. So he allowed me to come with Eustace."

Edith smiled and checked herself.

"I am glad to see you smile," he said. "It transforms you."

"There is little cause for smiling here."

"That is a pity."

"The King is not sure whether you have taken the veil."

"I have not."

"Then I have come in time."

The Abbess watching Edith and William Warren together was seething with indignation. How like the evil King of England to play such a trick on her! When she had made up her mind that in a very short time Edith would take vows from which it would be impossible for her to retract, this man had come.

She rose, her face white and tense with suppressed fury. "I can allow no more time," she said. "I must ask you to leave."

William Warren took Edith's hand and pressed it. "I will come again," he whispered.

The Abbess conducted the visitors to the door.

Edith and Mary went to Edith's cell.

"Edith," cried Mary, as soon as they were there. "Is this not a miracle? You as well." She added wistfully: "The Earl of Surrey is charming, is he not? Of course he is so much younger than Eustace. But just think of it. We are going to be free."

Edith was thinking of it.

It was another miracle. She was not entirely sure of her feelings for the young man. All she did know was that a way of escape had been offered to her.

*　　*　　*

She tossed on her straw, unable to sleep. Another opportunity. He was young and handsome; he was a grandson of the Conqueror. He was not repulsive to her and yet ...

What was wrong with her? Mary had been so determined to accept Eustace that she had made no complaint although he was not the handsome young man she had hoped for. She was in a happy state of euphoria. The world had taken on a new beauty. Mary had become quite beautiful and her black robes looked more incongruous than ever.

And I, thought Edith, who had believed I was to be left here without her, that I would have to go on battling with Aunt Christina, with the certainty that if I stayed here I must in time obey, have another chance.

She was not apprehensive but she felt no rapturous joy. Why should this be? What was wrong with her? William Warren was young, handsome, amiable. He had been courteous and she was being offered escape and yet she felt a vague depression.

She wanted to escape and yet...

What was it? Something she herself would not understand.

The Abbess came to her cell.

"So this man has come. Yet another of them."

Edith was silent.

"The King may give his consent. If he does so it will not be easy to prevent a marriage. But if you declared your determination to take the veil..."

"Nay," said Edith. "I will not take the veil."

"When I am dead you will be mistress of Wilton. Think of that. Here in this little world you would command all. You would be a ruler. Everyone here would obey you as they do me. If you marry this man, what will your life be? You will be submitted to indignities such as those I have warned you of. You will suffer painful childbearing, which is the lot of women who give way to the carnal desires of men. You still have a chance to escape it."

"I do not wish to take the veil."

"So you wish to marry this man. You have learned nothing. Have you forgotten your fears of Alan of Bretagne?"

"The Earl of Surrey is not Alan of Bretagne."

"He is a man."

"I want time," said Edith, "time to think."

A gleam of hope touched the stern features of the Abbess. So she had not been altogether seduced by the Earl's good looks.

"Then think of it," said the Abbess. "Think of what it means. Remember what will be expected of you. Remember that God once gave you a sign. He is testing you. Do not fail Him."

When she had gone Edith lay thinking of her and she told herself then: "But of course I shall take him. It is just that because of what the Abbess has told me I am afraid. I could love him, I doubt not, in time. And marriage with him would mean escape from Wilton and Aunt Christina."

* * *

83

The Abbess fell sick and was obliged to keep to her bed. It so happened that at this time the two suitors called once more at the Abbey. Christina was unaware that they had come and the two nuns who acted as her deputy, knowing that these men had the sanction of the King and that the object of Eustace of Boulogne was to decide whether he wished to ask for the hand of Mary, took them to the hall and the Princesses came down to see them.

There was a man in the party who had not visited the Abbey before; and it was his presence which wrought a subtle change. He was older than the Earl of Surrey by some ten years and it was apparent from the first that both the suitors were in awe of him.

There was an air of authority about him. His black hair parted in the centre and worn long in the fashion of the day fell about his shoulders in luxuriant curls, but there was nothing effeminate about him. His eyes flashed imperiously; his mouth was sensual but it could be suddenly hard and cruel. Christina's trembling deputies knew that they were in the presence of an important personage, and as soon as Eustace demanded that the Princesses be sent for they were brought.

When they came the stranger was the first to greet them for both the Count of Boulogne and the Earl of Surrey stood aside for him.

The Count said: "Prince Henry has accompanied us."

Both the girls curtsied. They knew that this man was the King's younger brother and in the event of the King's dying before him and leaving no heir, which he certainly would not do, Henry could be King.

Edith lifted her eyes and looked into his face. Never, she thought, had she seen a man so perfect. He was neither tall nor young; he must be ten years older than she was; but there was a gleam in his eyes when they met hers which showed his appreciation of her.

"I am pleased that I came," he said, his eyes studying her intently as though he were trying to probe what lay beneath the black robe. "Come, let us sit down and we will talk together."

William Warren was not looking very pleased. But

he accompanied Henry and Edith to the window seat. Eustace and Mary followed them.

The nuns sat some distance from them, their eyes watchful.

Henry said: "You may leave us."

"My lord," stammered one, "it is the wish of the Abbess and the rule of the Abbey . . ."

He waved his hand.

"We will change that rule," said Henry. "Pray leave us."

"My lord, the Abbess . . ."

"It is not the Abbess who commands now," he said.

They hesitated and looked at each other and then curtsying, retired.

He laughed, and Edith realized how little laughter there had been in her life.

"Now," he said, "the watchdogs have gone."

"I should like to see you deal with the old dragon herself," commented Eustace.

"It may well be that I shall have that pleasure," replied Henry.

He was smiling at Edith. "It grieves me," he went on, "that you should be imprisoned in this place. You are worthy of a better fate. And those black robes . . . but let me consider. They are so ugly that they draw attention to your fairness by the very contrast."

No one had ever paid Edith compliments before. She flushed with pleasure. She knew what was happening. She had had dreams. She knew now why she had so feared Alan; she knew now why handsome young William Warren had not appealed to her.

There was only one man in the world to whom she could happily go. It was strange that she should only have had to look at him to realize this. It was love, she supposed. At least she knew that nothing so completely exciting and exhilarating had ever happened to her before.

Eustace and Mary were deep in conversation. It was amazing what a difference the restraint imposed by watchful eyes could have.

"Tell me what you do here," said Henry. "How do you pass the days?"

"In prayer and work."

"A Princess should not work, nor should she spend over much time on her knees. Devotions should be brief. Do you not agree with me, nephew?"

William Warren mumbled that he supposed the Prince was right.

"I hear the Abbess is a stern jailer," went on Henry, leaning towards Edith.

"'Tis so."

"That such a lady should be so imprisoned! It angers me. Does it not anger you, William?"

"It shall not always be so," said William almost defiantly.

"Nay," replied Henry, smiling into Edith's eyes, "we must be assured of that."

"It is for the purpose that I am here," replied William.

"So I understood and because of this, nephew, I accompanied you."

"The King approves my coming," William reminded the Prince.

"Ay, and his consent will have to be given if you would succeed in your endeavours," said Henry.

"'Tis so," replied William defiantly, "and that of no one else."

"Certainly not mine." He turned to Edith with a wry smile. "My brother does not love me greatly. Nor I him."

"I am sorry to hear it," replied Edith.

"Do not let sorrow dim the brightness of those eyes. It grieves me not at all. As you know I am the youngest of the family. It is not good to be a younger brother. My father knew this well. He left Normandy to my brother Robert and England to William; and what of poor Henry? But he made a prophecy before he died. He said to me: 'Grieve not. There will come the day when you shall have all that your brothers have and more.'"

"You think this will come to pass?"

He had laid his hand on her arm and she had no wish to draw away from him.

"I know it," he answered. Then with a swift movement he did what Alan of Bretagne had done before him; deftly he threw back the hood of her robe and exposed her beautiful golden hair.

He looked at her intently. "'Twere a sin to hide it," he said. "I must set you a penance."

"If the Abbess could see..."

"By God's grace she lies on her sick bed. Long may He let her lie there." He put out a hand and touched her hair, caressing it lightly. "You are beautiful, Princess," he said. "Such beauty should not be kept from the world. I should like to see a crown set on that beautiful head. It would become it well."

Eustace, seeing that Edith was without her hood, pressed Mary to remove hers. This she did with pleasure and there were sounds of laughter in the old hall such as could never have been heard since the Abbess had ruled there.

It was the most enchanting hour that Edith had ever spent. Henry was gay and witty. She discovered that apart from the fact that he was a man who loved gaiety he was also learned. How glad she was that she had attended to her teachers; she had been chosen by Christina to follow her because she was clever; now Henry was interested in her because of it.

She understood the allusions in his discourse. She could speak to him on his own scholastic level; this delighted him and the more they pleased each other the more disgruntled became the poor Earl of Surrey.

Finally they left, much to the relief of the nuns, who were almost in tears. They knew that if the Abbess ever discovered that the Princesses had been alone with the visitors they would be in dire trouble. But who would be likely to give such an account? Certainly not the Princesses who had been more guilty than they had.

In Edith's cell Mary talked ecstatically of the interview. Eustace had given his word that he would ask for her hand and he knew that no obstacle would be put in their way.

"And the Earl," she said. "What of him? Have you made good progress with him? I feel so happy, Edith. We are free, both of us. For I confess that it would have grieved me greatly to leave you here. And what thought you of Prince Henry? The son of the King! Eustace says that he may well be King one day. But that will not be for a long time. Rufus is not so old that he can be expected to die, though he is older than Henry. What thought you of him?"

"He was different from the others."

"It is to be expected. He is the son and brother of a King. Your William is only a nephew. Eustace of course is quite different. He is a vassal of the Duke of Normandy, true . . . but he serves no king."

"I am pleased that you are happy at the prospect, Mary."

"Happy. I find it hard to wait. Oh, to be free of these hideous robes. Was it not exciting when Henry removed your hood? Eustace was happy to see my hair. He thought it beautiful. I kept laughing inwardly to think what Aunt Christina would have said. How quiet you are, Edith. Are you thinking of William Warren? And how exciting it will be to become the Countess of Surrey."

"Nay," said Edith slowly, "I was not thinking of that."

"But was that not the most exciting time we ever had in our lives?"

"Yes, there is no doubt of it," said Edith soberly.

*　　*　　*

He came again. This time with few attendants.

Eustace did not accompany him nor did William Warren.

He waved aside the protest that he could not be alone with her so imperiously that the two poor nuns were terrified. But what could they do when the brother of the King ordered them away?

88

"It is wrong. It is wrong!" they cried. "No man should enter the Abbey."

"Of a certainty no ordinary man should be allowed in," said Henry. "But I am no ordinary man."

He laughed aloud when they had gone; he sat close to Edith; he took off her hood and ran his fingers through her hair.

"How beautiful it is," he said. "I have dreamed of it."

"Why have you come to see me?" she asked.

"Because my inclinations first prompted me and then insisted. They would not be denied."

"The sisters are right. It is unseemly."

"That which is unseemly is often delightful you will discover."

"You know that the Earl of Surrey has the King's consent to become betrothed to me?"

"I know it."

"And . . . yet you come."

"Yes, I come to say it must not be."

"Why not?"

"You must know. I want you for myself."

"How . . . how could that be?"

Henry took her hands and drawing her to him kissed her on the lips.

She caught her breath; but she was not horrified, only delighted.

"Would the King give his consent to our marriage?"

"Nay. He has promised you to Surrey."

"Then how could we?"

"I do not always ask the consent of the King."

"Should not all subjects do that?"

"I am not his subject. I am his brother." He leaned towards her. "One day I shall be King of this realm. How would you like to be its Queen?"

She said: "I am the daughter of a King and I should be happy to return to the state in which I began my life. But I would not wish it if a man such as Alan of Bretagne were to be my husband."

He laughed aloud. "He came to woo you and you liked him not?"

"I liked him not."

"He is too old for you—my uncle by marriage. I am some ten years older than you. That is acceptable to you?"

She nodded.

"And *I* am acceptable to you?"

"I have never seen anyone like you."

"That tells me little. It may be that you have never seen anyone whom you found as repulsive."

"No, no..."

He was laughing at her. He took her hands suddenly and kissed her fingers.

"Then," he said, "you like me well."

"Yes," she answered. "I like you well."

"And when I am King you will be my Queen."

"I could ask nothing more of life."

"Will you be a good wife to me?"

"I will."

"And love me tenderly and bear my children?"

"I will."

"Why 'twould seem we are married already. Would there were a priest here who would marry us, and a bridal chamber where I could make you my wife in every truth."

"There is no priest and no bridal chamber."

He looked at her, his eyes gleaming. "Would we could do without them."

She was wide-eyed. "That is not possible, is it? How could we be married without a priest?"

"They have taught you much from books and little from life. How could they... in an abbey?"

"My aunt the Abbess told me what was expected of a wife." Her lips trembled suddenly. "I...I hated it."

"I would tell you a different story. Do you believe me?"

"Yes, I believe you."

"And you would be willing to learn?"

"With you I would be willing."

"And there is no bridal chamber where we can begin our lessons! Alas!"

His eyes were alight with merriment. He looked round the great hall, at the vaulted ceilings and a glint was in his eyes as though he were wondering how he could carry her off to a cell and there begin the lesson.

"What if the King will not give his consent?" she asked.

"The King will not give his consent."

"Then we are doomed."

"Never say that, my Princess. Happiness shall be ours. But we must needs wait for it."

"I will wait."

"You must refuse the Earl of Surrey."

"As soon as I saw you I made up my mind to."

"And before you had decided to take him?"

"No. Much as I hate a nun's life I knew there was something lacking. As soon as I saw you I knew what."

"You delight me. We shall be happy together. But we shall have to be careful."

"What must I do?"

"First refuse William Warren."

"If I do my aunt will try to force me take the veil."

"My poor little captive Princess! You must refuse to take the veil." His hands caressed her body under the rough serge. "To think they could condemn you to such a life. You were meant to be loved and love in return. You will be a ready pupil. Oh, I have such delights in store for you, my dearest love."

She felt she would swoon with delight already. Just to hear him address her in such a manner was enough.

"I must refuse Surrey and the veil. It will not be easy."

"Nothing that is worth while is ever easy. Hold off the Abbess. Tell her you are undecided. Tell her you need time to think."

"I have been saying that for years."

"Then you must perforce continue to do so."

"And in time . . ."

He brought his face close to hers so that his warm breath was on her cheek.

"I shall be King of this realm 'ere long and then none shall gainsay me. I shall say the Princess Edith is to be my Queen and I'll put to hideous death any who attempts to say me nay."

"No one would ever dare."

"They never would. So, my love, you will tell them that you cannot take Surrey and you feel it is very possible that you will choose the religious life. And you will wait . . . but not long. Then I shall come and claim you."

"I will do it," she cried. "I will keep myself free for you."

"And the waiting must not be long or I shall disguise myself as a wicked baron and take the Abbey; I shall carry off my Princess and begin to teach her how exciting love can be."

Then he drew her to him and kissed her once more. He wound her plaits about her wrists and pulled them so that he hurt in a manner which excited her. He thrust a hand inside her rough shift and caressed her body.

"Oh, to divest you of these abominable garments," he cried.

"It shall come to pass. I have vowed it."

He left her bewildered.

She could not speak to Mary or anyone.

Of only one thing was she certain. She would not marry the Earl of Surrey. She would not take the veil. She would wait for Prince Henry to become the King of England and claim her.

Brothers in Conflict

When Henry rode back from Wilton to Winchester he was feeling more than ever dissatisfied with his fate.

The Princess Edith was not uncomely; her innocence was amusing and she could give him some diversion which he could not find with his many mistresses. Moreover it was time he was married. He was thirty years of age and he wanted sons.

Edith had interested him; he had seen more beautiful women. Nesta, who was his favourite and the Princess of Wales, was one of the most fascinating women of the day; she had a sensuality to match his own and never failed to excite him. She had already borne him a child, and not only with her had he proved himself able to beget strong and healthy boys and girls. It was said that he had more bastards than any man in England.

He had four passions in his life: Women, the hunt, a love of learning—and more than any of these he longed for the crown.

Having seen the Princess and realized that he must

achieve his destiny soon, he was more restless than usual.

What bad fortune to be born a third son. And he might have been a fourth son, if Richard had not died in the forest when hunting. What hopes would he have had then? He must needs rejoice in Richard's death although he had been, as many had said, the best of the bunch. If only Rufus could have a similar accident in the hunting field!

Then he, Henry, would seize the crown without delay. Robert would no doubt claim it but Robert had no hope. The English would not accept a Norman. He, Henry, had been born in England; he had been educated by Lanfranc at Canterbury; he was the natural heir. Moreover Robert was a fool. All his life Robert had been a fool. First he had tried to pit his strength against that of the Conqueror. What hope had he had of succeeding there? Normandy had missed the strict rule of William I. And now, foolish Robert had put it in pawn to Rufus while he went on a Crusade. Men liked Robert; he was affable, generous—far too generous, for he squandered his fortune on those who flattered him—he was extravagant in the extreme; Robert as a man might be charming but as a ruler he was no good.

He had inherited none of his father's attributes, except his quick temper. Henry smiled to remember how he and Rufus when they were boys had thrown dirty water down from a balcony onto Robert and his friends and how Robert had been so incensed that he was ready to kill them and might well have done so if their father had not intervened. If he had harmed them he would never have forgiven himself. That was Robert's nature. He acted without thinking and then had to suffer remorse. He was unlike either of his brothers—most of all Henry.

Henry was too clever not to know himself, and that he was the most fitted to rule of all his brothers. His father had sensed that, for on his death bed he had shown a certain satisfaction in the belief that in the end both England and Normandy would come to Henry. He knew that Henry, cool and calculating, with a scholar's understanding and a lawyer's astuteness, would hold together the family's possessions with greater skill than either of his elder brothers.

But the waiting was long. Rufus was in good health. It was true that when he was enraged his face grew scarlet and the veins knotted at his temples and Henry had seen men drop dead when thus affected. But hot temper was no sure sign that death was imminent. Rufus merely had their father's temper, and his avariciousness, his skill—or some of it—in battle, his courage and determination to hold on to what he had. But he lacked the Conqueror's love of detail, his meticulous attention to the seemingly small matters which were in fact the foundations on which his rule was built; he lacked the passion for good rule and for justice.

All his sons, except perhaps one, thought Henry, lacked the essential qualities which had built William the Conqueror's domain and made him the greatest man of the age.

And now was the time for Henry to take over—now while Robert was in the Holy Land and Normandy was in pawn, now while the English were dissatisfied with Rufus, now while Anselm had been dismissed and was fulminating about the manner in which the King of England lived, while the names Sodom and Gomorrah were mentioned and the court of the English King was likened to those cities.

Yes, now was the time for Henry to take over the realm, but between him and the throne stood Rufus.

He thought a little of the virginal Princess to whom he had talked of marriage. She was in love with him already. She would be submissive. He liked a little spirit in his women; on the other hand variety was always enticing; and marriage would be a new adventure.

He would ride now over the border to Wales and visit Nesta; he had need of her company; he would like to see their son too. He would talk to her of the country's growing dissatisfaction with Rufus. They might be able to plan together. But Nesta was a wise woman; she would know that if he married it might be necessary to terminate their relationship. Although he could continue with his casual sexual encounters he could scarcely live as openly as he had been doing with Nesta. As yet though he need not consider that but could give himself up to the satisfaction of Nesta's bed and counsel.

There was always a welcome for Henry at the castle of Rhys ap Tewdur. Rhys, who was King of Deheubarth, was glad to be on such good terms with the brother of the English King. He felt this gave him an added protection, for his little realm was in constant danger of attack.

Henry was the lover of his daughter, the voluptuous Nesta, and Henry was going to be King of England in due course. Rufus, by his very nature, would as certainly as Edward the Confessor beget no children. So in due course it seemed likely that Henry would be King.

Henry rode into the courtyard where he was received with deference by the grooms and very soon the news of his arrival was spread throughout the castle. Rhys came down to welcome him and it was not long before Nesta arrived.

He stared at her with pleasure. She was a goodly sight. No matter what she wore she was beautiful in an entirely sexual manner. There was about Nesta an eternal air of promise. No matter how intimate a man became with her—and he could be very intimate indeed—there was always about Nesta a suggestion of as yet unexplored experiences, of sensations not yet probed. Moreover each lover was made to feel that there had never been and never could be any like him. This was the secret of her great fascination. No man could look on Nesta and not feel flattered by her.

Rhys said: "This is a happy day." And Henry had seized Nesta in a hungry embrace which indicated that he wished an early retirement to the bedchamber.

Nesta smiled in her lazy manner, implying that she was not averse to such a suggestion, and under the admiring gaze of Rhys and Gwladys her mother, who was a pale shadow of her daughter, they retired at once to Nesta's chamber.

Temporarily satisfied, Henry lay on the bed and

watched Nesta indolently lolling beside him, her magnificent hair seductively arranged to half-conceal her body.

She smiled at him, taking in his attractions, and if the greatest of these was perhaps the crown which could one day adorn his luxuriant black locks he was comely enough; a good and practised lover, she had long decided, and one of her best.

"What brings you to Deheubarth?" she asked him idly.

"What a question. Have I not told you with considerable eloquence?"

"There are women in England."

"But Nesta is in Wales."

She was satisfied with the reply for she knew that although he took women wherever he fancied them, and he fancied frequently, he could never have had such a mistress as she was.

"I notice though," she said, "that you are thoughtful. You brood. What schemes are in your head?"

"The usual thoughts are there," he said. "My brother lives too long."

"He has strange habits."

"Ranulf Flambard is still his shadow. He dotes on the fellow. The people hate Flambard as much as they hate Rufus."

"You think that they would like Henry and his favourite Nesta better?"

"You are a thousand times more beautiful than Flambard and the people understand a mistress. They like not Rufus's way of life."

"They fear him though."

"As subjects should fear their kings. My father taught them and us that."

"And so my Henry grows impatient, but impatience alone will not solve his problems."

Henry spread his hands helplessly. "What can I do but wait?"

She laughed at him. "Waiting was never a trick of yours."

"In love, nay."

"They say waiting too long quenches desire."

"I have waited long for the crown and my desire for it grows each day."

"And if it came to you what of me?"

"You would come to Winchester or Westminster to be with me constantly."

"They would expect you to marry."

He looked at her covertly. "Rufus has not."

"Nay, and look at him! His brother is ready to murder him for the crown. His son if he had one might have waited in a decorous manner."

"My ancestors favoured their children by their mistresses. My father himself was a bastard."

"But you and your brothers were born in respectable wedlock, and I doubt not the Conqueror's example will be followed in this matter as in everything else."

"If I were King I should follow my father's rules only where it seemed wise to do so."

"What of our little Robert?"

"How is the boy?"

"Eager for a glimpse of his father."

"Then I must needs make much of him."

"There is time after you have made much of his mother."

"Why, Nesta," he said, "you grow more desirable every time I see you."

"My fascination is not the only thing that grows." She patted her body. "Soon your seed will be grown so big it will be apparent to all who behold me."

"Mine!"

"Whose else? I reckon I am four months with child. Which means it happened during your last visit. That is a long time to stay away from me, Henry."

"It is far too long."

"Doubtless you have had other excitements in the meantime."

"Nothing to compare with these I share with you."

"And, if our child is another boy, he way well wear the crown after you . . . but Robert of course would come before him. I trust you would not put any other little bastard you have got on some light woman before our sons."

"Do you believe that?"

"Not if I were there to make sure of their rights."

"You will be there...beside me. Have no fear."

And he was thinking of the innocent young Princess whom he would marry if he had the crown. They would have children and the sons they would have would come before Nesta's. He remembered the pure adoration the Princess had been too candid to hide and he wondered how he would explain to her his situation with Nesta and the life he had led. She would be horrified, poor innocent girl; but he had said he would teach her what life was; and he could no more suppress his desires than Rufus could his.

There would be complications when he became King; Nesta would be one of them, for, although he talked glibly of keeping her with him and legitimizing her sons that they might inherit the throne after him, he knew this would not be. The Norman dukes who had done this in the past had not been head of a well ordered country such as the Conqueror had made England. But he would deal with these matters when they came and Nesta would never fret too much over one lover for there would always be others waiting to take his place.

And now she was pregnant with another child. He half hoped it would be a daughter. Daughters were not so ambitious and it often assured the loyalty of some wavering vassal to give him a king's daughter to wife. Daughters had their uses; but if they were legitimate the more useful they became.

He *must* get the crown.

Nesta moved close to him and put her arms about his neck.

"You are pleased about the child?"

"I am."

"And if he is a boy you will give him lands and titles?"

"When I have them to give."

"And you will not set him above the many children that exist in this country claiming to be yours?"

"Yours would always come first with me," he said,

abandoning all thoughts of his unsatisfactory position in her seductive embrace.

*   *   *

He was too restless to stay long in Deheubarth and he was soon riding to Winchester.

He did not go straight to the court, instead he called at the house of the Clare family to whom he had always shown favour.

They welcomed him and there was feasting in their hall. The venison tasted good. Rufus had given Sir Walter Tyrrell leave to hunt in the new forest. They were great friends, Tyrrell being a first class huntsman, and the King always enjoyed his company on a hunt.

Sir Walter had married one of the daughters of the Clare household and his father-in-law had bestowed lands in Essex upon him. They had always been ready to welcome Henry to their home, no matter on what ill terms the Prince was with his brother.

They had feasted and drunk, the minstrels had played and sung and the company was drowsy.

Tyrrell said to Henry: "You are thoughtful this night, my Prince. Are you dreaming of the beautiful Nesta?"

"Nay," said Henry, "of other matters." He laughed. "I grow old and I remain poor. I often think how unfortunate I was to be the youngest of my father's sons."

"If you do not possess great wealth now you have your hopes, my Prince."

"Hopes long deferred," mourned Henry.

Gilbert, Lord of Clare, Tyrrell's brother-in-law, looked a little uneasy.

"Serving men have long ears," he murmured.

Henry nodded. Gilbert was right to remind him. It was all very well to talk of his hopes with Nesta in her bedchamber; it was another matter to discuss them in a hall where many might hear.

He changed the subject but the next day when he went hunting with Walter Tyrrell and his brothers-in-law, Gilbert and Roger, he raised the subject again and there was no reason why they should not discuss it freely in the open air.

"Rufus," said Gilbert, "grows more and more under the influence of Flambard. The people are angry with the continual taxation, and they like not the manner of the King's way of life."

"They have taken to shaving the fore part of their heads as the thieves do, since you were at Court," said Tyrrell, "and they wear their hair long at the back so that from behind they look like harlots."

Gilbert added that men were wearing tails attached to their shoes so that it looked as though scorpions grew out of their feet.

"Nothing," added Roger, "is too ridiculous. And the aim of every courtier is to look like a woman. With long hair and rich clothes they mince about the Court. It is not easy to tell the difference between men and women. There are many who deplore the way things are going and the one they blame for it is the King. We all know how he extorts the utmost in taxation. Flambard's methods are detested throughout the country."

"They call the King a tyrant," said Walter Tyrrell.

"And so he is," cried Henry. "He is unfit to rule. If my father were here he would greatly regret having left England to him."

"And even more so to have left Normandy to Robert," said Gilbert. "If only he had lived long enough to see that there was one son who would have ruled in a manner like his own."

"He thought he had trained Rufus," replied Henry. "After the death of my brother Richard, Rufus was constantly in his company. I was too studious. I became more adept in book learning than my father and because of that he doubted I would make a soldier. Rufus became his favourite. Rufus was to have England. And see what Rufus has done to England. It would have been different had Richard lived. Richard was different from the rest of them. I think we are alike. Richard was calm of nature. Often he would step in and bring peace into our boyish quarrels. He would have been a good king."

"But he was killed when hunting in the New Forest."

"A terrible accident," said Henry. "It was said that it was a judgment on my father for taking people's homes from them to make the New Forest. Some poacher who had his eyes put out for killing a deer had laid a curse on my father, so they said."

"Rufus is as keen a huntsman as the Conqueror. He has kept what the people call the harsh forest laws."

"Perhaps," said Henry lightly, "some poacher will lay a curse on *him* so that the forest kills him as it did my brother Richard."

Gilbert looked cautiously over his shoulder. It was treasonable to talk thus about the death of the King.

The forest seemed suddenly still, as though all the wild creatures were listening.

The men exchanged glances. Something very significant was happening.

* * *

William Warren, Earl of Surrey, called at Wilton Abbey. The Abbess was still confined to her bed and it was the duty of her deputies to supervise the meeting with Edith.

Edith's disappointment was almost unbearable when she saw that he was not accompanied by Prince Henry. How insignificant he seemed! Yet he was handsome enough. It was merely that in comparison with the incomparable Henry he seemed of so little account.

They seated themselves on the window seat; the nuns took their place resolutely at a safe distance.

William had said: "You may leave us." But how he lacked the authority of Henry!

"We shall remain," replied the elder of them, and although he attempted to bluster they refused to go.

How different it would have been had Henry been here! thought Edith.

"I came to see you," said William, "because I am going to the King shortly. I am going to tell him that we are betrothed. I see no reason why we should not be married within a few weeks.

Edith said: "I have to tell you that I have been thinking on your request for my hand and I have been undecided for so long. I am no longer. I have made up my mind that I do not wish to accept your proposal."

William stared at her. "Not wish to marry!"

"I have grown accustomed to my life here and I have come to the conclusion that I cannot leave here to marry you."

"You would bury yourself for the rest of your life in this place! I cannot believe that you are serious."

"I am in earnest," she told him. "I know full well that I cannot marry you."

He could not believe it. What was wrong with him? He was young and women found him attractive. He had thought he pleased her. So it had seemed on the first occasion. Henry had been with them on the second and had taken the centre of the scene but she had given no indication that she was displeased by his attentions.

"You cannot mean that you wish me to look elsewhere for a wife?"

"I do mean that."

"I will not give up hope," he cried.

"That is for you to say, but I must tell you that you waste your time."

"It is impossible."

"Nay 'tis so. I wish you godspeed and may you find a wife more to your taste than I could ever have been."

"I had made up my mind to marry you."

"My mind is made up also," she told him.

"So you choose to spend your life here . . . to waste the years before you!"

She bowed her head.

The two figures rose from the seats.

They spoke gently to Edith.

"You wish to return to your cell, to meditate?" whispered one.

"I do," she answered.

"Then, my lord Earl, we will conduct you to the gate."

"Good-bye," said Edith. "May God go with you."

* * *

The nuns could not resist going to the Abbess's cell. She lay on her straw, weak but improving. Before her was a book of devotions and her eyes were closed as they entered. She opened them in outraged surprise and glared at the intruders.

"Reverend Mother," they said, "the Earl of Surrey has been."

She was alert. Her eyes stony, her mouth thin with suppressed anger.

"And so?" she demanded.

"He has gone, Mother."

"And the Princess has seen him?"

"She has sent him away. She says she does not wish to marry. She will take the veil."

The Abbess raised herself on one arm. "She has said this! She has said it of her own free will!"

"Yes, Reverend Mother, we heard and saw her rejection of him."

The Abbess sank back on her bed. She was smiling grimly to herself.

She believed she had won the battle for Edith's soul.

* * *

Mary was taking a farewell of her sister which was tinged with sadness.

"Oh, Edith," she said, "how I wish that you too were leaving this place to marry!"

"I could not take William Warren."

"I thought he was so handsome."

"He was not ill-favoured."

"So it is true then that you have made up your mind to take the veil and become like Aunt Christina?"

"I do not think that will come to pass."

"Edith . . . it was Henry. You changed after he came."

"Yes, it is Henry."

"He is the King's brother. Does he wish to marry you?"

"He wishes it."

"Then what should stop his making an offer for your hand? I believe our brother and uncle would accept it, for, although Eustace says he has no lands and very little money, he is the son of the Conqueror."

"He will offer for me, Mary."

"Have you told Aunt Christina?"

"No. How can I? There is nothing to tell as yet . . . except that I shall never take the veil."

"She will be furious."

"I know. She will hate me and be harsh with me. I am no longer a child to be beaten but I doubt not she will attempt to do so. I fear her, Mary. She is so powerful in this little world and she hates any who challenge her power. She will try to trick me. I know. Do not whisper a word of what I have told you. I shall lead her to believe that I have a taste for the sequestered life but that I cannot even yet make up my mind. I shall pray every day that Henry will come for me."

"But the King has promised you to William Warren."

"That is why I must feign to be preparing myself to take the veil."

"He could insist, Edith."

"I know. Oh, Mary, sometimes I am afraid. There is the King and Aunt Christina. One would force me to marry, the other to take the veil. But when Henry becomes the King he will claim me."

"Edith, how can he become the King while Rufus lives? Rufus is not an old man. He may live for ten more years or twenty. Are you going to defy the King and Aunt Christina all those years? In any case at the end of them you will be too old."

"I don't believe it will be long."

"Why does he not storm the Abbey and carry you off?"

"Without the King's consent? We should have to leave the country. And where should we go? To Normandy? That is in the King's hands now. To Scotland! Nay, I know I must be patient. And I know, too, how well worth while the waiting will be. Do not grieve for me, dear Mary. I rejoice that you are free and that your future husband pleases you. That is a great comfort to me."

The sisters embraced; and a few days later Mary left Wilton for her marriage to Eustace of Boulogne.

*　　*　　*

Flambard, who was constantly in the King's company, came to him to announce that his brother Henry was at Court.

"Ha!" said Rufus. "Depend upon it he wants something. If I were a soft man, Ranulf, I'd find it in my heart to be sorry for him. All that learning and hardly a mark or two to call his own. Nothing but the hope of what will one day come to him."

"He'll have to wait a long time to see those hopes fulfilled. *My* hope is never."

"It would go ill with you, Ranulf my dear, if he ever took my place. He'd have little time for my friends."

"That's another reason why your friends will guard you with their lives."

"Let's see the fellow and hear what he has to say."

Henry came into the King's chamber, and Rufus regarded him appraisingly. Seeming young in comparison with himself, lusty, sturdy with a wealth of good dark hair, a handsome fellow—but not of the kind he admired. Too virile, all man. Why did our father get two sons so different? wondered Rufus.

"Well, brother, how fares it with you?"

"Poorly," said Henry. He glanced significantly at Flambard and the King intercepting his gaze said: "Ranulf has become my chief minister and my bodyguard. I keep him with me at all times."

Henry glared distastefully at Ranulf who returned the look insolently.

"Do you think it fitting that your brother should roam the countryside so poor that he has but three or four attendants, no money to provide himself with horse to ride, and no land?" asked Henry.

"Alas," said Rufus, "we all need so much more than we possess."

106

"You are rich, William. Our father left you England and now Normandy is in pawn to you. I do not think you know the meaning of poverty."

"Do I not? Continually I must impose taxation to provide me with the money I need to rule this country."

"You are fortunate to have people to tax."

"There is a limit to what one can do in that direction. Oh, I sympathize with your poverty. It matches my own."

Henry was aware of a snigger from Ranulf. He thought: When I am King that man shall pay for his insults to me.

"I wonder what our father would say if he saw his son reduced to such poverty?"

"He would doubtless say it was what you deserved. You know what a hard man he was. He left you five thousand pounds in silver. What has happened to it?"

"You know that I lent Robert almost the whole of it."

"Ay, in exchange for the Cotentin. Of which he cheated you. And yet you gave your assistance to him. But for you Rouen would have fallen to me. You held the town for Robert, did you not? I remember what you did to Conan, the leader of those who would have put the town into my hands. You will remember too. You had him flung from the castle turret. You would be a hard ruler, Henry."

"I would be just . . . as our father was. It was the first law we learned from him. Normandy then belonged to our brother."

"And much good it did for you. For he returned not the silver you had lent him nor did he keep his bond to give you the Cotentin."

"Robert is weak. He makes promises which he believes he will fulfil and later he finds he cannot or forgets them."

"Normandy is now mine. I shall keep it. Do you think he will ever have the money to repay his debt?"

"Never! So he will try to win in battle what he cannot pay for. You will need help against him when the time comes. You will need a brother to help you."

"That time has not come and it may well be that

Robert will not return from the Crusade. And," went on Rufus, "when he would neither return the silver nor give you the land, you seized Mont St-Michel."

"And you both came against me and besieged me there. Brothers against brother. I wonder our father did not come back to haunt you! You would have left me to starve, William. It was Robert who helped me then. It was Robert who sent in wine for my table. If I went to Robert now, he would help me."

"So now we see where your legacy has gone. Most of it to Robert and the rest in attempting to defend Mont St-Michel against your brothers."

"Our father used to say that united we could hold everything against our enemies. It was when we divided that we put ourselves in danger."

"Our father is dead. He did not have our problems to deal with."

"He mastered all kinds of problems. He was the wisest man who ever lived."

Henry was thinking: And he prophesied that one day I should have more than either you or Robert. That day must come . . . soon. How could England go on suffering under Rufus with his mincing courtiers and his crippling taxation, his lack of attention to state matters? It would not be a sin to remove him.

England needed wise rule, the sort of rule which only a clever king could give it. The Conqueror had shown what could be done. He, Henry, knew exactly how to follow in his father's footsteps with the necessary adjustments to the times. Oh, it would be a blessing to the country if this paederast could be removed and a wise man set up in his place.

Rufus's face had grown suddenly more scarlet. The warning veins stood out at his temples.

"Our father chose to leave England to me. Doubtless he thought a soldier would make a better king than a lawyer."

"A country's laws are more important than its wars," retaliated Henry. "Laws bring order, wars inevitably chaos."

"Then I can give them both. Do you think I cannot make laws? I have brought Normandy and England together. There is not the conflict between Norman and Saxon as there was at one time. The people are beginning to live peacefully ... under my laws."

Harsh cruel laws, thought Henry. Eyes put out, noses and ears sliced off. Doubtless they were necessary. If one were fair one must admit that Rufus had not done badly. He had produced some fine buildings; he had defended the country and kept it strong; it was his private life that disgusted the people, for as always the manners of the court were reflected throughout the country.

Sensual in the extreme were all the brothers, but at least Robert and Henry were so in a natural manner.

"How think you the people like to see your brother in such straits?"

"I think the people are not over-anxious about the condition in which you live. They know that you are made very welcome in many houses and I have heard it said that wherever Prince Henry goes there is a warm bed waiting for him."

"'Tis good fortune for me since if I relied on my own resources I'd be sleeping under a hedge."

"But even there you would find a woman to comfort you. Such is my brother's charm, Ranulf, that he has but to lift a hand and the ladies flock to him."

"He is a lucky Prince, lord."

"So lucky that he should be content with his lot, eh?"

"Content indeed," echoed Ranulf.

"But I think he would like to share my counsels. He would like to have a hand in government. Is that so, Henry?"

"You are the King, William, the true king of this realm. All I ask is for a little help that I may live in a manner worthy of your brother."

"You are clever, Henry. Did we not always hear it. Robert was our mother's darling and Richard the favourite of them both, but Henry was the clever one. The scribe, the lawyer, the scholar. Poor Rufus, he was of no account."

"Until Richard died," said Henry, "and then our father bestowed on you, Rufus, that which would have gone to Richard."

"Ay, and I have given good service to this country. Have you seen my White Tower, Henry? It would rejoice our father's heart to see his Tower of London so embellished. Have you seen our bridge? Yes, I can be pleased with myself, for I have given good service for my inheritance. Through my laws Normans and Saxons live in peace together. That is my policy—to marry Norman to Saxon so that in a generation they become English. Why I have just given my consent to William Warren, our nephew and good Earl of Surrey, to take to wife the Saxon Princess Edith. The poor girl has been fretting her heart out in Wilton Abbey where her old aunt has been trying to make an Abbess of her. My good Norman, Warren, will take the Saxon girl. Their children will be English and that will please the people."

Henry's lips tightened. He thought of Edith, young, virginal, yet yielding. No, William Warren should not have Edith!

He was determined on that too. And the girl herself. She would hold out against Warren. He knew she would. His powers of fascination, at which Rufus sneered, had never been so potent as they had in the hall of Wilton Abbey.

"And so I can expect no help from you?" asked Henry. "I must go on in my impecunious way of life."

"I will relent. You may follow the hunt. Tomorrow we shall be in the forest. Join us there, Henry."

"But, brother, how can I do that when I am so poor that I have no steed suitable to hunt with you in your forest?"

"Oh, I'll be generous," said Rufus smirking at Ranulf. "I'll give you permission to follow the hunt...on foot."

Seething with rage, Henry bowed and left his brother.

*   *   *

The next day he was in the forest. How beautiful it was and how he longed to be mounted on a fiery charger to ride at the head of the party.

And here he was—the son of the Conqueror—too poor to buy a horse!

The hunt was the joy of his life as it was of all the family. They had been brought up to rejoice in the baying of the dogs and the glory of the chase. To see the bearers carrying in the deer or wild boar after the hunt was a goodly sight. Best of all was the chase itself.

He would shame his brother. People would look at him following the hunt on foot and say: "Poor Prince Henry has no means of living like a prince. His brother should have more respect for his brother."

But nothing could shame Rufus. He cared not what his people said of him. If it came to his ears that they had slandered him they would lose an ear, or the right or left hand. Few dared raise a voice against him. He was absolute ruler.

The King's nephew William Warren was at the hunt, mounted on a fine steed. When he saw Henry on foot he stared at him in astonishment. They looked at each other. Henry's gaze was ironical. How had Warren fared when he went courting the Princess Edith?

Henry went to him and said: "We have not met, nephew, since Wilton."

"Nay," answered Warren sullenly.

"A beautiful Princess ... your betrothed."

"I am not betrothed."

"Not so? I found her agreeable. You are hard to please, nephew."

"The Princess has decided to take the veil."

"The veil in preference to you! I don't believe it."

Henry's eyes mocked; the younger man was uneasy.

"Perhaps she liked you not. That is hard to understand ... a fine fellow like you. Could it be that her fancy has strayed elsewhere?"

William Warren flushed slightly. He knew. It was Henry then, Henry this lecher, this man whose reputation was well known at Court. Henry, the penniless Prince—with great prospects—who could not resist women and rode about the country seeking a means to live like a prince, taking his mistress wherever he fancied.

But he could not have taken the Princess Edith.

111

Even had she been willing this would not have been possible in Wilton Abbey.

What then? Had he promised her marriage? How could he, the penniless Prince, offer marriage to a Princess? And had not the King promised *him* the Princess? Even Henry would not dare go against the wishes of the King.

Yet some instinct told William Warren that it was due to Henry that the Princess Edith had refused him.

Hatred flared up in him. He would take his revenge for this. He was favoured by the King. He was after all his nephew just as he was Henry's. What a fool he had been to take Henry to Wilton! Trust Henry to make trouble where a woman was concerned.

But how could Edith have preferred this older man who lacked his good looks? He had that magnificent hair which he wore long and his many amorous adventures had made him very skilful in playing on female emotions. William Warren had to face the fact that Prince Henry was a man of deadly fascination to women, although it was not easy for him to define what this quality was.

They were enemies though. The successful lover against the one who had failed. And, thought William Warren grimly, of what use was Henry's success in that quarter to him?

He changed the subject abruptly. "I see you follow the hunt on foot, Prince Henry," he said, patting the head of his own fine steed. "Why you are in truth a veritable Deersfoot."

He rode off leaving Henry gazing balefully after him, angry because he, the Conqueror's son, had no suitable horse while his nephew should have such a fine one.

And when he heard people refer to him as Deersfoot he knew who had been responsible for the sneer.

* * *

Abbess Christina paced up and down Edith's cell.

"There is no reason for delay. You have made up your mind. You are no longer a child. You should take your final vows without delay."

"I am still uncertain."

"How can you be? Two men have offered for you and you wanted neither. Is this not proof enough?"

"I do not know."

"Then we must perforce insist that you do know."

But the Abbess knew that without Edith's consent there was nothing she could do.

Her pleasure at the Princess's rejection of William Warren had diminished, for Edith would not take the final step. All kinds of penances and punishments occurred to her but she knew that none of these would avail.

There was a stubbornness about the girl. It was as though some outside influence was at work.

"God will punish you," she told her. "You have witnessed His mercy. He has made it clear what He wishes of you and you ignore him."

Edith did not answer. It was clear that she cared nothing for threats from her aunt or from God. There was about her a set purpose. She was not going to be worried into taking her vows.

"We will pray together," said the Abbess.

"My knees are sore with praying," replied Edith.

"Mine are hard because of the hours I have spent on my knees."

"You are an abbess and a most pious woman. I beg of you be patient with me."

"All these years you have been under my care and still you hesitate."

"I must have time," insisted Edith.

In exasperation the Abbess left her. Edith did pray then.

"Soon, oh Lord, let him come for me. He *will* come I know. I have been saved for this. I will be his wife and we shall live together in harmony all the days of our lives. And if, by Your Grace, he comes to the throne I will be a good queen as well as a good wife to him."

She remembered how her mother had gone to church barefoot during Lent, how she had selected the poorest and dirtiest of the humble people that she might show *her* humility by washing and kissing their feet.

"This I will do, oh Lord. I will serve You with all my heart and soul if You will but give me Henry."

And so each day she prayed; and each day she held off the demands and harsh persuasion of Aunt Christina.

Her life had become a bitter battle of which at some times it seemed the Abbess would be the victor. Her love for Henry grew as time passed; she endowed him with all the qualities of the saints and the beauty of a pagan god.

And so the days passed, waiting, waiting.

The Forest Tragedy

It was August, a month when the forest was at its best, and the King, with a select party of his friends, those who shared his love of the chase, had come to Linwood Lodge in the heart of the New Forest.

Henry was a member of the party and with him was one of his most loyal friends, Henry Beaumont. The Prince's friends, the Clares, who were members of the party with Walter Tyrrell, had presented him with a fine horse, so that on this occasion he would not have to follow the hunt on foot.

The King had expressed his pleasure that Walter Tyrrell was of the party because he was known to be one of the best shots in England. It was his arrows which always appeared to inflict the mortal wound. The Clares, too, were very welcome, and it was a gay party.

There were some who were uneasy though. The servants had a way of looking over their shoulders as though they expected wild beasts to leap onto their backs. But it was nothing so tangible that they feared.

Henry heard them whispering together. "There are demons in the forest who come to life at night."

"The trees turn to monsters after dark; they dance wild dances and if any unwary soul should be wandering alone they would seize that one in their embrace and twist him this way and that in the dance of death and in the morning there would be another warped and twisted tree in the forest."

When riding through the forest it was no unusual sight to see the remains of a man hanging from a tree. He would be one of those ill-fated men who had thought to snatch something to feed himself and his family as his forefathers had been wont to do before the Conqueror came. To steal the King's beasts was one of the greatest crimes in the country. Men were hung from the trees without trial and left there to feed the carrion crows or to rot in the winds and weather. Better such a fate, though, than to have one's eyes torn out or destroyed by glowing metal.

Men had suffered for the forest. The forest was a monster. Homes had been destroyed to create it for the sport of the Norman kings and that was why it was generally believed that by night spirits walked abroad, and that the souls of men who had lost their homes, their eyes or their lives would haunt the forest bent on vengeance.

It was in this forest that Richard, the fairest of the Conqueror's sons, had met his death. There were many who believed that that was the revenge of the dead on the man who had torn up their homes and made harsh rules for those who took what the forest had to offer.

So on such occasions when the King planned several days of hunting and occupied his lodges in the forest this uneasiness always prevailed.

Linwood Lodge at this time was filled with the odour of roasting meat; there was laughter and merriment, for the King was in a good mood. He felt well and younger than his forty years. He always felt so during a hunting expedition.

The talk at table became ribald. The King always encouraged jokes against the churchmen; he had a special feud with them and, as he had often before declared, he had no fear of having to answer for his sins after death. He did not believe in such judgements, he said. No creator would like the weak men of the Church. He would favour a fighter and a good hunter. As for the churchmen their sins were as plentiful as those of other men only they would not admit to them. They were puling hypocrites all of them and he never ceased to congratulate himself on getting rid of the arch-hypocrite, Anselm.

Such talk in the lodge was listened to and applauded rather half-heartedly. It was all very well in the palaces of Winchester and Westminster. Here in the forest there was an air of foreboding. When night came it really did seem that the trees took on weird shapes; and the soughing of the wind in the branches could well be the moans of the dead calling for vengeance.

It may have been that even Rufus was aware of this, for during one night he awoke screaming to his attendants.

Ranulf was the first to reach him.

"What ails you, lord?"

Rufus sat up on his straw, sweating profusely.

"I know not. It was some evil thing that hovered over me. It was death, I think. It had an evil face. I felt it was suffocating me. Send for lights. I do not wish to be in darkness."

Ranulf obeyed and others of Rufus's retinue came hurrying in.

"Stay here," said the King. "You may pass the night in this chamber. I do not like this darkness. Let them bring candles. But stay here. Only then can I doze."

"Is it some sort of omen, think you?" asked one.

"Bah," retorted Ranulf. "It is a surfeit of venison."

"Think you so, my friend?" asked Rufus.

"What else? Our presence will restore you, lord. You may sleep knowing we guard you and warn off evil spirits. Thus you will ensure a good day's hunting tomorrow."

But in spite of the people and the lights, Rufus could not sleep. He remembered the profanities he had uttered at the banqueting table; he remembered the blasphemies. He did not think they had been any worse than at other times but now he was in the forest . . . the enchanted forest, the cursed forest as some called it . . . the forest which had been made at the expense of great suffering and hardship to so many.

"Nay, it was the venison," he comforted himself. "I ate too heartily and drank too much. There's nothing wrong that a good day's hunting will not kill."

The dawn came to outshine the candles. Everyone was relieved; and Rufus, laughing at his nightly fears, was in the best of spirits.

* * *

Breakfast was a lengthy meal because the party would not go into the forest until the early afternoon.

Rufus was hearty and full of good humour.

"So my brother Deersfoot is with us. Is it true, Henry, that you are as fleet as a deer?"

"Hardly that, brother. But I'm as fleet as most men."

"I rejoice. We might have been tempted to hunt *you*. You might not have cared for that."

"'Twould be a new experience," replied Henry in high good humour.

"Do not urge us to try it, brother. We might need but little persuasion."

The conversation was interrupted by the arrival of an armourer.

"What have you there?" asked the King.

"Six new arrows, my lord. I believe you will find them stronger and sharper than all others."

"Bring them to me, man."

Rufus examined them. "'Tis true," he declared. "They have a rare quality. Look you here, Tyrrell; you are the best shot I know. Tell me what you think of these."

Sir Walter Tyrrell examined them.

"It is indeed so, my lord. I rarely saw finer arrows."

"Reward the man who made them," said the King. "Here Tyrrell, you shall have two of them. I never knew a man better able to bring down a deer. You are a fine shot and worthy of the best."

"My lord is gracious," said Tyrrell.

"I shall be interested to know how you fare with them."

"I will tell you, my lord."

There was a commotion without which meant that there were new arrivals at the lodge.

"What means this?" asked the King. "Go and see who comes."

The page came back with the news that the Abbot of Gloucester was without and with him a man who had the appearance of a hermit.

"What want these holy men with me?" said Rufus with a grimace.

"They are begging to be allowed to speak with you, lord."

They stood before him and Rufus looked with distaste at the Abbot's robes and the tattered garments of the Holy Man.

"I am soon leaving for the chase. I have little time to dally with men of your calling."

"Lord, we come to beg you not to go into the forest today."

"Where else should I find fine fat deer, pray tell me?"

"I have a revelation," said the Abbot. "A dream came to me that I should find you here and that I should come to tell you not to go into the forest this day. This Holy Man arrived at my Abbey yester eve. He said to me: 'The King is near by. He must be warned. I have had a vision.'"

"What warning is this?"

"It is that you must not go into the forest this day."

Sir Walter Tyrrell was stroking the surface of the bow which Rufus had given him. Rufus watched him. "Your fingers itch to use it, Tyrrell," he said. "And these fellows would stop our sport."

"'Twould seem so, my lord."

"With talk of omens! Tell me what you saw in this dream?"

"Some danger threatens, lord, and it comes from the forest."

"Is that all?"

"That is all."

"And you, Holy Man?"

"Lord, I beg you do not go into the forest this day."

"I thank you for your coming," said the King. "You must be refreshed. Be seated."

The Abbot and the Holy Man sat at the table and partook of food.

Rufus said: "You churchmen know well my pleasure in the chase and it is your belief that that which is pleasurable is sinful. You rejoice in making others as yourselves and you wish to deny me the chase because you know how I enjoy it."

"What does my lord wish?" asked Ranulf. "Shall you not ride into the forest this day?"

"Not ride into the forest, Ranulf! Are you mad? Did I not come here to hunt?"

"These warnings following your dream . . ."

"A surfeit of venison, remember, Ranulf?"

"It may have been but the dream and the men . . ."

"What think you, Tyrrell?"

"It is for my lord to decide. Perhaps for today you would forgo the chase. Tomorrow would be a new day."

"Think you I would take heed of the churchmen, Tyrrell?"

"Nay, I would not think it, my lord; but if you did that is your will and would be mine."

"Come, to the devil with their omens. It's time we set out."

*   *   *

It was hot that August afternoon as the hunting party rode out from Linwood. The forest grew more beautiful every year. Rufus remembered it when the landscape had been scarred by the remains of cottages from which the owners had been turned out. Now these remains had become buried under gorse and bracken; only here and there was seen the pathetic remains of what had once been a humble and well beloved home.

Rufus had been a little uneasy—made so rather by his own disturbing dream than the prophesies. It was rather strange that one incident should have followed on the other but, as Ranulf said, these wise men were always prophesying in the hope that something they said would turn out to be true and they became re-nowned for it.

But the excitement of the chase was overtaking him. Always it was thus. He remembered how he and his father had ridden out together. It was the only time his father was human—that and perhaps in his relationship with their mother.

Tyrrell was beside him. He liked riding with Tyrrell. There was a man of whom his father would have approved—the best hunter of the party!

"Eager to try out your new arrow, Wat?" he asked.

"Ay, my lord."

"We'll expect good results, friend Wat."

"You shall have them, my lord."

"Come . . ."

They galloped ahead.

Walter Tyrrell and the King had ridden so fast and so far that they had left the rest of the party.

"Where are those laggards?" cried the King laughing.

"We've outridden them," cried Tyrrell.

"Look you," cried the King. "What saw you then? A movement in the undergrowth?"

"There's something there, my lord."

"A deer. Come."

Rufus rode on ahead of Tyrrell.

*   *   *

It was like the dream again. He lay on the grass . . . the grass of his beloved forest, that which had been called the New Forest because it had been made by his father. The grass was green. It should have been blood-red, some rebellious subjects had said. It was a beautiful forest; it had grown to its grandeur through the sufferings of people. Homes had been destroyed to make it; men had suffered torture and death for unlawfully trespassing in it. It had been the Conqueror's Forest and now it was the Red King's Forest.

The trees were taking on strange shapes. Was he in the forest or on his bed? Was this another dream such as that which had disturbed his night?

121

"A surfeit of venison..." He could hear Ranulf's mocking voice.

His friend Robert seemed to be there dancing round his chamber, throwing the long serpent's tail he had attached to his doublet around in a most amusing way. The elongated tips of his shoes danced like snakes.

He was very cold and there was a pain in his chest. There was something wet and warm on his chin.

"Where am I?" he wanted to shout; and it seemed to him that laughing voices answered, "In the forest, Rufus. The forest you and your father created from the blood of men."

There was something heavy on his chest. What had happened? He could not remember. He thought he was in his bedchamber.

Yes, he had been riding with Tyrrell. They had those special fine arrows.

The deer was fleet. They had followed it. Clearly it had thought to escape them and had run into the ruins of a building which had been destroyed to make way for the forest. And then...he could not remember.

He was cold...very, very cold, and growing colder. He tried to call Ranulf...Wat Tyrrell.

No one came and the darkness was overtaking him.

Rufus, the King, no longer knew that he was cold and that there was an oppressive weight on his chest, that his own blood was choking him. He lay inert on the cold, damp earth.

*　　*　　*

Henry, riding with Henry Beaumont, was surrounded by a group of hunters.

In the distance the bracken moved.

"A wild boar?" cried Henry.

"Nay, Prince," said Beaumont. "A fine plump deer, methinks."

"Then after him," replied Henry.

There was the deer poised for flight and Henry was about to shoot his arrow when the strings of his cross bow snapped suddenly.

"A thousand curses," he muttered.

"'Twill need to be repaired," said Beaumont.

"Alas, yes," answered Henry. "Ride on with the others and I'll go to yon forester's hut. The man will mend it for me. When he has done so I shall join the hunt. It should not take long."

The afternoon was hot and his disappointment was keen. He wondered whether his friends had succeeded with the deer. He rode over to the forester's hut and dismounting, tied his horse to a nearby tree.

He went into the hut where the forester's wife was baking. She told him that her husband was in the woods close by.

"Go and bring him to me at once," said Henry. "The string of my bow has broken."

The woman, flustered by the obvious nobility of the Prince, hurried out and as she was some time away, Henry left the cottage in search of her.

As he stepped into the glade an old woman came towards him. At first he was not much taken aback by her appearance, yet he did wonder what such a one was doing in a spot which the strict forestry laws had made almost sacred.

He was about to ask her when she, seeing him, hurried forward and as she did so, fell to her knees.

"Hail, King of England," she said.

He stared at her as she rose from her knees, and at that moment the forester arrived with his wife.

As Henry turned to look at him the old woman disappeared among the bracken and when he would have asked her for an explanation, she was no longer there.

"My lord, your bow needs to be put to rights," said the man.

Silently Henry handed it to him. While the man worked on the bow he wandered round the glade looking for the old woman, her words still ringing in his ears.

Who was she? Why had she spoken thus? Had she mistaken him for Rufus? Surely not. He was not redheaded and red-faced and even those who had never seen Rufus knew him to be thus by his very nickname.

"Hail, King of England."

He had lost his desire for the chase. He wanted to

ride back with all speed to Linwood. He would wait there until the hunters returned. And if Rufus came with them then he would think he had encountered a mad woman. And if he did not . . .

The prospect made him almost dizzy with excitement.

*   *   *

An old charcoal burner who had his cottage in the heart of the forest was returning to his home on the morning of the third of August, leading his thin little horse which was dragging a rough cart.

Suddenly he pulled up to a sharp halt. What was that lying there in the ruined walls of the old church which thirty years before had been demolished to make way for the forest? He paused. It was a man—his face blackened and distorted, his garments bloody, and protruding from his chest was the broken shaft of an arrow.

He could not believe it! But he knew that face. What should he do? As a forest dweller he lived in terror of breaking a rule of which he had not known the existence. Yet he could not leave a human being to be a victim to the carrion crows. The man's ghost might haunt him if he did not do all in his power to give him decent burial.

He lifted the body and placed it in his cart.

When he reached his home he called to his wife and said: "I found a man dead in the forest. He has been killed by an arrow."

She came out to look. "Why, Purkiss," she said, "he is one of a hunting party. An arrow meant for a deer has killed him. He must be of noble birth for only one of such would hunt in the King's forest."

"What shall I do?" asked Purkiss the charcoal burner.

"Wait here," she said and went to fetch some of their neighbours. They came and looked at the body.

"The King is hunting from Linwood," said one. "Mayhap you should take the body there. If it is a noble gentleman there could be some profit in it."

Purkiss decided that if some of his friends would accompany him he would take the body to Linwood Lodge.

*   *   *

Henry was in no mood for the chase. He did not remember any other occasion when he had not been ready to hunt. His thoughts were in a turmoil. The weird old woman had set his pulses racing with a wilder excitement than any other woman ever had before.

Impatiently he waited for the hunters to return to the lodge. How slowly the time passed. He wished that he had not come back yet; his mood was better suited to the wildness of the forest.

The first of the party to return was William Breteuil, a great hunter who was in charge of the treasury. His father had been Fitz-Osbern, one of the Conqueror's greatest friends and most trusted ministers. Henry had never greatly cared for him because he had taken little notice of him. He was a great friend of Robert, and Henry often fancied that he would have supported his elder brother against Rufus. On this occasion however, he was glad to see him.

They sat down at table together and gradually other members of the party began to return.

Darkness came and the King was still absent. Walter Tyrrell came in, but he said little to Henry.

A strange tension hung over the company. It could well have been that they had decided not to return to the lodge that night.

Henry sought an opportunity of telling Henry Beaumont of his strange experience in the glade because Beaumont was one of the few whom he could trust. Rufus had never liked Beaumont and there was an unspoken agreement between Henry and this man that if Rufus died they would work together.

"Who was this woman?"

"I know not. I could not discover."

"Could she have seen the King ... dead?"

"I cannot see how she could have done so."

"Doubtless she was a witch."

125

"She had the appearance of such."

"And she said 'Hail' to you and called you 'King.' Rufus does not return. There is one thing you must do if the King is indeed dead, and that is to take the Treasury. Once you have that in your possession you have only to win the people to you and the crown is yours."

"I know it well. We will not both sleep at the same time this night. I will keep watch for three hours, then so will you while I sleep. We must be fresh for the morning."

Morning came.

William Breteuil was asking everyone: "Where is the King? Have any seen him?"

But no one had.

It was in the middle of the morning when Purkiss the charcoal burner leading his horse and accompanied by a few of the local churls brought the body in his cart to Linwood Lodge.

Henry with the others went out to see what was in the cart.

When he saw the body, and in spite of the mire and mud recognized it, a great exultation came to him. The woman's words had been significant.

William Breteuil was there too.

He cried: "My God, this is the King."

"He is dead," said Henry.

"Killed in his own forest," murmured Breteuil.

Henry knew that there was no time to lose. If he did not claim the crown, someone might claim it on Robert's behalf. He knew what was passing in Breteuil's mind and without a moment's delay he ran to the stables. Henry Beaumont was already there saddling the horses and in a few moments they were galloping away on the road to Winchester.

Breteuil understood. He leaped onto his horse and was speeding after Henry.

Henry and Beaumont spurred on their horses. They knew that Breteuil's idea was to stop them and to claim the crown of England for Robert.

That must not be. The crown belonged to Henry. This was his great moment. He kept hearing the words of the weird woman ringing in his ears: "Hail, King of England."

King of England he would be and the next days were the most important in his life.

He was ready to take the challenge.

No one was going to stop him now.

By God's mercy, he thought, I must reach Winchester before Breteuil.

He would never forget that ride. The constant fear that his horse would fail; the anxiety that Breteuil would outdistance him; the great relief when he reached the door of the Treasury and found that he and Beaumont had arrived first.

"Open in the name of the King," cried Beaumont.

The startled custodian stared at him and Henry.

Beaumont had his sword at the man's throat.

"William II is dead—killed hunting in the forest. Henry I is King of England. On pain of death open the door."

The door was opened and Henry and Beaumont had command of the Treasury.

It was not long afterward when Breteuil arrived to find Henry and Beaumont at the door, their swords drawn.

"I claim the crown and regalia on behalf of Robert, the eldest son of William I," said Breteuil.

"I claim the crown and regalia as an English King born on English soil educated in England, and the son of the Conqueror," retorted Henry.

By this time many other nobles had arrived. The position was clear to them. Henry was on the spot. Robert was far away on a Crusade to the Holy Land. Normandy was in pawn. Henry had shown himself a good general; Robert was known to be feckless.

Those who supported Henry were firmly behind him, while Robert's adherents hesitated. Some of them, however, murmured together that this was a usurpation of the crown.

Henry spoke to them then. Being more learned than his brothers he had always been able to express himself with a force and logic which they had lacked.

"I am English," he said, "as none of my brothers ever

127

could be. My father was aware of this. It was for this purpose that he sent me to England at an early age and put me in the care of that great scholar Archbishop Lanfranc. The people of this country want an English King. I will marry at once. I have chosen for my bride the Princess Edith who is a member of the Saxon Royal Atheling family. Our children will be entirely English. Those who stand beside me will not be forgotten. There were many harsh laws made by my brother. These I will change. I have been educated to govern. Accept me as your King and I promise you peace and prosperity. Reject me in favour of my brother—who has been singularly unsuccessful in his own domain which is now in pawn to the English crown—and you will plunge this country into bitter war."

The realization of the truth of this, the promises Henry made, and the knowledge that he had qualities which would make him a better ruler than his brother were decisive. Grudgingly those Normans who had been ready to give their support to Robert gave way. Henry was proclaimed King. He took possession of the Treasury and Regalia.

"We must needs now win the same support in London," said Beaumont.

Within a few hours they were riding to London.

*   *   *

Henry had been called a lawyer. The Normans had nicknamed him "Henry Beauclerc." It was so rare to find a scholar king. Even the Conqueror had scarcely been that.

Henry knew that the consent to his accession could well waver; he had to consolidate his position, which meant pandering to those who might well stand against him ... temporarily of course.

He believed he would have the humble people with him, for their hatred of the Normans had persisted ever since 1066. They still looked upon them as the conquerors. So he would appeal to the Saxon section of the community.

He called together all the leading men of the towns and villages and spoke to them.

"My friends and liegemen, natives of this country in which I myself was born, you know that my brother would have my crown. He is a haughty man who cannot live peacefully. He openly despises you, believing you to be cowards and gluttons. He would scorn you and trample you under his feet. But I, a mild and pacific King, would maintain you in all your ancient liberties. I would govern you with moderation and prudence. I will give you, if you require it, a written promise to this effect, signed with my own hand. I will confirm what I write by my oath and my seal. Stand firm then, by me. For supported by English valour I fear not the mad menaces of the Normans."

It was a clever speech, calculated to move the oppressed people where they were most affected. Henry's lawyer's mind was already busy. He intended to govern sternly but justly as his father had. He wanted a prosperous kingdom and he knew how to get it. He was not sure how many of the promises he made at this juncture would be kept; he only knew that they had to be given.

He caused copies of the speech to be made; his seal was set on it and it was put up in all cathedrals and abbeys throughout the country.

The people were won over by this calm and reasoned statement. They told themselves that the cruel days of Rufus were over. They would have a King who would marry and give the country heirs. The last King's influence on the morals of the land would be over. There would be no more ridiculous fashion, with men apeing women and painting their faces and frizzing their hair. England would become a country of brave men.

Henry was accepted.

He was determined to show that he was no coward and ordered that his coronation should take place without delay in Westminster Abbey. There would be danger, he knew. It would be an occasion when his enemies might rise and make slaughter in the streets. He must take the risk. He could only feel safe when he was the crowned king of England.

So three days after the death of Rufus, Henry's ceremonious coronation took place.

* * *

Meanwhile Rufus's decomposing body was brought to Winchester by Purkiss and the five churls who had accompanied him. They took it to the close of St. Swithin's Minster and presented themselves to the Abbot.

"Lord Abbot," said Purkiss, "this is the body of the King. It is in urgent need of decent burial."

The Abbot took one look at the corpse and groaned in horror. Secretly he cursed Purkiss for bringing it to him. He hesitated; but he dared not send the men on with it. Where else would they take it? And if he turned away the body of the King, what then?

But he knew there was going to be difficulty in the burial.

He was right.

The Church had constantly been under the attack of Rufus. He had sneered at it and always baited churchmen. He had said he might be going to hell but at least he would have a good time on earth. Well, now he was in hell, so most people believed.

Stories about the dead king circulated. There was not the usual need to speak well of the dead, for Rufus had been a self-confessed sinner with no fears of hell. Some said they had seen the Devil in the form of a great goat in the sky, clutching the soul of Rufus. Rufus was damned. Therefore nothing too bad could be said against him.

His evil life was recalled. His vicious friend, Ranulf Flambard, should be punished with him, it was hinted. He had shared his vices. Everything would be different now. Rufus was where he belonged—in hell.

How could such a man be buried in consecrated ground? He would defile any place where he was laid. Yet what should be done with him?

Days passed. The corpse was now almost unrecog-

130

nizable and horrible to behold. Something would have to be done.

Henry made the decision. Rufus was his brother and had been a king. Therefore he must be accorded burial. Royalty must not be insulted, even evil royalty. A grave should be dug in the choir of the new cathedral and the body of Rufus should be put there. Although he would be in that spot where Saxon Kings lay, his burial should not be attended by any ceremony. The bells should not toll for Rufus, no alms should be given, and as he had so often declared that he cared for nothing for the future of his soul, no prayers should be given for its salvation. There should be no text, no cross, no symbols. Although he should be buried among kings— since he was a king and a son of the great William I— there should be no indication of where he lay.

Thus was the Red King laid to rest.

Shortly afterwards the great cathedral tower crashed to the ground and there was terror throughout Winchester.

This was God's vengeance on the city because its people had buried an evil king in a cathedral dedicated to Him.

At least the evil man was now in the custody of the Devil, but the stories about his wickedness were retold and exaggerated in the telling. They forgot that he was a great general and that although he had milched the Church he had given the country some fine buildings, the chief of these being the White Tower and the bridge across the Thames.

They forgot the few virtues and remembered the many vices; and they looked forward to the new reign of that benign—or so he had told them he was—and peace-loving monarch King Henry I.

A Royal Wedding

The most hated man in England was Ranulf Flambard. During Rufus's reign Flambard had been blamed for all the hardships that had been inflicted upon them. He it was who had collected the taxes for Rufus and devised vile means of doing so; therefore he, more than the King, had been regarded with loathing.

Henry, eager to consolidate his position and not to lose one little bit of the popularity he had gained through his declaration, decided that he must immediately perform two acts which would please the people.

The first would be to punish Ranulf Flambard and the second to marry the Saxon Princess.

Henry decided to deal first with Flambard. He had studied the man's methods often enough and had known that he was exceedingly clever. He had a mind to match Henry's. He had worked well for Rufus—and for himself of course—and would be an asset to any king for whom he was working.

Henry could have made use of him. He wondered whether he would be as devoted to him as he had been to Rufus because there had been a closer tie between the two of them than Henry could ever have with any man. Bribes might work with him. But no, that would be folly. To take Ranulf into his counsels would be in direct contrast to all that he promised the people. He was not in a strong enough position to do that yet.

Henry had a new adviser in one Roger, a priest who could say the mass quicker than any priest in the country. This had at first endeared him to Henry and, favouring him, he found him astute in many ways.

He discussed with Roger and with Henry Beaumont what should be done about Flambard.

Roger said: "He is too clever a fellow to lose."

"Yet the people wish to see him punished," insisted Beaumont.

"He never failed to raise the money my brother required," mused Henry, "and I am going to need money. If I am going to bring about all the reforms I wish to, I am going to need a great deal of it."

"Yet he must appear to be punished."

Henry agreed. "He shall be seized. It would please the people to know that he was imprisoned in the White Tower, for it was in raising money to build that Tower that he used the harshest methods."

"Then he must be imprisoned there. There will be great rejoicing when he is. And the people will applaud you and stand more firmly behind you."

"He shall be arrested without delay and conveyed there," decreed Henry.

* * *

Ranulf was making preparations to leave. Henry, being the clever man he was, would not, he knew, delay long in taking action. Ranulf had toyed with the idea of going to Normandy. Robert was away at the Holy War. What a fool Robert was! What did he think he was doing? Saving his soul! Ranulf had said to Rufus and this had amused the late King: "Normandy's a high price to pay for a soul."

He had often wondered what would happen when

Rufus died; he had not expected it yet in spite of the dream and the warnings. Rufus had been a strong man and he had never thought of such an accident. Was it an accident? Richard, the King's brother, had died in the forest, and Richard might have been King of England. Had memories of Richard's death put an idea in someone's head? If so, that someone would be a man, or men perhaps, who wished to see Henry on the throne.

How far was Henry implicated? Or was it an accident?

He had heard a startling piece of news. Sir Walter Tyrrell had left England rather suddenly. Why? Henry had been at Winchester very soon to claim the crown. It was almost as though he had been prepared.

But what was the use of speculating on the past? What was done was done and could not be changed. It was the future that was all important—the future of that clever fellow, Rufus had nicknamed Flambard, because he had taken his flaming torch into those lands and other possessions and robbed the owner of them in order to fill the King's coffers.

He heard the sound of guards outside.

Escape was too late. Foolish of him to have delayed so long—and all for the sake of gathering together his riches! Of what use would they be to him now!

"You are our prisoner," said the captain of the guards.

"On whose authority?"

"On that of the King."

Too late! he thought.

He was serious suddenly. What fate was in store for him? Not his eyes. He would die rather. Many a man had dashed out his brains against the stone wall of his prison when the hot irons were ready to tear out his precious eyes.

To the White Tower—that edifice which had special significance for him. How he had squeezed the money for that out of his protesting victims!

Ironical! How like the new King to send him there. And what would happen to him in that mighty fortress? What revenge would Henry take?

Into the Tower. He knew every bit of it. He had seen the plans which he had discussed at length with Rufus.

Here was his cell. He looked about him for the torturer.

Not my eyes, he thought. Anything but my eyes. It was a lesson to him. If he had left with a little he might be safe now. But he had been greedy and he had hesitated too long in an effort to salvage too much.

He was alone, apprehensive.

His jailer unlocked the cell and stood before him. Ranulf noticed at once that he was a little more deferential than was to be expected in such circumstances. There were no irons in his hand.

"You are not to be fettered," said the jailer.

Ranulf's spirits rose immediately.

"You will be allowed two shillings a day so that you may be supplied with wine for your comfort."

"On whose orders?" he asked.

"Those in high places," said the jailer. "Is there anything you could wish for your comfort?"

Ranulf asked for clean straw, and a stool.

These were brought to him.

He was almost elated. The King might well wish to use him. Henry was proving himself to be a man who did not want vengeance unless such would bring him benefit.

Henry had a clear incisive mind. Ranulf could appreciate that. They were not dissimilar.

To have sent Ranulf to the White Tower was the most popular move Henry could have made. He now set about making the second.

He rode in person to Wilton Abbey.

The Abbess received him. She must do so with deference for he was now the King.

"Pray send the Princess Edith to me," he commanded.

She hesitated and his anger rose—not the quick choleric temper of his brother and father but the cold kind which was equally deadly.

"My lord King, the Princess has already taken her vows."

"I don't believe it."

"It is so, my lord."

"Send for her," thundered the King.

The Abbess pretended to look bewildered. "It is against the laws of Wilton ... against the laws of God."

"To refuse would be against the King's law," cried Henry. "By God, woman, do you want me to sack the place?"

The Abbess shook her head and said that she would bring the Princess but she greatly feared the consequences.

Edith came into the hall accompanied by two nuns.

Henry strode towards her, took her hands in his and kissed them fiercely.

Then he turned to the nuns. "Go," he cried. And to the Abbess: "And you with them, Madam. Remember what I threatened and remember too that I am your King."

The Abbess obeyed; the nuns followed her trembling.

"I have come to claim you," he cried.

"I have long awaited that day," she answered.

"The Abbess says that you have taken the veil."

"I have not. I swear I have not."

"I rejoice, for had you done so our marriage might well have been impossible."

"I swear to you that it is not so. I wore the robes because she was so cruel if I did not. But I hated them. I have always hated them. And I determined to be free for you."

He kissed her.

"I could die for very happiness," she said. "I did not know it could exist and be so great."

"You have much to learn, my love." He led her to the window seat and they sat with his arm about her.

"We are to be married without delay. The people want it. They are delighted that I have chosen a Saxon princess. There is a strong Norman element in the country who will be against it, but we shall snap our fingers at them as you have just seen me do to the old Abbess."

"How happy I am that I held her off."

"She is a virago. She even attempted to defy me."

"So you are indeed the King."

"Ay, and determined soon to have a queen. We'll give them a prince by this time next year. What say you?"

She flushed a little. "You must forgive my ignorance. I have lived all my life it seems in an abbey."

"I would have it so." He thought of Nesta then, warm sensuous Nesta, who had had many lovers beside himself and was the most exciting woman he had ever known. He hoped Edith would not be frigid. Although there might be some variety in that—but only temporarily. Poor child, she had a great deal to learn about life and about him.

"I know that you wish to see your own children," she said.

And he thought: By God, I have seen many of them. Nesta would have another by now.

"And I shall do my best to please you."

"You could not fail to do that," he said and jeered at himself for the lie.

Well, she would grow up. She would learn about men's ways and his in particular. Men such as he was did not reach the age of thirty-two without a great deal of sexual experience and that meant children. How many of his were scattered about England and Normandy? Too many to be counted, he supposed. He hoped she would not be over-shocked when she heard it said that he had fathered more children than any known man.

But these thoughts were of no help. He now had to woo her, for the people wanted this marriage and it would be as popular as sending Ranulf to the White Tower had been.

"I shall send a retinue for you and you will leave the Abbey," he said. "As soon as can be arranged our wedding shall take place. You will be crowned Queen of England."

"I cannot believe it has happened at last."

He took her face in his hands. He was suddenly sorry for her. She would indeed be Queen of England but her dreams were too rosy.

He was tender suddenly as he knew well how to be.

She was not unattractive. Had she not been a princess ... well then he would not have wanted more than a transitory encounter. But when did he ever? It was only women with overwhelming fascination like Nesta, who could hold him for long. But marriage with Edith would consolidate his position. And if she so clearly adored him, the people would like that too. It would add to the image he wanted to create that he was a benign man, a peaceful man, a man who would govern well, his kingdom and his family. They would have heard rumours of his profligacy. They had taken them lightly because they preferred scandals concerning women to those of men with which Rufus had supplied them.

Edith was going to be a great help to him.

"There is one point over which you may hesitate," he told her.

"I cannot believe there could be one."

"There are many Normans in this country who will deplore our marriage because of your Saxon descent. I wish to please all my subjects where that is possible. As Edith the Saxon Princess you will delight the Saxons. If we could change your name to Matilda the Normans might forget your Saxon origins and be pleased with the match. It would be a compliment to my mother who was greatly admired. Would you do this?"

"Most gladly," she cried. "From this moment I will become Matilda."

"My dearest Matilda, how I adore you. I can see the happiest husband and wife in my kingdom will be the King and Queen."

He embraced her with a fervour which alarmed yet delighted her.

Then he departed, telling her to be in readiness to leave, for soon he would be sending for her.

* * *

The Abbess came to Edith's cell. Her eyes were blazing.

"You know," she cried, "that you cannot marry the King."

"I am going to marry the King," answered the Princess.

"The Church will never allow it. You are a nun. Nuns are the brides of Christ. They can never marry."

"I have never taken the vows."

"You have accepted the robes. You have lived the life of a nun for years. I shall never allow this marriage to take place."

"You will defy the King?"

"The Church will do that."

"You were very harsh when I was alone and unprotected. You can be so no longer. The King will take care of me for ever more."

"I can tell you this: You will never marry the King. I am making it known that you are a bride of Christ."

"Then you lie, Aunt Christina."

"I am saving your soul, you foolish girl."

"I am going to be what God intended me to be—a wife and mother."

"Edith, listen to me."

"I am no longer Edith. From henceforth my name is Matilda."

"What folly is this!"

"I feel as though I am re-born. I love and am loved. I have waited long for this day and now it has come. I shall throw off all my past wretchedness. Even my name is changed. The King has christened me Matilda. I like the sound of it. Poor Edith was a sad orphan, harshly treated. Oh, I do not forget how you stood over me with the cane. I do not forget those stinging blows. You have been very cruel to me, Aunt Christina, and I rejoice that you no longer dare. You can never harm proud Matilda as you did poor defenceless Edith."

"You are mad."

"Nay, only happy as I never have been in my life."

"Let us kneel and pray to God to deliver you from your folly."

"I will not obey you now, Aunt Christina. I will pray for you, though. I will ask God to forgive you your cruelty to me."

The Abbess was dumbfounded. That anyone should talk to her thus in her own Abbey! It was incredible!

And this ungrateful girl had the support of the King and Christina knew that with a stroke of the pen he had it in his power to take her Abbey from her, to put another Abbess in her place. It was a different matter to prevent the marriage of her niece with Alan of Bretagne or the Earl of Surrey. This was the King.

She narrowed her eyes. "God will not prosper you," she said. "If you go to your lecher king you will not find life easy. I have told you what you must expect from men. I know your wantonness craves just that. Go then. God will not prosper you."

"There is nothing you can say to me, Aunt Christina, to hurt me now. I am re-born."

"You heartless, ungrateful, wanton slut."

The Abbess raged out of the cell, and Matilda—for she would always think of herself as Matilda in future—threw back her hood and unbound her hair. Never again would she wear this hateful garment. She would have silks and velvets to caress her skin. Never never again the hateful serge which was almost horsehair.

She was ready and would wait eagerly for the summons.

Christina could do nothing to prevent her leaving, though she uttered threats to the effect that this marriage should not take place because the Church would not allow it.

* * *

The King rode out from Winchester to the Welsh border. News would in time reach Nesta of his proposed marriage with the Princess Matilda and he must be the first to bring the tidings to her.

As he rode he considered his relationship with Nesta. He had felt more deeply towards her than towards any other woman. It was a fact of course that a man who loved women as much as he did could never be whole-heartedly devoted to one. Nesta would know this. She was one of those women who had been born with all the knowledge which Eve must have acquired when she ate the apple. There were such women. They

140

were invariably irresistible. Love was their main preoccupation. They understood the needs of men, how to provoke them, how to satisfy them. There would never be a woman in his life to take the place of Nesta. Had it been possible he would have married her. But he had not been in a position to marry until now, and now he was in a position to marry none other than a Saxon Princess. He could not marry a woman who had been his mistress for many years unless of course her position warranted the match. No, Matilda was the bride for him. Sister to the King of Scotland, niece to the man whom many said should be the King of England—she was the perfect choice. A virgin too, a woman of impeccable reputation. Nesta would have to understand.

As he expected Nesta was eager to see him. The passion between them was as insistent as ever. It would have to be the last time, he told himself. Everything he did from now on would have to be considered. He doubted he would be a faithful husband but he wanted no deeply emotional relationships as this one with Nesta had been and could soon become again.

Their desire satiated, it was time to talk.

"So you are now a king?" said Nesta. "My little bastards are the King's bastards. You have yet to see Henry, a fine little fellow, the image of his father, and bearing his name. Our son Robert is delighted with him."

"I will see him and I swear to advance the fortunes of them both."

"That is well for you, my King, if you wish to please their mother."

"I wish that as I always have."

"Yet you stay away so long."

"I have risked much to come and see you."

"Why so?"

"Because I am recently King and my position is not yet as strong as I would have it."

"So I am flattered. But now that you are King..."

He dared not let her go on.

"Nesta, I have to speak to you very seriously. I have to marry."

She drew away from him, her eyes speculative.

He went on quickly: "They have chosen a bride for me."

"So you allow them to *choose* for you?"

"I must needs tread warily. There are many who would substitute my brother Robert if they could. I rely on the help of the Saxons. By marrying the Princess Matilda I please them. A Saxon Princess, daughter of one King of Scotland, sister to another, a niece of Edgar Atheling. You see what I mean."

"I see it perfectly."

"Nesta, you have been as a wife to me. No one have I loved as I love you. Would to God I could take you to Winchester with me and proclaim you my Queen."

"Are you not the King to do what you will?"

"A King rules by the will of his people."

"That was not one of your father's rules."

"He used to say that while one takes a firm hand in government the will of the people is important. This is my destiny. I have always known it. My father prophesied it on his death bed. It had to come and if I wish to hold my crown I have to please these people . . . for a while."

"Why not postpone your marriage until you are able to please yourself?"

"I would if I could. But I could lose my crown if I refused to marry Matilda."

"So I am not worth a crown?"

"You know better than that. It would not only be the crown that was lost but the head that carried it."

She let her fingers rest lightly on his neck. "I prefer you complete with head, my faithless lover."

"I knew you would understand. Let us talk in all seriousness. I shall not be able to see you for some time."

"You will be preoccupied with your bride. I wonder if she will please you as I did? Do you remember the first time?"

"Never shall I forget it. How could any please me as you do."

"There you speak truth. You are a man of wide experience but you must admit that Nesta was the best."

"I could never deny it."

"Remember it...always."

"I do. Now listen. I shall be occupied with affairs of state..."

"Including Matilda."

"She is in a manner of speaking an affair of state."

"One of the more enjoyable duties I trust."

"Nesta, I am concerned for you. That is why I have planned for you."

"A life which does not contain visits from you will have little savour."

"Nay. I have spoken to a good man, a friend of mine, who has always had my cause at heart. He is Gerald de Windsor. He is good-looking, a fine virile fellow."

"So I am to be passed to him."

"You will marry him."

"This is indeed the end, when you pass me to another."

"I swear to you that I should be the happiest man in England if I could make you my Queen."

"Alas, poor helpless King, who cannot marry where he will!"

"You have been constantly in my thoughts. I cannot rest until I know you are settled. I want our children to have a good home. I trust Gerald de Windsor."

"I have never heard of him. Is he rich?"

"He will be. I will give him a barony in Pembrokeshire on the day he marries you. There is a fine castle there, Carew Castle. Go and look at it. You will be enchanted by it. I will send Gerald to see you. It is for you to decide."

"And our boys?"

"Rest assured they will always be in my thoughts."

"And what is more important, recipients of your bounty?"

"I swear it on our love, Nesta."

"Is that a firm foundation on which to swear?"

"I would swear on that more fervently than anything else."

"You always had the right answers. I wonder if Matilda will find it so?"

"So you accept?"

"What else can I do? You are the King. It is different for a penniless prince to come riding this way and to find a loving heart waiting for him. But a king! All his actions are noted. What is Matilda like I wonder? Is she beautiful, tell me that?"

"She is not ill-favoured."

"As I am not?"

"You are as the sun, blazing hot, without which no man could live."

"Which is what you are proposing to do."

He ignored that. "She is as the moon."

"The moon is considered beautiful."

"I said she was not without a charm."

"A man can live without the moon, is that not so?"

"I know only that this parting breaks my heart."

"Now that is not worthy of my lawyer King. Your heart is sound enough, Henry, it's your head we are concerned with, not your heart."

"Have done," he said, and drew her to him.

"The last," she said.

"Let us make it as memorable as the first. But you know I shall come back."

"Could I be faithless to what is his name . . . Gerald?"

"Yes, I think you might."

"As you will be to Matilda?"

"It seems likely."

"Oh yes," said Nesta, "it seems very likely."

As he rode back to Winchester he congratulated himself that the interview with Nesta had gone off better than he had anticipated. But then Nesta was a woman of the world. She would understand.

However, when he returned to Winchester he was met by a concerned Roger, who told him that the Abbess of Wilton had made a statement to the effect that the Princess Matilda was a confirmed nun and that it would be an act of sacrilege to remove her from the Abbey.

*　　*　　*

Henry was furious. Matilda had sworn to him that she had not taken the veil and he believed her. The

144

girl was too innocent to lie. It was that wicked old Abbess who was lying.

"Nevertheless," said Roger, "the doubt will always be there. The Church will be against the marriage and that means that many of the people will be with them. It will not be the popular marriage you need. If you did marry the least little trouble would be laid to its door. Remember how ready people are to see signs and portents. Remember how they were sure the cathedral tower crashed because Rufus was buried beneath it, though it was well known that the work was too hurriedly done. If you are going to marry Matilda, it will have to be believed without a doubt that she never took the veil."

"She swears she didn't."

"That is not enough. You want the leading churchmen to confirm absolutely that she is able to marry."

"Churchmen! The clergy are more likely to support that old harridan of an Abbess than me. One moment. An idea occurs to me. You know my father was excommunicated for his marriage to another Matilda. For years he was ostracized by the Church. He had exiled Lanfranc and then reinstated him. Lanfranc went to Rome and the excommunication was withdrawn. There is a very clever churchman who had a quarrel with my brother. I have it. Anselm. I will recall Anselm."

"You think he will work for you against this Abbess?"

"Yes, for he will be grateful to me for recalling him."

"They say he lives in pleasant retirement. Is it at Lyons?"

"My good Roger, in spite of his piety he is an ambitious man. He lost the great See of Canterbury. What if I promised to return that to him? Do you not think that might prove irresistible?"

"We can but try it."

* * *

Anselm in the house of his friend Hugh at Lyons received the messengers from the King.

He read the dispatches and discussed the matter with his friend.

"Henry has become King. He is cleverer than his brother. He will make a better ruler than Rufus did. He will be more like his father. He is educated as Rufus never was. We shall be able to understand each other."

"Well, he is offering to reinstate you."

"It is clear why. He is determined to marry the Princess Matilda. If it is true that she has taken the veil he cannot do this. Such a marriage would be cursed."

"But you say the Princess denies this."

"Yes. She is, I have heard from her uncle, a good and pious young woman. It seems hardly likely that she would lie."

"Either she or the Abbess is lying. Would the Abbess lie?"

"The Abbess might well do so and convince herself that she was obeying God's will."

"Could you make the decision?"

"I doubt if I could alone. I would have to convene some sort of council."

"Well what will you do?"

"I think I should at least return to England and have discourse with the King."

*   *   *

Henry had impatiently awaited the coming of Anselm and when he arrived, greeted him warmly.

Henry said: "I intended to recall you in any case. It is not fitting that the Church of England should have no head. You are the Archbishop of Canterbury. Even though you were in a form of exile nothing could alter that."

Anselm bowed his head.

"I trust since you have arrived here you have been treated with all the respect due to an Archbishop of Canterbury?"

"I have nothing of which to complain on that score. Although a very important ceremony over which I should have presided was held in my absence."

"You mean my coronation?"

"I believe the Bishop of London performed that duty which rightly belongs to the Archbishop of Canterbury."

Ha, thought Henry, we are going to be a somewhat intransigent Archbishop and I shall not be ruled by the Church any more than my brother was. But at the moment Anselm's help was needed so he should be placated.

"The circumstances were such, my lord Archbishop, that they brooked no delay. It was for this reason that I allowed the Bishop of London to crown me."

Anselm said that he could understand the reason while he regretted the act.

"Now, my lord, I need your help. I am determined to marry the Princess Matilda. Her aunt, the Abbess of Wilton, had made other plans for her against the Princess's will. For years she has been ill-treating her and endeavouring to force her to take the veil. This the Princess refused to do; and now that I am ready to marry her, the Abbess insists that she has taken the vow."

"So it is a question of who is speaking the truth, the Abbess or her niece."

"There is no question in my mind and I want you to prove the Abbess is lying."

"This would be too big an undertaking for me alone. I should have to set up a council."

"Then, for the love of God, set up a council. But do so without delay. I am impatient for this marriage."

*　　*　　*

An emissary from the Archbishop arrived at Wilton. There was nothing Christina could do to prevent his seeing Matilda.

He stated what was expected of her.

"The Archbishop has set up a council to decide whether the marriage of the King and yourself can be proceeded with. It will be necessary for you to appear before that council and tell the truth."

"I always tell the truth," said Matilda warmly.

"You will have to convince the council that indeed you are free to marry. Will you do this?"

"I will," said Matilda, "with all my heart. I can stand before God if need be without fear and say that I have never taken the veil."

"That is well for you will be on oath to state the true facts."

He left and Matilda waited for the summons.

She rarely saw the Abbess. Christina was furious because it looked as though her hopes were going to be frustrated. She had rejoiced at first when she had heard that Anselm was back and would preside over a council. She had thought that as a good churchman he would have the interests of the Abbey at heart. But the King had sent for him. The King was urging him to discover that Edith . . . she would not call her by that absurd name Matilda . . . was in the right.

She was anxious; and when the summons came and her niece left the Abbey she was even more apprehensive.

* * *

The Archbishop announced that there was a report that the Princess Matilda had embraced a religious life. If this were the case and she had already made her vows to Almighty God, no power on earth would induce him to give her a dispensation. If it were indeed true that she had taken the veil then she must return to the Abbey of Wilton and could never be the King's wife.

Matilda was exultant. How glad she was that she had resisted her aunt's harsh persuasion! It had all been worth while, for now she could stand before the Archbishop and the council and, before God, with a clear conscience.

The Archbishop from his chair on the dais asked her to come forward and stand before him.

This she did.

"I ask you," said Anselm, "before God, is there truth in the statement that you are a confirmed nun?"

"There is no truth in this."

"Are you prepared to make this denial on oath?"

148

"I am prepared," answered Matilda firmly.

She took the oath and Anselm continued to question her.

"Was it the choice of either of your parents that you should take religious vows?"

"I believe my mother hoped I would. My father was against it."

"Did you ever in your father's court wear the black veil of a votaress?"

"Yes."

The members of the council looked at her intently and she went on steadily: "My Aunt Christina was at my father's court and she put the veil on my head and face. When my father saw it he was angry. He snatched it off and announced that the convent life was not for me, for he intended that I should marry."

"But you wore the veil in Rumsey and Wilton Abbeys?" persisted Anselm.

"I did."

"But it is the dress of a votaress."

"My aunt insisted that I wear it. I hated it. When my aunt found me without it she beat me severely. Often when I was alone I took it off and trampled on it."

"Yet you wore it constantly in Rumsey and Wilton?"

"I did so only because my aunt forced me and because often the soldiers came that way and it was some protection against their rough usage. I tell you before God that I never wished to wear these robes, that whenever possible I discarded them."

The Archbishop consulted with his council and a box of sacred relics was brought out and placed on the board supported by trestles.

"This coffer contains the bones and relics of saintly men. You are required to swear on them. You know that if you take a false oath you will be eternally damned and great misfortune will overtake you in this life."

"I understand."

"Now you are required to swear on this that you never took the veil, that you have made no vows to Almighty God, that you are free to marry the King."

"I gladly swear," she cried fervently.

She was taken from the council chamber.

Very shortly after that Anselm and the Council declared that they unanimously accepted the word of the Princess Matilda.

The King and she were free to marry.

* * *

The summer was past and November had come. It was three months since the death of William Rufus, St. Martin's day, and a Sunday, the eleventh day of the eleventh month of the year 1100.

Matilda's coronation was to take place immediately after her wedding, and crowds had gathered in the streets and about Westminster Abbey. There was a certain amount of murmuring, for many people still believed that Matilda was a nun who had denied her vows for the sake of marriage with the King.

Henry was uneasy. His position was not as strong as he wished it to be. What, he wondered, if this marriage was to rob him of the popularity he had gained? Was it a wrong step after all?

Anselm was strong. He had said that before the ceremony took place he would make an announcement from the pulpit that the Princess had never taken religious vows and was entitled to dispose of herself in marriage as she thought fit.

It had been a wise move to bring back Anselm. There was something about the man. He had an air of authority as well as sanctity. The people would believe that if he gave his support all must be well.

All the nobility were gathered together and Henry and Matilda stood before the Archbishop at the altar.

Anselm said in a loud voice, "Is there any man here who objects to the decision of the council regarding this marriage?"

Henry waited in trepidation, but immediately there came the reassuring shout which echoed through the Abbey. "That matter has been rightly settled."

The ceremony proceeded. The Princess Matilda was

married to Henry and afterwards crowned Queen of England.

*   *   *

Henry was the perfect lover. He had had practice enough. She was less afraid of him than he had feared she might be.

He could not stop himself thinking of Nesta and Gerald of Windsor. He supposed he would think of Nesta often. But his bride was pleasant, young, undoubtedly a virgin, and he could be fond of her if only because she so adored him.

She whispered to him of the revelation which her aunt had made to her when there had been a question of her marriage to Alan of Bretagne.

"It is so different," she cried. "That is because I am with you."

He responded as tenderly as she could wish.

There was no point in spoiling her wedding night. She would learn soon enough that the lover she adored was not quite all she thought him to be. Well, she who was so innocent of the world would have to learn, and when she did, as she inevitably must, she would after the first shock settle down to be a loving wife and when she produced the heirs of the kingdom she would be a good mother.

That should satisfy her so that when he strayed—as he surely would—she would come to accept this state of affairs as a natural course of events.

For the time though he feigned to share her ecstatic happiness.

Escape from the White Tower

Robert, Duke of Normandy, had had enough of his Crusade. His friends often reminded him of the need to go back and redeem Normandy. Robert, feckless, extravagant but of undeniable charm, was restless by nature. His enthusiasms waned quickly and his greatest excitement was in making grandiose plans which he deluded himself into believing would come to glorious fruition. That they never had in the past he refused to see. His was an optimistic nature and he always believed in the future.

He was a brave fighter and had distinguished himself in the Holy Land, but that little adventure was over. It was time he embarked on a new one. And that new one must be the recovery of Normandy. Crusading hero that he might be, he was, first of all, Duke of Normandy and he must win back his inheritance.

During the long journey back he made elaborate plans. He needed money. He knew Rufus; Rufus always wanted money, but he was of course hoping that Robert would not be able to raise that 10,000 marks. Nor could Robert at the time see any means of doing so.

He had ridden into southern Italy and had come to the castle of Count Geoffrey of Conversana. The Count greeted the hero of the Holy War with great warmth and begged him to give him the honour of entertaining him before he passed on.

"My good friend," said Robert, "your kindness is appreciated, but my dukedom needs me."

The Count said then he would hope for merely a few days of the Duke's company.

Robert, conferring with his friends, decided that it would be churlish to refuse such a gracious honour so they would stay for a few days, during which they would plan for the recapture of Normandy.

The Count's castle was a pleasant place; the weather was delightful—it was warmer than in Normandy and less exhaustingly hot than the Holy Land. It was a golden country, said Robert, a country which invited one to dally.

Robert had never needed a great deal of encouragement to do that and in this case the Count had a beautiful daughter, Sibyl, whom Robert found enchanting. They rode together; they talked together, and he told her of Normandy and his childhood there, of his great father who had never understood him and who had refused to recognize that he was a man so that he had perforce on more than one occasion taken up arms against him.

Sibyl was sympathetic.

And so the golden days passed. There was time to enjoy the Italian sun and the company of Sibyl before he recaptured Normandy.

*   *   *

In his prison in the White Tower, Ranulf Flambard was getting restive. He was not ill-treated; he had wine with his food every day; the jailers were his friends; and it had become clear to him that the King was uncertain how to treat him.

That Henry was shrewd, he had always known, and he believed Henry had some notion that he might make use of him at some time. Therefore the King was holding him a prisoner, but a well-treated one.

Ranulf had friends outside. He preserved the two shillings he received each day and determined to spend it wisely. The wine was a necessity for he had plans for that, but he would spend on nothing else save bribes to those whom he believed he could trust.

News was brought in to him. Robert of Normandy was on his way home. That was important. If he could get to Normandy he might offer his services to Robert. He would have offered them to Henry but Henry had imprisoned him. He knew Henry's reasons. It was to placate the people. Henry had disliked him when he had made jibes at him in Rufus's company, but Henry was too wise to waste time on personal vengeance, and was also shrewd enough to know a clever man when he saw one. But he, Ranulf, was unpopular in England. His work for Rufus had made him so. He would do better in Normandy so to Robert he would go.

Robert would be more amenable than Henry. Robert was easy-going; he needed a man like Ranulf. Henry was stronger. He would govern alone. Certainly Robert was his man.

Therefore his first task was to get to Normandy—but before he did that he had to escape from the White Tower.

There was only one way out as far as he could see. Through the window by means of a rope.

How get the rope?

It was not impossible. How wise he had been to feign a greater love of wine than he really had!

He asked that his brewer might come to see him as he wished to order some wine.

This was all right, said the guard, for orders had been that the prisoner was to have his two shillings a day to provide him with comforts.

The brewer was respectful. Ranulf had met him before when he ordered wine. They discussed the quality of the brews he had sent and Flambard not only astonished the man with his knowledge but amused him

154

by his wit—that very wit which had pleased King Rufus and been one of the reasons why he had held a high place in his affairs.

It was a risk, but he took it.

"I am confined here," he said. "A man of my abilities! And to tell you the truth, my good friend, I know *not* the reason why, for I have committed no crime."

The brewer was delighted to be called the good friend of such a cultured man. Ranulf watched the effect.

"I see you are a man of intelligence. You will not be influenced by the views of the rabble. You are a man who will make up his own mind. Therefore you are a man to whom I can talk." He lowered his voice. "I get precious little opportunity of doing so in this place, I assure you, my friend."

The brewer said that it was a sin that men should be imprisoned for breaking no laws and for a cultivated man—and he was wise enough to know one when he saw one—it was doubly irksome.

"I carried out the laws, but not on my own behalf, my friend. I did it for the King. I was his servant. I did for him what you would do for any of your customers."

The brewer nodded sagely.

"I am no ordinary prisoner. Although my property is in the hands of those who took it from me, I hope to regain it one day and when I do I shall remember my friends. But I am here, and while I am here I can do nothing."

"Where would your lordship go if you escaped from here?"

Ranulf pretended to hesitate. Then he said earnestly:

"I see that you are a man of wit and courage. Forgive me for hesitating. So much is at stake."

Flattered out of all good sense, the brewer said: "You may trust me, my lord sir."

"I know it. I would go to Normandy."

"How would you do that?"

"If I could get out from this place, if a horse was waiting for me, if a boat was waiting to take me over the water . . . then I could get to Normandy."

"How could this be, my lord?"

"I have friends. I shall regain everything one day and I shall never forget those who help me."

The brewer's cupidity showed in his eyes. The oaf is considering what he will gain, thought Ranulf.

He was right. The brewer was considering. He was easily prevailed upon to take messages to Ranulf's friends outside.

It was in this manner that he learned that the Duke of Normandy was dallying in Italy. He seemed to be so taken with the daughter of Count Geoffrey that he could not tear himself away from her. The months were passing and instead of returning to Normandy he remained in Italy.

Yes, Robert was the one for him. He could govern Robert as he had not been able to govern Rufus even.

The brewer had played his part well and it had come to the vital stages of Ranulf's plan. It was surprising how so much depended on this poor tradesman.

There were two casks of wine sent into him. He looked into one. This contained rich red wine; he looked into the other. Good man! Inside it curled round and round was a thick rope.

*   *   *

He said to his guards: "I have a new cask of wine. You must come and sample it."

They were nothing loath. In fact there was little they enjoyed as much as an hour or so in the company of this unusual prisoner.

He could amuse them with his stories of the late King's Court. What a place it had been by his account! He would mince round the cell describing the manners and customs of the King's friends until he had them helpless with laughter. And he always had a supply of good wine too. Very often they left his cell a little tipsy.

"Welcome, welcome!" he cried.

He looked round. There were three men to be taken care of: his own special guard whose duty it was never to leave him unobserved for more than a minute or two at a time; the keeper of the door of that part of the

White Tower in which they were; and another whose duty it was to prowl round every hour for inspection.

"Well, my friends, what think you of this brew?"

"Excellent. Excellent."

"Better than the last?"

"Well, my lord, I couldn't rightly say as to that."

"Drink up then and put it to the test."

They could not agree on it, by good fortune, so he kept them testing and drinking so that they lost count of the amount they had taken.

He then began to amuse them once more with stories of the Court, never forgetting to fill and refill their glasses.

The keeper of the outer door was the first to succumb; he slumped from his stool and lay on the floor in a stupor.

This unfortunately seemed to sober the others.

"We should drink no more, sir. Look at him."

"He could never hold his wine. He is something of a low fellow who has never learned the gentlemanly trick. Now you two are different. I have always known that. You could hold your drink with the rest of us. I'll warrant you can stand up to it as well as I can."

They had not been aware, the simple fools, that while they had been engaged in the testing, he had drunk nothing. Flattery was the weapon to use against these people. They could not resist it.

He knew that it would not be long before he had reduced those two to the state of stupor which had overtaken their fellow guard.

Nor was it.

There they were muttering to themselves—three men, overcome by the intoxication of good strong wine!

There was no time to lose; at any moment, one of these men might be aroused sufficiently from his stupor to know what was happening.

He drew the rope from the cask. He attached one end to the staple near the window. It was a pity it was not nearer, for the drop to the ground was far.

He looked out of the window and a feeling of apprehension overtook him. It was indeed a long drop and he had to rely on the security of the rope attached to the staple.

It was strong and coarse and he had bruised hands merely in tying it.

He let it out of the window, then cautiously clinging to it, lowered himself.

The agony! He had forgotten to ask for gloves. The coarse rope was taking the skin off his hands and they were raw and bleeding. He was dangling at the end of the rope which was far too short, and there remained a long distance between the end of it and the ground.

Fool, he thought. Why had not the brewer sent a longer rope? But the man had sent the longest that would go into the cask.

What now? Was he to wait here dangling at the end of a rope until he was captured? He could not if he wished to. His poor bleeding hands would not endure it.

He must take the risk.

He let go and fell.

Pain enveloped him; he was almost fainting, but he dared not do that. He could see the horse tied to a block a few yards away. His friends had done their part and he must get up. He must forget the pain. He stood.

Yes, he could stand, so it seemed his legs had not been broken.

He staggered to the horse, ready, saddled, waiting. They had not failed him.

He mounted and galloped off towards the coast.

* * *

Geoffrey Count of Conversana had watched the growing friendship between his daughter and Robert of Normandy, and it occurred to him that a match between them would be a good one as far as his daughter was concerned. The Duke of Normandy, if he could regain his lands, was a man of great importance and as there was a possibility that he might be King of England also, the marriage would be a brilliant one for Sibyl.

He found an opportunity of broaching the matter as

they sat in his gardens overlooking his vineyards and Robert remarked that it was time he moved on. Not that he necessarily meant it. He had been talking of leaving ever since he came; but there would always be something to detain him—a ball, a banquet, which Sibyl would point out would be spoiled by his absence.

"Yes, I must depart," mused Robert. "I have stayed over long."

"My lord Duke," replied the Count, "you could not stay too long under my roof."

"You have been a gracious host to me. I shall never forget you ... or your delightful daughter."

"I wish you all luck in your return to Normandy, my lord."

"I need it, Geoffrey. I need it as I rarely needed it before. I have heard that my brother Rufus is dead. Killed in the New Forest as my brother Richard was. And Henry has taken the throne of England."

"Has he a right to do this, my lord?"

"Nay. England should be mine. Rufus and I made a pact that if I died before him I would leave him Normandy and if he died before me he would leave me England. Of course I needed money to make my journey to the Holy Land and I borrowed from Rufus, giving him Normandy as security."

"You will redeem Normandy as soon as you return?"

"I have not the means to do this. 10,000 marks is the sum I need. I cannot do this. But I shall succeed. I shall not allow my brother Henry to take the throne of England from me. I shall regain Normandy, never fear ... and England too ... but I need the money if I am honourably to take Normandy out of pawn."

"And where will you find this money, my lord?"

"I have good friends in Normandy."

"Your charm and grace have given you good friends wherever you go."

"I trust that you are one of them, Count."

"My lord, you never had a better and I would be closer than a friend. Let me explain. You need 10,000 marks, the sum for which you put Normandy in pawn to Rufus. I have a marriageable daughter. Her dowry would be 10,000 marks if the Duke of Normandy would be prepared to take her."

"My dear good friend! I can think of nothing better. I love your daughter and I venture to think she does not regard me with distaste."

"Well then, 'tis settled."

"I will first ask the Lady Sibyl if she will take me."

"She will take you, my lord. Her father will insist on that."

"I would rather the lady chose me of her own free will."

He knew that she would do so most gladly. Nor was he disappointed.

Before he left Conversana he and Sibyl were married, and together and by slow stages, being lavishly entertained on the way, they made the journey back to Normandy.

The Chivalry of the Duke

Matilda was happy. The long years of incarceration in the Abbeys of Rumsey and Wilton under the strict rule of Aunt Christina were like an evil dream; yet she often told herself she could never have appreciated her happiness quite so wholeheartedly if she had not been able to contrast it with all that wretchedness.

Henry was a wonderful husband. He was tender and loving and not only this, he quickly realized that she was a woman of unusual education and as he was more learned than most men, this gave them a great deal in common.

He talked to her as though she were one of his ministers and more frankly, for while he must necessarily be on his guard with them, he knew that he never need be with her. She would be loyal in every way.

Henry himself was far from displeased with his marriage. His Matilda was no Nesta but it had not been expected she would be; all the same he very often thought longingly of his one-time mistress and envied Gerald de Windsor. But affairs of state occupied him to the full so perhaps it was as well that he must dispense with the tempestuous, demanding passion he indulged in with Nesta and should be content with the pleasant marital relationship he enjoyed with his wife.

He shared her delight when she became pregnant, and again and again she asked herself what joy there could possibly be in life to compare with bringing a family into the world. Sometimes she was afraid of her happiness. Was Aunt Christina right? Was it sinful to be so happy?

She remembered the vow she had made that if she could but be saved from the veil she would follow the pious habits of her mother.

As it was Lent she went to Westminster Abbey dressed in a shirt of hair cloth—a reminder of the Benedictines robe—and gave alms. At the same time she insisted on washing and kissing the feet of the poor.

On one occasion Henry, who had been unaware of this activity, came to the Abbey with one of his knights while she was engaged on this. He was astonished.

He went to her and cried: "Matilda! What are you doing here?"

"My duty," she answered. "Will you not join me?"

He shook his head and walked away. She thought he was displeased and this was the first cloud over her happiness.

She was apprehensive when they were alone together.

He said: "I had no idea that you performed such deeds."

"My mother did and I vowed that if I could escape from the Abbey I would do likewise."

"What if there were lepers among them?"

"My mother washed the feet of lepers."

He frowned and she asked fearfully: "Have I displeased you?"

He took her face in his hands. "Nay, nay, 'twas done from the goodness of your heart and that heart I have learned most gratefully is kind and loving."

"I feared greatly that you were angry."

"Nay, never with you, my Queen."

He was thinking: "The people were impressed by it and we have great need to impress the people."

"So you will not forbid this?"

"Nay, my love. Rather do I applaud it. But remember the child. In no way must we imperil that."

"You are so good to me, so kind," she said and there were tears in her eyes.

It was one of those occasions when he wondered what she would feel when she discovered the truth about him, which he supposed she would in due course. When he began bringing his illegitimate children to Court and bestowing favours on them, which indeed he must, he hoped she would not be too badly hurt. It might well be that by that time she would have more understanding of the world. But it was disconcerting when she showed so clearly that she looked upon him as a knight of shining purity. He supposed he was growing fond of her.

He was more at ease talking of affairs of state.

"Matilda," he said, "if ever I should have to go out of the country I should make you my Regent and for this reason you must know how I govern and what is happening in the realm."

She looked apprehensive and he knew it was not because she was afraid of the task but because he would have to go on some expedition which might be perilous.

"Why should you have to go?"

"Perhaps to Normandy," he said. "My brother Robert is claiming England."

"But he is the Duke of Normandy and Normandy is in pawn to England."

"The debt has been settled. He has married and the lady's dowry has paid his debt. Moreover she is with child. Men become ambitious for their children."

"He has laid claim to the throne then?"

"Ay and he has many supporters—not only in Normandy but here. Ranulf Flambard has escaped from the White Tower. He is in Normandy now. It is men such as he that I fear rather than my brother. Robert is too lazy to carry through any enterprise with success.

But when he is backed by men like Ranulf we must take the threat very seriously indeed."

"You think they will attempt invasion?"

"I do. Many Normans over here who support Robert's claim have already crossed the sea. But I have set a fleet to guard the Channel ports so that they can be prevented from landing."

"That is important," said Matilda. "If Harold Godwin had guarded his ports your father would never have landed so comfortably in England and it may well have been that the battle had gone a different way."

"In which case I should not be King of England, so let us rejoice in that lack of foresight."

"And profit by it," said Matilda.

"You will see that is what I intend to do. But, Matilda, I am surrounded by traitors. Ranulf Flambard should never have been allowed to escape. I could have used that man. I could have had him killed in prison. But I thought after a while to make use of his cleverness. I am disturbed that he thought there would be more advantages in serving my brother than myself."

"Could it have been that he knew you were a King who would rule your subjects and Robert is a Duke who would be ruled by his?"

He looked at her quizzically. "God has given me a clever wife. We'll stand together against them. My Queen, I thank God for you."

This was the peak of her happiness. Not only did she love and was loved, not only was her body fruitful but the years of study had given her an agile mind and she could bring to her husband many gifts which more than made up for her lack of dowry. He talked to her earnestly of his hopes.

"I have made promises which I shall endeavour to carry out ... if it is possible. It was necessary to make those promises. But I intend to bring law back to this country. I shall punish severely those who steal. We are plagued by those who clip coins and so debase the currency. I mean to bring back my father's laws. In his day men could travel without the fear of robbery and violence. That changed under Rufus. I will bring that back. The feudal barons must be made to understand that I will not have them roaming the country taking what they will and submitting to indignities the wives and daughters of peaceful citizens. I shall curb their power."

"The people will love you for it."

"They must, Matilda. I must make them see that I intend to prosper the country as my father did. They never loved him. He was a harsh man, but they came to respect him. And when Rufus reigned after him they appreciated him the more. I intend that they shall feel towards me as they did to my father."

"But you would wish them to love you?"

"If that is possible. But I intend to make this country rich and, by God, I'll do it. And I must make the people understand this. I have to bring the barons to order. You know that a band of them will set out together to plunder a market or a fair and will terrify the simple people who are enjoying these worthy pursuits. Some of them waylay merchants and kidnap them and hold them to ransom so that their family must squander their hard earned money on their release. They are cruel. They torture their victims. They raid a man's house and rape his woman under his very eyes. This I will stop and the people will see what my intentions are."

Matilda's eyes were shining. "You will be a great king, Henry."

He smiled at her ruefully. "If the people will let me."

"The forestry laws are said to be the most harsh."

Henry's lips hardened. He was not going to change those. His father had instituted them and the people had had to accept them. No, he would not give up his forests. The hunt was the breath of life to him as it had been to all his family. He and his brothers had been brought up to it; it was the greatest of pleasures—though perhaps women enchanted him slightly more, but not much; to ride through the forests, dogs in pursuit, the sight of a deer alert suddenly, and to see the graceful creature bound off; the smell of the forests; the excitement of the chase. No, not one of the harsh forestry laws should be lifted. They had perforce to accept them in his father's day and they should accept them now.

But he did not tell Matilda this. Like that other overwhelming passion it must remain one of those secrets which she would certainly discover in time—but not yet.

For the time it pleased him that she should live in this dream of perfection, which showed how fond he was of her.

A messenger had arrived and was brought to the King.

His face darkened as he read the message.

"Henry . . ." began Matilda.

He looked at her and a savage anger darkened his face. "The fleet which was protecting our shores has gone to Normandy. This can mean one thing. They have deserted me and instead of stopping Robert's landing they will help it."

*　　*　　*

These were trying weeks for Henry. Rumours were in circulation. He had been a member of the hunting party in which Rufus had died; he had already shown marked favour to the Clare family; their kinsman Walter Tyrrell had left the country. Could it have been that there had been a plot and that Henry, who had everything to gain, was at the heart of it?

Henry ignored these suggestions. He knew that what the people of England wanted was a good steady king who would amend the state of anarchy which had risen during the reign of Rufus. So he concentrated on letting the people know what reforms he intended to make, and he set about making them.

Henry had not been nicknamed Beauclerc for nothing. He was possessed of an energy and efficiency which was similar to that which had made the Conqueror such a brilliant administrator. The Saxon part of the community were of the opinion that he would make a better ruler than his brother Robert who had already proved himself to be feckless; but there were many Norman barons in the country who deplored the fact that Henry, having been born and bred in England, was removing the Norman influence, and these powerful Norman barons were giving their support to Robert.

One of the chief of these was Robert of Bellême—a man whose reputation was perhaps more evil than that of any other throughout England and Normandy. Henry's father had told him of the stories he had heard in his childhood of this wicked family who had terrorized the countryside. Nurses would warn him if he did not behave as they considered he should: "If you are not good the Bellêmes will get you." They tortured for sport and the entertainment they offered their guests at a banquet was the death agony of some poor prisoner. They would waylay travellers and take them to their dungeons. Men would be submitted to the slow death, women to all manner of indignities before suffering the same fate. The Conqueror had when a boy met a member of this family and had looked him straight in the face and in such a manner that the brute had quailed before him and turned away muttering that the boy and his heirs would bring disaster to the Bellêmes.

That prophecy should be fulfilled, Henry promised himself.

Robert of Bellême had until recently confined his atrocities to Normandy but alas, a few years earlier, he had bought the English estates of the Montgomerys and thus many castles and other property in England had fallen into his hands.

By the payment of this sum—£3,000—he had become one of the most powerful men in England as well as Normandy; and of course he would be in conflict with Henry whose new laws were aimed against such as himself.

"I shall be the one to destroy him," Henry promised himself, "and others of his kind. We do not want them here nor in Normandy."

He did not admit to Matilda that his hopes were not only to remain King of England but to take Normandy as well.

They were uneasy weeks. The Norman invasion was coming. He must be ready for it.

And in the midst of these preparations Matilda was brought to bed.

*　　*　　*

Her happiness was great when she held her child in her arms... although perhaps not quite complete, for the son for which she and Henry had longed had been denied them and they had a daughter.

Henry disguised his disappointment thinking: she is young; she has quickly shown she is fruitful. We'll get sons in time.

She watched him anxiously from her bed.

"Is she not perfect, Henry?"

Henry agreed that she was.

"I prophesy that she will be as great as any boy."

He kissed her and said, "We will have boys. Never fear."

"Yes, boys and girls. I never guessed how wonderful life could be until this child was born."

He smiled at her tenderly, thinking how strange that a woman who could be quite astute in matters of government could be quite simple in her knowledge of human nature.

They were at Winchester where it was fitting the royal child be born and Matilda was to rest there for a week or more.

It was necessary, said Henry. She must consider her health. He wanted her to be well that she might give him more children.

She talked a great deal about the child and never once did she ask about what was happening outside her lying-in chamber. He did not tell her that he hourly expected invasion and that more and more Norman barons were deserting England and that those who remained were of doubtful loyalty.

It seemed very likely that as bloody a battle as that of Senlac might soon be fought.

*   *   *

Henry left Matilda with stern injunctions that she was not to leave her bed until it was considered wise to do so, and he joined his troops at Pevensey. Here some thirty-six years before, William the Conqueror had landed without opposition. Matilda had said how different it might have been if Harold had been there to prevent the easy landing. Well, he would be on the spot to prevent Robert and his Normans having that advantage.

As he inspected his troops he thought of all the traitors who had turned against him and his suppressed anger almost choked him. Both his father and Rufus would have given way to a furious outburst. Not so Henry. He could take vengeance but in cold blood, which was so much more effective in the end.

It was sad that brother should fight brother. He thought of his mother—another Matilda—who had had to make a terrible decision between her son Robert and her husband.

His parents had been lovers all their married life. Theirs had been an ideal relationship, but it was never the same with them after Matilda helped her son Robert against his father. William never forgot it. It would have been one of the biggest blows of his life. But it had been a wonderful partnership. Could he hope for the same from his Matilda? Hardly. The Conqueror had never had time for any woman but his wife. He had been a faithful husband. Perhaps that was the secret of the great bond between them. If it were, he and Matilda could never be so close. He wondered what she would do when she knew of the hosts of mistresses with whom he had shared his life before he met her. He had not been faithful since the marriage. How could he be when he was away so much? It was against his nature. Women and the chase... they were necessary to him, and no matter what was at stake he could not give either of them up. That was his weakness. His calm judicial mind saw it clearly.

And Robert...Robert was a fool. Robert had been a fool throughout his life. Their father had been aware of it; that was why he and Robert had been enemies, mortal enemies. Robert should never have had Normandy. His father had known that too, but it was a long-standing promise which he had made to their mother and so he fulfilled it. Robert was doomed to failure. He was unfit to govern. He had made mistakes everywhere. It was only that charm of his which saved him from utter disaster. It always came to the surface in crucial moments. He had friends who loved him and helped him. He had found a rich woman to marry that he might redeem Normandy. It had always been thus with Robert but that did not mean it always would be.

No matter how strongly he came against him, he was going to defeat him.

Robert was not going to be the King of England. That honour was reserved for Henry. And, God willing, Robert should not long retain Normandy, for that was to be Henry's too. Their father would approve. What would he be thinking, looking down from heaven, of the terrible state of anarchy to which men like the Bellêmes had reduced Normandy? He would approve of Henry's rule in England; he was the king he himself would have instituted.

The spirit of my father will be with me today, thought Henry.

A messenger was brought to his tent. He was disordered and muddy and one look at his face showed that he had ill news to impart.

"My lord King, the Duke of Normandy has landed."

"Where, by God!"

"At Portsmouth. Piloted into the harbour by the fleet. They are marching to Winchester."

*　　*　　*

Robert surveyed his troops as they re-formed after the landing. Ranulf Flambard, who had done much to organize the expedition, was beside him. He was exultant.

"We cannot fail, my lord," said Ranulf. "We have

completed without opposition the most difficult part of the operation. Our spies have done well. Henry is waiting to receive us at Pevensey. Now to Winchester."

"To Winchester!" said Robert.

"A rather amusing turn to affairs," murmured Ranulf. "The Queen is lying-in there. She has given birth to a daughter."

"A daughter! My niece!" Robert smiled. "And lying-in at Winchester! Well, then we cannot march to Winchester."

"My lord?"

"Nay," said Robert, "for if the Queen is lying-in she would be disturbed by soldiers in the town. Moreover it might be difficult to control them. What if they broke into her lying-in chamber?"

"So much the better."

Robert looked with distaste at Ranulf. He had to admit that the man was clever and he had been eager to make use of his services when he had arrived in Normandy. He had been of great use for he knew by first hand what was to be expected in England. Having served Rufus in such an intimate manner he was well acquainted with the state of affairs in England. He could not have had a better guide. When Ranulf had arrived in Normandy, slightly crippled by his fall from the rope when escaping, his hands swathed in bandages because when he slid down the rope the skin had been peeled from them, he had seemed the perfect minister. He had suffered much to come to Normandy; he must believe Robert's cause was just to endure so much in his service, but now Robert clearly saw him as an insensitive oaf.

The fact was that Robert had been feeling more and more uneasy as he approached England. Brother against brother. It was not a situation he enjoyed. He had never been on good terms with Rufus, but he had always deplored it. And Henry was their younger brother, the one who had been left with very little. Their father had said that Henry would one day have more than either Robert or Rufus. He wondered what their mother would be thinking if she could know that they were preparing to go into battle against each other.

His chances were good. Ranulf was right there. He was in the superior position but he had very little stomach for battle against his own brother.

He had just returned from a holy war in which he had distinguished himself. He believed that he had been purged of his sins by his service to God; and now he was going to do battle against his brother. What if Henry should be killed? It seemed to him that all the honours he had won in heaven through his crusade would be lost to him.

Ranulf was looking uneasy. He drew his horse closer to Robert's.

"A goodly array," he said. "We shall be victorious. In a very short time now England will be where it belongs—in the hands of Robert of Normandy, King of England."

"That is in God's hands," said Robert.

"And in ours, my lord. We must take the city of Winchester."

"I say we shall not go to Winchester."

"It is the capital city of these parts, lord."

"It is the lying-in place of my sister-in-law."

"That cannot affect our plans."

"It can and it will." Robert's quick temper showed in his heightened colour. He had always been quixotic. He it was who when he and Rufus were besieging Mont St. Michel when Henry was there with his adherents, had sent in wine for his brother's table because they were dying of thirst. Rufus had cursed him for a fool just as Ranulf would be doing if he dared.

"These are my men," he said. "I am their commander, and I say that we shall not ride into Winchester."

* * *

Henry left Pevensey with a sinking heart. Robert would be marching on Winchester where Matilda was lying-in! He was afraid. What would become of her? He pictured her lying in her bed clutching the baby at her breast while Robert's soldiers burst into the chamber.

It must never be. He must prevent that. He cursed the fleet which had betrayed him. He cursed himself for being at Pevensey when they had landed at Portsmouth.

A messenger came riding up.

"My lord, the Normans are not riding to Winchester. They are going straight to London."

He was astonished. Surely they should have gone to Winchester? It was the reasonable road to have taken and at Winchester was the Treasury, his wife, his newborn child.

Seeing his puzzlement the messenger continued: "On the Duke's instructions, my lord. He would not go there as the Queen was lying-in."

A slow smile touched Henry's lips. How typical of Robert! Always chivalrous. He would lose a battle rather than act in an un-knightly manner. It was small wonder that his dukedom was a place of anarchy. Robert might be the most charming of men but he was one of the worst rulers any country could have. Rufus had been a good one compared with him. Odd, thought Henry, to think that we three were all fathered by one man and that man the great Conqueror!

But his spirits were lifted. He felt happier than he had since he knew that his fleet had deserted to his brother.

* * *

The two armies met at Alton. They drew up, their helmets glittering in the sun; and at the head of each army were the brothers.

Robert rode forward and Henry went to meet him.

"Hail, brother!" said Robert.

"Hail!" said Henry.

"This is a sorry state when brothers meet in conflict."

"A conflict of your making."

"I never had great heart for it."

Henry's own heart began to beat wildly with hope.

He knew that he was outnumbered. He could not be sure how many of those who were behind him now were true followers, and who would have deserted to the enemy by nightfall.

Henry said: "Yet you come at the head of an army."

"They seem to have arranged it before I returned to Rouen."

"Freed of your sins, but not for long if you kill your brother in battle," said Henry. "Are we to fight then? Our mother would be grieved."

It was a good allusion for Robert had always felt sentimental about his mother—and well he might as she had defied the Conqueror to support him.

"It is not meet that brother should fight brother."

"Perhaps we could come to some agreement."

"Why brother, that would please me."

An agreement! To sit down to a conference! Henry the lawyer would fare far better on such an occasion than the dreamer idealist.

"We must arrange it."

"We will."

Robert rode back to his men. He was smiling happily.

"There is to be no battle," he announced. "My brother and I have agreed to settle this matter amicably by a treaty."

Ranulf groaned. Did I almost kill myself for this? he asked himself. Did I arrange this excursion? Did I use my spies so that I knew what was happening in England, raise the money, manoeuvre the desertion of the fleet . . . all this for a fool? Had Robert not the advantage? He was crazy; he would never be anything but a foolish adventurer.

Ranulf had chosen unwisely. He should have served the wily lawyer, never the mad adventurer who could not call at Winchester because his sister-in-law was in childbed, who had every advantage, and who was prepared to have it all stripped from him at the conference table.

* * *

Each of the brothers had chosen twelve knights to sit with them at that conference table that they might work out the details of the treaty. Henry was in his element. He listened to Robert and whenever his brother made a point which was not quite sound he would seize on it so that all attention was focused on it. Robert did not understand this lawyer's trick and he was quickly out of his depth.

"The people of England," Henry explained, "want an English King as the people of Normandy want a Norman Duke. Our father was aware of this. If he were here now he would say that your place was in Normandy, brother, mine in England."

Robert saw the point of this.

"But as the elder I have the claim, Henry," he pointed out. "And Rufus and I had an understanding that if either of us died the other should inherit his possessions."

"You had pawned Normandy to Rufus."

"Ay, and redeemed it."

"From me," Henry reminded him with a smile as though that settled the matter. "You could not rule England and Normandy, brother. Admit my claim and it may well be that a pension can be arranged for you for so doing."

The thought of ready money always attracted Robert. True, he lost it almost as soon as he acquired it but that did not prevent his always being fascinated by the prospect.

The agreement was drawn up. For a pension of 3,000 marks a year Robert should withdraw his claim to the English throne and at the same time Henry would renounce his claims on Normandy.

That seemed fair enough.

"There is one other point," said Robert. "Many Normans who have estates in England came to my support. It must be part of the agreement that they do not suffer for this."

Henry hesitated. Ranulf Flambard. Robert of Bellême. His brother who was looking at him earnestly said,

175

"I could not agree without your promise. These men came to my aid. I could not desert them."

"And if I refused?"

"They would insist on fighting this out in battle."

Fighting it out in battle with superior forces and men of doubtful loyalty in his ranks! Henry was not really hesitating. He would give the promise but he might well find a way round it. He was not going to allow men like Robert of Bellême to flourish in his country. They were a menace to his plans for law and order. But the important fact now was to prevent a battle in which the enemy had superior forces.

He had come well out of this. Poor Robert! He would always fail.

So the treaty was concluded and even then Henry could scarcely believe his good fortune.

As soon as possible he rode to Winchester to tell Matilda about it.

* * *

So he had plucked peace out of what seemed like certain disaster. True he must pay Robert's pension—for a year at least. Then he must find some pretext of discontinuing it.

Now he could settle to this real business—that of ruling England. First though there was the christening of their little daughter.

Henry had said: "There is one name I should like her to have above all others. That of her mother."

So with a certain ceremony the child was christened Matilda.

She was a lusty girl, and showed signs of becoming a true granddaughter of the Conqueror, for she gave voice to loud yells of protest when anything she wanted was denied her; her parents were delighted with her.

* * *

Henry faced Ranulf Flambard, who was watching him covertly. This was the man who had dared cast jibes at him when Rufus was alive, who, when imprisoned in the White Tower, had made such a daring escape, and had gone to Normandy to plan the invasion of England, the man who would have snatched England from Henry and given it to Robert.

Such a man, thought Henry, I should send back to the White Tower, I should have his eyes put out that he might not escape again and plot against me.

They looked steadily at each other.

He knew what Ranulf was thinking: Robert is a fool and I was a fool also to throw in my lot with him. I would have been wiser to go with the clever brother.

Indeed, my friend, you would, thought Henry.

Ranulf was clever in a manner which Henry understood, for it was his own brand of wisdom. Could it be that he might use that wisdom in support of Henry? It was a brilliant move to have lured the fleet over to Normandy so that the force which Henry should have built up to protect him should have been the very means of destroying his protection. He could appreciate that.

"What would you say, Ranulf Flambard," he said, "if I were to return your lands in England?"

"I would say you were a most generous King."

"And you would live here?"

A crafty look came into Ranulf's eyes. "I am a grateful man. I return favour for favour. It might well be that I could show my gratitude if I spent some time in Normandy."

The man was shrewd. He knew what was going on in Henry's mind. Pay a pension to Robert? Only until his forces were out of England. And then why should not Henry turn the tables and cast his eyes in the direction of Normandy? And if he did Ranulf Flambard might well have an opportunity to show his gratitude.

"You are a clever man, Ranulf," said Henry. "There are not enough brains in the world that we can afford to destroy them."

Ranulf bowed, his eyes gleaming.

He was ready to change his allegiance, for here was a master whom he could serve while taking good care of himself. Moreover he was in Henry's hands now and if Henry was going to exact no payment for his deeds then he was indeed eager for his services.

There was complete understanding between the two men. Ranulf's estates would be graciously returned to him and he would live sometimes in Normandy, sometimes in England; and when the moment came for Henry to exert his claims, Ranulf would be his friend as he had tried to be Robert's.

Henry was not so lenient with Robert of Bellême.

Henry knew that Normundy was in a state of anarchy and that this was due to men such as Robert of Bellême. Since Robert of Bellême had acquired estates throughout the country he had attempted to set up a similar state of affairs in England. The Bellêmes had been brought up in cruelty. They had been practising for generations. There was a warped streak in the entire family and their great aim was to see everyone cringe before them. Henry was determined to crush them.

He discussed this with Anselm who was in agreement with him.

"I must," said Henry, "rid the country of this man. Yet I have vowed to my brother that those Normans who rebelled against me and showed their allegiance to Duke Robert should be forgiven."

"But," said Anselm, "this man has been guilty of many sins. It should not be difficult to bring charges against him on these scores."

It was exactly what Henry had in mind but he wanted Anselm to suggest that this action be taken, so that it did not come from him and he could not be said to have broken his promise to his brother.

It was not difficult to bring charges against Robert of Bellême. The man was a scoundrel of the first degree.

The result of the investigations was that Robert of Bellême was summoned to the King's court to face the charges.

Being accustomed to command and having held all Normandy in terror Robert of Bellême was not going to submit lightly to this upstart King. He began by fortifying his castles and preparing to defend them against the King.

This was a very different matter from facing a Norman army. Moreover Henry was in no fear of deserters now. There was not a man, woman or child in those areas near the Bellême estates who did not go in fear of capture by the wicked baron or his servants. The fact that the King was going into battle against this ogre was a cause for hope throughout the country.

The King had made harsh laws—particularly forest laws—but everyone knew them for laws which must be obeyed. They need have no fear if they obeyed them. How different was the rule of the Bellêmes when innocent travellers could be waylaid, when a man could be asked to dine and then to provide sport for the company which could end in his death. Bellême had been known to impale men and women on stakes and gloat over their dying agonies. There was no torture, no obscenity, no cruelty which he would not practise. It was not only the Saxons who hated and feared him; the Normans were also not immune from his cruelty.

Henry said: "I will not allow such practices to persist in my realm. I intend to make this country one where just laws will prevail. Those who disobey them will be punished, and severely, but I will not allow men such as Robert of Bellême to practise their evil deeds here."

With a party of troops he marched first to Arundel which had been fortified against him. It was not difficult to take that stronghold. It seemed that those who were holding it for such a master were not sorry to surrender.

The fortresses of Tickhill and Bridgnorth followed quickly and that left Shrewsbury which Robert of Bellême himself was holding.

This was a little more difficult but Bellême had no doubt lost heart and had realised by this time that Henry of England was not Robert of Normandy. Henry took the castle and Robert of Bellême was his prisoner.

The two men faced each other—the triumphant son of the Conqueror and the cruel depraved scion of the most notoriously wicked family in the world.

Henry despised and hated him. He would have liked to send him to the White Tower, to have inflicted on him the slow torture which he had made so many suffer. But Henry was not hot-headed. He saw a use he could make of this man. He had reduced Normandy to a state of anarchy before he had settled in England and tried to do the same here. If he were sent back to Normandy he could do the same again and it was men such as Robert of Bellême who weakened a country. A weakened Normandy could be very useful to Henry.

If he banished Robert of Bellême to Normandy he would be rid of him; he could take his estates which were considerable; he could give him an opportunity to disrupt the peace of Normandy and at the same time adhere to his part of the treaty in which he had promised leniency to those Norman barons who had worked against him.

There was great rejoicing on those estates where Robert of Bellême had lived and so angry was the Norman baron that he appeased his fury with the blood of his Norman victims.

Henry, outwardly shocked, was inwardly amused when Duke Robert had to take action against the conduct of his vassal, who was carrying out the most fearful atrocities on any who strayed into his path.

How typical of his brother not to be able to subdue the monster! How different from Henry! Robert was forced to make a truce with the Bellêmes and the atrocities continued.

When news of what was happening came to England people began to rejoice in their King. They saw that it was a mistake to have tried to replace him. If he had seized the throne when it should have gone to the eldest son, so much the better. In snatching victory from defeat by his clever treaty, by turning out Robert of Bellême and introducing law and order into the affairs of the kingdom, Henry had proved that he was going to be a good King.

It soon became apparent that rape and robbery were diminishing. Roving barons who had taken the law into their hands, an extreme example being Robert of Bellême, were punished and began to disappear. There was one law which had to be obeyed and that was the King's law.

There could be no prosperous country without a good

government, he insisted; and a good government there must be if all the petty barons who plundered and murdered at will were to be stopped. He was going to bring peace and prosperity to England. He was going to bring back the law and order which his father had instituted but which had been lost during the reign of his brother.

The people began to see what was happening. They were living in a more peaceful state than many of them had ever known.

It was due to the King's rule. They called him "The Lion of Justice."

Matilda's Eyes Are Opened

The just laws of the King and the piety of the Queen were beginning to have their effect. When they appeared together people would cheer them. It was gratifying to Henry when he remembered how uneasy the first months of his reign had been. As for Matilda she believed that she had achieved absolute perfection.

She had her dear little Matilda and she believed she would soon be pregnant again. Then, she was certain, she would have a son.

She told her attendants, "My happiness would be complete if I did."

The King was affectionate and tender, though she saw less of him than she had at first. State affairs, he told her, were constantly calling him away.

Sometimes when she spoke of the King and his goodness to her and his people and how she considered that she had achieved the perfect union, she could notice that there was often a heavy silence and once or twice she had seen her women turn away as though to control their features.

The poor gave her the title which in the past Saxons had bestowed on those queens who had been assiduous in their care for the needy: *Hlaefdige* which meant the Giver of Bread. She was glad that they had done this. It was an indication that she was carrying out her duties in the same pious manner as her mother had done.

She never failed to do some good deed whenever the opportunity offered itself. Discovering on a journey she made near Stratford that the people would find a bridge very useful at that point, she caused one to be set up. It was the first arched bridge to be built and the spot was called Bow after that. She founded the hospital at St. Giles's in the Field and another at Duke's Place.

These good works were noted and the people declared that England would be prosperous now that it had a Norman King—albeit he had been brought up as an Englishman—and a Saxon Queen.

But there were some to carp at them and to jeer at the affection they obviously had for each other. They did not behave as King and Queen, declared some of the courtiers who would have liked to see a return to the profligate court of Rufus. They sneered at them, calling them Gaffer Goodrich and Goody Maude, as though they were a married couple from one of the villages.

Matilda did not care. She was happy. She heard news from sister Mary whose marriage was not quite as idyllic.

Mary intended to visit her sister as soon as the opportunity arose. Eustace was a tolerable husband. He was many years older than Mary and she had discovered that he had a mistress. Mary wrote that she supposed it was to be expected in marriages such as theirs, because they were arranged for them.

Matilda felt indignant and extremely sorry for Mary. She could imagine nothing more sad than an unfaithful husband. She thanked God that He had given her Henry, the perfect one.

Poor Mary! She grieved for her. It seemed unfair

that one sister should have had so much and the other have to endure such sorrow.

All those years of wretchedness in the abbeys of Rumsey and Wilton were worth while since they led to this.

"You, of course," wrote Mary, "will understand too well what I mean."

Matilda read that through several times without understanding. Then she thought: She means because I am so happy in my marriage.

It was not a very pleasant encounter when William Warren, the Earl of Surrey, came to Court.

She was a little embarrassed because it was necessary for her to meet him. Henry was away on State business which he had told her had taken him as far as the borders of Wales. When he was away he left her, as he said, in charge. It was a little practice in case one day he should have to go say . . . to Normandy.

So at Winchester or Westminster she would receive certain nobles and she was able to talk to them of State matters, many of which she promised to lay before the King on his return. It was a habit for any who had a favour to ask to lay it first before Matilda. Often if she thought the cause a worthy one she would plead for it with the King and always secure a favourable hearing and sometimes the petition or whatever it was would be granted.

She was proud of her influence with the King but determined never to abuse it.

She was at Westminster when William Warren came to Court. She did not care for his manner right from the beginning, but she understood. Naturally he had been a little hurt because she had pleaded her interest in the religious life and made that an excuse for not marrying him, and then very soon after that had accepted the King.

As he sat next to her at the table, for his relationship to Henry entitled him to that, he said, "So you decided that a crown was more inviting than a veil?"

There was a faint edge of sarcasm in his voice.

"I chose the man," she said a little tersely, "not the crown."

"So it was only to a lesser man that you preferred the veil?"

"It would seem so."

"And I trust you found the exchange worth while?"

"Completely so."

"Well, a crown is a crown. One can close one's eyes to much for such a glittering thing, I doubt not."

"I have no need to close my eyes, my lord Earl. They are perfectly satisfied with everything they see."

"Of a certainty. They see the crown and the sceptre."

"And the man," she answered. There was something in his manner which was quite insolent. He was insinuating something and she was not sure what. She would have asked him to take a place farther down the table but she feared that would attract attention; and he was, she must remember, Henry's nephew, which no doubt he would consider entitled him to a little licence.

"So you *are* ready to shut your eyes to certain frailties?"

"You are speaking treason."

"Not in the family. *I* would have been a faithful husband."

"What are you suggesting?"

He put his hand to his lips in mock alarm. "Have I betrayed a royal secret? Why I thought 'twas common knowledge."

"What was common knowledge?"

"Holy Saints, then you do not know. You have never heard of Nesta de Windsor?"

"Of whom?"

"Then you have not! How did he manage to keep it from you?"

"What should I know?"

"Nothing," he said. "But clearly nothing. Forget I mentioned her."

"Now that you have I insist that you tell me what you mean."

"Clearly if the King had wished you to know he would have told you himself."

"I do not understand you."

"Then I am glad, for I have committed no indiscretion."

She wanted to slap his smiling face. He was staring before him delighted by her confusion and misgiving.

She noticed that several people were looking at her.

She began to talk of State matters.

*   *   *

In the solitude of her own chamber she could not sleep. She could not shut out of her thoughts the sneering face of William Warren. What had he been implying? It was something Henry had done, or was doing. What could he mean?

Henry was away a good deal. Of course he was. He was a king with a kingdom to govern. But where was he and whom did he meet on these occasions when they were separated?

She sat at her window until the dawn appeared. Then she sent for one of her women.

"I wish to have speech with you," she said.

"My lady?"

"Have you ever heard of a woman called Nesta . . . Nesta de Windsor?"

The woman immediately looked startled. She cast down her eyes.

"Come, tell me," said Matilda. "You have heard of her, have you not?"

"Y . . . yes, my lady."

"In what connection?"

"I . . . I believe she is a Princess of South Wales."

"And what have you heard of this Princess of South Wales?"

"I . . . I know nothing, my lady."

Matilda took the girl by the arm and shook her gently.

"You do know something and I want you to tell me."

"My lady, I dare not."

"You will tell me or suffer my displeasure."

"Others . . . may know more than I."

"That may be, but I will hear first what you know."

186

"My lady, I dursent. The King would be angry. My lady ..."

"Why should the King be angry?"

"Because ... because ... he has been her lover." The woman raised startled eyes to Matilda's face. "All know it, my lady."

"All!"

"Except you, my lady."

She closed her eyes and misery swept over her. All knew but his wife. While she was living in her blissful state he was no more faithful to her than Eustace was to Mary.

"When did this happen?" demanded Matilda.

"It has been happening over a long time. There are the children ..."

"The children!"

"My lord's sons by the lady. Oh, I have said too much. But you asked me. And all know save you."

She said: "Leave me."

And the woman went away and she was alone.

What was this wave of desolation which swept over her? Her dreams had become nightmares. The beautiful romance which she had built up out of the simplicity of her heart and mind had no reality.

He pretended to love her. He was practised in the art, and all his protestations of love, his endearments which she had believed had been for her alone meant nothing to him. It might well be that while he was with her he was thinking of this woman whom he had long loved and who had borne him sons.

*   *   *

Henry came back from the Welsh border, refreshed, gay and seeming delighted to be reunited with his wife.

She had been asking herself how she should deal with this new situation. What could she do? Accept it. Was it not the lot of royal spouses? Not all. He had talked to her of the love between his father and that other Matilda and she had believed that theirs was similar to that. She had often said: "But *I* would never

187

support any children I might have against you." And he had fondled her and said that their love match had everything that of his father had had and more also. And all the time he was going off whenever he could to visit his mistress!

She was not subtle enough to hide her discovery and as soon as he returned he knew that something was wrong.

"Why, Matilda, my dearest love, what ails you?" he wanted to know.

"You will not have far to seek for the reason," she answered.

As he looked nonplussed she went on: "I know that you have been visiting the borders of Wales, which is a very attractive part of the country in your eyes."

"Attractive. A troublesome spot, I do assure you."

"But with consolations. I refer of course to your mistress. Nesta I believe is her name."

He stared at her in dismay. "By God, who has told you this?"

"It is unimportant. Suffice it that I now know what has been common knowledge to everyone else—for how long? How long is it?"

"Listen. I will explain."

"What explanation is there? You must go to this trouble spot. It is not the first time since our marriage that it has been necessary to visit it. And there resides the irresistible Nesta, your ever attractive bedfellow and the mother of your children."

"Matilda," he said, "there is much you have to learn of life."

She said: "I am quickly learning that it can be very bitter."

"You must not take it so. You must be wise, my dear. You must understand that life cannot be seen clearly through convent eyes."

"I did not wish to learn. I have been happy. I know I shall never be so again."

"What nonsense is this? Have I not made you Queen of England?"

"I bear that title being married to a faithless husband."

"You have a loving husband, my dear."

"Loving to other women, I agree."

"And to you."

"I should be grateful to be one of a number, I suppose."

"You are the first because you are my Queen."

"I became your Queen because I am the sister of a King. I am Saxon and therefore it was wise to marry me."

"That's so."

"It is a pity that you had to perform the painful duty of marrying me because of my position."

"Let us not be foolish. It was no painful duty but one of pleasure. You know that is so."

"Not as pleasurable as it would have been with this . . . Nesta."

He hesitated and thought of marriage with Nesta. One thing was certain, he would never be having this conversation with her. She was a worldly woman; for all her experience of marriage and the bearing of a child, Matilda still retained a nunlike innocence.

He shrugged his shoulders. This revelation had to come to her sooner or later. A King who had illegitimate children scattered over the country and who was determined to remember them in due course could not keep his many indiscretions secret for ever.

He had always been aware that she would have to know sooner or later and this was as good a time as any.

"I see that you would have preferred her." With that Matilda threw herself down on the bed and gave way to tears.

He let her weep passionately for some minutes while he sat beside her stroking her hair.

He was fond of her. She was a good woman. She loved him sincerely. He almost wished that he could have been all she desired of him. That was folly. He was himself. He must try to explain to her. Once she grew up, once she understood the ways of the world, he would have no trouble with her.

"Matilda," he said gently, "I have known this revelation would come sooner or later. I want you to listen to me. Of course I would not wish to marry anyone but you. We have been happy, have we not? Answer me."

"Until now," she said. "Now I know I shall never be happy again."

"You are talking like a child, thinking like a child. When I came to the throne I was thirty-two years of age. Could you expect a man such as I am to have lived without women until that time?"

"I did," she answered. "You were not married."

"Oh, you are so innocent of the world. I have desires like most men, only in me they are more intense. It is nature's way. Some men need physical satisfaction more than others. Some need it so intensely that it cannot be repressed."

"If they prayed for help..."

"There speaks Aunt Christina. Nay, Matilda, you have much to learn."

"And this Nesta ... she was your mistress before our marriage?"

"Yes."

"And after?"

"Yes."

"Because you preferred her to me?"

"Because you were not there and she was."

"But you went to Wales to see her."

"You will never understand."

"I understand that you go to her when I am here. She is beautiful I suppose?"

"She has an appeal which is rare."

"I understand. And she has borne you children?"

"I have two sons by her."

"And you go to see them ... as well as her."

"I naturally see them."

"She should marry. Then she would have legitimate children and a husband of her own."

"She is married."

"And still..."

"And still. Matilda, you must grow up ... quickly. You must understand what goes on in the world. You are my Queen. I respect your intelligence. If I had to leave the country I could without fear leave you as regent. You are educated as few people are. That is

190

book learning. In the ways of the world you are completely ignorant."

"Does knowledge of the world mean that I must happily pass my husband over to other women?"

"With a husband such as you have, yes."

"Then I can never be worldly."

"You will be unhappy if you do not see that these matters are of scant importance."

"Then is my love for you unimportant?"

"Nay. You have an affection for me as I for you. But you do not see me as I am. I am a man who needs women and a variety of them. It has always been so from my earliest days. I am as I am. I have fathered many children. It is said in the Court—and you will hear it said—that I am the father of more children than anyone in my kingdom."

"So my daughter is but one of many."

"Our daughter is certainly not that. Our children are the most important in the land—in a class by themselves. They are the children of England for our son will inherit the crown after me. That is why I may have children wherever I fancy, but you, my dear Matilda, must never have a child that is not mine. If you were unfaithful to your marriage vows that would be treason, for by so doing you could foist on the nation a child who was not of the royal blood."

"I would not wish to. Nor shall I ever wish to bear a child again. It is not what I thought. Nothing is what I thought. Perhaps if I had known I might have taken the veil after all."

He laughed at her then and seizing her in his arms kissed her violently in an effort to arouse a passion in her.

She was surprised at her reaction. It was different. It was profane whereas before she had considered it sacred.

And afterwards she knew that she had changed. She knew that she would accept her fate and that her first violent disappointment was over.

Very soon after that she was pregnant once more.

She prayed for a boy.

Her marriage had turned out to be not what she had

thought it. But Henry was right. She must grow up. She must understand the ways of the world. She had her dear little daughter Matilda—that demanding child who was already making her forceful personality felt—and when she gave birth to a boy, she could be content.

The child was called William.

* * *

Although she would never be reconciled to her husband's infidelities Matilda made up her mind that she must accept them. She spent a great deal of time with her children who were a source of delight to her.

She was delighted to hear that her sister Mary had also given birth to a child—a little girl who, like her cousin, was called Matilda.

Mary hoped that the child would be educated in England, for, as she wrote to Matilda, their education had been of the best available and Matilda no doubt found as she had that the harshness of convent rule was good for the discipline of the mind, it made one able to endure the troubles of life; also the education received gave one an opportunity to be more than simply a mother.

Matilda agreed with her sister. When she looked back on the days spent under Aunt Christina's harsh surveillance she was sure that she was happier in the outside world—in spite of cruel understanding—than she could ever have been in the abbey.

To Henry's relief she did not mention Nesta or any of his other mistresses. A dream had been shattered and perhaps she would never feel the same towards him again, but she had the children and they—at least so far—had not disappointed her. They were two healthy children, intelligent, lively and although Matilda was more forceful than her brother, she could tell herself that no doubt that was because she was the elder.

She gave herself up to a study of state matters so that if the intimate relationship she shared with Henry was impaired, their partnership in state affairs flourished.

He was pleased with her. He was glad she was not going to prove a hysterical jealous woman. If she would shut her eyes to his occasional amatory adventure she was indeed the perfect wife.

He could wish that she were a little less pious, but even that was good for the country. He was rather more fastidious than most men and he did not care that she should come near him after she had washed the feet of the poor. However, his acceptance of these Lenten trips to the churches and her preoccupation with prayer, was given in return for hers of his desire for other women.

The marriage had survived the rocks of discovery, he assured himself; and because of it he was relieved of the burden of pretence.

He could now bestow honours on his illegitimate children without fear of Matilda's wanting to know why.

So when a difference arose with Anselm he was able to discuss the matter with Matilda just as he would have done before the revelation.

"These churchmen always want to interfere in state affairs," he complained. "As I see it there is beginning to grow a mighty conflict and in this the Church will be on one side, the King on the other."

"Rufus quarrelled with Anselm and he was almost excommunicated."

"Anselm can be a maddening fellow. As head of the Church in this country he feels he is on a level with the head of the State."

"Surely the Church and the State should work together?"

"They should, Matilda, but I for one shall not allow the Church to have the upper hand."

"Are you sure that is what Anselm wishes?"

"He wants the Church to stand aloof from the State. He wants the power to decide matters which should be for the King to settle."

"What is he asking?"

"He would deprive me of the right to appoint bishops. All Saxon kings appointed their own bishops. I insist on appointing mine."

"They are members of the Church ..."

"Powerful members of the Church, Matilda. I cannot have men of such power chosen without my sanction. They could be my enemies and work against me. If Anselm and I disagreed on some policy he would have the support of the men he had appointed. That is something I could not allow."

"And if Anselm insists on appointing his bishops ..."

"I shall insist on appointing mine."

"He will not agree with you."

"And I shall not agree with him."

"That is a stage which you have reached?"

"I fear so. I and my Archbishop of Canterbury do not agree, Matilda, as Rufus did not agree with his—and his and mine are the same man ... a stubborn fellow."

"What shall you do, Henry?"

"He insists on taking the matter to Rome. That's what angers me, Matilda. Every difference between the King and the Church must be taken to Rome."

"But His Holiness is head of the Church."

Henry narrowed his eyes. "My father would never allow him to have a say in the governing of the country. That is for the King. My father was a religious man but he would not brook interference from the Church. Rufus had no religion and so he stood more openly against the Church."

"And you, Henry?"

"I shall govern as I will, come what may."

She knew of course that the impasse between Henry and his Archbishop would persist. Neither was of a nature to give way.

She was right. Letters were sent back and forth between England and Rome. Henry stated his case; Anselm stated his.

The Pope was ready to agree with Anselm, which, said Henry to Matilda, was exactly what one would expect him to do.

"I will not relinquish my right to invest prelates and

abbots," cried Henry. "I have it in my mind to banish Anselm and sever England's connection with Rome."

"Henry you would never dare!" cried Matilda in terror.

"My dear Queen, I would dare much."

The outcome of the quarrel was that Anselm asked for permission to go to Rome and put his case before the Pope and as in the case of Rufus, the King was glad to give his permission and if the sorry question could not be settled, at least to have a rest from it.

The Pope was aware of the mood of the English King and, having no desire to lose any of his adherents, vacillated. But he could not do so for long. He must make a decision; and as Anselm was his representative in England he came down in his favour.

Henry was furious and declared that since Anselm was so well received in Rome he might stay there until his King was in the mood to recall him.

For the second time Anselm was in exile.

The Queen and the Duke

Robert Duke of Normandy was growing restive. Since his attempt to invade England had ended in a treaty the advantages of which had been largely on Henry's side, he began to consider new adventures.

To his great delight Sibyl had presented him with a son who had been christened William. He was known as the Clito which meant the Prince; and Robert was ambitious for him.

Normandy was in a state of chaos. Robert of Bellême, having been expelled from England, was back and, in an access of rage against Henry for banishing him, practised his vile cruelties with even greater vigour than ever before from his Norman strongholds. No one was safe. He would send his band of followers—almost as cruel as himself—to bring in victims for his entertainment and that of his guests. Young girls, young men, the elderly and the infirm, were not exempt. The name of Bellême was like a plague that swept through the countryside. Robert of Bellême gave up his time to devising new and more exquisite tortures and was in a constant fever of anticipation to try them out.

The custom of impaling men and women on stakes was a practice in which he delighted. That he was fiendishly mad was undoubted; the perverted wickedness of his actions was having its effect on Normandy and it became clear even to the Duke that if he was going to save his country from absolute disaster he must do something about it.

He decided that he would go into battle against the tyrant. Henry had satisfactorily driven Bellême out of England where he had attempted to establish the same diabolical rule that he practised in Normandy, so the Duke would follow his brother's example and take Bellême's castles one by one and if possible destroy him.

Alas for Robert, he lacked Henry's skill. He went into action but was very soon suffering from a humiliating defeat at the hands of his vassal.

Bellême concluded a treaty of peace with the Duke which was to the effect that he was to be permitted to live as he pleased in his own domain.

The troubled state of the country continued as before.

Robert had given shelter to many of the Norman barons who had escaped from England to Normandy, for they had proved themselves to be his allies and therefore he must befriend them. This gave Henry the excuse he had been looking for. The pension, he said, was to have been paid while there was friendship between him and his brother. To shelter the King's enemies could scarcely be called a friendly act, in which case the Duke had broken the treaty.

Ranulf Flambard, still chafing against his ill judgment in the first place, realized immediately that Henry was going to take an opportunity to seize Normandy. He had admired the manner in which Henry had extricated himself from a confrontation which could have been disastrous to him. He knew that Henry had not meant to pay that pension for long; his lawyer's mind had been searching for a loophole and he had found it. Ranulf was now eager to see Normandy pass to Henry. He knew what was in Henry's mind. As the son of the Conqueror he had inherited to an intense degree the avariciousness which was one of the strongest characteristics of his father. Ranulf was well aware that Henry yearned not only to remain King of England but to be Duke of Normandy as well.

Well, why not? Ranulf could grow rich and powerful in a prosperous land as he never could in one such as Normandy had become with the Bellêmes' power rising and that of the Duke diminishing.

"The King of England," he reminded Robert, "has not paid the pension which was granted to you."

"Nay," answered Robert. "He is cheating me of it."

"Will you allow this, my lord?"

"By Saint Mary, I will not, Ranulf."

"Nor did I think you would, my lord."

Ranulf's eyes were gleaming with the prospect of an enterprise which should be devious and cunning, such as his soul loved.

Robert said: "I should go to England and demand it."

"Would my lord take an army with him?"

"How else?"

"You did that before, my lord, and what resulted but this treaty?"

"I never cared to take up arms against my own brothers."

"Kings and rulers can be enemies as well as brothers. You made this treaty in good faith and Henry has not honoured it."

Robert's face grew scarlet with a sudden rush of temper. He smote his knee with his fist and cried: "'Tis so. I should teach him a lesson."

Ranulf surveyed the Duke through half-closed eyes.

"He complains that you have given shelter to barons who have displeased him."

"They are Normans. Why should I not?"

"Perhaps this is a matter which you should talk out together."

Robert looked interested. When they were making the treaty he had stayed at the English Court for six months. It had been a pleasant experience. He had greatly enjoyed the company of his sister-in-law Matilda—a charming cultivated lady and she had been very gracious to him because she said she had greatly appreciated his gallant gesture in not bringing his soldiers into Winchester where she was lying-in.

They had good beverages to drink at his brother's court and he had on several occasions drunk himself into a stupor and had to be carried to his bed. It had been vastly entertaining and he had been sorry to leave the English court. Perhaps he had had enough of fighting. He had distinguished himself in the Holy Land; but it was different fighting an infidel, from engaging in what could prove a death struggle with his own brother.

"To go in peace to my brother, discuss with him the reasons why he has not paid my pension, that seems a good idea."

"This suggestion of yours does seem a good one." It was always wise to shift the responsibility of a doubtful enterprise to other shoulders and Robert, like most men in his position, could always be persuaded to believe that an idea which seemed to him a good one had originated with himself.

"I am sure it is," cried Robert, his enthusiasm mounting. "I will take a few gentlemen with me and cross to England. Henry will then see that I come in peace and we can together discuss our difference. I am sure I can make him realize that he does in truth owe me the pension and that I need it desperately."

Ranulf nodded slowly. What a fool Robert was. Did he think that Henry was the man not to take advantage of every opportunity offered him? Did he really think that he could put his flighty mind against that astute lawyer's brain?

It would be interesting to see what came of this visit, and as Henry's very covetous eyes were almost certain to be fixed on Normandy—now that he was so admirably putting his own house in order—it might well be that Robert would never see Normandy again.

*   *   *

Henry was hunting in the New Forest when news was brought to him of his brother's arrival in the country.

The Count de Mellent who had come with the news was disturbed when he saw Henry's delight.

"He comes," said the Count, "with only twelve gentlemen in attendance."

"Can a man begotten by my father be such a fool?" cried Henry exultantly.

"He has said that he has come in friendship to speak with you. He wishes to reason with you about his unpaid pension, my lord," said Mellent.

"Now is my chance. I shall take him and put him in such a dungeon from which he will never be able to effect an escape."

"My lord, he is your brother."

"What mean you? Do you think I am not aware of that?"

"It would be considered a villainy."

Henry's cold rage had begun to rise. "You dare . . ."

"Yes, my lord, I dare," said the bold Count. "I dare because I serve you well. You are our Lion of Justice. The people are beginning to understand what it means to be ruled by a good strong king and most of all a just king. Do not allow them to doubt your justice, lord, for it is the quality in you they most admire."

"And think you it is unjust to imprison my enemies?"

"This is your brother who has come in good faith. It would become no great king to take as a prisoner one who came with only twelve attendants. If you will give me permission to talk with him I will send him back to Normandy and I believe I know a way in which I can give you acquittance of his pension."

"You have a high opinion of your talents, my lord Count."

"I would serve my King with all my powers and I believe you would regret deeply to lose the respect of your subjects."

"None would have dared talk to my brother William as you have to me."

"Your brother was no Lion of Justice, sir."

Henry said thoughtfully, "I believe in your loyalty

to me. My brother is unfit to rule the Duchy my father left in his hands. It could well be a wise act to seize this opportunity. But you say you can send him back to Normandy and relieve me of my obligation to pay his pension. I'll keep you to this. Do what you say you can. If you fail you will face my displeasure."

"My lord, I know that I can succeed."

Henry was not so sure. He continued to follow the deer but he was thinking of Robert and how foolish he had been not to take him prisoner.

* * *

The Count of Mellent rode to Winchester where the Queen sat with her women. She was embroidering cloth which would be made into a gown; it was an art at which she excelled and was practised to a great degree in England.

The Count was shown into her presence as he assured her servants that he came with some urgency.

He then told her that the Duke of Normandy was in England.

"Does the King know?" she asked.

"I have come from the King."

"He sent you to me?"

"Nay, he does not know I come to you."

She looked alarmed, and he told her quickly what had transpired between him and the King.

"And why do you tell me this?"

"Because I have an idea that you can be of great service to your husband."

"I do not see how."

"My lady, the King is incensed against his brother. Not because he comes here to remonstrate with him but because he has not paid him his pension."

Matilda was quick to understand that the King knew he had wronged Robert and therefore he hated his brother. He was now seeking an excuse to imprison him that he might make an easy conquest of Normandy.

"If the King harms his brother when he comes on

a peaceful mission he will regret it, I know," said the
Count de Mellent.

Matilda cried: "I am in agreement with you. The
King must not harm his own brother, particularly
when he comes in friendship." Her expression softened.
She had never forgotten how gallant Robert had been
when he had refused to disturb her lying-in; and afterwards when she had helped entertain him at the
Court she had found him charming. He was known to
be one of the most fascinating men of his day; he could
charm both sexes with the utmost ease; that he was
feckless and superficial and that the compliments were
lightly uttered, the friendship on no firm foundation
was something which was discovered later. It was Robert's personality which throughout his life had enabled
him to fail his friends and yet be able to win them back
to him.

Matilda was still smarting from her discovery of
Henry's infidelities. He left her frequently and she
knew full well that there were occasions when he could
have been with her but preferred some other woman,
some new light of love, perhaps the perennially attractive Nesta.

Robert with his admiring glances and his charming
compliments had made her feel a desirable woman and
since her discovery of Henry's waywardness she needed
to be reassured. It was not that she contemplated em-
ulating his example. She was far too pious for that, but
she did feel that she could enjoy the somewhat exciting
company of her brother-in-law; and now she would be
very ready to help if possible.

The Count of Mellent said: "I shall go to meet the
Duke and tell him that he may be in danger from the
King's anger. And I shall persuade him to come to you."

"Does the King know of this?"

"Not that I have called on your help. He knows only
that I wish to send the Duke back to Normandy un-
harmed and ready to forgo his pension."

"How can you promise that?"

"I believe you could help me. The King cannot pay
this pension. He has projects in this country. To raise
such a sum yearly would mean increased taxation and

you know full well how the people hate that. It was Ranulf Flambard's methods of extracting money from the people which made them hate him and the last King."

"But the people are beginning to understand that Henry is a great king."

"That is why they must not be over-burdened by this extra taxation."

"Yet the King has given his word to pay this money."

"He could do nothing else at the time. The Norman army was in England. The fleet had deserted. There could have been another Norman conquest and instead of our just King we could now be ruled by Robert of Normandy."

"So the King in truth cannot pay this pension."

"Not without inflicting hardship on the people."

"But if he was promised."

"My dear lady, there is more at stake than a promise. The King had to make that promise. He now has to break it."

"And you are asking me to help the King break his promises?"

"I am asking you to save the poor people of this land from further crippling taxation. I am asking you to do such service to the King your husband that he will never forget it."

"You convince me," she said. "Pray tell me what I must do."

* * *

The Count de Mellent intercepted Robert and his followers on the road to Winchester.

"My lord," said the Count, "what brings you here? How can you have been so ill advised as to come? The King regrets the treaty. He is determined not to pay you the pension. By coming here you have placed yourself in his hands. What do you think he will do? He will imprison you. He might even put you to death."

Robert and the twelve knights whom he had brought with him immediately realized in what danger they had placed themselves.

"Mayhap we should go back to Southampton," said Robert, "and return to Normandy without delay."

"The King will not allow you to do this. If you attempted to set sail you would be stopped."

"Then, my friend, what do you suggest we do?"

"The Queen remembers your last visit with gratitude. I think that she would receive you and I have no doubt that she would ask the King to give you free passage back to Normandy."

"The Queen is a delightful lady," said Robert with a smile. "I remember how kindly she received me before. I tell you this: I shall be glad of the opportunity to be with her again."

The Count de Mellent rode with the party to Winchester, where Matilda was waiting to receive them.

What a gracious woman she was, thought Robert, and if she was not as beautiful as some he had known, her grace and dignity and her clever mind put her well in the front rank.

She was beautifully dressed in a gown which she had embroidered herself. The work was exquisite. It was a Saxon art which they had perfected beyond anything that came from the Norman needle. The Saxons had a grace which made the Normans seem almost uncouth. They were a charming people if they did lack the warlike qualities of the old Viking stock. Her gown was of a blue which matched her eyes. The sleeves were exaggerated to such a degree that they hung at least a yard from the wrists; her skirts swept the floor as she walked and he noticed how the gown was laced at the waist to accentuate the trimness of her figure. Her main beauty was her hair which hung in two thick golden ropes reaching to her hips; there the plaits terminated in ringlets which were tied with ribbons the same colour as her gown.

Robert bowed low and declared himself speechless before such beauty.

"Welcome," said Matilda. "It rejoices me to see you."

"Your welcome is warmer, good lady, than that which I believe I must expect from my brother."

"The King is absent from Winchester at this time."

She was aware of a faint inward indignation. Where

was he? With some mistress at his hunting lodge in the New Forest? Or would the hunt take him in the direction of the Welsh border . . . accidentally of course.

"So," she went on, "you must be content with just a welcome from me."

"Nothing could delight me more. It is good of you to receive me so graciously."

"How could I be aught else but gracious towards you?" she said softly. "Think not that I forget easily those who show me kindness. I remember another occasion when you did not come to Winchester on my account. Now you have come and that pleases me."

She took his hand and led him into the castle.

He must be refreshed.

"I remember well the delicious beverages with which I was refreshed last time I was in England."

"You shall be so refreshed again. You must allow me to entertain you in the King's absence."

Robert brought into play all his gallantries in an effort to charm Matilda. De Mellent had said he must, for Matilda could save him from the King's wrath and perhaps procure for him a safe passage back to his Duchy.

She had wine brought for him and filled his glass herself. His followers were entertained by certain ladies and gentlemen of the court while she sat and chatted with her brother-in-law.

It was cosy and domestic at first. She said that before he left he must visit her nursery.

"A girl and a boy," she told him.

"My brother is indeed fortunate."

"And they tell me you have a son."

He glowed when he talked of his little William. "Such a bright boy," he told her. "And William like yours. I doubt not your son is named after his grandfather as mine is. I'll confess this to you, Matilda my dear sister, I am fonder of my father in death than I ever was in life. He was a tyrant. His word was law. He and I were in constant conflict."

"I have heard the story of how you saved his life in battle."

"Oh, did you hear that then?"

"Yes, of how you were engaged in combat against each other. The Conqueror was unseated and at your feet. But you heard his voice and knew him for your father and so you saved his life. It was a noble thing to do. I know from my own experience how chivalrous you can be."

Robert was delighted to bask in her approval. How wise he had been to come! De Mellent was right when he said that she might be able to plead for him with Henry. He could well understand how difficult it would be to refuse her anything.

She talked about her children. "My Matilda is very imperious. Is your William so?"

"He is young yet."

"Matilda is already aware that she is the daughter of the King of England, and she is not going to allow anyone to forget it."

"I doubt not she will grow up as charming and modest as her mother."

"Oh, my upbringing was very different." Then she was telling him about Aunt Christina and the convent and the struggle between them to make a nun of her.

"What a loss to the world!" cried Robert in horror. He took her hand and kissed it. "I rejoice that she did not succeed."

Then he talked about little Clito. "They always call him that. I suppose there have been so many Williams in the family. He is a bright little fellow. I think it would be pleasant if he and your little Matilda made a match of it. Let us drink to that."

He was of course drinking a great deal. He had quickly forgotten that he might be in danger. Robert's custom was to live in the moment. He felt that he had been snatched from a possible peril to a very pleasant interlude and he was going to enjoy that.

Matilda had had apartments made ready for him and when he retired he was a little hazy from the amount of potent liqueur he had consumed. His attendants helped him to bed and he was soon in a deep slumber.

When she knew that she was to entertain her brother-in-law Matilda had planned all manner of pastimes for his amusement. They rode together and she was able to show him the countryside; and she arranged for a tournament in the tilting yard. The gentlemen of the household had competitions in archery and with sword and buckler as well as tilting and wrestling, leaping and running. In some of these activities Robert took part and whenever he did Matilda always contrived that he should be the winner.

Robert excelled at all sports, even the quintain which was a novelty to him. This was an old Saxon game. The quintain was a strong post with a piece set in a crosswise direction moving on a spindle at the top. On this was nailed a board and a heavy bag of sand. The game was to strike a hard blow on the board and dodge back in time to escape a heavy knock from the bag of sand which, as the board was hit, swung round with great force. As many of the competitors were not quick enough to escape the blow there was a great deal of hilarity.

After the banquet tellers of stories entertained the company and there was dancing. Robert loved best of all the music and the songs of the minstrels; Matilda shared in his enthusiasm for this and it made an added bond between them.

Robert was enchanted when he and Matilda sang together; and during the evening he would partake heartily from the royal table, especially of the excellent beverages which he declared were superior to those of Normandy and all other parts of the world in which he had travelled. It seemed only courteous to show that he was sincere in his appreciation by gratefully accepting all that was pressed upon him with the result that he had invariably to be helped to his bedchamber. So enchanted with the company and the good wine was he that he completely forgot he was in an alien country, and since it was his dear sister-in-law who welcomed him to her board it would have been churlish to allow his friends to remind him of the precariousness of his position.

One evening when he was in a state of stupor he said to her in slurred tones: "My dear sister, I would I could show you my gratitude. If there was aught in

207

my kingdom that you desired most happy would I be to give it to you."

"I wonder if you would give anything I asked?"

"With all my heart," he stammered. "Tell me what you would have."

"I always need money. I give much to the poor. My mother always did and I have tried to follow in her footsteps."

"Ah, money," he said. "It is what we all need and what we never have enough of. Believe me, dear lady, anything I have is yours."

"I could not take it from you," she said.

"Do you not regard me as your brother then?"

"I do indeed."

"Then I should be affronted if you would not accept anything ... *anything* from me."

"You have one thing," she told him.

"What is that?"

"I have heard it said that my husband pays you a pension. If instead of paying it to you he paid it to me ..."

"Anything you want," repeated Robert. "Ask me ... and it is yours."

"This pension then ... you would give it to me for my charities?"

"Anything you ask, dear lady."

Matilda smiled. "My lord Count," she said to de Mellent, "you have just heard the Duke's most generous offer."

"I did indeed, my lady."

She looked at Robert who had slumped forward, his head on the table in a drunken stupor.

"I think the King would be most happy to learn of the Duke's generosity. Tomorrow morning, my lord Count, at dawn, you should ride to him and tell him what the Duke has given me."

* * *

Henry laughed aloud when he received the message. He must indeed be grateful to his clever wife. He lost no time in riding to Winchester.

208

There he embraced Robert.

Sobered by what had happened and no longer befuddled by drink, Robert had now realized what he had done but as his followers advised him, his plan now was to behave as though he had not given up his pension in a drunken stupor but out of affection for his sister-in-law. Once they were safe in Normandy they could consult with his ministers and friends and decide what could be done. The immediate need was a safe passage out of England.

Henry was so friendly that Robert was carried away by the situation.

"I came to see you out of affection," said Robert untruthfully in fact but so believing it while he said it that it seemed like truth. "We are brothers, Henry. Never should we forget that. I am older than you, but you are a king and have a king's crown, which is a greater honour than a ducal one. I seek nothing from you but friendship and I have given over to the Queen all you owe me for this kingdom. Let us exchange gifts as a token of our friendship. I will give you and the Queen jewels, dogs, birds ... such things as mark the amity between friends and brothers."

There were tears in Robert's eyes as he spoke and thinking what a fool he was Henry embraced him, for if he did not love his brother he loved his folly.

"Now that the King is here," said the Queen, "we will have an entertainment befitting the occasion. Robert and I have discovered a love for the same kind of music and we have a minstrel who sings like an angel."

"I shall look forward to hearing him," said the King.

In his chamber the Duke's friends said to him, "My lord, you should plead business in Normandy. You should leave as soon as you can."

They feared what other follies their Duke might commit and they were aware of the astute minds of the King and Queen of England.

Meanwhile the King warmly embraced his Queen.

"My clever Matilda! How did you do it?"

"He was drunk."

Henry laughed aloud. "How could I have such a fool for a brother!"

"I did not like doing it, Henry."

"Not like it! Why you have the art of a statesman."

"I am not proud of that."

"Oh come, Matilda, that conscience of yours will be the undoing of you. You have done good work for me and for England."

"That is my consolation. The Count de Mellent explained to me what the paying of the pension would mean in taxation to the people of this country."

"He did well."

"And I asked God for guidance. I believe that it is better for Robert to lose it than for the people here to pay and perhaps turn against you and begin to believe that the extortion under you was beginning to look like that under Rufus."

"I shall never forget what you have done, Matilda. I wish I could tell you what you mean to me."

"I know, Henry. You are fond of me, but not enough to love me only."

"You cannot understand. How could you, a woman who does not know of these mad desires which when they suddenly arise must be satisfied and then are forgotten almost immediately. They are not important, Matilda. Such is my nature that I cannot escape them but they are apart from my feelings for you."

She sighed. "I did wrong to refer to them."

"You do wrong to remember them."

"Alas, I cannot forget."

"In time you will come to understand."

But she knew she never would.

In a very short time Robert declared that Normandy demanded his attention and nothing was put in the way of his return. Henry and Matilda even went to Southampton to say farewell to him.

Robert embraced them warmly. He would send Matilda a set of jewels which would become her well; he had dogs too which he believed she would fancy.

He stood on the deck as his vessel moved slowly away from the shore. There were tears in his eyes.

But before he reached the shores of Normandy he began to see how he had been cheated and he fulminated against his brother, hating him as much as he had thought he loved him such a short while before.

"By Saint Mary," he said, "I shall not rest until England is mine. Am I not the eldest son? Does not all the fair land belong to me?"

His friends assured him that it did, but the way to get it was not to venture there with only twelve knights and to place himself at the mercy of the country's scheming King and Queen.

Henry, watching the ship depart, turned to Matilda and said: "To think my father's Duchy is in the hands of such a fool. It should not be an impossible task to wrest it from him and by all the saints that is what I intend to do."

Matilda was a little sad. She was ashamed of the part she had played in the interlude and she heartily wished that Henry would be content with England and leave Normandy to the Duke.

The Abduction

Nesta was not ill content with her lot. It was not her nature to seek adventure. It had always come to her. She was naturally indolent and had no great desire to take part in state matters. She was the kind of woman who was content to be a mistress and did not look for political influence, but she was determined that her children should not be overlooked although beyond that she made few demands.

Gerald of Windsor was a satisfactory husband in that he was complaisant. He had to be. The King had selected him and given him honours that he might marry his mistress. It was understood that he must not display the normal feelings a husband might have on seeing his wife entertain her lover. Certainly not when that lover was the King.

Gerald had a barony in Pembrokeshire and the magnificent castle of Carew was his home. They had not been bestowed for nothing. In taking the King's mistress Gerald's fortunes had soared.

The castle was a great fortress of stone standing on

its incline looking out boldly north, south, east and west as though defying any to come against it. Gerald should be proud to own such a castle and such new-found power which his wife had earned through her boudoir skills. Gerald understood perfectly. He was not a man who was capable of great passion. He was too old in any case; he already had two sons and they were being brought up at the castle with the King's two.

It was a comfortable arrangement.

Each day Nesta rose late; she had assigned the duties of chatelaine to a housekeeper. This suited her indolent nature; and because she was rarely out of humour she was popular both with the young and old of her household.

When visitors came to Carew Castle she liked to hear news of the Court but had no great wish to go there, although she knew that Henry had once thought of installing her near him. If he had been in a position to marry in the early stages of their liaison he might have married her, but when he became King and could have done so there was the need to unite the Normans and Saxons so he must perforce marry the Saxon Princess whose uncle had a claim to the throne.

Nesta did not think that the role of Queen would have suited her.

"You would have been too disturbing an influence at Court, my dear," Henry had once told her. "Moreover the Queen's morals must be above reproach. A king has to be sure that his son or daughter is of the royal blood."

"My dear Henry," she had replied, "that would have put too great a strain on my frail morals."

And they laughed together.

Now her cousin Owen son of Cadwgan had arrived at the castle and one encounter with the young man had been enough to tell Nesta that he would soon be attempting to share her bed.

She was amused by him. He was a fiery youth and as it was a long time since she had had a visit from the King, she was not averse to a new adventure.

Henry would not expect absolute fidelity from her

any more than she would have done from him. They were of a kind; and this had served them both well. There were never any reproaches when they met.

Owen could see nothing but Nesta and when in the banqueting hall at Carew they were seated side by side at the board his hand sought hers.

"You are the most fascinating woman I ever saw," he told her.

She smiled at him lazily.

"We must be together...alone," he went on urgently.

"Listen to the minstrel," she answered. "He sings a song of longing, of unrequited love. Is that not suited to the occasion?"

"Nay," cried the young Owen. "For I will not allow that to be. I have never seen any woman like you. I would rather die than forgo your favours."

"Shall I tell my husband? Perhaps he would send someone to despatch you to the other world."

"You jest, Nesta."

She studied him appraisingly. Young, impetuous. A good lover she doubted not. There was no real substitute for Henry and she knew that there was none to take her place with him, but he had his Matilda and perhaps she would test this Owen.

"You hesitate," he said.

"Under my husband's roof..." she began.

"Oh come, we know that the King often visits you...under your husband's roof."

"The King is the King and master of us all."

"Not in Wales. By God, no."

"Treason?" she said.

His hand was on her thigh. "When?" he said.

She pretended to consider.

He went on: "I will come to your bedchamber."

"And share my bed with my husband?"

"That old man, that...that...Oh God, I'll show you."

"I have been shown before, you must know."

"That is what excites me about you. I never felt so before."

"My dear cousin, if you are wise you will go back to
214

your father's castle and take a mistress or a wife of your own age. You will see the wisdom of this."

"Wisdom! What man was ever wise when he looked on you?"

"Gerald was wise. See what a fine castle he has got for himself for marrying me."

"And in his feeble way he loves you too."

"Go home, cousin, and forget Nesta."

That was impossible. Nesta was amused, wondering what he would do. She even believed that he would break into her bedchamber and take her before Gerald's eyes. Poor Gerald, he would be powerless to resist the strength of this young man who was growing more and more maddened by his desire for her every day.

He caught her eventually, as she intended he should. It was in the grounds of the castle where any might have come upon them. It gave a certain fillip to the occasion which pleased Nesta! and afterwards lying on her back staring up at the blue sky she said: "Now you are satisfied."

"Never!" he cried. "I could live a hundred years with you and never be satisfied."

"Alas, I cannot put you to that test."

She was amused by her cousin. They made love in various parts of the grounds and in the countryside, in the castle and in their bedchambers.

Then Owen's father called him home.

"I cannot leave you," he told Nesta.

She was beginning to be a little disturbed by the fervent nature of this young man.

"Your father calls for you."

"I'll take you with me."

"You are talking nonsense. Of course I must stay here. What think you the King would say if he came riding by and found me gone?"

"I care nothing for the King. I care only for you."

"Hush! That's treason."

"I care nothing for treason."

"You would if the King had your eyes put out."

That sobered him.

"You would plead for me, Nesta."

"Perhaps," she answered gently.

He seized her hand. "Would he be angered? You must have had other lovers."

"Yes, I have had others."

"And he knows?"

"We do not speak of such things. We are too worldly."

"And I am not? So you prefer him to me."

"He is the King."

"He married that Saxon woman. Did you know what they call them? Gaffer Goodrich and Goody Maude! She does good works and the King finds her very dull. Who would not seem dull after Nesta?"

"I believe the King to be well satisfied with his Queen."

"She has given him two children. You, too. By the Saints, Nesta, you shall bear my children."

"It's to be hoped not, cousin. I do not want too many little bastards about me."

"Nesta, you madden me."

There was nothing to do but make love.

He was a fair lover but he was too young and impetuous and she was not ill pleased when he was finally obliged to leave.

*　　*　　*

She should have known that that would not be the end.

Instead of satisfying him that she was just one of many women she had convinced him, as she seemed to have convinced the King, that she was unique. She was sensuous in the extreme, sexual desires were as demanding in her as in her lovers, and try as she might she could never stop herself implying that to each one he was the best lover she had ever had; and as she was known to have had many this was the greatest compliment she could pay, and such a one that it never failed to increase a lover's ardour.

Cadwgan, father of Owen, had heard rumours of what had happened during his son's sojourn at Carew Castle and knowing full well the unequalled charms of its chatelaine he was well aware of the effect she would have had on Owen. Therefore he would not allow his son to visit the castle again.

The desperate Owen sent one of his servants to the castle to entreat Nesta to come to him.

"He declares," said the messenger, "that he is mad for love of you. If you will come with me I will take you to him and he will defy the whole country including the King, and he will take you where you can live in peace."

"Go and tell him he is indeed mad," said Nesta. "We have had a pleasant friendship but it is over now. Tell him to obey his father for he is very young and he must forget me."

The messenger shook his head and said: "My lady he will never accept that."

Nesta was then a little uneasy and she was watchful night and day for what folly her cousin might commit.

* * *

Nesta awoke. Something had startled her. She looked at Gerald sleeping beside her.

Yes, there were shouts from below. She ran to the window and called down: "What is happening down there?"

One of the grooms looked up. "My lady, it is young Owen, son of Cadwgan, who is below."

She ran to the door and drew the heavy bolt. Then she turned to Gerald who was sitting up in bed.

"Owen is here. He is storming the castle."

"For what purpose?"

Poor old man! Did he not guess?

"I think he has come for me. Dress quickly. There is no time to lose."

"What shall we do?"

"He may kill you. He is a reckless, foolish young man. I would he had never come here."

Gerald was trembling and she felt a compassion for him. Poor Gerald, he had had to marry her because the King commanded it. And trust Henry to choose an old man who could not rival him!

And now if that headstrong Owen forced his way in, which he undoubtedly would, and saw Gerald in her bed he might be capable of any act of folly.

Already he was trying the door. Finding it locked he hammered on it.

"What do you want?" cried Nesta.

"You know full well. I come for you."

"Get you gone."

"When you come with me."

"I am in bed with my husband."

"I will run him through and take his place."

"I shall not come out. You can never break down the iron door. Go away. It will go ill with you if you do not."

"I have vowed to myself that I will not leave here without you."

She turned to Gerald who was hastily throwing on some clothes.

"This hot-headed young fool will do us an injury," said Nesta.

"We are safe here," said Gerald. "He can never break down the door. It is especially made for attack such as this. It is of iron."

There was silence from without.

"He has gone away," said Gerald.

But this was not so.

They heard Owen's voice suddenly. "If you do not come out I will burn you out."

"You cannot."

"I will. I will set fire to this room. I will burn you out like rats."

"He cannot mean this," said Gerald.

"He does. He is a young man gone mad!"

She set about pulling up some of the floor boards for she knew that under the chamber was a passage through which her husband could escape.

"Come then," he said.

"Nay," she answered, "if I do not go out he will burn down the house. There are the children to consider."

So Gerald concealed himself and Nesta unlocked the door and stepped out as Owen stood there, a blazing firebrand in his hand.

"You are mad," she cried.

"Yes," he answered, handing the burning brand to one of his men. "Made mad by my desire for you."

With that he forced her into the bedchamber. He saw the disarranged bed and as he flung himself upon her he said: "So your gallant husband has escaped me. Never mind. I have that for which I came."

"This could cost your life," she told him.

"It was worth it."

"You'll not say that when the irons enter your eyes."

"I would say it if they flayed me alive."

"You are a young fool."

"I love you, Nesta. No woman will do for me but you."

"So you would take me by force?"

"If the need arose. But it did not. You were willing. Don't deny it. Now I shall take you away with me."

"Abduct me!"

"You do not think I came here to stay."

"There will be trouble, Owen."

"Let there be."

"You are not considering what this could mean."

"Come away with me and you will see."

"If I refuse?"

"Then I must needs bind you and carry you off."

"I will come," she said, "on one condition."

"Name it."

"That I bring my boys with me and those of my husband's previous marriage."

"What do you want with them?"

"Two of them are mine and the others are their playmates. I want them with me."

"They shall come. See how I indulge your whims."

"Well, do you intend to carry me off now or spend the night in this bed?"

"Not the whole night," he answered.

*   *   *

"There is trouble in Wales," said the King.

Matilda raised her eyebrows. Real trouble, she wondered, or just the desire to see the lady of Carew Castle?

"And you must needs go to settle the matter, I doubt not?"

"That is so. Two houses are warring together."

"Can they not settle their own differences?"

"My dear Matilda, you know that aught that happens in this country is my concern."

She did not ask what the trouble was but she noticed that he went off with that expression of expectancy which she had begun to associate with his visits to Wales.

It was not long before she learned the truth. Nesta again! Sometimes she wished she could see this woman for herself. At others she was glad that she could not. She knew that the rest of his mistresses were in truth of little importance in the King's life. Not so Nesta.

Her attendant and friend Gunilda whispered to her that the war which was being waged on the Welsh border was due to a woman. She did not mention the woman's name but Matilda knew.

"Why should they be quarrelling over this woman?" she asked.

"Her cousin came and abducted her. He was so maddened by his love for her that he was ready to risk his life. His father is furious with him and the lady's husband enjoys great favour since ... since ... since ..."

Matilda said: "I understand. This woman is another Helen of Troy."

Another Helen! she thought; and how can I hope to compete with her?

Henry came back from Wales—reluctant she knew to leave this Circe.

"So you have settled this matter of war in Wales?" she asked him.

He had, he told her.

"And the lady is returned to her husband?"

He nodded, still smiling, the magic of those hours spent with Nesta still clinging to him.

At such times Matilda went to her nursery and there she stayed with her children. They soothed the hurt which would never quite heal. In time she promised herself she would forget the ridiculous romantic dream that had once seemed reality to her. She would live for the children.

Triumph in Normandy

In Normandy Robert was fulminating against his brother. He had been tricked out of his pension, he declared. He had been plied with wine and then lured into relinquishing it. He would be revenged.

Henry, listening to such reports, was delighted. He wanted Normandy. He could never forget his father's deathbed prophecy that he should have all that his brothers had and more. The Conqueror had meant of course that Henry would have England *and* Normandy.

Normandy, he told his ministers, was in a state of wild disorder. The country was ruled not so much by his brother as by barons like Robert of Bellême who terrorized the countryside. To take Normandy would be an act of clemency. It would be tantamount to a Holy Crusade. The people of Normandy deserved the good rule which those of England enjoyed under their Lion of Justice.

He decided first to put out tentative feelers. Would Robert be prepared to sell him Normandy? To offer a pension would be a little ironical at the moment when

Robert was just considering himself cheated out of the one he already laid claim to; but Robert could always be tempted by money. He was always in need of it because when he had it he squandered it on gifts given in unwary moments, or on extravagant clothes and living, and women of course.

"Robert is ruler in name only," he said, knowing that his remarks would be carried back to the Duke.

Robert was incensed when he heard this and railed bitterly against his trickster brother.

Henry's ministers warned him that to buy Normandy, even if Robert agreed, would mean excessive taxation. The money would have to come from somewhere.

Less taxation would be needed to pay Robert a sum of money than to make war in Normandy, Henry pointed out. The people would be made to see this.

"The people might think that life is becoming good in England so why consider Normandy."

"Because Normandy was my father's Duchy. Because men such as Robert of Bellême are ruining it. Because Robert is unfit to rule. And because I want it."

That was a good enough reason for Henry; and as Robert was not ready to come to terms with him, he prepared to go to war.

*   *   *

The people hated the taxes but they remembered Robert of Bellême who had briefly terrorized the countryside. Henry had made sure that they understood what this war was about. He had delivered his people from the wicked Baron and banished him to Normandy where he expected his brother to act as he had. But Robert had not done this. He had been unable to. Consequently Robert of Bellême flourished. He had the ascendancy over Duke Robert and it could be said that he ruled Normandy. He would very soon be turning his eyes to England. Before he was in a position to do that Henry was going to make war on Normandy. He was going to take it from his brother; he was going to set up there the just laws he had made in England and crush the Bellêmes for ever. The people must decide that they would willingly pay their taxes (for their taxes would be taken no matter what methods must be employed) remembering the threat of Robert of Bellême.

The people paid their taxes with less trouble than had been anticipated. And in a few months the King was ready to set sail for Normandy.

He talked earnestly to Matilda. "Oh, what a comfort it is to me to know that I can leave the country in such worthy hands."

She was eager to show herself worthy.

"There is one whose services I could wish were at your disposal, my dear. Anselm. He is a stubborn man but a good one and would be of use to you. All this time we are without an Archbishop of Canterbury. It is not seemly."

"But you are still in disagreement with him."

"I shall see him and we may come to some understanding. It would please me if he returned to England and was at your side to support you during my absence. My sister Adela is very anxious for me to see him. So I will call on her at Blois and if I can succeed in breaking down his stubbornness I will send him back."

"Yes," said Matilda, "he is a good man."

At a solemn ceremony Henry invested Matilda with the Regency and Matilda went with him to Dover to see him embark.

He embraced her warmly as he said farewell.

"Always remember, Matilda," he said, "that I was happy in my marriage."

She cried out in alarm: "You talk as though you are not coming back."

"Nay, do not say such things. My men would think them unlucky. Of course I shall return. You forget my father's prophecy. I am to have more than either of my brothers. This is what he means. Normandy will be mine as well as England. Have no fear, Matilda, I shall return."

"I shall wait for you."

"I can trust you with my crown, my heart and my life."

And at least she knew that at that time he would not have substituted her for Nesta.

*   *   *

In the castle at Blois Henry's sister Adela received him joyfully.

Adela was the fourth daughter of the Conqueror, who had married Stephen of Blois and Chartres. She had inherited the family ambition and believed that if Henry conquered Normandy it would be to the advantage of the family. Robert was charming in his way but he was unfit to rule, while Henry had proved himself to possess his father's flair. She was proud of Henry and she knew their father would have been.

Adela liked to have a hand in affairs and she it was who now contrived the meeting between Anselm and Henry for she knew that it was not advisable for the Archbishop of Canterbury to be in exile and such a state of affairs could lead to the excommunication of Henry which would not be a good thing.

She had arranged entertainments for her brother while he was at the castle but Henry was eager to begin the first stages of his campaign against his brother and did not intend to stay long. He did not wish Robert to have too much time to amass an army. Not that he believed he could very easily for he would lack the money. But men such as Robert of Bellême would be determined to drive Henry back and they were the real enemies.

Adela understood immediately and told him that she could arrange for a meeting between himself and Anselm at the Castle of L'Aigle the very next day.

"Then let it be so," said Henry.

After that he could enjoy an evening in the company of his sister and her family.

She was about four years older than Henry and because of this apt to play the big sister. Henry remembered well how angry she had been when Simon Crispin, the Earl of Amiens, had rejected her.

Simon had been a handsome young knight at the Conqueror's Court and the match had been arranged to everyone's satisfaction in the first place. But as the time for the wedding grew near, Simon had gone into deep melancholy, and much to the fury of the family had declared that he could not marry because he had chosen the monastic life.

Poor Adela, she had raged—for like most of the family she had inherited their father's temper—but she was soothed when Stephen of Blois was found for her, although Henry did not believe she had ever really recovered from the slight she considered Simon Crispin had subjected her to. As a result she had grown very dominating but Henry quickly showed her that she could not treat the King of England as her little brother.

There was no doubt that she admired his achievements in England and that she eagerly seized on all news she could get of her brother's country.

"Henry," she said, "I am so eager for you to meet the children. I am rather proud of them."

Of course, Henry said, he must meet them. He was interested in his nephews and nieces.

They were brought to Henry and he found pleasure in talking to them. He was particularly interested in the third son, Stephen, who was about seven or eight years old. He was such a handsome, bright little fellow.

"Well, young sir," said Henry, "what are you going to be when you grow up?"

Stephen said he would be a soldier and a king like his Uncle Henry.

"Why so?" asked Henry. "Do you think then that it is such a great thing to be a king?"

"Yes," said Stephen. "I would like to be a king like you."

Henry was delighted. "That is a bright boy," he told Adela.

"I have been wondering if he could be brought up in England," suggested Adela.

Henry considered this. "I would consult Matilda."

Adela raised her eyebrows.

"Does she dictate these matters?"

"I look after the State; she looks after the home."

"This would be a matter of State," said Adela.

Henry smiled at his sister.

"You need have no fear that I would not look after my nephew's interests."

"There might be members of her family whom she would put before him."

"You do not know Matilda. Her interests are mine."

"I can think of some fields in which her interest—or her knowledge—may not penetrate."

"Now, Adela, you play the censorious sister. Desist, I pray you. I am as I am and Matilda knows this well. If she accepts this, you assuredly must."

"A court follows the morals of its king."

"Then those who follow me will be discreet and brook no interference from their families."

"Guard your temper, Henry. You look just like our father when you frown! Do you remember how we used to tremble when we saw that look on his face?"

"I remember well and as I am so like him those who perceive my frown perforce should tremble."

"Come, no quarrels. This is a reunion to which I have long looked forward. Will you, in due course, take my son Stephen into your court? Will you look to his future which could be greater in England than it is in Blois? Henry, will you do this for your sister?"

"If she asks I may well. If she demands, most certainly I shall not."

"Then she asks most humbly."

"Her request is granted."

"In a few years then my Stephen shall join your Court to be brought up with your Matilda and little William."

"That affair is settled," said Henry.

* * *

In the Castle of L'Aigle Anselm awaited the King. Henry went forward and took his hands in his. By the saints, he thought, the man has aged.

227

"Anselm," said the King, "it has been a long time since we met."

"On your insistence, my lord."

"We have had our differences. Should we not try to solve them?"

"I have always wished to solve them."

"So have I. But you must admit, Archbishop, that you have been somewhat intransigent."

"The Church would say that of you, sir."

"Oh, the Church and the State, this perpetual quarrel."

"The Church must claim its dues, my lord."

"And so must the Crown. Let us speak seriously and frankly together. For settle our differences we should. You have excommunicated several of my bishops; you have even threatened to censure me."

"With just cause, sir."

"That I cannot admit."

"And therein lie our differences."

"Which must be settled. It is not meet that an archbishop should desert his flock. That must not be allowed to continue. You are lacking in your duty if not to me, to those who need you."

Anselm replied that he knew this to be so but while the Church and the State were in conflict he could not return.

"I will agree to a settlement of our difference," said the King. "If you will concede a little to me I will so do to you. You must withdraw the penalties you have placed on churchmen because they obeyed *my* laws. As my subjects you and your priests must do homage to the Crown. In all temporal matters they and you must bow to my will. If you will agree to this I will not claim spiritual investiture."

Anselm was thoughtful. He said he would lay this before the Pope and if permission was given for him to do so, he would comply with Henry's terms.

The Pope! thought Henry. It was always the Pope. There was a big conflict beginning to grow between the temporal rulers of the world and the man who thought himself above them all—the Pope!

He narrowed his eyes and studied Anselm. He

wanted him back in England; he wanted to pursue his Norman campaign. So he did not give vent to his irritation. He nodded slowly and said: "Do this then and when you have your overlord's permission to accept my terms, inform the Queen that you will be returning to England."

Henry then left for the first stage of his campaign against his brother. He had not planned to make immediate war. He was too clever for that. What he would first do was establish himself in his own stronghold of Domfront and reinforce his position while he sounded some of the more important barons as to whether they would be responsive to bribes in exchange for their help.

Once he had sewn the seeds he would return to England and prepare for the main attack.

* * *

Matilda was at Dover where she was awaiting the arrival of Anselm.

She was shocked by his appearance. He was indeed an old man.

She welcomed him warmly and he returned her greeting with pleasure. They had always been friends since he had called his council and proved to the country that she had never taken the veil. He knew her for a good and pious woman; he had heard of her Lenten activities and he thought her a noble spouse and a good influence on her more worldly husband.

"I know that you and the King have settled your differences," she told him, "and this affords me great pleasure."

"Ah, my lady," he replied, "it is not as simple as that. We have made a compromise and I trust that in future the King and I will have less cause for disagreement."

"I am sure the King is delighted by your return to office as so many good people will be. Let us hope that you can now continue in harmony."

"We will pray for it," he told her.

When she heard that both he and Henry had decided

that celibacy must be enforced throughout the clergy she immediately thought of those who had already entered into the married state.

She questioned Anselm on this matter and he told her that this was a rule which all clergy would have to obey and it had been a source of great disquiet to him that in the past the lower members of the Church had been able to obtain licences to marry.

She argued: "I understand of course that this rule is made and therefore those who enter the church must comply with it, but I think of those already married. What can you do. Unmarry them?"

"In marrying they have already offended the laws of Holy Church. There is only one course open now. Excommunication."

"But what will they do? They depend for their livelihood upon the Church. They are trained for the Church. If they are driven out they will have nothing."

"It will be a lesson to others. They sought to satisfy the lusts of the flesh. Now they must pay the price."

"But to enter into holy matrimony . . ."

"A priest is a priest," said Anselm. "Matrimony is no concern of his. He knows this and in the past asked for a licence to marry. It was given him though it never should have been and he took it. Now he must pay the price."

The Queen sighed. How hard were men! Henry who did not even need matrimony to satisfy his desires was ready to forbid priests to marry at all! Anselm of course had never wished to, being wedded to the Church; but did neither of them ever think of the hardship these priests would endure when cast out of office and mayhap forced with their families to beg for bread?

She decided that Anselm looked too frail to make the journey to London so she herself would travel on ahead of him to ease his journey by making sure that there should be good lodging for him on the road.

When Henry returned she would plead with him not to be harsh on the poor clergy who now found that they had erred unwittingly against the new law of the Church.

*　　*　　*

The King returned to England pleased with the first stages of his campaign. A less able general might have been misguided enough to continue the fight. Not so Henry. He had made valuable headway; he had ascertained that several barons in strategic positions were ready to betray Robert if satisfactorily bribed. Bayeux and Caen had surrendered to him. He had garrisoned them and they would hold firm until his return which would not be long delayed. He needed just enough time to raise more money and a bigger army. Then he would go into the attack once more.

Matilda met him at Dover. He looked in fine spirits and was glad to be back with her. She had proved a good Regent in his absence and once more he congratulated himself on his marriage.

The homecoming was marred for Matilda by the sight of members of the clergy who had come in a sad procession to waylay the royal party as it passed through the streets of London.

Such a sorry sight brought the tears to Matilda's eyes. Rarely had she seen such desperation in any face as she saw in those of this displaced clergy. Their feet were bare but they wore their clerical robes and they chanted as they went: "Have pity on us."

These were the members of the clergy who had married and were now excommunicated and deprived of their livelihood because of it.

"Oh, Henry," said Matilda, "could you not take them back? Make this rule for the future if you must but those who have already married when it was not illegal to do so should not be blamed."

"You don't understand," said Henry. "Too much is at stake."

"Surely a little pity."

"Be silent, Matilda. This cannot be. It is one of the conditions the Church has made. If I waive it the trouble will start again. I can't afford trouble with the Church while I'm engaged with Normandy."

One of the priests was trying to kneel beside the King's horse.

"Out of the way!" shouted Henry, and the man fell backwards onto the cobbles.

But some of those who pressed near had seen the compassion in Matilda's face and one man came close to her horse and said, "Lady, you could plead for us with the King. You could save us."

"If I could," she said, "I would do so. But I dare not."

They fell back in despair and for Matilda this could only be a sad occasion because she could not get out of her mind the faces of those miserable priests.

There was another matter which gave her great cause for sorrow. Her Uncle Edgar, of whom she had always been very fond, and who had accompanied Robert of Normandy on his crusade to the Holy Land, was now ranged on his side against Henry.

Edgar was the kindest of men, extremely cultivated but he was no fighter; and she trembled to think what his fate might be if he during the coming battles fell into her husband's hands.

*   *   *

Henry's stay in England was brief. He did not wish to delay too long. There must be just time to augment his army and prepare it for the campaign in which he was determined to capture Normandy.

Matilda once more accompanied him to the coast and waved him farewell.

She returned then to her children and the management of the country's affairs. One of the most pleasant of these tasks was the building of Windsor Castle, and she spent many a happy hour with Gundulph the architect, who was also a bishop, discussing the plans for this magnificent edifice.

She was also concerned with adding to the Tower of London. Rufus had built the imposing White Tower which had been an impressive addition; she and Henry were putting in the royal apartments. Henry had said that his father would be delighted if he could see what a superb building they were making of his original fortress.

She prayed for Henry's success, never entirely forgetting that this would mean the defeat of Robert. He had charmed her, this feckless brother-in-law, and she would always feel guilty because of the part she had played in robbing him of his pension, but she must remember that the people of Normandy were suffering under the tyranny of men such as Robert of Bellême and it was from this that Henry was rescuing them. Everyone must admire what he had done for England, as all admitted the just rule of his father, be they Norman or Saxon.

Henry had talked to her about the poor state of the clergy and expressed his sorrow at their state.

"But you will understand," he told her, "that in ruling a country one faces many important issues; and it is sometimes necessary to shut one's eyes to the injustice done to a few in order to protect the interests of many."

He had convinced her. She would add to her charities; she would see that a great deal of the money she gave should go to indigent clergy. She must not blame Henry. But this was a little difficult to remember after a conversation with her women Emma and Gunilda.

Matilda had just received a visit from Roger, Bishop of Salisbury, who was that priest who had first appealed to Henry because he said the mass in record time and so released Henry from the irksome business of spending too much time on it. Roger had risen high in the King's favour and the bishopric was a result of this. He was clever, astute and fast becoming a very rich man.

Matilda said: "The King is far-seeing. It is amazing that not long ago the Bishop was but a humble priest of Caen and the King, after a short acquaintance with him, realized his powers and now he is of great assistance in the governing of the country during my husband's absence."

"He is very clever indeed," said Gunilda.

"And loves his comforts," added Emma.

"He is able to enjoy them in spite of the rules which affect humbler men," went on Gunilda.

"What mean you?" asked Matilda.

The women exchanged glances and Matilda with a little rush of indignation asked herself: Why is it that I am always the last to hear what is going on in this kingdom? Why do people constantly protect me from the truth!

"Oh, he is clever," said Gunilda evasively, but Matilda insisted that she tell what was in her mind.

"It is well known, my lady, that the Bishop of Salisbury lives openly with his mistress, Matilda of Ramsbury."

"But how could this be so and he a bishop?"

"He is a very powerful bishop, my lady."

"But the King has expressly laid down the law . . ."

The women were silent.

"Does the King know of this?" asked Matilda.

There was silence, and Matilda said sternly: "I wish to know."

"My lady, the King often visits the Bishop and is very gracious to the Lady of Ramsbury."

A wave of anger swept over Matilda. She could not shut out of her mind the faces of those poor clergy who had implored her to help them. And Henry would do nothing; he had been stern and adamant. The few had to suffer for the good of the many, he had said, when all the time he was visiting the Bishop of Salisbury who was flaunting his mistress to the world. And the King looked on and was gracious!

Now that Emma and Gunilda had started to talk they could not stop.

"The Bishop's nephew who is also a bishop, Nigel of Ely, is married and makes no secret of it."

"I cannot believe it."

"It is true. But it may be that the King feels these are special cases."

Special cases! Favourites of the King! Was this The Lion of Justice?

She said sternly: "I would have to have proof of this."

The women were silent. They feared they had said too much.

*   *   *

Matilda wrestled with herself. She must find out if this were true. Women listen to tattle she told herself and there would always be scandal about those in high places.

Of course Henry would not countenance such behaviour. She would not dishonour the King by believing such gossip.

Then she laughed at herself because she knew that she did believe it and she was avoiding trying to discover because she feared what the result would be.

Then she knew she had to discover.

The truth was even worse than she expected. The Bishop of Salisbury was living openly with the voluptuous Matilda of Ramsbury. The Bishop of Ely was in truth a married man. This cruel edict had affected only those clergy in the lower ranks because they either did not enjoy the favour of the King or could not pay the fines he imposed on those who wished to keep their wives.

She learned that many of the rich clergy had been allowed to defy the law by contributing to the war in Normandy.

She was deeply disappointed. It seemed that she must continually be so. She imagined herself explaining her feeling on this point to Henry and what his reply would be. He would say: "Yes, I fined these men. They have provided money for the conquest of Normandy. Normandy will be saved from the anarchy which will always follow feeble rule. For the greater issue I have waived the lesser."

She could never reason with Henry. His lawyer's brain was too clever for her.

But once again she must regard her husband with bewildered dismay. She had accepted the sensualist, the libertine, but she had believed in his sense of justice.

He had always said there was much she had to learn of life. How right he had been.

                              *   *   *

There was news from her sister Mary.

She often thought of her sister, wrote Mary, and
wanted to come and see her.

"It is not meet," she went on, "that sisters should be
apart. We were closer than most, my dear Edith. (I
shall never think of you as Matilda.) I want you to
meet my daughter, my little Matilda, for I have a desire
to place her in an abbey that she may receive an education similar to that which you and I had. She is our
only child and I doubt we shall have another, so as you
can imagine, she is very precious to us. I long, too, to
meet your own Matilda and little William. These children must be friends. So very soon I shall be coming
to see you and would you in the meantime look about
and tell me which abbey you think would be most suitable? I shall certainly not send her to Wilton. I could
not allow our Aunt Christina to lay hands on my Matilda. I want marriage for her not the veil and I think
Aunt Christina might be tempted to make a nun of
her. This will be an anxious time for you, sister, with
the King in Normandy. I shall hope to hear from you
ere long. Your sister, Mary, Countess of Boulogne."

Matilda was delighted at the prospect of seeing Mary
and immediately began the search for a likely abbey
where Mary's laughter could be educated.

She agreed that the education so acquired was good
and that she owed a great deal of her ability to keep
pace with Henry to her grounding in the classics and
history.

She finally decided on the Abbey of Bermondsey, the
Abbess of which, realizing that she would receive mu-
nificent gifts from the Countess of Boulogne if she
promised to educate and care for her daughter, declared
that she would be delighted to take the young Matilda
with the object of giving her the best possible education
which would prepare her for a good marriage.

Mary was pleased with all she heard of Bermondsey,
immediately sent a gift to the Abbey and made her
preparations to leave Boulogne with her daughter.

*   *   *

The battle of Tinchebrai took place exactly to the day on the fortieth anniversary of the Norman Conquest. This was seen to be significant.

It was the year 1106 and the 28th September; and it had been on September 28th of the year 1066 that William the Conqueror had landed at Pevensey.

And now here stood his son Henry before Tinchebrai in conflict with his brother Robert. So on the date when their father had begun his conquest of England, the two brothers wrestled with each other for the conquest of Normandy.

Many said that the spirit of the Conqueror brooded over Tinchebrai on that fatal day and that he gave the victory to the son who could best preserve that for which he had spent his life in conquering and holding.

The castle of Tinchebrai belonged to Robert of Mortain, the Conqueror's half-brother; and the battle was lost from the beginning because so many Normans had been bribed to fight under Henry's banner and his forces as well as his generalship were immensely superior.

Robert of Bellême, commanding the rearguard of the Duke's army, and becoming aware that defeat was inevitable, made his escape, and not only did Robert of Mortain fall prisoner to Henry but Robert of Normandy also. Perhaps more important, too, one of the captives was Robert's little son William, known as the Clito. The boy was six years old and Henry, realizing that although at this time he could be said to hold Normandy in his hands and that the battle of Tinchebrai was a decisive one, like his father before him he would have to hold the Duchy and this would be no easy task. His father had found it one of the utmost difficulty even before he became King of England, and to hold both titles, King and Duke, had meant a life spent in battle.

There would be uprisings and Henry wanted to make sure that there was no heir of Normandy who could win adherents to his side. Robert had proved himself useless as a ruler and even the staunchest Norman was realizing this, but a child was always appealing.

He discussed with his generals and advisers what would be done with the prisoners. Duke Robert and Mortain should be taken to England and held there. The boy too.

No, said those Normans who had been won to his side. That would be disastrous. There would be an immediate uprising if the boy was taken out of Normandy.

"There will be risings if he remains," countered Henry.

"When he grows older mayhap, but to take the boy to England and imprison him would mean the indignation of the people would be aroused to such an extent that they would immediately rise against you. Beaten as they are they would rally to this cause and fight with more spirit than they have shown at Tinchebrai."

Henry was at length persuaded to this point of view and agreed that the boy should be placed in the hands of one of his many kinsmen. He saw the wisdom of it but he knew that while the boy was free he would have to be very watchful.

Robert, brought before him as a captive, was too proud to plead for himself but he did ask that his son be well looked after.

"What will you do with me?" asked Robert. "Shall you remember our boyhood days?"

"What I shall do with you you will discover. Yes, I remember our boyhood days. There was an occasion when you were ready to kill Rufus and me because we threw water down from a balcony on you and your friends."

"I was young and headstrong and you were children to be taught a lesson."

"You would have killed us if our father had not prevented you."

"It was just a flash of the family temper."

"Robert, you have been a fool throughout your life . . . from the days when you attempted to pit your strength against our father. Now you have done the same towards your brother. You were doomed to failure in both these enterprises. Take your reward now and blame no one but yourself."

"Nor shall I if you preserve my son."

"Rest assured he shall not be harmed as long as he obeys his Duke."

"I shall see that he obeys me."

"You forget, Robert, there is a new Duke of Normandy and that is not you."

"You are a hard man, Henry, as hard as our father."

"You could not compliment me more than to make this comparison."

Robert turned away in desolation. He knew that he could expect little mercy from Henry.

Very soon after he was sent to England, there to be lodged at Wareham.

"He is my brother," said Henry, "so let him have some comforts. But in prison he must remain."

His uncle, Robert of Mortain, was less humanely treated. His eyes were put out as a warning to any who did not obey Henry, the new Duke mf Normandy. None would be spared however close to him, as they would see from the example of Robert of Mortain, the remainder of whose life would be spent within the walls of a prison he would never see.

He meant this as a warning to those who hoped in due course to set up William the Clito. What he had ordered should be done to an uncle would also be done to a nephew should he warrant it.

He was very uneasy that the boy should be left free in Normandy, but he saw the wisdom of not alienating his new Norman subjects.

Another who was taken prisoner at Tinchebrai was Edgar Atheling. The King asked that he be brought to him and when he saw the old man he felt a mingling of contempt and pity.

"So," he said, "you fought against your niece's husband. What do you think Matilda will say to that?"

"Matilda must know that I must be loyal to my friends," replied Edgar.

"I had thought I was your friend."

"I deplore these wars," said Edgar.

"Of a certainty when you are on the losing side."

"Nay, Henry. I would we could all live in peace. Robert was ever my friend, as you know, and I felt it my duty to support him. England is yours and as I see it your father intended him to have Normandy."

"You know full well my father hated Robert. He saw through him as a feckless fool."

"But he left him Normandy."

"Because of a long-ago promise to our mother."

"Nevertheless it was his."

"Know this, Edgar Atheling: I had my father's blessing at Tinchebrai."

"You had better troops, and a better general."

Henry laughed. "Well, you are in my hands now."

"And you must do what you will to me."

"I shall release you for two reasons. One because I have nothing to fear from you and the other because you are Matilda's uncle and she is fond of you. It would grieve her if aught ill befell you. You may thank her for your release."

Edgar lowered his head and the King went on: "You will come to England and there keep out of further mischief."

"I thank you, Henry."

Henry waved his hand dismissing him.

There were some men in life, he mused, who were doomed to failure. Robert his brother was one and Matilda's old uncle was another.

* * *

Henry was fully aware that the battle for Normandy had only just begun. He might call himself the Duke but he had yet to win over his new subjects. Just as he was accepted in England because he had been born on English soil and educated there, so in Normandy he was reckoned an alien. If he was to win the people of Normandy to his cause he must constantly remind them that his father had been the greatest Norman of them all and, even though circumstances had been such that his parents were in England at the time of his birth, he was none the less the Conqueror's son.

He made himself agreeable to his new subjects. First of all he wanted them to understand, as his English subjects did, that he wished to bring law and order to their country.

He knew that he would find most favour with the people if he showed himself to be of a pious nature so he made a point of going to church when he passed through every town.

He had always been very proud of his hair which he wore long and in ringlets. It was his finest feature and many said it was the second reason—the first being his crown—why so many women found him irresistible. He wore it in long curls which hung about his shoulders; he also flaunted a luxuriant beard and side pieces. As the King adopted a fashion as a matter of course so did his Court and the men's hair was as much an adornment as that of the women. The fashion had started in the reign of Rufus when court manners and mode of dress had been decidedly effeminate. There was nothing effeminate about Henry except his luxuriant curls and it was solely because he possessed such bountiful growth that he had allowed the fashion to remain.

The Normans had been astonished by the appearance of the English and had mistakenly thought that they would be easily beaten in battle. It was a Saxon custom to wear the hair long but the fashions set by the men of Rufus's court had been greatly exaggerated.

In the church of Seez where the Bishop was preaching, Henry and a party of his followers took their places in order to join in the service and show the inhabitants that they were a godly band. They were unprepared for the sermon, the theme of which was vanity.

"Men who look like women," thundered the Bishop, "are the prey of the Evil One." He went on to talk of the fashion which could only be offensive in the eyes of God. He believed that those who flaunted their locks as women might be forgiven for doing, would find them consumed eternally in the fires of hell. Such hairy men reminded him of goats.

Everyone was awaiting their cue from the King. Would he rise and demand the arrest of the Bishop? Have his eyes put out declaring that since he could not look with pleasure on the hair of Englishmen he should not be able to look at all?

Henry was indeed angry. How dared the man speak thus to his conqueror. His father would have fallen in one of his wild rages. But who could imagine the Conqueror with curls? Henry's anger was cool; it gave him time to reason. He had to win these Normans and he would do so.

He pretended to be affected. "Yes," he answered the Bishop, "we have been sinful. We have been over vain of our hair. We have displeased God by our vanity."

The Bishop came to the King and said: "My Lord, I see that you are as wise as men say, and that you will repent in time and set a good example to your subjects."

"It is what I shall always strive to do," said the King.

The Bishop then took a pair of scissors from his robes.

"Then, my lord," he said, "you will give those assembled here the opportunity of seeing that you are a man who means what he says. If your lordship will be seated I will remove that which is offensive to God, and the people of Normandy will rejoice in their Duke."

Henry was aware of his men watching him. It was an awkward moment. He could snatch the scissors from the fellow's hands and order his arrest. But only for a moment did he hesitate. Then he sat down. Whereupon the Bishop triumphantly cut off his curls and not content with that cut off his beard and side pieces also.

Nonplussed but determined not to show it, Henry ordered the Bishop to shear his friends also.

That day he sent out an order. No man was to wear his hair long. The fashion for curls was over.

*　　*　　*

Crossing back to England Henry was elated. He had ceased to regret his hair. He had his prisoners; he had his dukedom; he was victorious.

When he landed he was greeted not only by Matilda but by his cheering subjects.

On the very day of the month forty years after the Normans had conquered England the English had conquered Normandy. Henry was English born, English bred. He was their King. He was their Lion of Justice, and although they had suffered cruel taxation to finance the war it had been worth while.

Matilda was at first shocked and then amused by the shearing of his locks. He himself was able to laugh at the incident now and ask himself how a great King and conqueror could ever have thought it admirable to look like a woman.

All had been well in his absence and he was longing to see his children. He was prepared to enjoy for a brief respite the cosy domesticity of his home.

He told Matilda of his triumphs and that his brother was his prisoner and should remain so that he might not make trouble again.

"He will be well treated," said Matilda apprehensively.

"I knew you would wish that," replied Henry. "Yes, he will be treated well, but you understand that I must keep him in close confinement."

Matilda nodded.

"There is something else I must tell you. Your uncle Edgar is my prisoner also."

He saw the alarm in her eyes and for a moment let her imagine the horrible death which could overtake her uncle if her powerful husband gave the word.

"Do not fear," he said tenderly "No harm shall befall him. For your sake I have pardoned him. He will never rise against me again, but will live in peace. He has learned his lesson."

He was rewarded by her gratitude. At least, he thought, if I am not a faithful husband I am a considerate one.

He wanted to hear more of what had been happening and she told him that her sister was sending her daughter to Bermondsey and they might have her at Court from time to time; he replied that as his nephew Stephen of Blois would be joining them in due course they would have a merry family of children.

She assured him that very soon they would be able to hold court at Windsor for Gundulph had excelled himself and she was sure the King would be pleased with his new castle.

But first home to Westminster where they would feast and revel because of his safe return. There the finest deer would be roasted and she would see that some of his favourite lampreys were prepared for him.

It was a wonderful homecoming and he was determined to enjoy it, for he knew in his heart that Normandy, though it had fallen into his hands, was going to be as slippery as an eel to hold.

Weddings in the Family

In Cotton Garden, at the Palace of Westminster, the royal children were at play. This was Matilda's own garden which she often tended herself, growing herbs which she used for medicines and the flowers she liked best.

They had been warned not to pick the flowers unless given special permission but the young Matilda for this very reason must show the others that such rules did not apply to her.

"*You* may not pick them, but I may."

"We were told all of us were not to," William reminded her.

She looked at her brother. "That does not mean me."

"But it does," insisted William.

Their companions, children of the Court nobles, looked on with interest. There were often differences of opinion between the royal pair from which Matilda invariably emerged the victor.

Matilda said: "You are younger than I so be quiet."

"I am the heir though," William reminded her. "Not you."

"You are not," she said hotly.

"But," put in one of the other children boldly, "the boy is always the next King."

Matilda's eyes flashed. "If you talk of the next King that's treason because it means my father has to die first. You will be taken to the White Tower and your eyes will be put out."

The frightened child put his fingers to his ears but William said soothingly: "You won't. I shan't allow it."

"You!" said Matilda scornfully. "You will do what you're told."

"And so will you," replied William. "Now let us play a game. I shall hide and you will find me."

Before Matilda could reply he had run off shouting: "Count ten first and hide your eyes."

As Matilda could never resist the game she counted with the rest and was certain that she would be the one to find William for she knew his favourite hiding-place was in the courtyard behind the great buttress close to the stables.

Matilda always wanted to lead; in all games she must excel; so must she in lessons. She had once heard her father say that it was a pity she had not been born a boy. She thought it a pity too for if she had she would have been heir to the throne.

She had asked her mother how she had felt when she was born. Was she sorry that she was not a boy?

"As soon as I saw you I was glad you were just as you were."

"Was I very beautiful then?"

"No, but you were mine."

"Whose did you expect me to be?" asked Matilda, and her mother repeated what she had said to her father to show what a clever little girl they had.

It seemed that her mother was always trying to make up to her for being the elder and not a boy. Her father, of course, while affectionate towards her, could not hide his greater interest in William. It was for this reason that Matilda must always assert herself, and with her nature that was not difficult.

"You will be your grandfather over again," said her father.

Her grandfather had been the great William the Conqueror. She liked to hear of his adventures. He was a man to be proud of, but listening to an account of his exploits only made her wish all the more that she had been born a boy.

She was however not going to allow that fact to affect her. She was going to show everyone that even though she might be a girl she was as good as any man.

William had not hidden in his usual place and there were sounds of arrival from a little way off. Who was visiting them?

She forgot the game and went to see.

There was a retinue of very rich-looking men. Their clothes were colourful but strange and they spoke in unusual tones.

Her father and her mother were there to greet them and so they must be very important people.

She heard a shout of triumph. Someone had found William. That was the signal to go back to the Cotton Garden. She ignored it. She always liked to know what was going on. She kept her ears and eyes open. Then she could talk to the others as though she had very special knowledge.

She did not go back to the Cotton Garden but watched the visitors instead. Her father was talking with one of them and leading him into the palace, her mother with another.

They were ambassadors from abroad. How she would love to know who they were and what they had come for.

It must be wonderfully exciting to be a King and have such people come to talk to you.

She felt a fresh resentment because that silly little William would be the next King of England while she, Matilda . . . what would she be?

*   *   *

Matilda was not long is discovering the object of the strangers' visit.

Later that day her mother sent for her.

The two Matildas were so unlike each other that they would never have been taken for mother and daughter. The Queen often thought the one thing we share is our name and that is not really mine. But it was so long ago that she had been Edith that even she had come to think of herself as Matilda.

The Queen held out her hand and Matilda came to her and kissed it.

Matilda thought her mother quite handsome in a meek kind of way which would never be her daughter's. She looked as though she had become resigned to life. Young Matilda had heard that she had been brought up in an abbey and how her Aunt Christina had tried to make a nun of her. I should like to see anyone try to make a nun of me! thought Matilda with eyes flashing. But her mother was so meek she wondered often why the ogre Christina had not succeeded. The Queen wore her favourite colour blue and her mantle was scarlet. The blue kirtle had gold buttons and her fair plaits hanging over her shoulders ended in ringlets.

The dress was formal and her daughter guessed that it had been donned because she knew that the important visitors were coming.

"Now, my daughter," said the Queen, "I have something very important to say to you."

"Has it anything to do with the visitors?"

"You saw the visitors?"

"Yes, we were playing hide and seek and I came into the courtyard near the stables to look for William."

Why was it that Matilda was always in some strategic position at important moments, wondered her mother.

"Then you may have guessed that they have come on an important mission."

"Yes, my lady."

"It concerns you."

Matilda's eyes sparkled. "How?" she cried. "What does it mean? Oh, my mother, what *does* it mean?"

The Queen smiled and laid her hand on her daughter's head. "This may come as a great surprise to you."

"That they came about me? No, my lady..."

"You believe yourself to be of great importance I know."

"I am the daughter of the King," replied Matilda proudly.

"You are shrewd beyond your years. A very great honour is about to befall you. You are asked for in marriage."

"In marriage! Oh, my mother! Who wants to marry me? I shall not take him unless he is the greatest King in the world but that is my father and I cannot marry him. It will have to be the second greatest king. Who is that?"

"Matilda, Matilda, you are too hasty and too proud. But you have reason to be proud for the Emperor Henry V of Germany is asking for your hand in marriage."

"Oh, my mother, I shall be an Empress!"

"That is so, my child."

"And is an Empress as great as a Queen?"

"Some would say greater."

Matilda clasped her hands together and raised her eyes in ecstasy. "When shall I be married?"

The Queen smiled. "My dear child, you are seven years old."

"But the Emperor wants to marry me."

"People do not marry at seven."

"Then why does he ask for me?"

"It is the result of friendship between our countries. Your father is now the Duke of Normandy as well as King of England and that means that he will have influence in Europe and his friendship is important there. So the Emperor wants this alliance."

"Will he wait?"

"He is prepared to do that."

"For how long?"

"Until you are of an age to marry."

"But when will that be?"

"My dear daughter, are you so anxious to leave us?"

"Oh, no, my lady, but to be an Empress . . ."

"I see you love the prospect of honours more than your family."

Matilda considered this. "I love you and my father,"

she answered. "But it is not fair that I am a girl and not my father's heir. I would be a better ruler than William."

"You must not say such things. William is little more than a baby. Your father would be most displeased. You must try not to be so ambitious Matilda; it is not becoming."

"How can one try to be what one is not, my lady?"

"Every one of us must curb the weaknesses in our nature."

Afraid that in a short while her mother would be suggesting they kneel and pray if she did not change the conversation Matilda said hastily, "I will try, my lady. What is the Emperor like?"

The Queen hesitated.

"He is older than you are."

"How old?"

"He is forty years older."

"Forty years! Then he is an old man for I am seven. That makes him forty-seven."

"He will be kind and gentle because he is old."

Matilda lifted her shoulders philosophically. "Still," she said, "he is an Emperor and much can be forgiven him for that."

The Queen shook her head over her daughter. She was a true Norman—ambitious and already showing signs of that love of possessions together with the quick temper which were an inheritance from her paternal grandfather.

Most children would have collapsed into tears of horror at the thought of marriage with a man forty years older and the Queen had been prepared to soothe the child and tell her that it would be many years before she must leave them.

But Matilda was no ordinary child. As soon as she had heard that she would be an Empress she was completely contented with her lot.

From then on she gave herself new airs. She was no longer the King's daughter merely; she was the Empress Matilda.

*   *   *

Anselm was very ill and it appeared that he had not long to live.

The Queen sent kind messages in which she assured the Archbishop the King joined. Henry however did not view the imminent death of his Primate with any real dismay.

He needed money badly. The war in Normandy had proved expensive; it seemed very likely that he would soon have to make an expedition to that troubled land. It was hardly possible that the barons would not take an opportunity of rising against him; they would use the young Clito as an excuse. So that was something for which he must be prepared.

He was flattered and honoured that the Emperor of Germany should have asked for the hand of his daughter; but naturally he would seek some advantage from the match. For instance Henry would have to provide a dowry and it would have to be a handsome one.

Anselm would have reminded him of his promises to the people. Had he not on his accession sworn that he would abolish the cruel taxes which his brother Rufus had demanded?

Yes, yes, thought Henry. I had to. What would have happened if I had said I would need money for my various enterprises? Would Anselm have had him not make those promises? Would he have wished England to have been passed over to the feckless Robert? And now he had Normandy and there was need to hold it. There was need to strengthen alliances with those countries close to Normandy. And therefore he must provide a dowry for his daughter.

He talked of these matters with the Queen as always.

"We must find the dowry before the proxy betrothal takes place," he explained. "There will have to be new taxes."

"But you have promised the people..."

"Not you also," groaned Henry. "Tell me where I am to find the money for my daughter's dowry without taxation?"

"Perhaps it would be as well not to accept the proposal."

"Not accept the proposal of such a powerful man! The Emperor of Germany asks for your daughter's hand and you say perhaps we should not accept it! Are you mad?"

"Nay, only suggesting how you might keep your promises."

"Promises . . . promises . . . what are promises compared with the safety and prosperity of the country? I need strong allies in Europe and the best alliances are made through marriage."

"Perhaps it would be better if you had not taken Normandy. You will have to defend it and this will take you away from England."

"My dear Matilda, I have brought England to a state of peace and prosperity. Everyone knows that. The people may be taxed but it is so that they may continue to enjoy peace and prosperity. I shall have to go to Normandy of a truth but I can leave the government of this country in good hands—the chief of these my Queen and good Roger of Salisbury."

"He who keeps a mistress?" she asked.

He burst into laughter. "A fine and comely woman."

She shrank from him. "It is wrong . . . *wrong*, Henry."

He kissed her full on the lips and held her against him.

"Did I not tell you you had much to learn of the world?"

"To learn that a poor priest is outcast for doing what a rich one may do with impunity?"

"These poor priests are of no use to the country. Roger is of the greatest use. He is a man who cannot do without women. As you know there are some like that in the world."

"Then they should not be priests."

"They become so and then discover their needs. Come, Matilda, there must be leniency for those who serve us well. Let him enjoy his warm bed. The people can sleep safer in theirs because he is in charge of affairs while I am away."

"If you had not taken Normandy . . ."

"Have done, Matilda. I was meant to conquer Normandy. My father prophesied that I should. But the people will have to understand that I need money and they, who reap the benefits, must provide it."

Matilda knew that she could not remonstrate with him either to take a stern view of Roger's way of life or to keep his promise to the people.

There was murmuring throughout the country now, for the new tax was three shillings on every hide of land and burly men were sent all over England to collect it.

Matilda heard stories of great hardship, for many families who possessed a little land had no money to pay the tax. In these cases the house owner was thrown into prison or his goods were taken and the door of his house removed so that any passer-by could enter it.

Many of the victims of this new hardship escaped into the forests and there became bandits who emerged from their hiding-places to rob their more fortunate fellow countrymen. The fact that these people hid in the forests was an indication of their desperation, for the forestry laws of Henry I were as harsh as those of the first William and Rufus and any man found trespassing was most viciously and horribly punished.

People began to murmur against the King. They said that life was as cruel in these days as it had been in the preceding reigns.

In the midst of this Anselm died.

Matilda wept for the man whom she regarded as an old friend; Henry assumed grief but he felt little. Anselm had always been a trial to him and now that he was dead Henry could seize the See of Canterbury and all its wealth.

Thus was the dowry provided for Matilda's match with the Emperor Henry V, and Henry I of England found the means to equip his army for Normandy where he knew full well he would shortly be needing it.

*   *   *

With all due honours the young Matilda was betrothed by proxy to the Emperor of Germany.

Matilda was delighted with the pomp which accompanied her proxy marriage. Many guests had been arriving at Westminster for the occasion and among these were her cousins Theobold and Stephen.

They were older than she was. Stephen was about twelve years old, Theobald some years older.

Matilda thought Stephen the most beautiful young man she had ever seen and she took an opportunity of waylaying him.

*　　*　　*

She caught him on the way to the stables.

"Good day, cousin," she called. He turned to look down at her, for he was tall for his twelve years; and although she was not small for her age he towered above her.

"I'm Matilda," she told him, "the Empress Matilda."

"Already?" asked Stephen.

"I am married by proxy to the Emperor, you know."

"You don't look like an Empress."

"Do I not? My brother says I put on the airs of one."

"He may well be right in that."

Stephen was smiling at her and she noticed what beautiful teeth he had.

"You are handsome," she told him in her forthright manner.

He bowed. "I am delighted to hear that I find favour with you."

"Who are you? I know that you are my cousin and that is why you are here. But you are not an Emperor."

"Alas," he said ironically, "I cannot compare with the Emperor of Germany. He is forty-seven years of age and I am but twelve."

"But it is not only in age that you are different."

"Nay, he is an Emperor and I am not even the eldest son of a Count."

"Still you are the Conqueror's grandson, as I am his granddaughter."

"Which is the reason why you and I are cousins."

Matilda viewed him frankly.

"It is a pity you are not an Emperor," she said.

"A great pity, but if I were I should not be here, and I am going to stay here for some time. Did you know the King has promised my mother that I shall live at his Court and finish my education here?"

"I did not know, but it pleases me." She sighed. "How I wish you *were* an Emperor...I wish you were the Emperor of Germany."

Stephen smiled at the colourful, bold-eyed little girl and said: "I wish it too, with all my heart."

*   *   *

Stephen, son of the Count of Blois and his wife Adela, settled in to the Court very happily. The King had a special liking for him; he reminded him of his favourite sister, he told Matilda.

"When the time comes," said Henry, "I must make sure that Stephen is well looked after. He shall have estates and a good match."

"Mary's girl at Bermondsey will be needing a husband ere long," said Matilda.

"It may well be that we can make a match there. The daughter of the Count of Boulogne to the son of the Count of Blois. That could be possible. Unless I need to marry Stephen to someone who will bring me more good."

"Stephen is a charming boy."

"I like him well. I could wish that he were my son."

"Well, we have our William."

"Only one son," sighed the King. He wondered why it was that he, whom so many boys claimed as father, could only get two legitimate children.

He took an opportunity while in England to go to see Nesta.

Voluptuous as ever, she was delighted to welcome him.

The trouble with Owen seemed long ago. The war was over and she had returned to Gerald of Windsor and had become, so Henry heard, the mistress of the Constable of Cardigan while she continued to live with Gerald.

Whatever lovers she had she would always be pleased to see the King, and on this occasion she had something of special importance to say to him.

It concerned their son Robert. She was proud of the boy. She told Henry he should be proud of him too.

"I'll warrant he is the most kingly of all your sons."

When he saw the young fellow he was inclined to agree with her, and heartily wished Robert had been Matilda's son.

"You must promise me to find an heiress for him," said Nesta. "Robert has all the virtues except a fortune. But as he is the son of the King of England that ought not to be denied him."

"I think I know the woman for him."

"Who is that?"

"Mabel, daughter of Robert FitzHaymon, Lord of Glamorgan."

"She seems a likely choice."

"Indeed she is. Her father has just died and she is his sole heiress."

"Of considerable wealth?"

"Indeed his wealth is considerable. She will own all the lands and honours of Gloucester which my brother Rufus bestowed on her father for services rendered. These lands came to our family through my mother who confiscated them from a certain Saxon gentleman named Brihtric Meaw. It was said that when my mother was young she fell in love with this young Saxon and offered him her hand which he refused. When she became Queen of England she took his lands from him and he died soon after . . . in prison."

"She must have loved him dearly!"

The King laughed. "She loved her pride even more so. That will teach you, my dear, not to refuse the requests of sovereigns."

"When have I ever?"

"I will say that you have been generous to this one from our first meeting."

"Tell me more of Robert's heiress."

"I have told you that the lands and honours of Gloucester are hers. What more could you ask?"

"And they shall be Robert's."

"I promise that they shall."

"And this is one of the promises that you will keep?"

"Have I ever not kept my promises to you?"

"You have not come to see me as often as you promised for a start."

"Only state matters could keep me from you."

"Well, since your visits are so rare and becoming rarer, let us settle this matter of Robert's future now."

"It will be simple," he said. "Mabel's father left her in my care when he died. I am her guardian. I will tell her that I have found a husband for her and that shall be Robert. Let him ride back to Court with me. There is no reason whatever why the marriage should not take place without delay."

"Presuming the lady is agreeable."

"You are not suggesting that she will attempt to disobey her King."

"So she will have no choice in the matter. I do not pity her. She could not find a more worthy husband in the kingdom than our handsome Robert."

And when the King rode back to Westminster his natural son Robert rode with him.

*　　*　　*

Henry was so proud of his son—who looked a little like Nesta and had inherited a modicum of her charm—that he made no secret of their relationship.

Matilda knew he had natural children. There were plenty more of them who would need a start in the world, so Matilda would have to grow accustomed to seeing him bring them forward.

He told her what he proposed for Robert.

The boy needed a rich wife and one who could bring honours to him.

"I shall give him Glamorgan's heiress Mabel. I pray you summon the girl to your presence and tell her that we have a husband for her."

Matilda said: "Do you think such a great heiress will accept this young man as a husband? He has no fortune, I believe, and he is a bastard."

Her lips quivered as she said that word and Henry laughed aloud.

"There is a great difference, my dear, between a

commoner's bastard and a king's. The only rank above a king's illegitimate son is his legitimate one."

"We shall see if the young lady agrees with you."

Henry's temper rose suddenly. "I tell you Mabel FitzHaymon is going to marry my son Robert and be glad to. You will inform her of this fact."

The Queen accordingly sent for the heiress. The girl, although but sixteen, was as Matilda expected, a haughty young woman. She knew that she had been one of the greatest heiresses in the country and now that her father was dead, was the possessor of great wealth.

"The King has asked me to speak to you," said Matilda. "He is your guardian and he wishes to place you in the hands of a husband who will care for you."

"I am able to take care of myself," replied Mabel. "And when the time comes I shall doubtless marry."

"The King appears to think that that time is now. He has chosen his son Robert as your husband."

"Robert, my lady? Do you mean the son of Nesta of Wales and the King?"

"I do."

Mabel laughed scornfully. She was bold for her years. She said: "My lady, I must ask you to tell the King that the ladies of my family do not marry bastards."

"Do you indeed wish me to give this answer to the King?"

"I do indeed."

"You know it will displease him."

"Then displeased he must be for that is my answer."

Matilda herself was not displeased to do so. It would show the King the general opinion of his philanderings and that the children he had so thoughtlessly scattered about his kingdom were not regarded with any respect by the noble families of the land.

*   *   *

When he heard Mabel's reply the King narrowed his eyes and the sudden rush of colour to his face told Matilda that he was angry.

He said: "Send for the maiden. I will speak with her."

She came defiantly and not in the least fearful. Matilda trembled for her. Evidently she did not know how fierce the wrath of the King could be.

"Now," he said, "the Queen has told me that you do not care for the match I have arranged for you."

"My lord King," answered the bold girl, "I care for it not in the least. I cannot marry a nameless person."

"I do not ask you to."

"Then I am mistaken. I had thought that you were offering to me Robert the bastard."

"I offered you my son Robert."

"A bastard nevertheless."

"You foolish girl, do you know that the greatest man of his age—my father whom all men honour—was a bastard?"

She held her head high. "I can only tell you, my lord, that the ladies of my house do not marry men of no name."

"Then I will give my son a name. He is Robert Fitzroy and do you know a greater name than that?"

"Whatever the name, sir, he has no wealth. No lands. Of what use is a name however honoured without these?"

"You are a shrewd maiden, I see. A true daughter of your father. So shall you be to me. For I like your boldness. I have decided to endow my son with the lands and honours of Gloucester, and from this day he shall be known as Robert of Gloucester."

"The lands of Gloucester were my father's . . . they are mine . . ."

"While the King pleases to allow you to hold them."

"But . . ."

"Come, my clever girl. You have not lost your lands for I am giving you the chance of sharing them with Robert of Gloucester."

There was no avoiding the King's ultimatum and shortly after that interview both Henry and Nesta were delighted to see their son united in marriage with the heiress of Gloucester.

* * *

It was a happy day for Matilda when her brother Alexander, King of Scotland, visited Henry's Court. The fact that her uncle Edgar had been against Henry in the battle for Normandy had upset her deeply, and she had been grateful for Henry's leniency towards him. He might so easily have imprisoned her uncle as he had his brother. It was a relief therefore that Alexander should come in friendship.

The Scottish royal family were more or less vassals to the English throne since Rufus had helped it regain the crown from the traitor Donald Bane, but Henry treated Alexander with great respect because, he told Matilda, he was her brother.

Mary joined the Court briefly, for her husband was away on a crusade and she was residing for a while at Bermondsey, the Abbey where she had placed her daughter Matilda and which she now honoured with her patronage.

The sisters talked a great deal of the old days when they had been children together, before that terrible time when their father had been murdered while their mother lay dying.

Henry insisted on entertaining Alexander royally and knowing her husband well Matilda believed that he had some reason for being so delighted to receive his brother-in-law.

She soon discovered that reason when a certain young woman arrived at Court.

"I wish you to take Sybilla under your wing," he told her. "She is the daughter of the Count of Meulan's sister. I should like to find a suitable husband for her."

"And who is her father?" asked Matilda with a sinking heart.

"Come, my dear, you should guess."

"Another of them?"

"I fear so. I told you there were many of them."

"And after the clever manner in which you made

260

poor Mabel take Robert, you would like to repeat the action?"

"I would like to do my best for this girl. And I ask you to help me."

He laid his hand on her arm and smiled at her beguilingly. "Come, Matilda. Help me with my responsibilities. I shall soon have to leave you. Let us be good friends while we are together."

"To leave me!"

"There is trouble brewing in Normandy," he said.

"But you have conquered Normandy."

"Would that I had!"

"But surely the battle of Tinchebrai was decisive?"

He shook his head. "I captured Robert. He is my prisoner. I listened to what I believed all along to be unwise counsel and the Clito goes free. I have enemies. The King of France is not pleased to see me become so powerful. I must watch him closely. Robert of Flanders, Robert of Bellême, Fulk of Anjou. I do not trust these people for one moment. Depend upon it they are biding their time to rise against me. I shall be in Normandy soon to quell rebellion after rebellion. So, as I say, let us make the most of the time we have together."

"You are the King," she said. "If you command me to help you to find wives and husbands for your illegitimate children I must needs do so."

"I would have you do it willingly."

She shook her head sadly.

"I would . . ." she began.

"I know," he interrupted. "You would I had been the hero of your romantic dreams as you made me out to be before you discovered my true nature. But now you know me for what I am and in spite of all you have an affection for me."

"'Tis true," she said, "but . . ."

"But?" He smiled at her wryly. "We must all make the best of what we have, Matilda, my wife. We must curb our needs and desires to what we can attain. Come, be my good friend. Help me find this girl of mine a husband."

She smiled. "I will do it," she told him.

She was a little disturbed when she learned a few truths about Sybilla.

The young woman was by no means a virgin; nor was she of any special beauty. It would not be easy, Matilda decided, to find a husband for her. She told the King so.

He smiled at her indulgently.

"You have no need to worry yourself further," he answered. "I have found the very husband."

"And he has agreed?"

"Not yet, but he will when he knows that it is my wish."

"I am sorry for him."

"Oh, he is capable of looking after himself." Henry was smiling, well pleased. "Would you not like to know his name?"

She said she would.

"Alexander, King of Scotland."

"My brother! But . . . it's impossible."

"No, my dear, it is quite possible, and when my good vassal knows my wishes in the matter I have not the slightest doubt that he will be happy to do my will."

"But I could not allow it."

"*You* could not allow it, my dear Matilda?"

"It was different with the heiress of Gloucester."

"Nay. There was a similarity. You saw how quickly she changed her mind when she knew my wishes. You will see that the King of Scotland is every bit as amenable."

"Henry, please choose someone else for him."

"But I wish him to take her. I shall be well content to see her married. It is a pleasure to see one's children settled in life as you will know when our own Matilda and William are given in marriage."

She was hurt and angry; and she was surprised when without a demur her brother, who was known as The Fierce, meekly allowed himself to be betrothed to Sybilla.

Such was the power of the King of England.

Young Matilda and Stephen

Henry was right when he said that it would not be long before he left for Normandy.

Philippe of France had died and his son Louis had ascended the throne. Philippe had been lazy and preferred the comforts of his court to the battle field. Louis however had a score to settle with Henry. He remembered when they were boys and Henry and Rufus were visiting his father's Court, he, Louis, and Henry had engaged in a chess game. Henry had so incensed the French Prince when he won that he had thrown the pieces at him, to which Henry had responded by smashing the chess board over his head. War between the Conqueror and the French had grown out of that incident and it was at the ensuing battle that William's horse had trodden on a burning ember which had resulted in the great King's death.

It was no wonder that Louis had a score to settle. More than that it was becoming politically impossible to endure such a powerful enemy on his borders.

Stephen of Blois and his forceful wife were natural

supporters of Henry since Adela was his sister and one of the sons of the house was actually being brought up in the Court of his uncle Henry of England. It was different with Flanders and Anjou.

Henry knew that if the King of France could be robbed of the aid of Flanders, Anjou and the diabolical Robert of Bellême he would be more or less powerless against Normandy. He often reminded himself that he had made two big mistakes in his policy. One which affected the present was the release of Bellême. He had had the man in his power and instead of dispatching him, or robbing him of his eyes, he had banished him to Normandy. A perhaps greater error which had yet to be realized to the full was to have allowed the Clito to escape from his hands.

In the years to come it seemed certain that the Clito would be a figurehead to which men would rally. Fortunately he was but a child at the moment and his father was safe in prison. Robert had been moved from Wareham to Devises and then to Bristol and shortly was to go to Cardiff. Henry had not wished him to stay too long in one place for fear attempts to rescue him might be carried out.

Now Henry knew that the King of France was conspiring with his enemies; he could safely leave England in the hands of Matilda and his trusted ministers headed by Roger of Salisbury and so he set out for Normandy.

Luck was with Henry. The first news that reached him when he set foot in Normandy was that Robert of Flanders, one of the greatest enemies, had been killed when his horse threw him on the Meaux Bridge.

This was a good augury, he told his followers, and because of their superstitious natures and their certainty that this was so, success seemed to come their way. But Henry was the first to realize that these successes were temporary and the whole picture could suddenly change.

His great fortune was that England remained peaceful and he had no need to worry about events there, so that he could give his attention to Normandy and this he did.

A year passed and he was still there. He dared not leave. Messages came from England that all was well under the wise hands of Matilda and Roger. He heard news of the children. Matilda was growing more forceful each day and was undoubtedly Queen of the nurseries; William was gentle, kindly and doing well at his lessons both indoor and outdoor; their cousin Stephen was a charming boy, inclined to be a little lazy at his lessons, but always with a reason for his misdemeanours and such a charming way of delivering it that he was always forgiven. He and young Matilda had become the greatest friends and sometimes the Queen thought it a pity that she was betrothed to the Emperor of Germany for they might have made a match for her with Stephen. Then she could have stayed with them or at least not so far from them. Germany seemed very far away and when the Queen considered that it would not be long before their daughter would have to leave them to go and complete her education in a strange land she was sad. But she did not wish to burden Henry with these domestic details. He would be pleased to know that all was well in England and he need have no qualms about leaving the country while he settled the affairs of Normandy.

* * *

Henry could scarcely believe his luck. Trust Louis to be so foolish. Henry could never quite forget that plump boy of about fourteen who had become so incensed when he was beaten at chess. Louis was in difficulties and he wished to call a truce that some sort of conference might take place. His choice of envoy would have been comical if it had not been so utterly stupid. What sort of man did he think Henry was?

When Robert of Bellême stood before him Henry could scarcely believe his eyes.

"I come from the King of France in good faith and I expect you to show the same."

Henry, seated in the ornate chair on which he received envoys and which was a kind of throne, looked up into that cruel perverted face. This was the man

265

who had brought misery to thousands, the man whose name had struck terror into innocent people; those eyes had looked on at a thousand indescribable tortures. And now they were fixed on the King of England in a manner which could only be described as insolent.

"You are bold to come to me, Robert of Bellême," said Henry slowly.

"I come as a mediator."

"Whatever you come as you are always my enemy," said Henry.

He called to his servants. "Arrest this man."

"How can you do that? I come as an envoy."

"I can do as I will, Robert of Bellême. Have no doubt of that. Once before you were in my hands and unwisely I allowed you to go back to Normandy. What have you done since then? You have worked against me. You will always be my enemy."

"I am your enemy," said Robert of Bellême. "You have robbed me of my lands in England."

"I shall now rob you of your vile and filthy pleasures. Let me tell you you shall never have an opportunity of torturing my subjects whether in Normandy or England . . . never again."

Protesting, Robert of Bellême was dragged away. He was put in prison at Cherbourg until such time as he could be taken to England, where he would be doubly secure.

Two of his enemies were removed. First Robert of Flanders and now Robert of Bellême.

"There is Anjou now," said Henry. "When he is my prisoner then the King of France will be of a certainty not well served against me."

This was good fortune, but still he could not leave Normandy and so the government of England remained entrusted to Matilda and her advisers. She was both mother and Queen and often she thought of Henry and wondered what adventures he was having in Normandy. Sometimes in the night she would awaken and think of him and she wondered then who was sharing his bed.

*   *   *

It was almost two years since Henry had left England and he still remained in Normandy. He was eager now to return to England. He was longing for a sight of Matilda and his family. He was weary of the conflict, but although he had had success in Normandy he could see that the final battle was yet to be won. In his heart he wondered whether it ever would be and when he contemplated the future he admitted that before him stretched years of campaigning in Normandy.

There was another stroke of good fortune, or perhaps it should be called strategy, when Alençon fell into his hands. This lay on the borders of Maine, that constant trouble spot, and Fulk of Anjou was obliged to sue for peace.

Maine was forced to recognize the suzerainty of the King of England and believing that the best way of cementing an alliance was through marriage, Henry suggested that Fulk's daughter—yet another Matilda—should be betrothed to his son William.

This was a dazzling prospect for Fulk. His daughter to be the future Queen of England! True her rich inheritance would pass into the hands of her husband but it was a bait that was irresistible.

The alliance was made, promises were given by parents of the betrothed, and now that Louis of France was denuded of the most powerful of his allies, Henry thought that he might well return to England.

*   *   *

What a joyous homecoming that was!

"Two years is far too long to be away from my home and family," said Henry sentimentally.

Matilda was delighted to see him. She met him at Dover and they rode triumphantly back to Westminster, the people cheering them on the way. The Queen's piety and goodness to the poor had always been applauded. The King was harsh but he was a good king—

as kings went—and he had wiped out the humiliation of the conquest in the minds of the Saxon community by winning victories in Normandy.

"Welcome to the King of England and the Duke of Normandy," they cried.

It was indeed good to be back.

The children had grown. His eyes lingered on William, a goodly boy. He would have to teach him the art of kingship. That would be a pleasure. And Matilda; she was growing handsome and how proudly she held her head and how her eyes flashed!

He said: "How is my young empress?" He spoke ironically, for she was not entitled to the title until the marriage was solemnized. That day was not far off. But Matilda saw nothing ironical. She already saw herself as the Empress.

"And Stephen, my nephew."

Stephen bowed gracefully. He was a handsome young fellow and growing fast.

"Why, Stephen," said the King, "you will soon be joining me on the battle field."

"It cannot be too soon for me, sir."

"So you want to be a soldier eh?"

"I want nothing more than to be at your side and to put an end to all those who are traitors against my lord King."

"Well spoken. Very soon then. Next time I go to Normandy I may take you with me. Your brother Theobald gives a good account of himself and that pleases your mother."

Stephen bowed his head, full of respect for the returned warrior.

The Queen watching thought that Stephen had more grace than her own children. William was perhaps too gentle; Matilda was too proud. Henry would be able to report very favourably on his nephew to his sister Adela.

There was a banquet at which the children were present and the King ate heartily of his favourite dish of lampreys.

Yes, a very pleasant homecoming.

It would be advisable, Henry believed, now that he had returned, to show himself to his subjects. So he arranged with Matilda a succession of tours throughout the country.

They were well received in most places. The only dissatisfaction with Henry was his harsh taxation (which he always declared was necessary if he was going to subdue the rebels of Normandy and prevent England's being invaded by men such as the cruel Robert of Bellême) and his even harsher forestry laws. The latter Henry's better judgement warned him to modify but he would not forgo his great passion for the hunt any more than his father could. He needed the exhilaration the chase could give him. He spent much of his life in battle—or he had since the conquest of Normandy—and he must have the only relaxation that meant anything to him: hunting, whether it was the deer, the wild boar or a woman. He was not sure which of these gave him the greater satisfaction, but that satisfaction he must have.

Now for a while he would be the faithful husband of Matilda. She was not uncomely with her long fair hair and her swan-like neck, and it pleased him to congratulate himself on his temporary virtue. Moreover they needed more children. Two was a poor tally. Daughters were as valuable in the game of statecraft as pawns were in the game of chess. Young Matilda had proved that through the alliance with Germany. He had his son and heir it was true, but there should have been more. When he thought of his brother Richard's death in the New Forest he remembered the grief in the home, but his father had remarked: "By the grace of God we have other sons." And so he had—too many as it turned out. Robert, Rufus and himself . . . and not enough land for poor Henry. But he was no longer poor Henry, for he had more than either of his brothers had had, which was what his father had prophesied.

But what would have happened if Richard had been the only one?

What was the matter with Matilda that she had suddenly become barren? It was since she had discovered his peccadilloes and was almost as though her body declared that since he had fathered so many others he should have no more from her. Which was absurd, for she longed for more children even as he did.

So be it, he would be a faithful husband for the sake of his conscience and the hope of another son or even a daughter.

The great Abbey of Hyde which they had founded and endowed was now ready to be opened and Henry decided that they would make a grand ceremony of the opening; and since he felt, after his long absence in Normandy, he had need of placating the Saxon element of his country, he decided to honour one of the greatest of their kings.

The bones of King Alfred and his Queen Alswitha had been buried in Newminster chapel in Winchester and this seemed to Henry an appropriate moment to remind the people that not only was Matilda descended from Alfred the Great but he was also, for of Alfred's three daughters one of them, Ethleswitha, had married Baldwin of Flanders and it was well-known that Henry's mother Matilda was the daughter of another Baldwin of Flanders.

So in a brilliant ceremony the bones of the Great Alfred were taken from Newminster to Hyde and there Henry told the people that he found great satisfaction in honouring the greatest Saxon king from whom not only the Queen but he himself had descended.

The children accompanied their parents, for now that they were growing up Henry liked them to be seen as much as possible.

They had watched the ceremony of the burial of the bones with great interest and when they were alone together discussed it.

William said that he hoped when the time came for him to rule he would be as great a ruler as King Alfred had been.

"You never will," retorted Matilda. "I should have

been born the boy. I know it, and I am sure everyone agrees."

"They do not," declared William hotly. "Our father is pleased. He told me so and when he next goes to Normandy I am to go with him."

"To marry that girl! She is only the daughter of a vassal of our father. When I go it will be to marry an Emperor." She looked at Stephen and her expression softened. "But I don't want to go now," she added. "I don't want to go one little bit."

"You won't hate your going half as much as I shall," said Stephen, his face growing melancholy, which Matilda thought made it look more beautiful than ever.

"Dear, dear Stephen! The Emperor is an old man. I wish he were young and beautiful." She and Stephen exchanged smiles and she went on: "*You* think I'd make a better ruler than William will, don't you, Stephen?"

Stephen was never at a loss for words. "I think you would both make the very best rulers it is possible to have."

Matilda went to him and threw her arms about his neck. She loved kissing Stephen. She thought him the most beautiful creature she had ever seen. Stephen returned her kiss lingeringly.

William watched them and said: "Stephen always says what people like hearing, but it is not always what he means."

"William is trying to be clever," retorted Matilda watching Stephen.

"He doesn't have to try, he is," replied Stephen, always the diplomat, making sure that his replies could never be taken amiss by any member of the company.

Stephen had the cleverest tongue of all the young people at Court, it had been said. He was very popular with the women. Matilda knew that he often did what he should not do. Many of these women had husbands. She had heard it said: "He will be another such as the King."

Matilda would have liked to share Stephen's adventures. It was a little game between them. There was so much he would like her to share with him but always he remembered that she was the King's daughter, an

271

Empress to be, and Stephen's position at the Court was one which had been given him by the bounty of his uncle. His home was really in Blois and his parents had impressed on him that when in England he must do nothing to displease the King or Queen for if he did such action might result in his being sent back to Blois, his prospects in ruins.

He knew the King and Queen well. The Queen must never hear of his little adventures; if the King did—and he believed he had—he would shrug his shoulders and laugh, for he had had very similar adventures when he was Stephen's age. But of course if Matilda were involved in those adventures it would be a very different matter.

Matilda knew this too. It was a titillating situation though. She wondered how she would have felt if she had been able to marry Stephen. Very excited she believed and looking forward to the consummation.

But Stephen was not for her. He was merely a humble son of the Court of Blois and not even the eldest son. He was only at the Court because his mother was her father's favourite sister and she had asked the King to look after Stephen's future.

Matilda was reserved for a far more glorious match; but she was not sure now whether she would have preferred to be the wife of Stephen of Blois or the Emperor of Germany.

Until Stephen had begun to fascinate her with his good looks, his lazy ways and his gallant speeches she had been absolutely sure that the finest thing in the world was to be a great Empress.

*   *   *

It was spring when the embassy arrived from Germany. From a window the young Matilda watched their arrival. She knew, of course, for what purpose they came. For the first time she began to feel afraid. It was one thing to be told when one was seven years old that great honour had been done to one, the result of which was that one would be the wife of a great ruler and an Empress. But when one was twelve years old and began

272

to understand something of the meaning of marriage, it was a different matter.

She was going to a man she had never seen. He was forty years older than she was. She would be conducted to his country with great ceremonies which her proud heart loved and that was well enough if only she did not have to arrive. But she would, and in the not very distant future. Then there would be the greatest ceremony of all, and after that . . . she shivered.

She was frightened. She, Matilda, the bold one, who had sworn to William and the other children that she was never frightened of anything! She was frightened of this old man who would be her husband; and she did not want to leave her home to go and be his Empress.

Someone was standing behind her. She knew who it was before she turned, for he too would come to see the arrival.

"Stephen," she said with a little catch in her voice.

She turned to him and threw herself at him. He put his arms about her and stroked her hair.

"This means I shall soon be gone, Stephen," she said.

"I know."

"Oh, Stephen, what am I going to do?"

He did not answer. He went on stroking her hair.

"I don't want to be married to him. I don't want to be an Empress."

"You'll be all right. He will love you dearly."

"I don't want him to. I don't want him. I want to stay here."

"You will be a great Empress, Matilda."

She brightened a little at the thought, but only momentarily. "Oh, Stephen," she said, "I wish . . ."

"I wish it too," he told her.

"I wouldn't mind not being an empress . . . I wouldn't mind anything . . ."

"We have to marry those who are chosen for us, Matilda. It happens to us all."

"Perhaps . . ."

Speculation shone in her eyes. She did have the wildest fancies. Somewhere in her mind was the thought that she, Matilda, could do anything she wished simply because she was Matilda.

Stephen was not like that. Stephen was lazy; he would do nothing to offend the King because he feared that if he did he would be sent back to Blois and that was the very last thing that must happen. Perhaps she liked Stephen so much because he was so different from herself.

Stephen said: "I shall think of you all the time."

She nodded. That must be her consolation.

*　　*　　*

There was little time for grieving. The ceremonies to entertain the embassy occupied all her time. She must be presented to this one and that and she was aware of the new respect with which she was treated and this gave a little balm to her feelings.

If only she could stop thinking of Stephen, and how beautiful he was, how young and amusing. And the Emperor was forty years older than she was. That made him fifty-two! He was a very old man . . . older than her mother and father.

Bishop Burchard of Cambrai, in whose charge she was to be put, was very stern although, like all the others, respectful. He told her that she would continue with her education in Germany after her marriage. The Emperor wished her to speak German so she would have to work hard at that, for everyone around her would be speaking German. She would learn to live like a German, to *be* a German.

She felt angry and resentful. She was English she wanted to say, and so she would remain, but she merely regarded the Bishop haughtily and replied that she would do what *she* judged to be her duty.

Her father sent for her that he might make her fully aware of the importance of what was happening to her.

"My daughter," he said, "you are fortunate indeed. This is a great match and you are doubly blessed, for you will be an Empress, the wife of a great ruler, and you will bring great good to your country. Never forget that you are English and that it is your duty to make sure that you bring good to me and your family. Never forget that."

"I shall not forget," said Matilda.

"You are a good brave girl," he said.

Her lips trembled slightly as he embraced her.

"I'm proud of you, Matilda," he went on; he left her, for he did not wish to know that she was apprehensive. It disturbed him. Poor child, she was only twelve years old. He was thinking that she had always been self-reliant. Once she had children, if she did, all would be well, as long as she remembered her allegiance to her father's kingdom.

It was different with her mother. The Queen was gentle, remembering that this was the little baby who had filled her with tenderness when she was born, and had continued to do so until Matilda had shown herself to be in no need of tenderness, and was indeed a little impatient with it. Matilda had always wanted admiration beyond all else.

But now the child looked a little forlorn. It was a long way to go from home to a strange land and a husband whom she had never seen. She would know nothing of what marriage entailed. The Queen thought of herself at that age and did not know that Matilda was unlike her and not entirely ignorant as her mother had been at that age.

"My dearest daughter," said the Queen, drawing the girl into her arms, "you are going far from us and we shall miss you sorely. But you will have a husband to care for you. You must love him dearly. You must promise me to do so."

"How can I until I know I can?"

"You must strive for this."

"My lady, can one strive to love?"

"One can strive to do one's duty."

Matilda said suddenly: "I don't want to go."

"My child, this happens to Princesses. They must leave their homes. They must marry where it will do good to their families. It happens to many of us."

"It did not happen to you."

"No." The Queen smiled thinking of Henry's coming to the Abbey. How wonderful he had seemed, a shining hero coming to rescue her from the harshness of her Aunt Christina. And it had not turned out quite as she had hoped. The chivalrous knight had turned out to be a lecher, a man who, while he was courting her, was living in intimacy with another woman, perhaps several, so that she was never surprised when some new young man or woman was brought to Court and she discovered him or her to be yet another of her husband's bastards. "Your father came and courted me and I loved him before I married him. Love will come to you after marriage."

Matilda said nothing.

She was thinking of Stephen, for as the day of her departure drew nearer she thought more and more of Stephen. He was always in her company; they both knew that they wished to see as much as possible of each other for when she went to Germany and he maybe followed his uncle to Normandy, they would have only memories of each other.

The last day came.

Matilda was dressed in a kirtle of blue, edged with gold embroidery; the little cap on her head was covered in precious stones and her long hair fell under it in two long plaits. She looked very handsome and slightly older than her twelve years. There was a faint colour in her cheeks because in spite of the fact that she was about to leave her home she was the centre of attraction and that had always meant a great deal to Matilda.

Down to the coast she travelled with her parents and the members of the embassy from Germany. Stephen was of the party, and he was never far from her side.

Sadly he watched her and Matilda thought often of how different it would have been if instead of being her poor cousin he had been a great king.

Her parents bade her a tender farewell; she boarded the ship which was to take her to her new life. She was the centre of all attention, for all this pomp had been devised for her.

She stood on deck watching the last of England fade away.

Somewhere on the shore which would soon fade from her sight was her dearest cousin Stephen, but he was not meant for her. She turned her face from the white cliffs and looked out to sea.

She must put away childish romantic dreams and begin to think of her new role of Empress.

The Passing of the Queen

The Queen's sister Mary came to Court. Matilda was delighted to see her as always, for they still both enjoyed talking of the old days under Aunt Christina and congratulating themselves on their escape.

"Although," Mary admitted, "it wasn't quite as wonderful as I used to think it would be when as a prisoner in the Abbey I dreamed of love and marriage; and I know it was not for you either, Edith."

"How it takes me back to those days to be called Edith. No one calls me that now except you."

"If I called you Matilda I should confuse you with my daughter and yours. It is my daughter I want to talk to you about, Edith."

"How fares she in the Abbey of Bermondsey?"

"Very well indeed, I think. Her lot is different from ours. As you know I visit her when I am here and I make an opportunity of coming whenever I can."

"So you do not mind leaving Eustace?"

Mary grimaced. "Eustace is always concerned with planning a crusade and then going on it and planning another. I believe he has led such a sinful life that he has much to be forgiven and he thinks this is the way of washing his sins away."

Matilda said: "Oh Mary!" in shocked tones, which made Mary laugh.

"Oh, I will say what I mean," she said. "And so should you. We know that the men we married are not saints so should we pretend they are? You especially, Edith. All know you are married to the biggest lecher in Christendom."

"Mary, I beg of you!"

"You may beg of me all you wish but nothing can change this. How many children has he? I'll swear even he does not know. He only has to show favour to a young man or woman and the young man is said to be his son and the young woman his latest mistress."

Matilda shut her eyes and shivered.

"Forgive me, sister," went on Mary. "You are too good for the world; but I believe in speaking my mind. We were frank with each other in the Abbey. Should we not be so now? I know that you endowed Henry with the virtues of the perfect knight. Well, he is gallant enough." She leaned forward and laid her hand over her sister's. "Do you fret because of his habits? Cheer up. When he gets older his desires will lessen. It is in the nature of things."

"Mary, could we talk of something else?"

"With pleasure. We will talk of that which is uppermost in my mind. My daughter's future. She will need a husband."

"And Eustace has plans for her?"

"Eustace! He is piqued because she was not a boy. He thinks I should have given him a string of sons. How typical of these men! They never doubt their own manhood. They always blame us. He is so much older than I, yet he thinks the reason we have no son is due to me."

"So it is you who make plans for your daughter."

"I will, with your help."

"My help? How can I help you?"

"By speaking to the King of course."

"You had someone in mind at this Court. Who?"

"Stephen . . . Stephen of Blois."

"Why, that would seem an excellent match."

"I am glad you are in agreement with me. Stephen is not greatly endowed but I hear he is a personable young man. He is the son of the Count of Blois and his mother is the daughter of the Conqueror and your husband's sister."

"He has little prospects."

"Little I agree, but in view of his relations with the King, it may well be that he will one day be not so ill-endowed."

"So you wish me to speak to the King and to ask him if he would approve of the match?"

"I should be grateful if you would."

"Well," said Matilda, "there is no harm in mentioning it to the King. He has not said he has other plans for his nephew."

*   *   *

How strangely quiet were the children's apartments without Matilda.

They constantly talked of her and often said: "Now if Matilda were here . . ." and then they would realize how much they missed her.

Stephen regretted her going more than any even though there were plenty of women who were ready to console him and he was eager to be consoled.

William said to him: "I shall be married one day, Stephen. Then I shall be gone, too."

"You will be married soon, depend upon it," replied Stephen. "Your marriage is so much a matter of policy."

"Perhaps you will be allowed to choose."

Stephen contemplated that and wondered. It was possible that he would not be, for he was not far from the throne. Suppose William did not have any children, would he, Stephen, ever have a chance? There was Matilda to come before him. He had often cherished the idea that one day he might marry Matilda and even though she had been betrothed to the old Emperor he had gone on hoping. The Emperor was a very old man.

Sometimes old men died on the night of their weddings when they were married to young girls like Matilda. Suppose the Emperor died and suppose Matilda was a widow and came back to England and needed a new husband.

Matilda would have taken him readily . . . as readily as he would have taken her. His feeling for Matilda had never been expressed except through innuendo, and hopes that could never be realized. It could have been so different.

Sometimes Stephen wished that he had been bolder. Who knew what might have happened then? Danger! What if he had got young Matilda with child? He believed that she was passionate and would conceive readily. He shuddered at the thought. The King could be ruthless. Sometimes he had imagined himself caught in a passionate relationship with Matilda which both of them were unable to resist, and wondered what the King's reaction would have been. In his nightmares he imagined himself groping his way blindly through his prison, dark sockets in his face where his eyes had been. That could have happened to him if Matilda had been delivered to her Emperor anything but an unsullied virgin.

Nothing was worth the loss of eyes, of freedom; certainly not a woman. There were so many of them and very few who were not ready to be gracious to a handsome young man like Stephen.

The King sent for him and smiled in a friendly fashion when his nephew entered his chamber. He was a fine young fellow, thought Henry, who could never see him without wishing that he was his son.

"My dear nephew," he said, "can you guess what I wish to say to you?"

"I hope, my lord, that you are going to tell me that I may accompany you when you next leave for Normandy."

"Ha, that may be sooner than you think. Rest assured, nephew, you shall be with me. But it was not of that I wished to talk to you. What say you if I tell you I have found a bride for you?"

Hope leaped up. Matilda's husband was dead. She

was to have a new husband. Stephen had been chosen. If William died he and Matilda might reign together . . .

Wild dreams! Matilda's old husband was a few steps from the tomb yet. He had let his imagination run on too far.

"Pray tell me, uncle, whom you have chosen?"

"I have chosen Matilda," said Henry.

The colour rushed into Stephen's face. "Then, sir, it is so. The Emperor *is* dead . . ."

Henry looked at his nephew in amazement. "What say you?"

"You said Matilda."

Henry burst into loud laughter. "You are thinking of my daughter. Nay, nephew. She is well married and bedded by now I doubt not. The Emperor wants an heir before he is too old. There are many Matildas, Stephen. There is one now in the Bermondsey Abbey—a daughter of the Count of Boulogne and the Queen's sister. That is the Matilda I had chosen for you."

Henry was amazed by the expression on his nephew's face for Stephen's hopes had been so raised and they so fitted his dream that he was unable to hide his dismay.

Henry was amused. "So you thought it was my daughter. She would be a handful, Stephen. I trust this other Matilda will be more meek. It should be so for she was brought up in an Abbey and in such places they give a good grounding for meekness."

Stephen was still silent.

"My daughter Matilda would give a husband a merry dance I doubt not. She has something of me in her and my father and my mother. She does not take after her own mother at all. Be content with this Matilda I have chosen for you. By all accounts women are inclined to be gracious to you. Well, you'll have little to complain of I'm sure. Do not look for too much pleasure in the marriage bed. Do your duty and look elsewhere for enjoyment. It is often so—and I know full well that you are one to come to a quick understanding of these matters."

"I shall, my lord, be happy to marry whomsoever it is your wish to choose for me."

"That is the spirit, nephew. I've no doubt you'll make the lady happy. The marriage should take place soon, for it is time you married."

Stephen bowed and left the King; then he went to his chamber and brooded on his future.

He was a fool to think that he would have aspired to that other Matilda. If she had been free a man in a very much more important position would be found for her. He was not even the eldest son of the Count of Blois and it was only because his mother was Henry's favourite sister that he received his present favour.

His family would consider this marriage a good match.

He must resign himself to Matilda of Boulogne instead of Matilda of England.

*   *   *

Mary was delighted and went to Bermondsey to acquaint her daughter that she was to be betrothed to Stephen of Blois.

The Queen missed her. She missed her daughter too, for the children's apartments were so quiet without the dominating Matilda. And now Stephen was to marry and presumably would leave Court. The next would be William; but at least he would not have to go away.

It was comforting to have Henry in England although he must keep a continual watch on the situation in Normandy, and at any moment he would be called away to deal with some rising.

He had not been to Wales to visit Nesta for some time and she knew that he prayed that a son might be born to him and the Queen.

She did not tell him that she was often very tired and suffered from breathlessness at certain exertions. She tried her best to disguise her ill health. Henry did not like sick people about him, and he could not understand why it was that she did not become pregnant. The fault could not be his; he had proved that many times over.

"Only two children," he brooded. "'Tis not for want of trying."

He could not understand it. He only had to spend a week or so with a new mistress and she would be telling him she was enceinte very soon. It was particularly galling to have so many fine sons and daughters born outside wedlock and to have merely two legitimate ones. He was pleased with them. Matilda was a daughter to be proud of and the German alliance would set the King of France shivering in his shoes. He wished he had six daughters that he might marry them to the enemies of the King of France; he would plant them all along his borders and that would show fat Louis that Henry was capable of beating him at more than a game of chess.

William was the delight of his life; and the more barren Matilda seemed to have become the more was he drawn to William.

William was a fine-looking boy . . . and a good boy too. He had inherited the Norman characteristics of the family. He was gentle-tempered though—something rare—yet brave and making progress in the art of chivalry. A son to be proud of. He would be a good king of England.

"If only there was another boy," Henry used to say to Matilda. "I'd give him Normandy, but I'd make William and him swear to be allies. This fighting in families brings no good."

"Why does it have to go on? Robert is your prisoner in Cardiff Castle. You are Duke of Normandy as well as King. Why do not these miserable risings cease?"

"Because I allowed the Clito to go free. Had I imprisoned him as was my intention there would be no figurehead to rally them. Clito is only young as yet but he is the thorn in my side, Matilda. In future I shall take my own counsel. That boy should be in an English prison with his father, not roaming the Duchy held up as the rightful duke by my rebellious subjects."

"But now that you have affianced William to Anjou's daughter."

"William is young for marriage. I must needs postpone the ceremony for a few years."

"But the betrothal is firm?"

"Ay, and Louis likes it not. But I don't altogether trust Fulk of Anjou."

"But surely he would do nothing to prevent his daughter's marriage to the heir of England?"

"I think not. But it is long ere the marriage will be celebrated. I would to God we had more children that I might make matches for them."

This was a reproach which stung Matilda to retort: "Perhaps God has given you so many out of wedlock that He has seen fit to restrict the number within it."

"He has given us an indication that the fault does not lie with me."

It was a near quarrel, for this subject was a sore one with Henry, but they avoided it. Quarrelling was not the way to get children.

*　　*　　*

Mary had arrived at Court with her daughter. When the young Matilda met the man who was to be her husband she was enchanted with him. Stephen was some seventeen years of age; he was good-looking but his charm of manner would have made him attractive even had he been less handsome. He had a habit of putting everyone at ease; even the humblest were treated well by him. He was indolent by nature; to charm required little effort from him, and he was shrewd enough to realize that the popularity he acquired by this would be useful to him.

Even his uncle, the King, was affected by his manners and had favoured him because he could not help liking him.

Stephen's reaction to his bride was not so enthusiastic. She was fair enough but very young and quite innocent. At his age he preferred mature women. Poor little Matilda would be a trifle dull, but her adoration was pleasant so he set out to charm her—such an easy task which offered no challenge and was therefore not very exciting. But he must remember that she was the Queen's niece and that he was not an eldest son, so he must be grateful for such a match. He was a fool ever to have thought of that other Matilda.

The King was amused by the bride's obvious infatuation with her husband-to-be. He talked to Stephen about it. "She reminds me of the Queen before our marriage," he said. "She was abbey-bred and as innocent as your bride. She took too high an opinion of me, just as this child is taking of you. It is, alas, a shock to them when they discover our true natures."

He took Stephen to the Tower Royal, a palace situated close to Watling Street and Cheapside. Henry had built it not long before. He asked Stephen what he thought of this new palace.

"A palace!" replied Stephen. "Why, sir, it is a mighty fortress. It is almost as solid as the Tower of London."

"I like it well," said Henry, "and the reason I shall give it away is not that it has found disfavour with me. It is yours, Stephen. It is my gift to you and my niece."

"My lord, you are generous."

"I forget not your loyalty to me. While it lasts, nephew, you will have my favour."

"I shall pray to be worthy of your kindness, sir."

"We are of a family. Your mother was always my favourite sister. It has pleased me greatly to do something for her son."

"My lord, I shall serve you with my life."

The King bowed his head and an expression of rare softness came into his face.

"I would you had been born my son, Stephen," he said.

Stephen replied, "Those words, sir, give me greater pleasure than your magnificent gift."

*　　*　　*

The wedding ceremony took place without delay, and Stephen of Blois and Matilda of Boulogne were husband and wife.

There were feasting and ceremonies; and the Queen and her sister were constantly in each other's company.

When the married pair settled in the Tower Royal Mary went back to Bermondsey where she decided to stay for a while before she made the journey back to Boulogne.

As the King remained in England he decided it would be good to travel about the country, staying in the castles and palaces of his loyal subjects as he went.

Like the rest of his family he delighted in fine buildings and admired the best architecture, so it was always a great pleasure to visit castles which either he, his brother Rufus or his father had built. They were indeed becoming part of the English countryside and it was impossible to go far without coming upon the formidable-looking piles with their turrets and arches. The latest to be built was Woodstock, a palace to be proud of, and the park was delightful.

Also like his father and Rufus, Henry loved wild animals. Not only did he wish to hunt them, he liked to observe them. He discussed with Matilda the possibility of filling the park with wild animals. These of course would have to be kept in enclosures; and he believed a great deal of pleasure would be derived from sauntering through the park and watching the animals from as close quarters as was possible.

Matilda thought it an excellent idea and together they set about obtaining animals to fill the Woodstock Zoo.

Harry did not look for deer and wild boar and such other animals as were familiar in the English forests for he decided Woodstock should be famous for the animals which did not normally live in England.

How would he come by such animals? Matilda wanted to know.

"In their travels to the Holy Land, men have passed through countries in which wild animals flourish. I would wish some of these to be brought to England."

"Is it possible?"

"They could be caged and brought. I should like to see lions and the strange animal which my brother Robert told us of when he was with us. He saw it in the desert and it will carry a man on its back through sand and heat. It is called a camel. I should like one or more of that type."

Henry recovered from the strain of the Normandy

battles in his enthusiasm for his Zoo and the day finally came when he had gathered together lions and leopards; he even had his camel. These animals were put into enclosures that they might be watched from afar and keepers were engaged to care for them. Everyone was talking of the wonders of Woodstock Park—a change from the continual talk of war.

Henry and Matilda presided over the opening of the Zoo; and rarely had Henry been in better humour. Many of the leading nobles were lodged at the New Palace and Henry explained to them how he had managed to procure the animals.

A special favourite was a porcupine which provided a great deal of amusement when its prickles shot out.

The Queen was happy on that day. She felt a little better than usual, although far from well; but she was at least able to disguise her weakness from the King.

Just before the opening of the Zoo messengers arrived from Germany. The Queen was very eager to hear news of her daughter and was delighted to receive letters from Matilda implying that she was content with her lot. The Emperor was very old but very kind. She was taking German lessons, and there had been a splendid ceremony at Mentz.

The Queen questioned the messengers. Had they seen the Empress?

Oh, yes, they had seen her. She had made a progress through the streets of Mentz in her bridal gown, the Emperor beside her in the carriage.

"Did she seem happy?" the Queen asked.

"None happier. She seemed very pleased to be among the German people and they expressed their liking for her in loud cheers. They called her "the little Empress" and they had thought her very handsome. She had spoken to them in German and told them that she loved their country already and would do her best to serve them. The people had been delighted."

"And her husband?" asked Matilda.

"He could not be better pleased. He finds her handsome and amusing. He is pleased with his marriage."

She might have known that Matilda would be all

right. All Matilda needed to make her happy was homage.

She took the messengers to Henry who listened with approval and when they were alone he said: "You see how useful these marriages can be in families such as ours. Now I have secured the Emperor's friendship. He cannot take up arms against his father-in-law. Would I had more daughters to place strategically throughout Europe."

And because of the sudden pain she felt which was often followed by periods of lethargy she said: "I doubt not you are surprised that honours cannot be picked up so easily for those children you have got on other women. It is only my children who are of use to you."

"It seems unnecessary to call attention to the fact that my legitimate children can marry in higher places than my others." He turned on her, with the temper beginning to flare up in his eyes. "But let me tell you this, any child of mine will be well looked after to the best of my power and you, Madam, will add your help to mine in this matter."

"You ask a great deal, Henry."

"I have given you a great deal. But for your marriage to me you would be in a convent in your hair shirt and veil."

"Our marriage brought advantage to you, Henry. You forget that I am the daughter of the royal Saxon house."

"You would not allow me to forget it an I would."

She felt ill suddenly and had no heart for the quarrel. "Oh, Henry," she said, "you are here in England and that rejoices me. Let us not spoil the pleasure of this by harsh words."

He did not wish to quarrel either. He said: "I am content, Matilda. I love you well. I am only sad that we cannot get more children. If we could but have another son . . . and if you would cease to harp on these others I have had, I should know complete happiness."

"The first I cannot help for that is in God's hands, for the second I will do my best not to refer to the matter again."

"I bless you, my dear," he said; and they went out to the opening ceremony of the Zoo.

While Henry talked merrily of the habits of the animals, Matilda was aware of the nagging pain within her. The terrible notion that she would never have another child could not be dismissed.

The ceremony over, the feasting in the great hall of the palace began; and it was while this was in progress that a messenger arrived from Bermondsey.

Mary had very suddenly been taken ill and within a few hours was dead.

* * *

Matilda was shocked into illness. For several days she did not leave her bed. Mary, who had seemed so very much alive but a short time before ... dead! It was inconceivable.

The messenger had told her that the Countess had risen from the table and fallen in a faint. She had been alive when they carried her to her bed. She had spoken of her sister and how happy she was that her daughter was safely married. She had asked that her dear sister Matilda be asked always to look after her namesake. Then within an hour she had passed away. As she had always expressed a desire to be buried in the Abbey of Bermondsey her wishes were respected. That Abbey to which she had entrusted her daughter had benefited greatly from her generosity and it seemed fitting that she should be laid to rest in a spot where she had found peace during her lifetime.

The young bride wept for her mother but she had her handsome young husband and the novelty of marriage to comfort her. It was Matilda, her sister, who felt her death more keenly.

"It happened so suddenly," she said to Gunilda. "It could happen to anyone. One day one is well and the next dead. I had thought to go long before she did."

"We can never tell when our time has come," replied Gunilda, "and often those of us who seem most likely to live for a long time go first."

All the same Matilda was becoming increasingly

aware of her failing health and she often wondered how long was left to her.

It was shortly after the death of Mary that rebellion broke out once more in Normandy. The King left for that troubled country and he took with him his son William and his nephew Stephen. Matilda hated parting with her son, particularly to the wars; she was apprehensive for his welfare and wished as she had on so many occasions that Henry had been content with England and had left Normandy to his brother Robert, who was still languishing in Cardiff Castle. But she gave her time up to comforting Stephen's young wife and as they sat together over their embroidery she shared with the young girl confidences of her life in the Abbey under her harsh Aunt Christina and she told of her joy when Henry had come courting her.

*   *   *

When the King had left there was no longer the necessity to keep up appearances. Matilda could spend days in her apartment with only her women about her.

Gunilda and Emma were growing more and more worried about the state of her health because it was becoming clear that she was very ill indeed. Often she lay on her bed asking nothing but to be left in peace. There she liked to think over the past and most of all those days when Henry had first come to court her. She had loved him deeply and believed that she could have gone on loving him had she not made too perfect an image of him in the first place. Often she believed that had she been brought up in a court instead of an abbey, she might have been accustomed to the ways of men. But because she had led such a sequestered existence she had believed in romantic knights who remained faithful till death.

A pity! Her daughter Matilda had been different. Matilda was knowledgeable of the world and this would doubtless help her in her relationship with her husband.

She wondered whether the marriage had been consummated or whether the Emperor had taken pity on his young bride and delayed that part of the marriage. He could not delay too long, for he was growing old.

Life was strange. One must needs learn all one could of it and adjust oneself to its demands.

She tried to impress this on her special friends, the two women who had been with her all her married life, and the other, Christina, who had joined them a little later.

"When I am gone, what will you do?" she asked them.

"Gone, my lady!" cried Emma in bewilderment.

"I mean when God has called me from this earth."

"You mean . . . *dead*!" said Gunilda shocked. "Oh, my lady, do not speak of such things."

"Come and sit beside me," said Matilda, "and you too, Christina. You must know that I am going to die."

"No, my lady," said Emma firmly, "except that one day that is something we must all come to."

"My time is not far off."

"No, my lady. What will the King say?"

"Life and death is something the King himself cannot control."

"He will be desolate."

She turned her face away from them and a sad smile played about her mouth. Would he be? How much had he loved her? Never with the over-powering love which she had been ready to give him. She had believed theirs would be the greatest love story of their times, because she was young and innocent, and he had cared for her in a certain way, though not as he had cared for Nesta. Or did he care for Nesta? He had desired Nesta as he never desired any other; and he wanted Matilda for his wife. One was sensuous, able to slake his sexual thirst; the other was the daughter of a royal house who could give him the support he needed from his Saxon subjects.

We both had our uses, thought Matilda a little sadly.

And when she was dead would he mourn? A little. But not for long. He would say: "I will marry again. There is still time left for me to get a son."

"The King will recover from his grief," she said. "But I speak of you."

Emma, the soft-hearted one, wept surreptitiously.

"I beg of you, my lady," whispered Gunilda, "do not

speak of these matters, for we should never go from here while you needed us and if you did not ..." her voice broke. "It could mean but one thing."

"It is in fact that of which we speak," said Matilda. "We must perforce look into the truth. You could not marry now."

"Nay," said Christina, "we would have no wish to, were it possible."

"Stay together then. You are good friends and will have the friendship of each other. Perhaps you would be happy in a priory or an abbey."

Emma had started to weep so heart-brokenly that Matilda agreed not to discuss the matter further at that time. But that did not mean that it was not uppermost in their minds.

For their sake Matilda attempted to bestir herself, but it was difficult, for with each passing day she grew more feeble.

*　　*　　*

It was November when Henry returned.

When he saw Matilda he was horrified by her appearance.

"Why, you are ill!" he cried.

"It will pass," she told him.

"Why was I not told?"

"Blame no one. It was on my orders."

"I would wish to know if you were unwell."

"You had your campaign in Normandy. I did not wish to disturb you with unpleasant news from home."

"I wish to know *all* that is going on in my kingdom."

"You are kept informed of all matters of importance."

"And you think your health is of no importance to me?"

He took her hand and kissed it. Remorse struck him. She was a good and gentle creature; and perhaps he had not always been a good husband. But she must understand that he was a king and that duties weighed heavily on him. Other women? How could he help that? They were as necessary to him as breathing and how could he ever make Matilda understand that he saw his relations with other women as something apart from marriage?

He would stay with her, he told her, and they would have *merry* revels at Christmas time. When he left—for alas his stay could not be extended over more than a few months for the situation in Normandy was far from secure—she would be as well as she ever was.

"I long to see William," she told him.

"Alas, William is not with me. He remains in Normandy."

Alarm seized her. Her son in Normandy without the protection of his father!

"It was necessary," said Henry. "If I had brought him home with me there would have been reproaches. It was necessary to leave him as a kind of hostage."

"A hostage!"

"Oh, not in the usual sense. But to leave him there gives those of my men who must remain a sense of security. They know I will be back soon since my son is there."

"So we shall not have William for Christmas?"

"Let us content ourselves by knowing that he is doing his duty."

Matilda in Germany, and William in Normandy. Even Stephen no longer here.

She wondered: Shall I ever see them again?

*   *   *

It was scarcely a gay Christmas. In spite of Henry's insistence that Matilda rouse herself and enjoy the festivities she was unable to do so. As for Henry, he was concerned most of the time with what was happening in Normandy.

He talked to Matilda about the perfidy of the Norman barons and that he could not trust them; and that immediately his back was turned he knew they would be brewing trouble.

"We must get William married to Fulk's girl as soon as possible," he said. "It's the only way to ensure his loyalty. I would not trust him but for the bait of this marriage."

"And how is William at the prospect? Does he like well his bride?"

"William is eager to do his duty. And when the marriage is celebrated it would be well if you could join us in Normandy."

The thought of crossing that unpredictable strip of water so appalled Matilda in her state that she could not suppress a shudder.

"My mother crossed often from Normandy to England," he reminded her. "I was born here."

"When William is married then," she said.

"That will be this coming year," said Henry.

This coming year! It was a long way away. Where would she be then? It would not surprise her if she had left this earth by then.

Soon after Christmas Henry sailed for France, and making a great effort, Matilda accompanied him to Dover.

She was rather relieved when she had waved him farewell and the ship which carried him disappeared from view.

Now she could give herself up to the comfort of accepting the fact that she was a very sick woman.

* * *

All through the spring she was in decline. She became so tired that she did not leave her room.

Gunilda said: "The King should be told of your illness, my lady."

"The King has much with which to occupy himself."

"Should not the sickness of his wife be his first consideration?"

"Not if he is a king with a dukedom to hold."

"Madam," said Emma, "would you not like to see your son?"

"More than anything," she answered.

"Then should you not send for him?"

"How could he come and the King not know it?"

"I think the King should be told," said Christina.

"My dear friends, you must not say such things. The King must not be disturbed. He has great tasks to perform. He must not be worried by these domestic details. I have lived for nearly forty-one years and eighteen of those I have been married to the King. I know him well."

"But, my lady..."

She silenced them. "I know and you know that my end is near. But the King has affairs of great moment which require his attention. He must be in Normandy. What do you think would happen if he were to leave the battle there for the sake of a sick wife?"

Gunilda shook her head and went into the ante-room where she talked in whispers with Emma and Christina. The Queen was a saint. They spoke of all she had had to endure, of the King's infidelities, of his numerous bastards, all that which emphasized the saintliness of his Queen.

"He should know," said Christina emphatically.

The others agreed but there was none who dared tell the King.

*   *   *

She lay in her bed. The light was fading fast. She felt wonderfully peaceful. There were moments when she was not sure whether she was in her bed in the palace of Westminster or in her convent cell.

There were shadows on the wall. The candles cast such a flickering light—elongated shadows that looked like a woman in the dark Benedictine robe, a woman who had a stern face and a cane.

"No," she whispered. "Never. Not now that I know Henry..."

"You did not know Henry," whispered a voice within her. "You never knew Henry."

Such men as her husband were complex people. He could be kind to her; he had been a good husband. All those other women, they were like a long procession marching through her bedchamber and at the head of them was Nesta of Wales. Naked she danced and the King with her.

"No!" cried Matilda. "No."

And she was in her bed again.

It was only a dream, she told herself. They were not here. But what had he been like with those others? She knew that she had never been able to give him what they had. There were but the two children—the girl and the boy. How she would love to see them now! Little Matilda, an Empress, flashing scornful eyes, proud and bold, and gentle William, her darling son. How cruel that she must leave this life without one more look at them, with no loving word of farewell from their lips.

But they were royal. They were not supposed to have the feelings of ordinary people—Matilda's marriage with the Emperor of Germany; William's with the daughter of Fulk of Anjou; Henry's battles with Normandy—all these were of more importance than a dying mother and wife.

And so farewell my children who are far away, farewell my husband. There will never be another son now, Henry. But you have William . . . and there is Matilda.

How dark it was. Who was that by the bed? Emma? Gunilda?

Bless them. Good and faithful, kind friends. What would they do without her?

"Emma . . ."

"My lady."

"What will you do . . . ? Where . . . ?"

"Do not fret for us, my lady. You should make your peace with God."

"Is it time then?"

There were many at her bedside. There was the cross to hold before her eyes. She remembered hazily a long ago day when her mother lay dying, grasping the black cross in her hand as she did so. A terrible day . . . when the news of her father's murder had come to them and that awful desolation had descended upon them. That was in a way the beginning. Was that why she thought of it at the end?

Her hands were limp about the cross.

Very soon now it would be over. They would take the news to Henry ... to Matilda ... to William ...

"Farewell my dear ones ..."

The tears ran down Emma's cheeks and Gunilda took her arm.

"It is over now," she whispered; and they stood for a moment looking down at the still face of the Queen.

*   *   *

It was May time, the beautiful month, when the trees were in bud and new life was bursting out in the lanes and fields.

But the Queen was dead.

The bells of Westminster tolled for her and it seemed fitting that she should be laid beside that great King of England, Edward the Confessor. She was of his royal house; she had brought together the Saxon and Norman houses; she had been a saintly woman who had been a good and faithful wife to a sometimes harsh and not always faithful husband.

And when her obsequies were over and she was at rest in her tomb the messengers were sent to Germany and to Normandy that her family might learn the dismal truth.

A Horse and a Bride
for William

They brought the news to Henry when he was preparing to go into battle. Matilda dead and buried! "It is not possible," he cried, as though by denying it he could prevent its having happened.

The messenger bowed his head, not daring to contradict the King, yet being unable to agree with him.

"When?" cried Henry. "How?"

She had passed peacefully away in her bed. Her women had known she was ill for some time.

Deep in his heart he had known it too. He thought of her sitting beside him at Woodstock, pale and remote, as though her thoughts were far away. He knew that she had been in pain and seeking to hide it from him.

She was too young to die. Ten years younger than he was. It was eighteen years since he had taken her from the abbey and married her. Eighteen good years!

He had never regretted his marriage even when

there had been those uneasy scenes which he hated, when she had reproached him for his infidelities and he had been irritated by her innocence of the world and men such as himself.

Matilda . . . dead! Life would never be the same without her.

But there was a war to be fought and won. He had a kingdom and a dukedom to hold; and for such as he personal grief must not come between him and his duty.

* * *

"William," he said, "your mother is dead."

William's face puckered. "No, sir . . ." he stammered.

"Alas, my son, 'tis so. That good woman has passed away. We are going to miss her sorely."

"But to happen while none of us was with her!"

The King nodded.

"Should we go back, sir?"

"Back to England! At this time. Are you mad? The King of France would move in in triumph. The Clito is gathering men to his side every day. To go back now could lose us Normandy!"

William was abashed. He should never have made such a foolish comment.

"And of what use?" asked Henry. "She is dead now and buried. Nay, we must perforce do our mourning here in Normandy, and take our revenge on our enemies that they have caused us to be absent when your beloved mother passed away."

When he was alone Henry thought of the future without Matilda. He was no longer young but not too old to take a wife. The Emperor of Germany had married Matilda who was forty years his junior. Perhaps he should consider marriage. Yet he had his son, William, his heir whom he was preparing to follow in his footsteps.

To marry again! It was a little soon to be thinking of that but kings were not ordinary men. Brides would be offered him doubtless—young nubile women. He was free now with an easy conscience to take his women where he fancied them. Not that marriage had prevented him but he often remembered those occasions when Matilda had reproached him. Why should he marry again—unless of course a marriage offered him great opportunities and what marriage could make Normandy safe for him? Where in Normandy was there a vassal strong enough to guarantee the submission of that troublesome dukedom? William was to marry Fulk of Anjou's daughter. They were betrothed. That was enough. Nay, he would not marry. He would go to seek comfort of Nesta when he was back in England.

In the meantime he would mourn Matilda, his good wife, and mourn her with unfeigned sorrow; but his first thoughts must be for battle.

*   *   *

The battle raged fiercely. The King of France had allied himself with the Clito's forces, but the Clito seemed to have inherited his father's inescapable curse of failure and Henry had never had much respect for the King of France since that long ago game of chess. Henry's forces were superior and Henry was a great general. When he rode into battle it seemed to him that the spirit of his great father rode with him. William the Conqueror had never been defeated in battle save once when he fought against his own son and had been unseated. Then Robert could have killed him but he could not bring himself to harm his own father in spite of the long-standing conflict between them. Poor ineffectual Robert! He had so little luck and when it did come his way he would not know what to do with it. He had not taken advantage of his victory because he, like all the family, had been brought up to believe that the Conqueror had some divine right of victory and that this must be maintained no matter with what results. Poor idealistic futile Robert! Even on that occasion his father had despised him for not making the most of his advantages.

"Oh, my father," said Henry, "I should never be guilty of such folly. This young man who comes against me is my nephew, your grandson, but by God and all the saints, if I come face to face with him in combat I

301

shall slay him, nor should I admire him if he having the advantage did not slay me. You prophesied that I should have more than either of my brothers and by this you meant both your dukedom of Normandy and the England you conquered. I know it was your dream to make one country of these two and that is what I shall do. Let your spirit ride beside me and I shall be sure of victory."

So he prayed not to God but to the spirit of his great all-conquering father.

It was inevitable that he should rout the enemy. He had the superior forces; he was a greater general than the King of France ever could be and poor Clito was too inexperienced as yet.

During the battle Clito was unhorsed; he managed to escape but the horse was captured—a magnificent creature caparisoned in the most elaborate fashion. None could doubt that such a horse had belonged to the son of Robert of Normandy for so magnificent was it that it must have cost a fortune to make it so.

Henry laughed aloud when the horse was brought to him.

"The Clito's horse, sire. He was unseated."

"And escaped?" asked Henry.

"Alas, sire. As soon as he fell he was surrounded by a strong force who held off his attacker who was slain. Before more of our men should take him he was hustled away."

"I would rather have him than his horse," said Henry, "for while he lives he will find men to rally to his banner."

But the battle was won; the Clito had been unhorsed, the King of France was in retreat. It was a victory.

"William," said Henry, "see what a fine horse your cousin rides?"

"I never saw a horse so richly caparisoned, sir."

"These riches should have gone into equipping his men. One does not win battles with gold and bejewelled saddles, my son."

"Nay, father."

"Never make the mistake of extravagance. Your grandfather never did that."

William nodded. He had been lectured many times on the need never to waste money. Henry knew to a penny what was spent on his campaigns and on his household. He had not been nicknamed Beauclerc for nothing. He could wield a pen as readily as any scribe and he enjoyed working with figures which must always balance.

"Learn all you can of your grandfather's campaigns. He was the greatest ruler ever known. Listen to my advice, for I follow him. One day, William, you will step into my shoes. The death of your mother who was more than ten years younger than I brings home this truth. I cannot live for ever. Then you will be King in my place. You must be ready, for as your mother was taken when we least expected it, so could I be."

"Father, I beg of you ... stop. The subject is so distasteful to me."

Henry laughed. "There, my son. We kings must face facts. There is little time in our lives for family feelings. You must be ready when the time comes. But a king cannot afford to make mistakes. Learn from the folly of your uncle Robert and the Clito who a wanderer, one might say in search of his inheritance, yet spends a fortune on a horse which he could—and has—lost in battle. Your grandfather was a richer man than Clito could ever be. He was the richest man in England and Normandy, yet he would never have wasted a penny as I do not. Nor must you. Take this horse then. I give it to you. Make what use of it you wish."

William took the horse and left his father.

*　　*　　*

In his tent, he thought of the horse—a noble creature. He fancied it had a sad lost look in its eyes; and he thought of his own horse bereft of its master. The finer the horse the deeper its feelings. This was Clito's horse and he loved his master.

He went out to the stable and looked at the horse again. He patted its neck and he felt the aloofness of the creature who managed to show him a disdain he understood, as though it were saying: Do you think I am yours because you won me in battle?

Clito had loved this horse. He had decked it out in this fashion because he wished to give it accoutrements worthy of it. William understood that though his father did not.

How could he take his cousin's horse when it belonged to him? It was not like a town or a jewel. It was a living thing. Nothing on earth could make this horse his. It would fret for its master.

William knew then that he could never be a king as his grandfather had been or his father was. He could not count his possessions and revel because they were so large and plan how to enhance them. William wanted to live. He wanted to be a king, yes; and he knew that a king had to go into battle. It would always be necessary for a king to fight to hold what he had, to gain more than he had. It was part of kingship.

He was joined by his cousin Stephen who had come to look at the horse.

"What a beauty!" cried Stephen. "Look at this cloth! These jewels are worth a fortune."

"So my father says. The Clito is a fool to have wasted money which could have gone into more useful things."

"But what a sight! And it is yours."

"I feel I have no right to it."

Stephen surveyed William intently. William was too gentle, too honest for kingship, he decided. He wondered what would happen to the kingdom under him. He would be his close friend and cousin and William would honour him. Their lives would be bound together. How often had he wished that he had been Henry's son instead of his nephew; being older than William he would have been the heir. Sometimes he thought that Henry wished that too.

"You have a right to what has been honourably won in battle," said Stephen.

"This horse pines for its master."

"It would soon forget."

"I think not."

William continued to stroke the horse. "You see, he does not respond to me. He resents me. There is only one thing he wants from me and that is that I should send him back to the master he loves."

Stephen laughed aloud at the thought; but William turned on him almost angrily. "That is what I am going to do," he said.

Stephen stared in dismay. "Your father . . ."

"I shall do it first and he will hear of it when it is done."

He called a groom and said, "I want this horse taken into the enemy's camp. It is to be delivered to William the Clito with my compliments."

The groom thought the Prince had gone mad, but one did not question one's master's orders; one obeyed them.

*　　*　　*

The King said: "So you sent the horse back?"

"Yes, sir."

"With a fortune on its back!"

"I am not a thief, my lord."

"You are a fool," said Henry. "A man is not a thief for enjoying the spoils of war."

"I could not in good conscience take it."

"William, you are a fool."

"Yes, sir."

"And fools do not rule kingdoms."

"But a man must be at peace with himself, sir, and if he is not how can he hope to be at peace with others? Peace is necessary to the prosperity of any land and to have kept my cousin's horse would have seemed to me a violation of the rules of chivalry."

Henry said: "Go, my son, I will think of what you say."

Surprised, William left him. His father's reception of the news had been much milder than he had believed possible. Was he perhaps in a subdued mood because of the Queen's death, or did he in fact understand?

Later Henry spoke to him of the matter. "I believe you were right to send back the horse," he said.

The expression of affection on his son's face was rewarding.

"I am not sure about the rich caparisons."

"Nay, father, to have returned the horse without them would have seemed to me churlish."

Henry nodded. Then he laughed aloud. "My son," he said, "you have noble thoughts. You and I will spend more time together. You will have to learn when to be generous as you have been this day and when it is necessary to be harsh. This gesture was not without merit although it has lost us the cost of those jewels. But our enemies will see with what men they have to deal and that is not a bad thing. They will know us to be just and virtuous in our thoughts. It may be that your actions will bring those who are wavering to our side. Then it would be worth while, as you see."

William did see, but his father's motives and his were not quite the same.

"So," went on Henry, "we have lost a valuable horse and his splendid accoutrements. Let us hope we have gained in good will. But you have done this thing without consulting me and it would seem that you now fancy yourself as a man capable of rule. Well, then, it is time you married. The ceremony must be delayed no longer. I fear your father-in-law may grow restive. Your wife is young...twelve years old, but Matilda went to her German Emperor at that age."

"I would lief wait awhile, father."

"Come, you are a laggard. And we cannot wait on your whims. This marriage must take place without delay. We have routed the enemy; now we must consolidate our gains. I need the help of Fulk of Anjou and only when his daughter and my son are wed can I be sure of it. We shall leave for Burgundy forthwith and there a very impatient young bride will be awaiting her husband."

*   *   *

She was very young and her name was Alice, although the King said that he wished her to be known as Matilda.

"It will give me great pleasure if this be done," said the King, "for deeply do I mourn my beloved and virtuous Queen. And it will give her pleasure if when looking down from Heaven she sees her son married to another Matilda. My mother too was Matilda, my wife was Matilda, though she was christened Edith, and this beautiful child, this Alice, shall be another Matilda too."

Fulk did not care what his daughter was called as long as she was the future Queen of England.

As for the girl herself, she was so enamoured of the handsome, gentle youth who was to be her husband that she was as happy to change her name to Matilda as her father was for her to do so.

In the town of Lisieux there were great celebrations. Fulk was delighted with the honours done to him and that he had succeeded in making a brilliant match for his daughter. The King was under no illusion. He knew that this marriage was the price Fulk asked for his loyalty but he felt it was wise to pay it.

The young couple were charming to look upon and there was great revelry in the neighbourhood for everyone hoped that this marriage would bring the peace they so desired.

William was tender with his little bride, aware of her extreme youth. His cousin Stephen chided him and said that he was no husband, but William had no intention of frightening the child.

"'Tis a pity," said Stephen, "that we cannot marry where we will." He was thinking of another Matilda, such a one as he had never known before, nor ever would, and his young meek Matilda who was now his wife. So many Matildas and all different! Only one was bold and exciting and what was she doing now? He did hear that her husband was indulgent towards her. Stephen laughed. Poor old man, trust Matilda to make sure of that. She was popular with her husband's German subjects. She spoke German well; she was cheered when she rode into the streets.

He could imagine her, bold, proud and exciting Matilda!

If he could have married her ... If William had been killed in battle and the King too and Matilda were Queen of England and she married Stephen ...

He was being foolish, indulging in impossible dreams; but in dreams he often saw a glittering crown that was being put on his head.

It was ridiculous. How could it possibly happen? There were too many in between, so he must be content with the lands his uncle would give him, and he must try to be satisfied with his mild little Matilda. There were other women and always would be. He would follow his uncle in his way of life. Others had done so before him. He and Matilda must get children and he would obtain grants and blessings for them from his uncle; and his cousin he guessed would be even more generous when he came to the throne.

It was a promising future, but he was near enough to the crown to covet it and not near enough to be able to grasp it.

And so he gave himself up to the revelry and often his nights were charmed by some fair maiden of Burgundy. His little wife was safe in England, no doubt longing for his return. That would not be long delayed for the King had been away from England for more than a year.

Matilda the Queen had died; and William the Prince was married.

It was time the royal party returned to England to assure themselves that all was well there.

The White Ship

Henry could congratulate himself. For the time being at least there was peace in Normandy. He had friends in useful places and he could afford to return to England from which he had been away for two years.

With his cavalcade he arrived at Barfleur where his ships were waiting to carry him home. Among these was the beautiful *White Ship*, undoubtedly one of the finest in his fleet. He was filled with pride as he watched her dancing on the waters.

He was in his tent making the last preparations for leaving which he liked to superintend himself and which gave him a chance to display his special talent and to assure himself that all details were correct when the captain of the *White Ship* asked for an audience.

Captain Fitz-Stephen was a man he respected and Henry was pleased to hear what he had to say.

"I have a request to make, my lord," he said.

"Well then, make it," replied the King.

"I would like the honour of carrying the heir to the throne to England, sir."

Henry who had planned to sail in the *White Ship* himself was momentarily silent. He could not sail in the same vessel as his son. That was a rule he had made and it seemed fitting to him that the King should sail in the finest ship.

"My lord," went on Fitz-Stephen, "my father was captain of your father's ship the *Mora,* and he had the honour, of which he talked often, of carrying Great William to England in the year 1066."

"That was before I was born, Captain."

"Ay, sire, and he never forgot it. He made a sea captain of me and he said that he hoped one day I should enjoy as great an honour. If I could but take the Prince of England, sire, my father would look down in such pride that the angels would sing for us."

Henry laughed.

"So you would carry the Prince, not the King."

"I would follow your wishes, my lord."

"But you asked to carry the Prince."

"It came to me that I would like to carry the heir of England."

"So be it," said the King. "I will not travel on the *White Ship* but will sail with my men. Let the Prince sail on that ship and choose those of his friends whom he would wish to accompany him. I wish to sail with my gallant soldiers who have helped me to win this victory."

Fitz-Stephen bowed and left to make his preparation.

Then Henry thought of all he had heard of that great occasion when his father had set sail in the *Mora,* the ship which his mother had built for him and presented to him for the great enterprise. He had often studied the work on the tapestry which was now in the Bayeux Cathedral and which had been worked by his mother.

How many times had he heard the story of that great Conquest which had changed the course of his family's history and made kings of them and which was a great example never to be forgotten?

Well, his father would smile on him this day.

He went down to the shore and watched the ships being loaded. Very soon they would sail for England.

*   *   *

They would sail at the end of the day with the tide and if the wind was with them they would soon see the white cliffs of home.

William was happy to be going home. He had left his bride behind in France. Poor child, she had wept at their parting. But she was so young. When he returned to her side she would be more of an age to be a wife.

He was touched that Fitz-Stephen had begged for the honour of conveying him and the Captain told him that all the members of the crew were celebrating because they were to have the honour of taking him to England. He said at once that he would choose who should accompany him and immediately went to Stephen.

"I am to sail in the *White Ship*," he told his cousin. "You will accompany me, will you not?"

"With pleasure," replied Stephen. "She is the greatest ship in the fleet. I wonder your father does not sail in her."

"Fitz-Stephen asked that he might take me and my father will sail with his soldiers. He wishes to show them that he appreciates all they have done in Normandy. So I am choosing my companions. I shall ask Richard and the Countess of Perche. That will please my father."

Stephen nodded. Richard and the Countess Matilda of Perche belonged to the King's numerous family and it always pleased Henry to see them honoured.

William then began to enumerate the friends he had decided to take with him on the *White Ship*. They were all young men. He said: "We will have a very merry time and there shall be much revelry aboard."

Because he wished the crew to know how delighted he was to sail with them he ordered three casks of wine to be sent on board for them before they started.

Consequently there was much merrymaking on the

White Ship all that day and every sailor drank the Prince's health not once but many times.

* * *

The afternoon was coming to its end.

Stephen went on board. He could hear the sounds of singing coming from below. The ship reeked of wine.

He found William and said: "Many of the crew are drunk. They are in no fit state to take the ship across the sea."

"Nay," cried William, "we have the best ship in the fleet."

"Of what use a fine ship with a drunken crew?"

"Fitz-Stephen is the best captain afloat. Are you suggesting he cannot manage his ship? His father took the Conqueror across on that all famous occasion."

"I'll warrant the crew of the *Mora* were not drunk."

William laughed aloud. "By all I hear of my grandfather he himself was never in that state."

"Nay, and he was said to be the wisest of men." Stephen was thoughtful. "I have changed my mind, William. I shall not sail on the *White Ship*."

"Why ever not?"

"I like not to sail with a drunken crew."

"They will stop their merrymaking when we sail."

"They'll be too fuddled for anything by the look of them. Nay, William, I'll not sail on the *White Ship* and if you are wise now you will wait until tomorrow."

"What mean you? I have promised myself that we shall be the first to reach England."

Stephen shrugged his shoulders. "I wish you a good voyage."

"You cannot really mean you are leaving us!"

"I shall join the King's ship."

"What has come over you?"

"Just the notion that I will not sail this time in the *White Ship*."

"You're joking. I know you."

"Nay, I shall leave you now."

"You'll be back before we sail. Don't leave it too long, Stephen."

Stephen did not answer but went ashore.

When he turned and looked at the vessel he thought it looked like a ghost ship.

* * *

"Come," cried William. "I have sworn we shall be the first to reach England. Is she not the finest ship in the fleet?"

"She is my lord," said the Captain. "But she is doing all she can."

"She'll be beaten at this rate. I have promised the men ... I have promised myself. The oars must increase their speed."

"Not easy, my lord."

"But they must."

In ten minutes the order had been given. All the sails were out; the oarsmen were pulling with all their might.

The Captain was disturbed, for he believed this high speed was putting the ship into danger.

He tried to remonstrate but the Prince and his young friends were delighting in the speed. They were taking wagers as to by how long they would beat the rest of the fleet.

The distracted Captain urged them to be reasonable. The *White Ship* was known to be the fleetest on the seas. She would be home first. He was sure of it.

"Captain," cried Richard, son of the King, "I have a wager with the Countess my sister on this. I cannot afford to lose. For my pocket and the honour of the ship do not slow her down."

"My lords, my lords," cried the distraught Captain. "We are not yet free of the rocks. I beg of you do not ask me to act against my judgement."

But it was already too late for the *White Ship* had struck one of the sharpest of the rocks.

"The *Catte raze*!" cried the Captain. "By God, my ship will founder."

He called: "To the boats." His one thought was to save the life of the heir to the throne.

The ship was filling rapidly with water; she would

sink at any moment. There was no hope of saving everyone on board. But the Prince must be saved.

With great relief the Captain saw one of the boats lowered and the Prince with some of his companions climb into it.

"Get away fast!" shouted Fitz-Stephen. "Back to Barfleur. You can do it."

They were away.

* * *

William looked back in dismay at the sinking ship.

The men were pulling at the oars trying to get clear of the vessel, knowing that if they could do so in time there was a chance of saving their lives.

William could hear the sound of crying.

"It is terrible," he said to his brother Richard. "We are safe but those souls are in danger."

"Look," said Richard, "there is our sister."

It was true. The Countess of Perche was clinging to the rail on a deck which would be swamped at any moment.

"Brothers! William . . . Richard . . ." Her arms were stretched out appealingly.

"We dare not go back, my lords," said one of the boat men. "We'll be caught up and dragged down if we attempt it."

"But we cannot leave my sister!" cried William.

"'Tis death to attempt to go back, sir. We ourselves are in danger even now. We must get away from the ship without a second's delay if we are to save our lives."

"Nay," replied William. "We cannot leave her. We must do our best to save her."

"'Tis death, sir. 'Tis death, I tell you."

"Turn back," commanded William. "We shall not leave my sister."

The Countess saw that they were rowing towards her.

"God bless you, William . . ." she called.

"We are coming," shouted William. "Soon now, sister . . ."

But he never reached her for at that moment the ship went down taking the Countess with it, and the small boat carrying the heir to the throne was swallowed up in the wake of the *White Ship*.

*   *   *

Captain Fitz-Stephen was clinging to a broken spar. There was nothing but sound and fury all about him. He had lost his ship but he believed he had saved the heir to the throne. The boat carrying him and his friends could reach the coast of France for they were not far out. At least he had done his duty.

How foolish to have allowed the Prince to make his sailors drunk! How wrong to have followed the boyish wish to exceed a safe speed! Oh God, he prayed, if I could but live the last hours of my life again. But his consolation was that he had saved the Prince.

Clinging to the top of the mast which was just visible above the water was a man.

The Captain called to him.

"Hi, man, who are you?"

"I am Berthould, Captain, the butcher."

"Are you the only one there?"

"Yes, Captain, I climbed here right at the start. So far I am safe."

"The Prince got away. Did you see him go?"

"Ay, sir. But he came back for the Countess of Perche and the boat went down with the ship."

The Captain cried: "It cannot be. I saw him leave. He would have got away."

"I saw him, Captain. Went down with the ship! The Countess too and the Princes. Everyone, sir. You and I, Captain, are the only ones left."

The Captain's hands were limp on the spar. They felt cold and dead.

How could he face the King? How could he tell him: "I have lost the *White Ship* and the White Hope of England."

The waters swirled about him; he was exhausted.

He let the spar slip away from him and he sank down into the water.

*   *   *

Henry was amused. He and his soldiers had reached England before the *White Ship*.

"Stephen," he said, "what ails you? Why are you so nervous?"

Stephen said he did not know that he was.

"You are back in England now, my lad. The fighting is behind us for a while. I think never have events in Normandy augured so well for peace. We must be eternally on the watch of course, but the signs are good. The *White Ship* is not sighted yet. I will ask Fitz-Stephen what he means by bringing in the fastest ship of all the last."

Stephen did not answer. He could not get out of his mind his last glimpse of the *White Ship*.

The King's Resolve

They had brought the news.

The butcher had been picked up and taken back to Normandy. He had seen what had happened.

The *White Ship* lost with all on her—except butcher Berthould who had climbed the mast and seen the ship go down.

They brought the news to Stephen for he was now considered to be nearest to the King.

"How can I tell him that his son is lost?" asked Stephen.

"Someone must, my lord."

"Ay," said Stephen, "someone must."

There came a time when the King could not be kept in the dark any longer.

Stephen went to him.

"Uncle, there is bad news."

The King turned his head slowly and looked full at his nephew. "It is William..." he began.

Stephen nodded. "The *White Ship* foundered not far

out of Barfleur. She sank and all went with her save one butcher who lived to tell the sorry tale."

The King said nothing; his lips moved but no sound came.

Then slowly he got to his feet. He would have fallen had not Stephen caught him.

The news had been such a shock to him that he had fainted.

* * *

The King shut himself in his chamber. He wanted to see no one. Only Stephen ventured near him and for a few days he did not speak even to him.

Then there came the day when Stephen went to him and he said: "Sit down, nephew."

"My lord," said Stephen with a smile of compassion which seemed beautiful in the King's eyes.

"My boy," said Henry, "I wish you were my son, then the tragedy would seem less severe."

It seemed to Stephen then that he felt the crown upon his head. The dreams that seemed so wild were wild no longer. Was it possible? There is no male heir, those words kept hammering in his brain. There is Matilda but she is the Empress of Germany. If I could have married Matilda there would be no doubt.

"I would I were," he answered the King vehemently.

"You are a comfort to me, Stephen, in my bereavement."

"My uncle, there is nothing I would not do to bring you comfort."

"I know it well. I rejoice in you. You shall not suffer for your devotion to me. You see a man bowed down with sorrow."

"But a great King, sire."

"I have done what I thought best for my people."

"And will for many years to come, please God."

"There is life in me yet, Stephen."

"It is clear to all who behold you, sire."

"I have suffered much tragedy of late. I lost my wife, my good Matilda, and I was hoping for more sons from her until the last. And then my son and heir, the future

318

King. It seems God would punish me for all my sins. I lost two other children on that ship, Stephen—my daughter the Countess Matilda, my son Richard. Three children with their lives before them went down with that accursed *White Ship*. You see a man bowed down with misery."

Stephen said: "I see a great King, sire, who will rise above his adversity."

Stephen had always had a golden tongue. The King smiled at him affectionately. "You are a comfort to me, nephew. I've told your mother that I shall do well by you."

"Thank you, sire. You have been so good to me. I would ask nothing more but to serve you to the end of my days."

"Talk to me, Stephen. Tell me what the butcher told you. Tell me of William's last hours. The butcher saw him go back for his sister. He was a saint, Stephen."

Stephen thought: And so do we all become in death. But he said: "A saint, sire."

"I sometimes thought that he would have had too gentle a nature to be a king. For we have to be harsh, often, Stephen, to do what is best."

"You have always done what is best for your subjects, sire."

Oh yes, there was great comfort in Stephen.

When Stephen left the King he could not help feeling exultant.

Who is there? he asked himself. Why should I not be the next? The King loves me. If he does not get himself an heir ... why should the next ruler not be King Stephen?

*　　*　　*

Henry had come out of stupor. A king cannot mourn forever. We should have had more sons, he thought. Better too many than not enough.

He went to the window and looked out.

Across the courtyard walked a comely young lady of the Court. He felt the familiar stirrings which invariably assailed him at the sight of a nubile girl.

I am not old, he thought. I am not as old as the Emperor of Germany—yet *he* took a young wife.

Why should I not get sons, a prince who will follow me? I have the time; I have the vitality.

It was the answer.

Then he would stop grieving. He had loved Matilda; he had loved his son; but they were lost.

He was not old; he was full of vigour. His desire for women had not yet begun to fail.

The King had made up his mind. He would take a young wife and that without delay.